Coming of Age

Volume One

In the beginning...

Jane Jantet

www.tynebridgepublishing.org.uk

First published in the UK in 2018 by
Tyne Bridge Publishing, City Library,
Newcastle-upon-Tyne, United Kingdom
www.tynebridgepublishing.org.uk

Copyright © Jane Jantet 2018

The right of Jane Jantet to be identified as the author of this work has been asserted by her in accordance with Sections 77 and 78 of the Copyright, Design and Patents Act 1988.

All rights reserved. No part of this publication may be reproduced, stored in a retrieval system or transmitted, in any form or by any means, electronic, mechanical, recording or otherwise, in any part of the world, without the prior written permission of the publisher.

This book is sold subject to the condition that it shall not, by way of trade or otherwise, be lent, resold, hired out, or otherwise circulated without the publisher's prior consent in any form of binding or cover other than that in which it is published and without a similar condition, including this condition, being imposed on the subsequent purchaser.

This book is a work of fiction.

To Bernard, Sebastien, Fiona, Edward, Angus, Henry and Lucinda, with special thanks to my sister Anna, editor in chief.

CHAPTER One

Winter, 1947

It was on a piercingly cold February day of the winter of 1947, that coldest of cold winters, that Laura Martin, aged ten, decided she had had enough of life and walked into the half-frozen lake in the grounds of the prestigious Baynes School in the north of England. She was wearing a woollen vest, thick cotton knickers, a liberty bodice, a blouse, a tunic, and a blazer. Inside her wellington boots were long grey knee socks, and a thick winter coat and scarf covered everything up. Yet she was colder than she had ever been before, with a cold which had started deep inside her and which had nothing to do with the weather.

It was nearly four o'clock, and although almost the whole school was outside, making their way to their various boarding houses to change for tea, there was no one near the Pond, as it was known, which was in any case out of bounds to Juniors. The day was swiftly dying, the light seeping back into the sky, and the trees round the Pond darkened the day even more, the faint tracery of their branches beginning to merge with the evening. As Laura, looking neither to right nor left, marched into the water, her boots started to fill, the water so freezing that for a second she almost gave up, but her resolution was strong, her thoughts bleak. She started to sink, feeling herself falling, and as she fell she let out an involuntary moan, eerie in the half-dark, and fought against the pull of the water to stand upright again.

Slowly two small girls emerged from the shrubbery, one fair, one sandy haired. The fair one took in the situation immediately, flung herself into the half-rotten boat at the Pond's edge, cracked the thin ice round it with an oar and pushed herself off from the bank towards the floundering Laura.

"Get someone, Harry," she shouted. "Get someone who speaks French!" The other girl, who had been standing transfixed with horror, turned and ran up the path towards the lights of the school.

Georgina stood up in the boat and thrust the oar towards Laura, who instinctively pulled on it. When the boat was near enough, Georgina grabbed her hand and tried unsuccessfully to heave her into the boat. She let go of Laura's hand and placed it firmly on the boat's edge.

"Take off your boots," she said slowly, pointing to her own, but Laura looked at her uncomprehendingly. Her teeth were chattering and her face turning a bluish colour. Georgina swiftly and decisively removed her own boots, coat and blazer and jumped into the water, just as Laura lost consciousness and her hand slipped from the side of the boat. She manoeuvred her arms under Laura's and started dragging her towards the bank. It seemed to take ages for them to move at all, and then in the distance she heard the sound of voices, and within minutes stronger arms than hers were dragging both of them out of the water. It was almost completely dark now, and the bobbing torches of the rescuers cast strange shadows under the trees. A woman's voice was saying over and over in French to Laura, *"Qu'est ce qu'il y a? Qu'est-ce qu'il se passe"?* and Georgina thought, good for Harriet, she did get someone who speaks French, before she allowed herself to be wrapped in a blanket and led away, shivering and dripping.

Laura and Georgina were put into the school San by Matron, known as the Bun, her small eyes in her porcine face as black as currants. Georgina revived quickly, warmth from a stone hot water bottle taking the chill off the sheets, and she was almost asleep when George Maxwell, the school doctor, arrived.

"Let's have a look at you first," he said to Georgina. He was a large man with a homely red face, on which a smile could usually be found, in contrast to the grim-faced Bun.

He took out his stethoscope and bent over her, moving the cold end around which made her flinch. "Open wide," he said, putting a flat stick on her tongue and looking carefully down her throat with a torch. "Nothing amiss here, Matron. This one," – he looked at the card in his hand – "Georgina, can go back to school tomorrow." He looked at Georgina. "You come from North Shields?" he said, his voice surprised.

"Tynemouth," Georgina replied, wary, determined to give no inkling that he was right, and that her accent was far removed from that which had been hers only two years before.

He frowned. "Oh. The card says North Shields."

"It's the postal address," Georgina lied. "Something to do with the boundaries ..." and willed him to go away.

"Anyway, you'll do, Georgina Charlton." He patted her shoulder, and crossed the room to Laura, who was staring at the wall. The room was big, and although Georgina strained to hear what they were saying, only a low murmur reached her, and after a while she moved down into the warmth of the bed, sleep overcoming her. When she awoke, the other bed was empty.

Later, supper was brought to her in bed by Ruby, the maid who brought the Juniors' supper over from the kitchens. Ruby's dull brown eyes were shining with curiosity, her voice avid as she said in the thick local accent, "Eh by gum, Miss Georgina, what 'appened? How did you and that French girl end up in t'water?"

Georgina told her, exaggerating the time she'd spent in the Pond with Laura. "Well, you're a proper 'eroine, you are, Miss," Ruby stated with awe. "It was me, you know, what fetched Ladd. You should get a reward or summat. 'Ere, if you doan't want that sweet I'll tek it away. She won't see," – she meant the Bun – "she's down in t'bathrooms, 'arrassin' your friend 'Arriet." She piled the plates on the tray.

"Harriet was there too, Ruby," Georgina said. "She did more than I did – she ran to get help. It's not fair if she doesn't get any credit."

"Well, it's your tunic that's dryin' in front of the fire, not 'ers." Ruby replied. "I'll iron it meself, and check your blazer and coat. It's a good thing you took 'em off. That French girl's clothes'll all 'ave to be thrown away. What a story!" Ruby lifted the tray and moved towards the door. "Now you get some sleep." She switched off the light and closed the door, and Georgina lay back, hearing faintly the noises of the house, familiar and safe. Warm light came in through the mottled half-glass of the door. In a few moments she was asleep again.

She woke much later to the sound of voices through the wall, a murmur and inflexion that she realized after a while was probably French. She thought about the strange French girl who had arrived last term and who had a perfectly ordinary English name but who could not or would not speak a word of English and refused to try. When called by her Christian name, she said *"Je m'appelle Laurence, pas Laura,"* and then sat white and silent. She picked at her food with an expression of distaste on her face, and when she was told to finish it pretended not to understand, until finally the prefects and staff had given up. None of the other pupils seemed to know much about her, though they knew that she had spent all of her life in France, and they guessed that she had been sent to Baynes to become anglicised. Every day she went to a special lesson with Mademoiselle but Georgina had listened outside the door one day and had heard her answer a monosyllabic *"non"* to what were obviously questions.

The voices continued next door as Georgina strained to listen, and later, in her dreams, she heard sobs and wails, and the cry of what sounded like "Mama" and "Papa" and weeping which seemed desperate.

***

Harriet felt left out, although it was she who had raised the alarm, running up to the school determined that her paralysing shyness must not overcome her now. Breathlessly, she had torn across the lawns, up the steps to the terrace and round to the forbidden front door. It was just closing behind the imposing figures of a school prefect and another sixth-former. She grabbed the prefect's arm and hung on, speechless with running.

"Why, it's the little Church Mouse," said the prefect. She was referring to an incident of the previous year, when Harriet had manifested her uncontrollable temper for the first time at school, marching up the classroom and hitting a Junior School mistress who had accused her of being as silent and timid as a church mouse. Harriet fiercely resented the name. The prefect turned back to Harriet. "What do you want? You're not supposed to come in this door, you know." She looked more closely. "What on earth's the matter ...?"

Harriet blurted out, "It's the Pond! Laura Martin's tried to drown herself. You've got to get someone. Someone who speaks French," she added, remembering George's command.

"Oh, God," the prefect said and turned towards the headmistress's study. "Get Mademoiselle," she said to the other girl. "I'll fetch Morry. You stay here," she said to Harriet, but Harriet was already tearing up the forbidden front stairs to the dining room, an immense round room on the first floor filled with long tables covered with white cloths, set at this time of day with piles of bread and margarine and bowls of what Harriet knew to be revolting tomato jam. The room smelled of hot tea, and the windows were misted up. Harriet plucked at the sleeve of the teacher nearest to the door.

"What do you want, Harriet?" she said brusquely, preoccupied. "And why have you not changed, or even taken your coat off?"

Harriet took a deep breath. "Laura Martin's drowning in the Pond, Miss King," she said clearly. "I told a prefect, but I think Mr Ladd should go." Ladd was the handyman and gardener.

The mistress looked closely at Harriet. "You're not joking, are you," she stated, and turned to one of the maids. "Fetch Ladd, Ruby, and send him down to the Pond with lights – and a rope. And be quick about it. It's an emergency." Ruby scurried out of the room.

She turned to the young, lithe-looking teacher of gym and games. "You come with me, Miss Rose," she said, already halfway to the door.

Now the girls were crowding around Harriet and pushing towards the windows on the south side of the dining room, where they could see running figures and the flash of torches.

Harriet was gratified to be the centre of attention, although she wanted to rush back to the Pond. She turned towards the door, but a prefect was herding the girls back to the tables. It would be useless to try to leave.

"Come on, Harry, tell us what happened," the girls at the Junior table were clamouring.

"Come on, come and sit down. I'm starving," said one, a bossy, attractive girl whose looks Harriet admired but of whom she was instinctively wary. She patted the chair next to her.

"You can sit next to me. Shove over, Mary," she said. Her name was Meredith – the sort of girl who would have a name different from anyone else's, Harriet had thought after observing her for a term. "Mary, you go and get Harry some tea," she added.

Harriet told her story, but in retrospect it seemed she had very little to tell.

"So you don't know why she did it?" said one girl, and another intervened, "Of course George is terribly brave. Have you seen her climbing Old Oak?"

The conversation turned to the braveness of Georgina and the reasons why Laura should have walked into the Pond. Mary slopped down a cup of tea beside Harriet, making sure it spilt into the saucer.

Harriet was not popular; the more she tried, the more her shyness made her awkward and clumsy. But she was observant, and she knew that Georgina Charlton was no more brave than she herself, but just very determined to succeed, in popularity and everything else, and that she possessed the happy knack of making people like and admire her. She had not worked out yet why Georgina had picked her, Harriet, to be her best friend, but just thanked God that she had, otherwise she might be as lonely as Laura.

"Her parents were probably spies," someone was saying. "Stupid, she hasn't got any parents," interrupted another girl. "Morry told my mother, and she also asked my mother to ask me to be nice to her."

"Why aren't you, then?" muttered Harriet, but no one heard her except Meredith, who looked thoughtful for a moment and then held her hand up for attention. When she had it she said slowly, "I think we'd all better say that we've tried to be nice to her. Otherwise they'll think it's all our fault."

"It probably is," said a quiet girl with a face that looked older than her ten years. "It's no use pretending. We haven't been nice to her."

"Well, you can say what you like, Alison," Meredith said, "but I'm not going to take any of the blame. It's her own fault. She hasn't been friendly to us."

"Don't any of you understand?" said Harriet. "I saw her. I saw her face. She looked ... she looked desperate. And you're a pig, Meredith, because you've been nastiest of all to her."

In that instant, Harriet saw that Meredith had categorised her as an enemy.

"Speak for yourself, Harry," Meredith said. "I don't sit and stare at her like you do. In fact, I was going to ask her out next time my mother came."

"Liar," said Harriet, rage beginning to boil up inside her. She knew that in one minute it would overcome her and she would do something awful. She started to push her chair back.

The bell rang. Everyone else pushed their chairs back and in the push and shove for the door Harriet found herself separated from Meredith. The rage started to subside, although she banged her chair in with such force that one of the teachers still there looked over in surprise.

Alison came round the table. "Don't worry, Harry," she said. "Meredith's just jealous that you and George were there, not her. What were you and George doing there anyway? It's out of bounds to us."

"I know *that*," said Harriet. "We were being sleuths" – pronouncing it *slerths*, and Alison laughed. "Sleuths," she said, pronouncing it properly.

"Oh, sleuths, then. We were following Laura," said Harriet, who had read a large number of books but mispronounced many of the long or unusual words. "Anyway, we were there. Luckily. You know, my grandmother asked me to be nice to Laura, too. She knows her grandmother. She said Laura was sent here because I and one or two other girls were here, and I didn't do anything about it, because it was too difficult. I tried a bit at the beginning of last term, but she just looked away as if I hadn't spoken. And then everyone seemed to hate her and Meredith was so foul to her that I knew she'd be foul to me too if I was nice to her."

They had almost reached the classroom.

"Well, I was just as bad," said Alison. "She's in my dorm, but she never says anything. It's like talking to a brick wall. That's what my mother says about one of my father's sisters, and now I know what she means. I mean, Laura just ignores everyone."

She pushed open the door. The gas fire was on and although the lighting was harsh there was a cosiness in the room. Someone was making toast at the fire, with a piece of bread stuck on to the point of a compass. Others were sitting at their desks, reading or drawing, and Meredith was perched on a desk in a position that showed off her long muscular legs. Footsteps were heard coming along the corridor. The toast maker snatched the toast off the compass point and thrust it into the nearest desk. The door opened, and Miss Rose came in. She sniffed, and smiled.

"I thought you'd all like to know," she said, "that Laura is perfectly all right, although very wet, and that she and Georgina, who behaved most sensibly, are both in the San, for tonight at least."

"Can we visit?"

"Why did she do it?"

"Will she be expelled?"

The questioners crowded round Miss Rose, who laughed and pushed them away by holding her hand up.

"I don't know anything more," she said. "Shouldn't you lot be on your way to bed?"

The Juniors went over to bed incredibly early, their supper being eaten in the Junior boarding house, not in the dining room with the rest of the school.

They groaned and looked at the clock. "We've got fifteen minutes yet, Miss Rose," said Meredith, who always spoke for the class. Miss Rose opened the door. "Enjoy your toast," she said, laughing, as she went out.

Later, trailing over to bed, Harriet felt gloomy and let down. The clouds had cleared and it was freezing again, the stars brilliant in the dark blue sky. Each blade of grass was stiff with frost and crunched when you stood on it, and some parts of the path were black and icy. But Harriet's knees were cold between her socks and her coat and she did not feel like joining the other juniors sliding and skidding their way to June's, which was what the Junior boarding house was called, though no one could remember if this was because an early Matron had been called June, or if it was a shortening of Junior. No one had thanked her for sounding the alarm and George wasn't here to defend her against Meredith. Also, it was bath night.

As she crossed the black and white diamond patterned hall of June's (a big house that must once have been an imposing family seat set in its own gardens but was now absorbed into the immense grounds of the school), Harriet cast a covert glance at the San's door, but nothing could be seen through the mottled glass panels. Matron appeared on the stairs.

"Harriet, Alison, Mary, Hilary, Judith, Susan," – she listed the names – "it's your bath night tonight."

"As if we didn't know," muttered Harriet.

"Harriet? Did you say something? You don't by any chance feel sick, do you?" said Matron. She had made Harriet's life a misery in her first term, when homesickness had made her feel physically sick most of the time.

"No, Matron," said Harriet glumly.

"I hear you were involved in this afternoon's drama," Matron continued. "Though Georgina's the heroine of the day." Pig, thought Harriet.

"I expect Miss Morrisson will want to see you tomorrow," Matron went on. "You shouldn't have been down at the Pond at all."

"Then Laura would have drowned and you'd all have been sorry," said Harriet rudely, feeling the rage again.

"That's enough, Miss," replied Matron, her hand squeezing Harriet's shoulder painfully. She gave her a little push. "Get to your dormitory. We'll see who'll be cheeky tomorrow."

Harriet climbed the stairs to her dormitory, banged the door open and then banged it shut.

The dormitories each held six white-counterpaned beds, two or three shared chests-of-drawers, a washbasin and a large chamber pot under one bed. There was no privacy.

The bathrooms were in the basement, a dank yellow-painted cavernous room subdivided by wooden panels into four bathrooms. The doors could not be locked. At any moment, Matron might come in. The steamy cellar with its smell of carbolic soap and damp wood, its suspect, spider-filled corners, and its wet walls dripping with condensation filled Harriet with horror. Later in life the smell and the hollow sounds of the bathwater running away came back often in dreams.

Tonight, though, Harriet went down the stairs without fear, too cross to think of anything but her own resentment. She was carrying her flannel, her soapbox and her Viyella pyjamas, made by her mother in a white and blue flowered pattern. She ran her fingers along the line of the hand-stitched hem – it seemed to bring her nearer to home, from which she had been removed so abruptly the previous year.

She had her bath unvisited by Matron, ate with the others in the kitchen the unappetising supper brought over by Ruby, swallowed with distaste the spoonful of thick brown Radio Malt spooned out to all the Juniors each night, and finally pushed her feet between the freezing sheets of her bed. She pulled the tartan rug up from the bottom of the bed, and on top of that laid her thick woollen dressing gown. The dolls that Granny Carruthers had made her for Christmas, with their embroidered brown eyes and wide red mouths and that she had named Dinah and Dorinda after the girls in *The Wind on the Moon*, were little comfort tonight. George's bed looked abandoned, and as Harriet curled down under the now faintly warm covers silent tears were snaking down her cheeks. She fell asleep thinking how much she hated Baynes and longing for the soft touch of her mother's hand.

***

It was only as she started gulping mouthfuls of the freezing Pond that Laura's determination faltered. Instinctively she fought against the pull of the weed-clogged water, but each mouthful she swallowed seemed to pull her down further into its depths. She was hardly aware of the voices of Harriet and Georgina and scarcely realised herself when her determination to drown was replaced by a determination to survive.

Suddenly, the boat was there, an oar thrusting itself towards her. She pulled on it weakly. It was the girl called Georgina, Laura thought without surprise, for if she had expected anyone to come to her rescue it would have been the resourceful and calm Georgina. She felt Georgina's strong pull, but her feet were stuck to the bottom, and for a moment it looked as if Georgina would fall into the water with her.

"Take off your boots," Georgina said clearly and slowly, but although Laura understood – her grasp of English was much stronger than anyone guessed – she could not comply. Her teeth were chattering, her knees shaking with the cold, and a darkness kept coming towards her until she felt her head slipping under the icy water. She heard a splash and felt hands under her arms holding her upright, and then everything went black.

Slowly she became aware of voices calling from far away. One was saying in English, "Wake up, wake up," over and over again, while another, in the familiar language of her upbringing, was demanding to know what had happened.

Someone seemed to be sitting on her back, and there was sour earth and snow under her head. She retched and a man's voice said in a dialect she was beginning to understand, "That's right, lass, let it out. Yer doan't want that dirty Pond water inside yer."

The water came out with a gush, choking and disgusting her, so she could not stop coughing and vomiting. She heard herself giving little cries and then someone was wrapping a rug around her and was carrying her away, and there seemed to be no gap between the time she was lifted up and finding herself in bed. She opened her eyes. There was an unknown man standing by the bed, a stethoscope round his neck. He was talking to Matron in a low voice, but not so low that Laura could not hear.

"Well, we've done what we can, Doctor," Matron was saying, "But she won't respond. She pretends she doesn't understand a word, but I'm sure she understands more than she lets on. She won't eat, won't speak, won't even look you in the eye."

"Has it occurred to you, Matron, to try to imagine what this child has gone through?" replied the doctor. "She spent the war years in occupied France, I gather from your headmistress, and was then uprooted from what she thought was her family and sent to England, and then here, without anyone seeming to think of the psychological damage such arbitrary treatment could result in. I'm not surprised that the child felt suicidal – don't try and fool me, Matron, it was a suicide attempt, wasn't it?"

Matron looked uncomfortable.

"I really couldn't say, doctor," she replied. "All I know is that she and Georgina Charlton were found in the Pond, sopping wet and half-drowned."

The doctor glanced at Laura and saw that her eyes were open.

"Ah, Laura, you're awake." he said in passable French.

Laura looked at him blankly. The desire to reply to him in her own language was strong, but the instinct that had forbidden her to make any response to these alien, English people was stronger.

The doctor smiled.

"*Je comprends,*" he said. "But you've made your protest, and now I'm going to do something about it." He examined her quickly, pronounced her physically undamaged and turned back to Matron.

"I'm going back to have a talk with Miss Morrisson," he said. "There's a French doctor here, attached to the hospital. Her name's Miriam Stein. I'm going to arrange for her to come to talk to this poor child. She may even be able to come tonight." He looked at Laura and repeated the gist of what he had said in French.

"Now I want you to eat and to sleep," he finished.

Laura shook her head minimally.

"Try and get a little warm milk into her," the doctor said to Matron. "And I think it might be sensible to move her into the isolation room so that if Dr Stein can come tonight she has some privacy ..." He looked towards Georgina's bed, and saw that she was asleep again.

"I don't want anyone gossiping about this, Matron. If Georgina Charlton wants to know where she's gone, just tell her she's in the isolation room so that they can each have some peace. Georgina can go back to school tomorrow, but this one – well, let's wait and see." He put away his stethoscope and closed his black bag. "You just make sure, Matron, that Laura in particular is kept warm – I suggest you put a hot water bottle in the bed before you move her and give her another blanket." He patted Laura on her unresponsive cheek and strode out.

Matron followed, but not before she'd whispered to Laura, "I know you understand English, Miss, and this special treatment won't last for long."

Later, lying in the isolation room, with two stone hot water bottles that warmed her outwardly but did nothing for her inner cold, Laura thought that if she was going to acknowledge that she understood English it would not be to this fat woman with the piggy eyes. She might, she thought, if she found she had to, admit it to the girl who'd pulled her from the water. Or the other one who had gone to fetch help. She'd observed them, standing together outside the circle of girls who always surrounded the tall dark one. They were outsiders, just as she was. Through the window she could see the cold stars shining in the clear, frosty sky, and thought of the times she had stood with the woman she had thought was her mother and counted the stars with her brothers and sisters, and wondered if they were looking at them in France. She felt the tears welling up, and with all the self-control she could find she willed them back. Why had she not let herself fall into the water? Water which had been welcoming her and pulling her down into its embrace. She felt despair overcome her again. What could she do, to escape this terrible place where she had been sent without explanation? When Ruby brought in her supper she pushed it away. Ruby must have told Matron because Matron came back later with a glass of warm milk and, quite gently for her, spooned a few mouthfuls between Laura's unwilling lips.

CHAPTER Two

The milk that Matron had brought tasted disgusting, thought Laura. She had allowed Matron to give her a few mouthfuls, but as soon as the immediate pangs of hunger were stilled she turned her face away. She wondered what they would do with her now. I don't care, she thought. Nothing worse can happen to me than has happened in this last year. The only thing I want is to go back to my family in France, and never leave them again.

She lay quite still in the narrow bed, listening as the house grew quieter. The light in her room was out, but the top half of the door was panelled in mottled glass, allowing light from the hall to penetrate. She heard Matron go upstairs to her room, then the maids come up from the basement. The hall light went out and the house was silent, the tick of the big clock in the hall the only noise. Then, much later, she heard a car crunch on the gravel drive, and stop. A door opened and shut, and someone knocked on the front door. She heard Matron come heavily down the stairs, and the hall light came on.

This was what she had been waiting for, she realised. Without consciously admitting it, she had taken in what the English doctor had said, and had been waiting for this Dr Stein to come. Footsteps came towards her door and Matron said quietly, "I think she may be asleep."

A foreign voice spoke. "I'll wake her, then. This situation cannot go on any longer, Matron."

The door opened and a tall, dark haired woman came towards the bed. Her features were clean-cut and bold, a long defined mouth, a slightly curved nose.

"Laura," she whispered in French. "Are you awake?"

Laura took in a great breath as if she had come to the end of a race.

"*Oui*," she whispered. "I'm awake."

Miriam Stein's voice was deep and warm, the French so welcome after all the months of English.

She sat down on the bed, held out her arms and pulled Laura up towards her. An involuntary sob convulsed Laura as she tried to resist. Then Dr Stein put up a hand and smoothed her hair, and the gesture, so reminiscent of Maman – Tante Marie-Claude, as she had to call her now – broke her determination and with a sigh she collapsed and cried. She smelled the perfume, felt the softness of the woollen sweater against her face. As Miriam whispered over and over in French *"Ma pauvre petite,"* she felt the stored up misery coming out of her. She did not care that she had never met this woman before. Her arms were almost as comforting as Maman's, the words she was saying were the familiar endearments she had heard all her life and she recognised that she could no longer keep her story hidden inside her, that it was making everything so painful that she had wanted to end it all.

She pulled back from Miriam, and took a deep breath.

"My name is not Laura Martin," she said in French. "It's Laurence Bonneville."

Gradually the story came out, supplemented for Miriam Stein by the facts she had gained from Laura's grandmother. She was glad now that she had telephoned, for she had hesitated, wanting to hear without prejudice what Laura Martin herself had to say. George Maxwell had been adamant that something was seriously wrong.

"This child tried to kill herself this afternoon," he had said, pushing his way into Miriam's warm flat, putting his hat down on the papers on which she had been working. "Walked into the lake in the school grounds – the Pond they call it, but it's bigger than a pond. And no one seems to know anything about her.

Apparently her father was English, living in France when the war broke out, and the mother was dead. The grandmother thought both the father and the child were dead, until she got a letter from some French people saying the girl was not dead and had been living with them all through the war. So the grandmother ups sticks and goes to get her, and sends her to Baynes. What on earth can she have been thinking of? The child can't speak a word of English ... neither Edith Morrisson nor Agnes Becquet can get a word out of her."

Miriam knew Agnes Becquet, a dried-up stick of a woman who had been teaching French for decades, and who understood nothing that did not come out of a textbook. She was not surprised that Agnes had not been able to persuade this girl to speak.

"So you want me to talk to her?" she said drily. "Why do you think I'll be able to get more from her than Agnes Becquet?"

"Oh, come off it, Miriam," replied Maxwell. "Who else but you? You're a doctor, you're French, and you're a psychiatrist. And you're the antithesis of Mademoiselle Becquet, and all the other spinsters in that school."

Miriam laughed. It was true. Although she had been Jewish and Russian first, she could not deny that French was her first language, with English now running a close second, and she was, as George said, a doctor and a psychiatrist.

"OK George," she said. "I'll see her. But you must let me deal with it in my own way. I'm not sure, but I think I'd better speak to the grandmother first. Anyway, give me her telephone number. Where did you say she lived?"

"Newcastle upon Tyne."

They discussed the situation for a few moments more, while Maxwell drank a cup of the bitter coffee of which Miriam seemed to have an endless supply, before he reluctantly left the warm book-filled room.

Miriam picked up the telephone and placed a trunk call. She had been to Newcastle once, and remembered it as a cold, dark, grey city, quite grand, but sombre.

When the telephone rang, a voice that Miriam identified as old and not very confident answered.

"Mrs Martin?" Miriam said.

"Speaking," said the voice.

"I'm telephoning about Laura," said Miriam tentatively. "Do you know ...?"

"Miss Morrison has already telephoned me. I'm coming tomorrow. This is all very distressing ..."

Miriam explained who she was.

"I'm at my wit's end. I'm not used to children. It's a long while since my son was a child." Mrs Martin sighed and Miriam heard regret in the old voice. "Now Laura is all I've got left but she's a closed book to me."

"Tell me about her," said Miriam. "How does she come to speak only French?"

"It's a long story," replied the grandmother. There was a pause and then her voice came back more strongly. "However, you'd better have the gist of it. My son, Robert, lived in France. He very rarely came home. He married an English girl he met out there and Laura was born in 1936. Unfortunately, the mother died when Laura was born and Robert never got over it. He didn't reply to letters."

"You never visited him?"

Mrs Martin hesitated, and then said, "The situation was complicated. We'd not been on good terms with him, well his father hadn't ... and when his father died nothing really changed. Robert came to the funeral but, well, we still didn't get on. Robert did ask me to go to the wedding, but I'm not strong ... the journey. Then he wrote to say his wife had died and that he wanted to be left alone ..."

"So you never saw Laura as a baby?"

"No. And he never came back to England. Then the war came, and we could find out nothing." Miriam could hear the disbelief in her voice. No one who had not had to find something out could understand the impenetrable curtain which cut off one country from another in time of war; the blankness, the impossibility.

"I had a brother there," she said. "I understand. Do go on, Mrs Martin."

The old voice continued. "After the war I wrote to the Mayor of the local town, and I received a letter back telling me that nothing had been heard of Monsieur Martin since the German occupation and that the child had died. He sent me a copy of the death certificate. The cause was noted as *scarlatine* – scarlet fever." She stopped and Miriam felt a shiver go through her.

"But she hadn't died?" she said.

"No." said the grandmother. "She hadn't. Last year, more than a year after the war ended, I got a letter from a family called Bonneville who had apparently looked after Laura since she was a baby. It said that Laura was alive and that their consciences could not allow them to go on pretending that Laura was dead. I don't really understand what happened ..." she sighed. "But it's all legal. Laura *is* my grandchild ..." Her voice died away.

"Just tell me what you know," Miriam said.

"As far as I can understand, because of the war and the fact that Laura's father was in the Resistance, and an Englishman, this family, the Bonnevilles, had to pretend, when her father was caught and the Germans came to find her, that it was Laura who had died, when actually it was their own daughter. Even the priest was in on the deception, so no wonder the Mayor, who just looked up the facts, searched no further for Laura."

"And what about her father?"

"They said in the letter that they presumed he was dead, but no one knew for certain. He just disappeared."

Miriam shivered again. Just like Nathan, she thought.

"Mrs Martin," she said. "Many people disappeared without trace in Europe during the war. If he hasn't come back, well, I think you should accept it ... I'm sorry. But no wonder the poor child is ..." she tried to think of a tactful word "... confused – she probably has no idea who she is or what's happened to her."

"I should have been more careful," said old Mrs Martin. "I was just so relieved to find her that it never occurred to me that the problem would be anything other than a linguistic one. I thought that if I sent her to Baynes, she would learn English more quickly from her contemporaries."

Unbelievable, thought Miriam. She said carefully, "So she would, in the normal course of events. But in Laura's case, much more important than the language is the identity. One day she's a French child living with the people she thinks are her parents. The next, she's told she's English, and has no parents, and before she knows what has happened she is here, alone. I have my own views on English boarding schools."

"So I gather," said Mrs Martin. Miriam could hear her sigh over the phone. "But don't be too hard on us, Dr Stein. Some very worthwhile people are turned out by our boarding schools."

"At what cost?" murmured Miriam.

They had arranged to meet the following day. Miriam had then telephoned Edith Morrison, the school's headmistress, whom she had met and found interesting, if not entirely likeable, and now here she was with the subject of the evening's conversations in person, clinging to her so closely that she could hardly see her. She gently loosened the girl's hands and pushed her slightly away from her, though not letting go. She would have to be very, very careful, she thought.

"Let me look at you," she said.

She saw a small, dark, sallow-complexioned girl, very thin – she hasn't been eating, thought Miriam. The hair was dark and short, and the green eyes, now shiny with tears and small and red-rimmed, slanted upwards slightly, giving her a faintly cat-like look.

"I want you to tell me everything that has happened, Laura," she said. "Everything. I know a little. I know that you lived in France with a family after your father died."

"*My* family," said Laura passionately. "*My* family, *my* mother and *my* father. I can't remember the man you now all say is my father. And my name is Laurence, not Laura."

That must have been confusing to her classmates to start with, thought Miriam. And no wonder she can't remember her real father. Apart from the fact that she probably doesn't want to, she can only have been three or four when he disappeared. In fact, she discovered later, Laura Martin had not seen her real father since she was four years old, in the spring of 1940.

"All right, Laurence," she said with a smile. "With me you'll be Laurence, until you decide to be Laura. Now, tell me Laurence's story."

***

Georgina wondered for a second, in the grey light of dawn, where she was. Then she remembered and with the memory came a sharp sting of anxiety. How close that nosy doctor had come to learning her secret, which no one here must ever know. She had changed so utterly since coming to Baynes that she could hardly remember what she had been like before she won the scholarship, two years and one term earlier, and hoped that no one who had met her then could remember either. That hated name, Gloria. How could her mother have called her that? But in the rough streets where she lived, down by the docks in North Shields, there were many Glorias.

"Glo...ree...aa." Georgina shuddered as she heard in her head the moronic sound, rising at the end so that it never seemed finished. She loathed it every time she heard it. She wondered if she would really miss home if she never saw it again. I'd miss Mam – my mother, she corrected herself – but none of the others, she thought, and felt guilty because she had not included her father or her two brothers. I'd miss Baynes more than I've ever missed home, she thought, and wondered if it was wicked to feel like this. She loved Baynes, everything it was, everything it stood for. When she first saw it, she had thought she would die if she couldn't come there.

The school was famous, founded in the late 1890s by a disciple of the formidable Miss Buss. This first headmistress, Elizabeth Baynes, had purchased the small Georgian manor house that still stood at the centre of Baynes, but over the years the school had grown in size as well as in stature, and the original house had been built onto in numerous different ways. Other nearby houses had been bought, so that now the school grounds were immense, sweeping down to the river that was the boundary to the south. Playing fields and tennis courts had been carefully planned not to spoil the original garden, which still flourished beneath the terrace running the length the old house.

Elizabeth Baynes had set her school on the outskirts of the town where she herself had been brought up. This cold northern town had welcomed the school, and now enjoyed the fame the school brought, for quite swiftly it had become recognised for its academic worth and its modern attitude towards education for women. Baynes girls became doctors, lawyers, teachers and university lecturers, missionaries and staunch pillars of their communities, though a few who refused to conform would slip through the net, as Harriet would.

Georgina had come to Baynes through Dotty Brand, teacher, friend, and old Baynes girl.

"I've got a pearl for you," Dotty Brand had said to the headmistress, a woman who had been head girl in Dotty's time. "She's very, very bright."

"Put her in for a scholarship then, Dotty," replied the Edith Morrisson. "I suppose she's one of your lame ducks?"

Dotty had once or twice before tried to get places for children she thought were deserving but poor, but the Baynes rules were strict: win a full scholarship or pay the fees.

"Well, yes, in a way," replied Dotty. "But this one *will* get a scholarship. I've only got one worry ..." she frowned. It was embarrassing to talk about class, something that she and Edith Morrisson had never had to worry about. "It's her accent. Pure Tyneside. She'll get dreadfully teased."

"She'll soon learn," said Edith. "Others have. They copy, at that age. What's the family like?"

Dotty felt embarrassed again, at having to describe in Edith's terms the stubborn, determined woman who had brought Gloria to her at the age of five. She could hear her words now.

"I want her out of that, Miss," she had said, indicating with a wave of her hand the seedy streets lying only a mile or two away from Dotty's school. This school, in the next small town along the coast, was in more salubrious surroundings, though not so far away that Dotty couldn't almost always smell the fish and guano.

Dotty had liked Gloria's mother with her blunt honesty. "Her father's a layabout," she had said. "Would give up his job tomorrow if he could, and spend his time in the pub, if he didn't have to support us – I've got two boys older than Gloria. Steve and Geordie. Me eldest, Davy, he was killed at Dunkirk, last year. He were only nineteen ... and the best of the bunch, save her." Mrs Charlton's eyes filled with tears, which she wiped away with a hand.

"I'm sorry," said Dotty. The man she had been going to marry had also been killed the year before, on leave in London where a bomb had found him, so that he had not even been killed in action.

"War's always taken the best," said Gloria's mother, and went on to tell Dotty the ambitions she had for Gloria.

Gloria had been a late addition to her family, she said. Unexpected, but now a blessing. And clever.

"Could read when she were four. I taught her. I diven'na where she gets it from." Probably from you, thought Dotty, who guessed that there were untapped resources in Gloria's mother.

Mrs Charlton produced a newspaper cutting from her bag. It told the story of a girl in Dotty's school who had gained a scholarship to one of the well-known schools in Newcastle.

"This is why I've come to you," she said. "You can get wor Gloria out of this. I want summat better for her." Dotty found Mrs Charlton hard to understand – she had the harsh accent, the glottal t's and d's, the peculiar dialect of Tyneside to a stronger degree than most of the parents in Dotty's school.

"It doesn't entirely depend on me," she replied. "It will be up to Gloria. We'll see how she gets on."

"Oh, she'll manage," asserted Mrs Charlton, with a faith in her daughter that Dotty understood when she started teaching Gloria.

She was a remarkable child. Not only was she good at reading and writing, maths and nature study, she also showed talent for the piano, which Dotty started to teach her. She was good at games and gym. Above all, thought Dotty, she's nice. I can't think of a better word. I think of her as a friend. She laughed to herself. Whoever heard of a headmistress having an eight-year-old pupil as a friend? And yet ... that's what she is. She enjoyed her after-school teaching sessions with Gloria, preparing her for the scholarship she was sure she would get.

Dotty had not been sure which one to put her in for. In a way she resented the thought that one of the big Newcastle schools would get her prodigy. She'll disappear from my life, she thought. But if she went to Baynes there was her own connection … Impossible. How could the family ever pay for the uniform, the extras, the travel? How could a child from the back streets of North Shields ever get to a school like Baynes? But once the idea had come to her, Dotty found that she could not let it go. She had decided to consult Edith Morrison.

Now she said to her, "The family's very poor. It's the mother who has the ambition – and I haven't even told her that Baynes might be in the running."

"Probably never heard of it," commented Edith.

"Well, for the moment her sights are set on the Church High or the Central High in Newcastle."

"Well, wouldn't they be better – they're closer and they wouldn't involve boarding?" said Edith.

"In the short run, yes," said Dotty. "But in the long run I have to think of Gloria, and a school like Baynes would be so much better. Lift her right out of it …"

"You're just a snob, Dotty," said Edith. "You just want to turn her into another middle-class child like you were."

"You haven't seen the deprivation, Edith," replied Dotty. "Remember, I chose to teach in the state system, unlike you, and I've taught in some pretty rough places. This school is better than most I've taught in, because it's in a fairly well-to-do part of the area, but where Gloria comes from it's really hard. There's bomb damage everywhere, streets filled with rubbish, the houses all damp and falling to bits. I could go on and on."

"I get the picture," said Edith. "I can see why you want to get her out of it, but why her? There must be hundreds of deserving children living in just such circumstances."

"I can't be a guardian angel to them all," replied Dotty. "Isn't it better to do something for just one than none at all? At least some of my guilt for having had all this might be assuaged."

She gestured towards the school from where they were sitting on the lawn under the ancient cedar tree. It was an untimely warm and sunny spring day in March, with daffodils and tulips filling the borders. Through the big windows looking on to the terrace she could see girls at their desks. A few walked past them, heads bent towards each other in the intimacy of adolescent friendships. From inside the school came the ringing of the bell which had been placed in the front hall by Elizabeth Baynes herself, and a hum of sound came from the open windows as classes came to an end for the morning. It was a Saturday, and an afternoon of hockey matches, lacrosse games or walks into the country lay in front of the pupils.

"There's a new scholarship, Dotty," said Edith, getting up. "An Old Girl endowment for eight-year-olds all the way through. Your Gloria could sit for that in May, and then she could come straight away, next September. If she won it, of course." She looked sceptical, and Dotty found herself saying in Mrs Charlton's confident tone, "She'll manage," before all the implications of this new scholarship hit her.

All through lunch, taken in the elegant, big round dining room up on the first floor, where she sat at Edith's side, and felt like a pupil again as silent grace was said and portions of fairly awful food were put in front of her, she thought about Gloria and the possibility of getting her here. All round the soaring walls of the room were the varnished wooden boards engraved in gold with the names of Prize Winners and Head Girls, who year by year had achieved the best for themselves or for Baynes. Would Gloria's name be there one day? The pros and cons went round and round in Dotty's head.

First, this was not what Gloria's mother had asked for. Maybe she wouldn't tolerate the child being away from home. Secondly, Dotty had been relying on another two years of tuition under her own capable hands before Gloria sat for an eleven-year-old entry to the Newcastle schools. Another two years, too, she thought wryly, of trying to improve that dreadful accent. Gloria's voice had softened a bit since she'd been with children from more middle-class homes, but after every holiday Dotty found herself newly horrified at the strength of the accent. Really, it shouldn't matter, she thought to herself, but of course, it will.

She listened to the girls sitting at her table, a mixture of all ages, for even mealtimes were considered educationally valuable at Baynes, and the girls were not allowed to sit next to their friends but were allocated what were called Mealsides, the girls they sat next to for the duration of each term. Sometimes thought cruelly hard on the shy or timid, or very young, the system in the end paid off, each girl knowing girls throughout the school.

The voices she heard were clear, confident young voices being groomed for a world in which what they said would carry weight. In their bottle-green blazers and square necked white blouses they looked like a young army, a unified body that would give any outsider a feeling of inferiority. And that was another thing, she thought. How on earth would the Charlton parents afford the clothes that Gloria would need? It was more than just a blazer and a tunic. It involved afternoon dresses and Sunday dresses, indoor shoes and outdoor shoes, games clothes and hockey sticks, all the paraphernalia that a school acquires when it has been building a tradition over many years. Any school starting today would not need those blasted afternoon dresses, thought Dotty disloyally, a thought which she had voiced once to Edith, only to be told that part of the girls' education was to learn to wear the right sort of clothes for the right occasion. "School tea hardly qualifies for that," Dotty had said, but Edith had been adamant. "It's part of the tradition," she had replied, "and once you start chipping away at that there's no stopping. Then you find you've destroyed valuable, intangible things in trying to streamline everything."

Dorothy was brought back to the present by the sudden cessation of noise. Edith had rung her little silver bell for the end of lunch and the girls were pushing their chairs back under the tables, filing out in a neat queue of green.

"You've been miles away, Dotty," Edith said. "Come downstairs, and I'll get you the papers. She'll face stiff competition, mind."

When Dotty discovered that the scholarship covered uniform and games equipment too, in fact everything a pupil might need, her mind was made up. The exam would be sat in May, and over the school holidays she would give her extra tuition. Now all she had to do was to persuade Gloria's mother.

In the event, little persuasion was needed.

"Baynes?" Mrs Charlton had said. "Why of course I know about Baynes, it's one of the best schools in the country. If she could go there, it'd be grand. But what about the clothes? I've a bit put by, for the uniform like …"

"It's all in the scholarship," said Dotty. "It covers tuition, clothes, books, the lot. And …" She hesitated. "Mrs Charlton, I hope you will take this in the way I mean it. I'm unlikely ever to get married now," – she glanced at the photograph on her desk of her dead fiancé – "and therefore I'll never have the pleasure of being able to give presents to my children. I wonder, would you let me help provide for Gloria in a small way, like a godmother almost?" Her voice fell away as she thought how dreadful this sounded, as if the Charltons were a charity case.

But Edna Charlton recognised the appeal in Dotty's voice. If Miss Brand wanted to concern herself with Gloria, she would have an ally, someone who could tell her what Gloria needed for this venture into the unknown.

"You're a very generous woman," she said. "You tell me what she needs, if she gets the scholarship, mind, and then you and me can work it out together. We'll not bother her father with the details." She picked up the glossy brochure that Dotty had brought back with her.

"By, it's grand place," she said. "Who'd have thought it, wor Gloria ..."

A smile of triumph crossed her face and Dotty smiled back, a bond of complicity between the two women.

And so it was that one May morning Gloria Charlton found herself walking up the drive with Dotty Brand. She had seen the brochure, read the descriptions in it of what Baynes offered, but nothing had prepared her for the school in action. The big classrooms were airy and light; the teachers seeming like lots of Miss Brands, and the girls were terrifying. The older ones looked polished and sophisticated, and the younger Baynes girls swung along confidently in their matching tunics and coloured girdles, which signified the House they belonged to, Gloria knew from Miss Brand.

Even in the Junior classes, which were where she would go if she won the scholarship, the girls looked different from her friends at home. They stared coolly at Dotty and Gloria, who had come early so that Dotty could show Gloria the school. One girl giggled and whispered something behind her hand. Gloria knew instinctively what it was. It was the awful coat she was wearing, a purple coat handed down to her by her aunt, and accepted by Edna because she couldn't afford to turn away hand-me-downs. She took it off, claiming to Dotty that she was too hot, though the day was in fact quite cool, and thought in that moment, I *will* come here, and I *will* be like them, and I *will* belong.

One of the girls to whom Dotty had been talking turned to Gloria.

"What's your name?" she said in a clear, upper-class voice, the sort of voice Gloria had heard on the wireless and had secretly imitated in her bedroom.

Gloria looked at Miss Brand, willing her to keep silent.

"Georgina," she said, using a passable pronunciation. "My name is Georgina."

Dotty opened her mouth to say something, and then thought better of it.

After Gloria had come out of the room where the scholarship exam had been taken, a room where seven very nervous children had bitten their pens and frowned over the questions, and one completely confident child had worked quietly through the paper and finished in excellent time, Dotty asked her why she had said that her name was Georgina.

"Why, Gloria? It's not your name." Though it's a darned sight nicer than Gloria, Dotty thought to herself.

Gloria looked at her, her face set. "You can't be called Gloria in a place like this," she said. "From now on, my name's Georgina. Like the girl in the Enid Blyton books."

And of course she had won the scholarship and had become a Baynes pupil whose name was Georgina Charlton.

***

Harriet had never thought of her parents as a unit. There was her mother, who was always there, and her father who came and went. So when her mother told her that there was going to be a divorce, Harriet was not really worried. It was only when she realised that everything she had ever known was going to change that she took in the full impact of what it would mean.

Firstly there would be no more living in the country and going to the village school. There would in fact be no home at all, because her father was going to London and she and her mother were going to live with Granny Carruthers in the house in Newcastle for a time. It was 1945, the war coming to an end, so living in the country was no longer necessary for Harriet's safety.

"Just until I get settled, darling," Isabel Bolton said, her face carefully showing no emotion. "Then we'll have a house again."

"Here?" demanded Harriet, who as far as she could remember had always lived in the remote Northumbrian countryside.

"No, darling. In Newcastle," replied her mother. Harriet felt dismay. She dreaded the great grey city, which she hardly knew. She felt the anger that was inside her boiling up, a feeling that she gave in to increasingly, and with increasing satisfaction. Her face became red.

"I won't go, and I hate you both!" she yelled, crashing her foot down on the sitting room floor. Isabel Bolton's face became even whiter than it had been when she had started this conversation. Harriet was becoming impossible. Alec was right – she would have to go away to school, and even if circumstances had not forced it she might have decided to send Harriet away early anyway.

Now she said quietly, "It's no use shouting, Harriet. We are moving to Newcastle. Your father is going to London, and you are going to Baynes School. That was always planned but now you'll go a little earlier than we'd thought. And personally I can't wait to get away from here. Now go upstairs until you've calmed down."

Later, calm after her storm of tears, Harriet gazed forlornly out of her bedroom window at the peaceful countryside with its brownish-green grass stretching away upwards until it met the smoky purple heather of the high hills. She couldn't bear to think of life going on here without her. The smells of farms and animals and crushed grass, the mysterious woods and coppices, the clear streams running with peaty water, the frosty nights burning cold, the hot summer days when the only thing that moved was an aeroplane wheeling lazily in the sky – all these things were part of her and would remain so for ever. She could not know that the remoteness of this place that she so loved had mortally damaged her mother with the loneliness it had thrust upon her, and had caused wounds of neglect and dismissal that would never entirely heal.

That night she cried again, not knowing exactly what she cried for – was it for the loss of her father, who was already packing his things into boxes, taking his busy presence away? Or was it for the loss of her childhood? Or was it fear of going to boarding school, which she knew of through books but not through anyone she knew, and had not expected yet? Or was it for her mother who looked so white and frail that Harriet thought she might just blow away? Harriet had never really thought about her parents. They were just there, just parents. Now she thought how different they were from each other.

Her mother was quiet and gentle. She read a great deal of the time, and only occasionally went out with her father when he came up from Newcastle. Often she would shut herself away in the drawing room and Harriet would be left to her own company, which she didn't mind because she could make up games on her own without having to explain them to anyone. She had an imaginary friend with whom she could spend whole days.

Her father liked noise and bustle and people, having them in for drinks or dinner, which her mother always said exhausted her. He liked picking Harriet up and letting her ride on his shoulders, and he made up stories about people who didn't exist. She didn't quite know what her father did – he was not in the war for some reason, though he had been at first. Then there had been letters and telegrams, and the words "pneumonia" and "invalided out" had swum into Harriet's hearing, and after a while her father had been at home for quite a long time, resting. Then there had been a long and terrible quarrel between him and her mother and now he did things to do with the war, which was why he was often in Newcastle.

Thinking these thoughts, Harriet realised that in a way she had been waiting for this to happen. There had been too many quarrels. In a way, it was a relief. At least she would not have to go through any more of the occasions on which she could see a row beginning and then find herself asked to take sides. She hated it, her loyalty lying always with her mother but her intelligence telling her that sometimes her father was right. Now there would be no more of that. Instead there would be the great plunge into the unknown.

Gradually her sobs lessened and she slept. When she woke the next morning, she found that she was resigned to the coming changes. Resigned, but not accepting.

Throughout that last summer in the country, Harriet looked at everything through the eyes of the condemned. Everywhere she went, she felt she was seeing for the last time: the woods, the streams, the lonely roads She remembered winters when the river that she crossed on the way to school had filled and overflowed its banks, a fullness of water which both thrilled and frightened her in its shimmering silver immensity. Would she ever see it again? She thought of the satisfying noise her steel-rimmed clogs had made on the frost-hard road, clogs that she had persuaded her mother to buy when her shoes wore out, because they didn't need coupons. She would never wear a pair of those again.

Harriet had loved her wartime childhood. Years later, when she learned of the unthinkable horrors that had gone on across the North Sea, she could not believe that not a trace, not the smallest hint of what was happening, had intruded on her childhood.

It was unfortunate that her first day at Baynes was her ninth birthday.

"I won't stay!" she had screamed, pulling at her mother's coat, watched silently by the fat white-coated woman into whose charge she was to be given.

Her mother put her arms around her again.

"It won't be long, darling," she whispered. "You'll soon be home. We'll come to see you."

"No you won't," cried Harriet hysterically. "You can't drive, and Daddy's going away ..." She stopped speaking, overcome by tears.

The day was coming to an end, and dark clouds were sweeping across the sky, bringing a few drops of rain to the gravelled drive in front of the Baynes Junior boarding house.

"I think it would be better if Harriet came with me, Mrs Bolton," Matron said, coming down the steps and inserting her fat bulk between the crying child and her mother. She took Harriet's hand, seeming not to feel her pulling her hand away.

"Say goodbye to your parents, Harriet," she ordered.

"I won't!" screamed Harriet as she was pulled inexorably towards the door.

Her parents turned towards the car from which her new trunk had been unloaded. "Be a good girl, Harriet," her father said as he opened the car door. "We'll see you soon." Her mother waved weakly, but Harriet had already disappeared, pulled bodily by Matron into the front hall of June's.

It was not an auspicious beginning.

Everything seemed strange. Her whole world had been changed, and the only things that remained reliable were possessions, to which she clung with a passion. Her rag dolls, Dinah and Dorinda, meant more to her than any of the children around her. In her pencil case she found a pencil the she had drawn with at home, before any of this had happened. The pencil was gold, with a fat lump of fake gold embossed on the end of it. She went to sleep clutching it and during the next weeks the pencil became a sort of talisman, as did the dolls. These were the first of the objects Harriet was to cling to for reassurance that, although people might come and go, things remained; a habit she was to know for the rest of her life.

But that was all in the undiscovered future. At Baynes in the autumn of 1945 Harriet was learning that no matter how much she shouted and cried it would not change the reality of school. She also learned that homesickness could provoke physical sickness and spent much of the first term in bed in the San, having once again vomited her unwillingly eaten supper, or having had to be led out of the dining room at breakfast when something called Polony had made her go white and then green.

Life to Harriet had never seemed bleaker. The only compensation was the entry of Georgina into her life.

Harriet first saw her standing under the Edwardian stained glass window gazing at her dispassionately from the landing half way up the stairs.

"Don't stare at me!" she had shrieked. "I hate all of you," she continued hysterically, until Matron had taken one of her sandy plaits and pulled it quite hard, stopping a scream by the force of her tug.

"You'd do well to note how Georgina Charlton behaves, Miss," Matron said. "No hysterics from her when she first came."

The fair-haired girl on the stairs smiled and walked away, up the stairs to the dormitory, where her bed turned out to be next to Harriet's.

"It's not that bad," she said when, after a traumatic supper, which Harriet had refused to eat, they had been sent to bed. "Can I see your dolls?"

Harriet, finally subdued, had handed Dorinda and Dinah over silently. She pulled on her winceyette pyjamas, fingering the stitches sewn by her mother.

Matron appeared in the doorway.

"Lights out in five minutes," she announced. "Into bed, all of you." The six girls scrambled into their cold beds, which had been made with the sheets pulled so tight they could hardly slide their feet between them.

Harriet sat up in bed and lifted her head, for the first time looking round at the others. She smiled tentatively.

One girl, older than Harriet, smiled back.

"It's quite good fun here, really," she said. "I've been here for a year, and now I quite like it. Except for her," she gestured towards the door. "Matron's awful. We call her the Bun because she looks like a bun, with currants for eyes."

Matron came back and put her fat hand on the light switch.

"Night, night girls, sleep tight, mind the bugs don't bite," she said with what Harriet knew to be a false smile on her face.

"Goodnight, Matron," chorused the other girls and Harriet thought she heard someone whisper "Bun", but then the light was snapped out and the room was in total darkness. It was the last straw. She was afraid of the dark. The tears welled up and rolled down her cheeks until her pillow was sodden. Suddenly, in the darkness, she sensed someone standing by her bed.

"It's me, Georgina," whispered a voice. "I can hear you crying. You'll be all right, it's just tonight, the first night away. But it will be all right." Harriet's tears lessened. Who was this girl, who seemed to have her own wellbeing at heart?

"Where do you come from?" she whispered.

"Tynemouth," came the reply. Harriet had heard of Tynemouth. "Is it near Newcastle?" she whispered.

"Yes – it's just on the coast," replied Georgina. She touched Harriet's cheek. "You've stopped crying," she whispered.

Harriet felt an immense tiredness come over her. She yawned.

"I'd better get back," whispered Georgina, just as one of the other girls murmured, "Shhh, I can hear the Bun." The door opened and Matron stood there. "What's going on in here?" she said suspiciously, flicking a torch over the beds, but no one replied and everyone lay seemingly asleep. Even Harriet's sobs were stilled – she had fallen asleep from sheer exhaustion.

But now, a year and a half later, waking up to another Baynes day, reluctantly leaving behind her dreams, nothing for Harriet had changed much. She still resented every moment away from her mother, chivvied and chased by the Bun, teased by Meredith and her friends, spanked with a hairbrush by Matron for feeling sick.

The door opened and Georgina walked in, carrying her tunic and blouse like a trophy. Everyone crowded round her, but it was to Harriet that she spoke. "You saved Laura's life, Harry," she said. "I couldn't have held her up much longer when they came, and she would have drowned," and Harriet's world brightened. At least someone recognised what she'd done.

The Bun came in. "That'll do," she said. "No more talking. You should all be dressed. Now get a move on."

CHAPTER Three

Laura tried to remember as far back into her childhood as she could. Her earliest memory was of a picnic by a river, with a high arched bridge above. Maman was there, and Papa, and her brothers and sisters and another man, a shadowy figure but someone familiar. She tried to put the memory into place for Miriam: was it before the war, or later, after the Germans had come?

"Don't try to work it out, Laurence. Just tell me what you remember," said Miriam, who was beginning to have an idea of what must have happened. It was to be many months, however, before she, and more importantly, Laura, learned the full story.

The girl who called herself Laurence Bonneville had not been born that at all. She had been born Laura Martin, to English parents living in France. Whatever she may have felt, Laura Martin had no French blood in her veins, though for the rest of her life she was to feel the pull of the language and customs of her earliest years.

To begin to understand the confusion Miriam Stein, later that year, had to go painfully back with Marie-Claude and Paul Bonneville to a night in the autumn of 1940. In June, France had capitulated to superior German forces that occupied the North and set up the short-lived Vichy Government. Under German rule Marie-Claude and Paul had led a life of compromise, fear and deprivation. But none of that concerned them as they, the doctor and the priest kept vigil over their youngest daughter Laurence, aged four-and-a-half, and ill with scarlet fever.

Marie-Claude refused to believe that Laurence was dying, although to the doctor and to the priest it was clear that she would not last the night. The fever which had swept through the villages had taken many children from families already touched by the horrors of war, and yet it seemed unbelievable to Marie-Claude that one of her own precious five should be so arbitrarily picked out. She leant over and touched the hot cheek of the semi-conscious child, willing her to hold on for just one more night although in her heart she knew it was hopeless. She looked up at the doctor and recognized in his eyes what she had been denying to herself. Laurence had been in the grip of fever for too long. Nothing would bring down her temperature.

She sat down by Laurence's bedside and took the hot little hand in hers. It would happen tonight, she realised. Why else would Père Xavier Guy, the priest, have stayed?

Silently, Paul, her husband, came over to her and held her shoulders. The hours passed slowly, as they watched the fight go out of their daughter's face and heard her breathing get weaker. They saw the features become calm and then, finally, still. The doctor moved over to lift the child's inert wrist as the priest murmured a prayer, his voice muted and solemn.

In the dim light of early morning the movement at the door was hardly seen, but Marie-Claude heard, and turned her tired face towards it. A small figure stood there, her sharp cat-like face pinched and ugly, the colour drained from the sallow skin. She looked uncannily like the dead girl now that Laurence had lost her rosy plumpness. Only the eyes were different; Laurence's had been brown while this girl's were green.

"What has happened to Laurence?" she whispered. Marie-Claude stretched out the hand that had been holding Laurence's, and pulled the little girl to her.

"Laurence is dead, Laure," she said flatly. She had expected to feel resentment that this other child had been spared, but she felt nothing.

Laura stretched out her hand and touched Laurence's cheek, then walked silently out of the room. Paul started after her, but with a touch Marie-Claude stopped him.

"Let her go, Paul," she said.

Marie-Claude felt more tired than ever in her life before, a weariness that she felt no sleep would touch. Yet life had to go on; she had four other children to feed and care for, let alone Robert's child, Laura, who had spent most of her life with them. Slowly she got to her feet and pulled the sheet up over Laurence's face, and turned to her husband and touched his cheek with a small hopeless gesture. He started to speak, but she shook her head and left the room, her step heavy and slow. In a few moments the men left in the room heard from downstairs the squeak of the door into the kitchen, and then deep, heartfelt sobs as Marie-Claude wept in the arms of Fernande, her housekeeper and friend.

For days the big house was silent, the children – thirteen-year-old Nathalie, Jean-Claude who was eleven, nine-year-old Sabine, and Olivier, at eight now the baby of the family – coming warily into Marie-Claude's bedroom where she sat silently on a hard chair, a photograph of Laurence in her hand. When they saw their mother's face, staring so whitely at nothing, they went away, wishing for her to come back to them, to become once more the heart of the house.

"Give her time," their father said, himself worried that his wife would make no arrangements for the funeral, which could not be put off much longer. Fernande nodded in agreement. "She's strong. She'll recover. Even death recedes in time." She looked at Laura. "Even for you, too, Laure, it will get better," she said firmly, but Laura turned her head away.

"When is her father coming?" Fernande asked, passing the meagre meat dish to Paul.

"I don't know," replied Paul. He looked at Laura who appeared to be staring out of the window but who was certainly listening. "Soon, I hope." He shrugged, his expressive face showing the worry his words belied.

Paul Bonneville was a lawyer. His family had always lived in Belay, in the house built half into the hill, where generations of Bonnevilles had been born, lived and died. The village of Belay was hidden high in the hills above the coal-mining town of St Didier in central France, near Vichy, but just within the occupied zone. Paul's work took him daily into the town, which he found hot and dusty in summer, and gloomy in winter, and it was with pleasure that at night he returned to Belay, his relief on finding everything as he had left it stronger now that the war had turned every day into a gamble. Many of his friends he guessed were in the Resistance, but he himself had never been approached, for which he was thankful, for much as he loathed the Germans he had seen the reprisals they could take, and Paul Bonneville had too many hostages. His English friend, Robert Martin, Laura's father, was, he was certain, heavily involved in Resistance activities. Luckily, Paul thought, most people had forgotten that Robert was English, so French did he seem, and it was many years since he had become a French citizen. But while local people might accept Robert's position as a Frenchman, any German looking at the records would assume that Robert's position qualified him automatically for work as a spy. After the war, he learned that, as he'd guessed, all naturalised foreigners were known to the Germans.

Paul had no idea whether the English had contacted Robert, and nor did he wish to know.

"The less I know the less I can tell them," he had said the last time he had seen Robert, when it had seemed that Robert might be about to unburden himself; and a tight, guarded look had come into Robert's face.

"There's nothing to tell, old boy," he had said, reverting to the English that Paul liked to practise whenever he could. "Just, if you could go on looking after Laura for me when I'm away. Business is quite good at moment, surprisingly."

Robert was a restorer and valuer of pictures, and had a small antique shop in a more picturesque town than St Didier, a business that was successful enough to keep him and his wife, when she was alive, and now his daughter, in comfort.

Now, thinking back on that conversation, Paul thought that Robert might have meant more than was apparent in asking Paul to "to go on looking after Laura for me". For the child had lived, ever since she was born, more at the Bonneville house than at her own.

***

In 1932, Robert, who had for years refused to commit himself to any of the many women who had fallen for him, had met, in one of those casual meetings which on looking back seem so carelessly to have been allowed to happen, an English girl called Caroline Orme. Robert had been visiting a farm in a valley a few kilometres from St Didier, examining a painting found in an attic by a farmer he slightly knew, when one of the farmer's children had come, red-faced and puffed, from across the fields to say that the Marquise de Sauvigny, who lived in the chateau at the head of the valley, had broken down in her newly acquired motor car, and would Monsieur le Brun please come and help.

"I know nothing about such contraptions," grumbled M le Brun, getting up heavily from the table and swallowing the rest of his wine at a gulp.

"But I do," said Robert. "I'll go if you like?"

In the end they both went, to find the handsome Marquise de Sauvigny waiting beside her steaming and immobile car, accompanied by a creamy-skinned shy English girl who had come to be the Marquise de Sauvigny's companion and to learn French.

Robert inspected the car, pronounced it to be beyond his help, and drove them both home to the imposing Chateau Sauvigny, where he was invited to take a glass of wine with some cake, and to tell the Marquise what an Englishman was doing in this remote region of France. The silent, grave-faced Caroline had fixed her cool grey eyes upon him and he found himself telling the story as much to her as to her employer. They spoke in English, which the Marquise spoke well, for the sake of Caroline.

"I came to France many years ago," he told them. "I'd loved France since I spent two years in Paris with my parents before the war. That's where I learned to speak the language." He shrugged. "Friends say I have no accent, but I can't quite believe that."

"My dear man, it is quite true," said Mme de Sauvigny. "The fact that you learned it at such a young age explains it. After the age of ten, they say it's impossible to learn to speak French as a Frenchman. As you will learn, my dear." She turned towards Caroline. "You will learn to speak French with me, of that have no doubt. But you will never learn to speak it as Monsieur Martin does." She turned back to Robert.

"If you hadn't told me yourself, Monsieur Martin, I would never have thought you to be anything but a Frenchman. And that, I can tell you, is a compliment."

"It is indeed," smiled Robert. "I might believe from you what I don't believe from my friends. It's a strange thought, that I could pass for a Frenchman whenever I want to." He laughed. "Though I'm not sure when that would ever be necessary." Later he was to remember his words, as the necessity to appear a true Frenchman became imperative.

"Anyway," he continued, "After the war I came back to France. I spent a year in Paris, working with a French auctioneer who specialised in art, and living on a small allowance from my father. He didn't approve. Didn't like *les grenouilles*." He turned to Caroline. "The frogs."

"Any more than I like many of the Englishmen I have met," replied the Marquise with a laugh. "By the way," she turned to Caroline, "When you can say *grenouille* the way Monsieur Martin can then you too will be admitted into the company of those who can speak perfect French. It's one of those words that foreigners just cannot get their tongues around." She turned to Robert. "Please go on – you said your father didn't approve of your love for France?"

"No, he didn't. Wanted me to become a lawyer, like him. Thought anything to do with art was soft – not a job for a man. So I was lucky that he continued my allowance." He paused, not wanting to go into the arguments and rows that had filled the big house in the cold grey northern town of Newcastle.

"I haven't been back since ..." He looked out of the window, calculating, not seeing the formal gardens or the sweep of the land across the valley to the steep-sided hills. "It must have been 1926, when my father died."

"And your mother?" said the Marquise. "Is she still living in England?"

"Yes, she is. She's alone now, in that great house ..." He saw the massive house sitting squarely in its dark suburban garden, far enough away from its neighbours not to be overlooked; silent, heavy, the dark shrubs outside the windows making the inside even darker, casting a pall over the heavy brown furniture unrelieved by any bright or cheering colour. Only his mother's bedroom, for which she had been allowed to choose the decoration, had lightness and pale colours.

"But that's enough about me," he said, and the conversation moved on.

As he left, promising to arrange for the local garage to deal with the car, Caroline got up and saw him to the door. "I'm awfully glad you're here," she said in English, her grey eyes still shy but smiling now. "I was beginning to feel so lost. It's a horrible feeling, that you can't understand anyone and that no one can understand you. And the Marquise won't normally let me speak a word of English."

"Very good for you," laughed Robert. He looked very French as he said it, dark-haired and olive-skinned, with the taut, thin-hipped figure more often found on a Frenchman than on the bigger-boned English. "I hope you can understand me, though," he added. "I don't suppose the Marquise will let me call on you unless I promise only to speak French to you."

Caroline blushed. "At least I could ask you in English to explain whatever it is I don't understand," she said. "Please do come." She held out her hand in correct French fashion to wish him goodbye, and as his fingers touched hers, cool and smooth, a frisson ran through him, a feeling almost of foreboding.

Their romance was swift, helped along by both the amused and secretly envious Marquise, who remembered her own sweet days of youth and the young Marquis who had left her a widow at fifty, and by Marie-Claude Bonneville who had for a long time felt that Robert's eye had been roving too far afield. She liked Caroline when Robert brought her to one of her big Sunday lunches, where the guests sat long over the many courses. At first Caroline did not understand much, but she liked Marie-Claude and in particular Paul, who spoke slowly and carefully and listened equally carefully to her clumsy replies; and soon her French had progressed enough for her to begin to understand most of what was being said.

All through that perfect summer she and Robert met whenever he could get away.

Robert learned that Caroline was an orphan, her parents having been killed together in a road accident less than a year ago.

"There was a lot of bad luck that year. Daddy had had to sell the house where I grew up and we'd moved in with his Aunt Eleanor while he looked for a new house, and then my parents were both killed, just before Christmas." Her features started to dissolve, and she fought back the tears.

"I don't want to talk about it. Anyway, that's why I'm here. Aunt Eleanor thought a complete change would do me good, and wrote to the Marquise, whom she'd met many years ago, during the war. She smiled. "I think Aunt Eleanor was right. I mean, it is a complete change and it is doing me good. I've stopped thinking about them so sadly, and I've stopped worrying about where I'm going to live when I go back to England. I don't want to live with Aunt Eleanor forever ... I suppose I could get a job and a flat. Maybe I could teach French?" She laughed. "Though recently my lessons from you seem to have stopped ..." Robert thought that he had never heard her talk so much, and thought too that there was really no need for her ever to go back to England. Not if she became Mrs Robert Martin.

By the end of the summer it was decided. Caroline went back to England to collect her things and to bring Aunt Eleanor back with her to see her married; but Aunt Eleanor had been unable to come, the first sign of the illness that was eventually to kill her suddenly manifesting itself.

Robert arranged for the civil ceremony to take place in St Didier.

"No church service in Belay?" said Marie-Claude, shocked. Staunchly Catholic, she believed that marriages could only really be made in church, but Robert reminded her that only the civil ceremony was binding in France, and was obligatory.

"It's more important here to be married in the eyes of the Law than in the eye of God," he quipped, and then, seeing her shocked face, he said more seriously, "Neither Caroline nor I are Catholic and it would be hard to find a Church of England around here. And we do want to have the wedding here in France. Tell you what, though," he continued, thinking as he spoke, "If you could arrange for Père Guy to give us a blessing, it would be wonderful. Caroline would be pleased – I know she feels that a civil ceremony isn't quite the same as a church wedding."

And so when Caroline came back it was all arranged. First the civil ceremony in St Didier, then a quiet blessing in the ornate little church in Belay, with its statues of the Virgin Mary and its elaborate altar, so different from the English churches Caroline was used to. The only guests were Paul and Marie-Claude Bonneville and the Marquise. Robert's mother, to whom he had written imploring her to come, had written back saying that her health was as usual not good enough to allow her to travel, although she wished them both luck and enclosed a cheque for £100 as a wedding gift. He kept his disappointment quiet, and spent the money on a new bed and some essentials for the kitchen of the small cottage where he lived, ten minutes down the road from the Bonnevilles' house.

Caroline looked heavenly, thought Robert on his wedding day, dressed in a cream shantung silk dress, so light and pale it was almost like gauze, with a little hat of apricot velvet, matching the late roses she carried. Her thick pale hair hung straight and heavy to her shoulders, contrasting strangely with the dark lines of her brow and the black eyelashes that fringed her grey eyes.

They had two perfect years of marriage, living in Robert's old cottage, Caroline making it more feminine and learning from Marie-Claude the routines of a French housewife. She and Marie-Claude became close, though Marie-Claude was to realise some years later how little, in fact, Caroline had divulged about her former life.

Then in the summer of 1935, Caroline discovered that she was pregnant. She was delighted, and even more so when she found that Marie-Claude was in the same interesting condition, though a little more advanced than Caroline.

"What a pity they couldn't be born on the same day," she said smiling, radiant with the bloom that had never left her since her marriage. Gradually, though, as the pregnancy progressed, that bloom did leave her. She became tired, envious of the energy that Marie-Claude still possessed.

The doctor became concerned as Caroline's blood pressure rose and she was confined to bed. Fernande took to bringing meals for the two of them to the cottage, and eventually Marie-Claude suggested to Paul that Caroline and he move in with them until after the birth.

"I don't like leaving her alone," said Marie-Claude, a worried frown creasing her usually unlined forehead. "It would be better if she were here, where there's someone always around. I worry about her."

Robert, too, was worried about his wife, as he watched her face become ever more strained, the thick pale hair become lank, and he saw the effort she had to make even to raise herself in the bed.

"I have no energy," she said to him. "It's all gone to make this baby."

He went to the doctor alone.

"I don't know," said the doctor. "She has high blood pressure, but there's something else. I would feel happier if she were in hospital where she could be observed more closely."

But Caroline, with a show of spirit that cheered Robert, refused to go. She was only having a baby, she said, she was not ill, and she was not going to spend the rest of her pregnancy surrounded by people who could not speak her language.

"I would feel so ... so alien, so ... *forgotten* almost."

Under the protestation Robert detected fear and panic, and realized that although she seemed to have adapted so well to her new country, it was hardly more than three years since her parents had died and her life had changed so fundamentally. So, although the move was made to the Bonneville's house, no more was said about hospital, and when next he saw her the doctor seemed relieved.

"Well, at least the baby is strong and kicking," he said. "Stronger than its mother," he laughed. "And now you're here, with the redoubtable Fernande to look after you, I'm reassured. She's probably brought as many babies into the world as I have. However," Dr Jacquot continued, "I will be taking you into hospital before the birth. All right, all right, I'll leave it as late as I dare," he said hurriedly as he saw Caroline's face. "But I want you in for the last two weeks." He turned to Robert. "I must insist on that."

As it happened, he was not able to insist, for the baby was born prematurely, four weeks before it was due, in the high wooden bed in Marie-Claude's spare room, when the doctor was on the other side of the district delivering a child in a house without a telephone. By the time a message could reach him, it was too late to move Caroline, and by the time he got there, too late to save her.

Fernande had done her best.

"There's too much blood," she said to the doctor as he arrived at a run, tearing off his jacket as he leapt up the stairs. Caroline lay exhausted and white, a new contraction racking her body every few minutes, leaving her spent and faint in between. Marie-Claude, her own body extended in what must have seemed an unfair parody, stood on one side, holding Caroline's hand and smoothing the fair hair back from her forehead with a damp cloth, while on the other side Robert, white and drawn and yet trying not to show how frightened he was, stroked his wife's tensed hand and murmured encouragement to her.

The doctor examined her rapidly then said, "I'll have to operate. It will have to be a Caesarean. And we can't move her – the birth is too far on." He turned to Robert.

"She has *placenta previa*. The placenta is in the way of the birth canal. I should have suspected it, but the symptoms were not present, and the high-blood pressure distracted me. It is my fault. I should have insisted she came into hospital."

As he spoke he was pulling things rapidly out of his bag. He scanned the room quickly.

"I'll do it here. Fernande, fetch clean sheets and towels, as many as you have. And boiled water – you know what to do." He turned to Robert.

"You'll have to give the anaesthetic. It's chloroform – can't use anything more sophisticated here. We'll put her out for as little time as necessary. Wash your hands thoroughly when Fernande brings the water."

He handed Robert a pad of cotton wool and a brown bottle.

"I'll put the right amount on when the time comes. Then you'll just have to hold it."

He busied himself with the sheets. Marie-Claude helped him to arrange them to leave just the space for the incision. "We must keep it as clean as possible," he said. "Thank God I've got some sterilised instruments.

Caroline gave a low moan. She seemed to be only half-conscious, and the contractions had died down.

"What's happening?" she said in English, her voice frightened, her eyes imploring. Robert leaned over.

"It will be all right, my darling," he said, trying to keep his voice calm and steady. "The doctor is going to give you something to make you sleep."

"He's going to operate, isn't he?" said Caroline. She gave a shaky laugh. "This blasted baby seems to have gone to sleep itself, thank God. It's giving me a tough time. It must be very strong."

Robert tried never to think again about the next hour. The operation was a success as far as the baby was concerned and his own work with the bottle of chloroform kept his wife asleep as the doctor cut into her and brought out the scrawny but visibly tough little girl whose sharp cry sounded like an announcement to the world that she had arrived. He cut the cord.

"Thank God the baby is all right," said Fernande, who had acted as nurse. She took the child away to wash her, but the doctor hardly heard her, and the child's father never looked at his daughter, as they both stooped back over Caroline. Robert watched her face for signs of waking, while the doctor mopped and repaired. Caroline's face was greenish white.

"She's lost too much blood," the doctor murmured to himself. "And she's still losing it."

Robert looked up, his own face white. He knew from the expression on the doctor's face that all was not well, but even so he heard himself saying, "She will be all right?"

The doctor did not reply, and with a chill certainty Robert realised that although the baby might have been saved, it could well be that it would be motherless.

"We must get her to hospital," the doctor said. He looked up, and saw Marie-Claude waiting by the door, her face pale but composed.

At that moment Caroline stirred and opened her eyes.

"God, I feel awful," she said, and then, remembering where she was, she asked, "Is my baby born?"

Marie-Claude turned heavily in the doorway and called to Fernande, who came running with the baby, washed and wrapped now in a white woollen shawl. Fernande handed the child to Robert who was murmuring to his wife, stroking her forehead and telling her that everything was fine, the baby was born and she had no more to worry about. He took the baby from Fernande and placed it in the crook of Caroline's arm.

"It's a girl," he said.

"I'd like to call her Laura," Caroline murmured, so low that only Robert heard her. She moved her head weakly on the pillow.

"I think I'm rather ill," she whispered. "Pick the baby up, Robert, and show her to me."

Robert lifted the child, and as he did so a fierce love warred within him with the fierce anger he felt that the child had put her mother in such danger. He pulled the shawl back and held the child so that Caroline could see her.

"I feel so happy," Caroline said softly. "It was all worth it. But I'm so cold ..." She shifted her head and seemed to shrink in the bed. The doctor looked up. "Take the baby back to Fernande," he said to Marie-Claude, "And then go and get some rest yourself, or we'll have trouble with your baby, too."

Marie-Claude looked at Caroline but her eyes had shut and she seemed to be sleeping. Robert handed her the baby, and when she had gone, turned to the doctor whose face looked ominously grave.

Before he could speak the doctor said harshly, "It's too late. She's lost too much blood. I blame myself ..." he shook his head and turned away from Robert, angry at the unnecessary tragedy. Robert went over to his wife and touched her cheek, but there was no response. He took her hand, called her name.

"It's no good," said the doctor. "She's gone."

Robert never knew how he got through the next few weeks. Marie-Claude's baby, also a girl, was born two nights later, without trouble, and Fernande looked after both children, holding them like twins on her ample lap, putting them to sleep in the same room. As Marie-Claude fed her own daughter, Fernande gave Laura her bottle.

Robert was grateful. He wanted no distraction from his grief over Caroline and in fact the best gift that Marie-Claude could give was to take the responsibility for looking after Laura from him. He felt no anger any longer with the baby, only a deep overwhelming love, mingled with pity that this ugly, scrawny child should never know her mother. His anger was directed more at

God, at whom he railed and cursed, and at himself for not seeing that Caroline had been much more ill than anyone had realised. He did not even blame the doctor, who had wanted Caroline in hospital, but who had allowed Robert to talk him out of it.

After the funeral, which was conducted by the same French priest, Xavier Guy, who had blessed their marriage, Robert moved back to the cottage. He left the baby with Marie-Claude, but came most days to watch her and play with her. As the weeks went by, and the baby thrived under Fernande's care and the Bonneville family's love and warmth, Robert became more and more silent. Often he left without eating.

"I'm no company," he said gruffly to Marie-Claude when she implored him to stay. "I blame myself, and I can't forgive myself."

"We're all to blame," said Marie-Claude. "I saw that Caroline was not well, and yet I encouraged her to stay here and not go to the hospital."

"And even with all my experience, I did not sense that anything serious was wrong," interjected Fernande who was sitting in the nursery with the two babies lying on a rug at her feet. She tickled their feet and both babies gurgled with pleasure. Marie-Claude's baby had been christened Laurence, in spite of its similarity to Laura, in memory of a favourite aunt as Marie-Claude had planned. She was bigger and stronger-looking than Laura, but they both had the same dark colouring, Laura from her father, Laurence from both her parents, and now that Laura was beginning to thrive her strong personality was already starting to show in the demanding way she grabbed the toys Fernande and the other children dangled in her cot.

"It doesn't really matter whose fault it was," said Robert flatly. "It happened. Marie-Claude," he turned towards her, "I've got to get away. Will you look after Laura for me? I've got to ... forget, and I can't do it with Laura here reminding me every day of what I've lost. I don't know how long I'll be away." He shook his head; as if to shake off the doubts and longings that filled him. "I just don't know …"

"Robert." Marie-Claude stopped him. "You can go away for as long as you like. Laura is already like a daughter here. You know that and you need never worry about her. But we'll worry about you. Where will you go? Back to England?"

"Not to England. Anywhere. I don't know." He took out a packet of Gitanes and lit one with a sharp, fierce gesture. "I just can't bear being with all of you, without Caroline." He brushed his face with the back of his hand, smoothing away the tear that had begun to form. It was the nearest Marie-Claude had seen him come to an outward show of grief.

Fernande picked up the two babies, one under each firm arm.

"You go, Monsieur Martin," she said. "We know you'll come back to see how this one is growing. No one can father a child and not want to see what it becomes …"

Robert sighed and got heavily to his feet.

"Come downstairs," said Marie-Claude, taking his arm. "Paul is back, and would like to see you. And if you're going away there are things we should arrange."

That evening it was decided that Laura was to stay indefinitely with Paul and Marie-Claude. Robert wanted to sell the cottage where he and Caroline had been so happy.

"I can't face sorting things out," he said. "There's too much, all her clothes, her books …" His face seemed to crumple and he turned away, fingers gripping the arm of his chair.

"Don't sell it," Marie-Claude said quickly. "You'll regret it. One day you'll come back. I'll deal with the clothes, but all Caroline's other things – they're yours and now Laura's. She must one day have something from her mother."

Paul was pouring a stiff brandy for Robert.

"Drink this," he ordered. "You need it." The strain of dealing daily with Robert's almost tangible misery, and the guilt he felt when he looked with love at his own new daughter and slid his arm round his strong and beautiful wife, were beginning to exhaust him.

"Laura will stay here for as long as you like," he said. "The cottage we'll shut up and you can go away for as long as you need to. But when you come back there will be a home and a daughter here for you. Your life here is not ended and one day you'll want to come back to it."

Robert shrugged. "Perhaps you're right. As you say, Marie-Claude, Laura must have some knowledge of her mother one day, and she'll like to look at her things, though to me that seems so far into the future ..." He shook his head. "*D'accora*. I keep the cottage. If you'll shut it up for me?"

Marie-Claude smiled. "As long as you come back soon, Robert," she said.

"I'll come back. But perhaps not soon." He put down his glass. "Paul, I am putting you *in loco parentis*. Whatever decisions need to be taken, you take them. I'll come into your office tomorrow and arrange the finances. Now, I'm going to spend a last night in the cottage" – he waved away Marie-Claude's invitation to stay and eat – "and by tomorrow evening I'll be gone."

Both Paul and Marie-Claude sensed the relief that he felt. He left the room, and they heard him run up the stairs, say something to Fernande and go into the babies' room.

"It's as if he can't lay her ghost unless he goes away," said Marie-Claude.

"I can't imagine how I would feel if it were you," said Paul sombrely. "I might have to do the same."

He looked round the room. Though formally furnished, as most French salons, with heavy pieces of dark furniture and hard, uncomfortable chairs and sofas, Marie-Claude had softened its severe looks with plants and pictures. In one corner sat an elegant table covered with a collection of delicate china cups and saucers, while on another an array of photographs showed her four elder children in poses from babyhood. She would have one taken of Laurence soon, she thought, and decided that she would add one of Laura, too, as it looked as if she might be here for a long time. Maybe forever. The thought slid into her mind, but she dismissed it as foolish, little knowing that one day she would have to make the terrible decision for Laura as to whether she did or did not stay forever.

Robert came back into the room. "I'll say goodbye now," he said to Marie-Claude. He kissed her formally on both cheeks, then held her face in both hands, looking into her eyes.

"Guard her for me. She's all I've got." He turned to Paul. "I'll see you tomorrow."

It was almost two years before Robert came back. The babies grew strong and healthy, Laurence becoming bigger than Laura, more solid like her mother, with dark hair and brown eyes, Laura remaining smaller, with a dark, sharp, triangular face which reminded Marie-Claude a little of a cat, straight black hair like her father's, and small, slanted, green eyes.

"She's inherited nothing of her mother's looks," Marie-Claude said ruefully to Fernande one day.

"She's no beauty. But you can't help but love her. There's something so endearing about that sharp little face. And you know, those two babies copy each other – they make the same gestures. They could well be sisters. But this one ..." – she indicated Laura – "this one will be a devil when she's older. She's got such a determined little nature."

It was true. Laura already had a way of making sure that everybody knew she was there. When Marie-Claude came to kiss the babies goodnight she would put out her hand and hold Marie-

Claude's face, as though to say: I need you more. When the older children played with them, Laura made more noise than the more placid Laurence, and tried to keep their attention, and cried more when they went away. The other four soon forgot that Laura was not really one of them, and treated her like another sister. Soon she was greeting Marie-Claude with "Maman" and Paul with "Papa".

Marie-Claude was worried. "How can I tell a child so young that she's not mine? And yet she isn't," she said to Paul. "However much I feel she's as dear to me as the others, she's not ours. What will Robert say when he comes back ..."

"If he comes back," interjected Paul. "He was pretty determined to go away and not look back."

"Then what would we do?"

"I don't know."

His lawyer's mind had already told him that their position was difficult. People who did not know them well had already assumed that the babies were twins, and although, whenever he got the opportunity, he would emphasize that one them was not theirs – "Laura, the smaller one, is not ours. We're looking after her for a friend" – he knew that people really couldn't be bothered to listen properly, and the next time he saw them would ask, "and how are your little girls?"

Of course, the Priest, Père Guy, and the doctor knew what the position was, but as time went on and Robert did not reappear it became more and more difficult to think of Laura as having any home other than the one she was being brought up in. The cottage was shut up and deserted, though every now and again Fernande went in and made sure everything remained clean and undisturbed.

"I don't know what we'll do if he doesn't come back," repeated Paul. "I just don't know."

But Robert did come back, nearly two years after he had gone. He wrote out of the blue from a village many miles away, near Nantua, and appeared a few days later looking fit and well, but older. His dark hair was touched with grey and his face thinner, with new lines round the eyes and mouth.

He watched with delight as the children were brought in, Fernande holding Laura's hand tightly as she took the tentative steps she had just learned to take. On Fernande's hip sat Laurence, her arms stretching forward to the new strange man.

Robert looked puzzled.

"This is awful – but which one is she?" he said. Then Laura looked up at him and smiled and he laughed.

"Of course. She's very like my mother."

And she was, a miniature reminder of his mother whom he had only contacted once since Caroline died, to tell her of the tragedy and of the birth of the child and to warn her that he was going away for an indeterminate time. He expected there were some letters for him at the cottage, but they could wait.

"Come on then," he said to Laura, and held out his arms, but Laura pulled back, suddenly shy and unsure who this new man was.

Marie-Claude said worriedly, "She thinks Paul and I are her parents, Robert. I've tried to tell her, but she's too young. She doesn't understand."

She turned to Laura.

"Papa," she said, pointing to Robert. "Laura's Papa."

But the child turned her face away.

"Papa," she said and pulled Fernande towards Paul, who was sitting quietly in a corner, wondering what to say.

Robert laughed.

"Don't worry," he said. "If she thinks you're her parents, that's fine by me. When she's old enough, we'll tell her. In the meantime, I'll be the strange man who comes home sometimes and bring special presents for her. If you don't mind ...?" He looked suddenly worried. "Of course, if you don't want her any more ..." he began, but Marie-Claude interrupted.

"Robert, of course we want her. She's just like another daughter, and we love her like one. I just worry that it will come as a terrible shock to her, when we have to convince her that we are not her parents." How much of a shock, and how many years later, Marie-Claude was not to know.

Robert was full of talk of war during the few days that he spent back in Belay again later in October of the same year. It was just after Chamberlain had been to Germany and come back with his piece of paper and his policy of appeasement.

"The man's a deluded fool," said Robert with conviction. "He can't stop Hitler. No one can. I tell you, there's going to be war. And it's going to be a war like no war has ever been before."

He looked sombrely round the dining room of the Bonneville's house. It was late. Fernande had gone to bed, and the house felt warm and safe, the six children asleep in their beds, the door locked against the outside world. The three adults, Marie-Claude, Paul and Robert, their appetites satisfied with Fernande's robust pork cooked with prunes and her famous *tarte au pommes*, were enjoying being together again, as they had been so many times before Caroline had married Robert, though the ghost of Caroline hovered ever-present. Robert took a sip of cognac, and swirled the liquor around in its glass, watching it without seeing it.

"Life as we know it will never be the same if war comes, he said. "I've seen and heard a few things recently ... dreadful things. Most people don't know what's happening inside Germany. Hitler's a monster," he said forcefully.

Paul looked at him. "If it comes, this war, which you're so certain about – and I hope you're wrong – if it comes, will you go back to England?"

"I don't know. Probably not." replied Robert. "This is my country now. And anyway, there's no certainty that England will be any safer. If the Germans move into the Netherlands there's only a few miles of sea between them and England. Why shouldn't he want that too for his *Lebensraum*?"

"He won't get France," said Paul with conviction. Robert looked doubtful.

"You don't seem to understand what the civilised part of Europe – France, England – is up against. It's not going to be like the last war. Hitler is an extraordinary phenomenon; he has the ability to make people do things they're not usually capable of. I don't put anything past him."

Marie-Claude, who had been watching Robert as he spoke, said: "You know more than you're telling us, Robert, don't you."

"I might," said Robert. "People talk to me. I've been in Germany recently. I can't betray confidences, but being forewarned is being forearmed. I just want you to know that if war comes, it will affect everyone. You, me, the children ..."

"What about Laura?" said Marie-Claude.

She felt as though a small dark cloud had appeared ominously, far off, in a clear sky. Her future, she had thought, would be composed of the same elements as the past – slow, happy days of children growing up, the routine of Paul's coming and going from St Didier, the familiar passing of the seasons. Now Robert, with his talk of war, was making this future seem uncertain. And what would he want to do with Laura?

"If you'll keep her, Laura will be as safe here as anywhere," Robert said slowly. "She's French, by birth if not by blood, and this is where she belongs."

Marie-Claude was to remember that statement a year or two later, but now its significance meant little to her.

Robert continued, "But I feel it's a lot to ask. She's my daughter, and it's unfair to you that you do all the work and then

I just appear out of the blue. I ... I find it hard to come back here, with all its memories ..."

"You don't have to make a decision about Laura now, you know, Robert," she said gently. "She's perfectly happy, and we love her, and as you said, if there is a war, which I doubt ..."

"You mean you don't want to think about it," Robert interjected.

"... If there is a war," Marie-Claude went on, "Laura will be as safe here as anywhere."

Paul said nothing. He was thinking of the unpleasant rumours he had heard in St Didier that week, rumours of hidden camps in Germany where criminals and others who were considered undesirable were sent. A Jewish friend of his, only the other day, had announced that he would be emigrating to America as soon as he could.

"Europe's not safe for Jews," he had said. "I'm going to be as far away as possible when everything erupts. Neville Chamberlain has no idea what he's dealing with. Hitler is not a man like you and me, and you can't deal with him as if he were. I have Jewish friends in Germany from whom I never hear any more – and I can't find out what's happened to them."

Now Paul thought that the rumours he had heard were probably true, and wondered if his Jewish friend, whom he had thought was exaggerating his fear, was after all right in removing himself from the expected fields of war.

"From what you say, Robert, and from what I've heard, nowhere in Europe is going to be safe. But England may be a little safer, as there's a sea between it and Germany, and you could take Laura there, to your mother ...?"

"No," Robert interrupted explosively. "I don't want her brought up in that dead atmosphere. Never. Anyway, I'm staying in France. I'll be around even if I'm not here very often, and if you'll have her she'll stay too."

So it was again agreed that Laura would remain with the Bonnevilles indefinitely.

Robert spent as much time with her as he could during the few days he was in Belay, but Laura was shy and difficult, running back to Fernande or Marie-Claude whenever she could. Once, they went for a picnic down to the river, where the railway crossed the valley on a viaduct seemingly miles high in the sky, and ate homemade paté and pungent soft cheese with ripe tomatoes and fresh baguettes, and peaches from Robert's garden. Laura sidled up to Robert once or twice, but when he tried to take her paddling in the still warm shallow river, she refused, hiding her head in Marie-Claude's skirt. Another day, he came down to breakfast to find Laura sitting alone at the table in the kitchen, a sticky piece of bread and jam in her hand. As soon as she saw him, she jumped down from her seat, her bottom lip sticking ominously out. "I don't like you," she said defiantly and threw her piece of bread at him. Robert picked it up resignedly from the floor.

"I'm not sure that I like you, either," he said, but he was smiling and said it so quietly that she didn't hear as she ran with her usual energy into the garden.

Only for one afternoon did he feel that he had made any headway with her, when he took her down to the cottage and showed her some of her mother's things. Laura had enjoyed playing with a sewing box Caroline had brought from England, which had two drawers concealed within its padded interior. Inside this were some pearl buttons and a pearl brooch.

"You shall have this one day," he said, and pinned it on her dress She was delighted, and ran to the mirror, preening herself as she had seen Marie-Claude do in front of her mirror.

"That belonged to your mother," said Robert. "Not Marie-Claude. *Your* mother Caroline. My wife. I am your father. *Ton père. Je suis le père de Laura.*"

He pointed at himself, but Laura would have none of it.

"Non, non," she said. *"Tu n'es pas mon père. Mon père n'est pas ici. Mon père est à la maison."* And she let go of his hand and ran to the door.

"OK, OK," said Robert. "We won't go into it."

It hurt him that Laura refused to recognise him, but he reasoned that in time she would be old enough to understand, especially when he could come back permanently to Belay and move back into the cottage with her. But for now, there was no time. He had to go; he had business in Nantua, which was nothing to do with antiques or picture-restoring, and which was overridingly important now.

He enticed Laura back to him, and found some picture books that Caroline had bought when she first found she was pregnant. With Laura on his knee, he showed her the enchanting little pictures and read her the childish text. For an hour, they sat thus, father and child, immersed in each other, and then Laura scrambled down.

"I'm hungry," she said. *"Laure a faim."*

And back they went to the big house, where Fernande gave Laura a piece of bread and some dark chocolate, and she ran off to show Laurence her new books.

"She doesn't want to know me, Fernande," said Robert ruefully.

Fernande smiled her warm countrywoman's smile.

"You can't expect her to, Monsieur," she said. "All her life she's known no other parents than Monsieur and Madame Bonneville. Everyone treats her like another sister, and she's too young to understand the truth. Don't you worry, though. When the time is right, we'll make sure she knows who her father is."

But when the time was right, everything had changed.

War had erupted, and France had been overrun by Germany. Dunkirk had come and gone, and the news seemed ever blacker as the days went by. St Didier was full of Germans, as was all of France in the occupied zone. And now, in November 1940, at the age of four-and-a-half, Laurence had died. The house was full of silence.

***

Paul Bonneville stood up from the desk where he had been sitting thinking about his friend Robert, Robert's child, and his own dead daughter. He was thankful that they had Laura, for without her the gap where Laurence had been would seem even bigger. But he was worried about Marie-Claude. She couldn't seem to come to terms with the death. And the funeral had yet to be arranged.

He went to the window and opened it to reach for the shutters. It was late afternoon, and the raw grey day was quietly turning into evening. The garden looked desolate, the bushes and trees merging into each other in the going of the light. Then, as he leant out to pull the shutter round, there was a movement at the gate and Père Guy came hurrying across the gravel. His face looked grave and he was breathing fast, as if he had run up the hill from the church.

Paul was surprised. This was the hour when the priest was usually preparing for Benediction, but he was glad to see him. Perhaps he would be able to persuade Marie-Claude to think about the funeral. It was four days since Laurence had died and a decision had to be made.

But when he opened the door to the priest, it was Père Guy who spoke first, and urgently, his voice not much more than a whisper.

"Thank God you're here," he said. "I've got news of Robert. Come in here," and he pushed Paul into the study as if he were the host and Paul the guest.

"What's happened?" said Paul. "I was just thinking about Robert ..."

"We haven't got much time," said the priest. "Robert's been taken by the Germans. Near Nantua. You know he's with the Resistance?"

"I suspected," said Paul. He went to a cupboard and brought out the cognac and glasses. He poured one out for each of them and handed one to the priest, who took it gratefully. "Go on," said Paul.

"There's nothing we can do for Robert," said the priest. "His own people will get him out if they can, but I doubt it – once they've got someone they rarely return. It's the child. They'll take her, too."

"Surely not," said Paul. "What on earth would they do with a child that age?"

"Blackmail. Use her to make Robert talk. You can put nothing past them ..."

Paul caught his breath. Of course the Germans would use Laura, if it would help them get from Robert the names of his associates.

But what could they do? He thought rapidly. How could they hide her? Or could they send her away – but where? Where in this country full of Germans, full of people asking for your papers, could she become invisible?

He said as much to the priest. But Père Guy, priest though he was, was already more used to dissimulation and deceit than he wanted to be, dealing as he had to with an occupying force and being closer than Paul to the people in the village and the villages around.

"What if she were dead?" he said to Paul. "They couldn't use her then, could they."

"What do you mean, dead? We couldn't ..." Paul stopped, and understanding flooded into his face.

"You mean if it had been Laura who had died and Laurence who was still alive?"

"Precisely," said the priest. "I know it's a terrible thing to ask, but at least this way Laurence wouldn't have died for nothing."

Paul was thinking. Because of the war, the family had not circulated as much as they might have. Laura and Laurence had not yet started school. Only their own immediate family knew them, people in the village not well, if at all. Laura's colouring was similar enough to their own for her to pass as a Bonneville, even if she didn't look particularly like any of them. And they had been so much together that only those who knew them well could swear to which one was which. Laura had been allowed to go on calling them Maman and Papa and now Paul was grateful that they had not had the heart to force her to stop.

What other obstacles were there? Marie-Claude would know better than he ...

"I must get Marie-Claude," he said. He ran up the stairs to the bedroom where Marie-Claude still sat, her thoughts miles away with her daughter. She had not heard the priest arrive, but when Paul said he was there she rose stiffly and said, yes, of course she would come down to speak to him.

Paul blocked her way and pulled her to him as she moved towards the door.

"Wait, *chou*," he said. " Let me explain. Something terrible has happened. We need you, you must wake up." He shook her gently. "It's time to stop grieving this way. Alone. Nothing can bring Laurence back, but this, what's happened, might make some sense of her death."

Marie-Claude looked at him. "What do you mean?" she said. "What could ever make sense of a four-year-old child dying?" Her lip trembled, and Paul pulled a handkerchief out of his pocket and wiped her eyes.

"This might," he said and told her what had happened to Robert.

"If we could do it, it might save Laura," he said.

"I couldn't, Paul. It seems a dreadful thing to do. We would have to bury Laurence as Laura. I can't. It would be like denying her life."

Paul sighed. "I feel the same," he said, "but if the Germans come, and I think they will, they'll take Laura away, and we'll lose both of them. I haven't told you of how people seem to disappear these days. I didn't want to frighten you. But in St Didier people I knew have just ... gone. Do you remember David Benjamin, the jeweller? His shop is shut, all the jewellery gone from the window, and no one knows what happened to him. He was there one day and gone the next. And there are others ... Think, Marie, think of what it might mean. We'd lose both children, and the second one to a fate no one would wish on anyone, let alone a four year old child. *Les Boches* are monsters. I've seen and heard things I've kept from you, they're so vile, but if you knew ... we have to do this, *chou*. It's not denying Laurence's life, it's making her death mean something positive." He stopped. Had his wife sensed the urgency, understood the consequences of leaving Laura a hostage?

Marie-Claude shook herself, just as Paul had shaken her a minute or two ago, but this time it seemed to clear her head. A little colour came back into her cheeks. She remained silent for a minute or two, while Paul consulted his watch, willing her to hurry. There was so little time. Then she spoke.

"You're right, Paul. We have to do it, however painful it is," she said. "We have to, for Robert's sake." She looked at the photo she still held in her hand, and turned it over. The back was blank. She went over to the little desk she had in their bedroom, and picked up a pencil.

"This is the sort of thing we'll have to do," she said, and wrote on the back: *Laura aged 3, 1939.*

Paul hurried her down the stairs. The priest had to get back to say Benediction. Nothing must seem different in the village where Robert's daughter would be found to have died in the scarlet fever epidemic. The Germans might arrive at any moment.

"The funeral will be the day after tomorrow," Père Guy said with relief. "It's a good job your house is a little outside the village – not too many people have been to call, I expect? They know in the village there's been a death in the family, but I know I just said one of the children, and many of them are taken up nursing their own."

"No one's been in," said Paul. "Marie-Claude was too distressed, and Fernande's turned any callers away. Not that there have been many. We'll ask her."

He called Fernande, who had been busy preparing the children's supper in the kitchen, and told her succinctly what had happened.

"Père Guy must go," he said. "We'll have to work out the details."

The priest drained what remained of his cognac and, gathering his skirts around him, hurried out into the dark. He had ten minutes to get the church ready, but already he had his excuses for any who were waiting. Poor Madame Bonneville, with the little Laura dying and no way of notifying her father. Did any of them have any idea where he was? Not by anything would he give away that he knew that Robert had been captured. You never knew, these days, who was a traitor. Not that he suspected any of his congregation, but still ... you couldn't be too sure.

At the Bonneville's house Marie-Claude, Fernande and Paul sat at the kitchen table, Marie-Claude eating a piece of bread spread with jam. She could feel strength coming slowly back into her, and thanked God that the dreadful blankness and hopelessness that had overtaken her was lifting. Even though the reason for it lifting was so terrible. She thrust thoughts of Robert from her mind. What she had to do was save his daughter.

She was worried that Laura's features were different from the other children's. "Although her colouring's the same, she doesn't really look like any of us," she said slowly. "If only we had someone in the family who looked like her ..."

Fernande opened her eyes wide. "There could be, Madame, there could be," she said. "Well, not in your family, but in hers. We could bring it here."

"What are you talking about, Fernande?" said Marie-Claude.

"There's a photograph of Monsieur Martin's mother in the cottage. His wife made him hang it up, she didn't like it lying in a drawer where he had it, so he put it in a dark corner of the dining room. Laura is very like her. We could change it for the picture you have of your aunt, the one Laurence was christened for."

"You're a genius, Fernande," said Paul. "I wonder what Robert had against his mother? He never talked about her, or about his father."

"Well, we'll never know now," said Marie-Claude. "The important thing is to get that photograph. I'll go." And she ran from the room, snatched her coat from its peg, and went out into the dark night. This was like a catharsis, this necessity to protect Laura, and by doing so prove that Laurence would not have died in vain.

The cottage was dark and cold. No one had been there for weeks, and Marie-Claude was careful to touch nothing, to disturb the dust as little as possible. There must be nothing to show that anyone had been there. Carefully she lifted the picture off the wall. She had never noticed it before. It showed a middle-aged woman in a formal pose, her hair swept up and pinned on top of her head. She had on a high-necked blouse and wore a cameo at her throat. She was not a beautiful woman, but there was no doubt about her relationship to Laura.

Back at the house, she took the photograph of Tante Laurence from the table where she had all the children's photographs, and those of their grandparents, godparents and various nieces and nephews. Carefully she prised the back off it, and noted that the photographer in St Didier had put his stamp on the cardboard backing of the frame. One more piece of verification.

She took out the photograph of Tante Laurence and compared it with the framed photograph she had brought from the cottage. The two women were contemporaries, at least, although they looked quite different, the French woman more fashionably dressed and altogether more approachable looking.

Deftly, she changed the two pictures over, replaced the frame, bringing it slightly further to the front of the table. Laura's grandmother, Robert's mother, looked quite comfortable among the other photos. Now all she had to do was replace the picture in Robert's house. She could hear Paul in the study. He was talking to the stonemason in the next village.

"I know it's late," she could hear him saying, apologising. "But we want it done quickly."

She knew Paul was ordering the wording to be added to Caroline's gravestone. "And of Laura Caroline, beloved daughter of Robert and Caroline."

It would add verisimilitude to the story. She felt a sob well up for the daughter who was going to be obliterated, and vowed that when this awful war was over she would have another service, put in place Laurence's own stone. But for now ... there was nothing else they could do.

She ran down to the cottage and slipped in, using a torch half-covered by her hand so no light would show. She hung the reframed picture of Tante Laurence on the wall. Now it had a frame on it with an English photographer's name stamped on the back. It should fool the Germans.

Now, had Robert any photographs of Laura lying around to give away their deception? Luckily the two children had almost always been photographed together, and she remembered that the one that Robert usually carried was one of both of them. Though surely he would not have been so foolhardy to carry it on any mission he'd been sent on?

Swiftly she traversed the rooms. There was nothing obvious to give away the deception. Robert had barely spent a night here since Caroline had died. The rooms looked deserted, unlived in. There was a photograph of Caroline in the bedroom. With dismay, Marie-Claude saw she was wearing the pearl brooch Robert had given to Laura, and which the child loved and wore whenever she could. She would have to take it away, hide it. Laurence, as Laura was to become, would not own a brooch belonging to Caroline.

Dousing the torch, she shut the door quietly behind her and, taking her courage in her hands, decided to face the villagers. The small congregation for Benediction was dispersing, golden light spilling from the church door, and Marie-Claude mingled with them. She went up to Père Guy who was standing at the door, and said, "*Père,* have you any news of Monsieur Martin? I'm so worried that we can't let him know about his daughter."

The priest shook his head. "No. Nothing. I've tried but it's impossible these days to reach anyone. However, the funeral must go ahead." He shrugged, his expressive face showing regret, worry and resignation at the same time. Marie-Claude thanked God he was a good actor, as they would all have to be.

"Yes, you're right, *Père,*" she said. "The day after tomorrow. Good night."

She turned away, and one of the villagers touched her arm. "I heard one of the children died," the old woman said, her face pious under her ugly black hat.

"Yes, indeed, Madame Bozon," she said. "It was Laura, Monsieur Martin's child. It's so sad, because we could not get word to her father. She's been living with us since her mother died, you know." She knew the news would go round the village. Madame Bozon was a notorious gossip.

"Poor child," said the old woman, and crossed herself. "She's gone to God ... along with quite a few others, so I've heard."

Marie-Claude wondered why the woman sounded so satisfied that so many innocent children should have gone to God, as she put it. She smiled slightly and said piously herself, "Yes, you could look at it that way. What's our loss is God's gain. Goodnight, Madame Bozon, and thank you for your sympathy."

She turned away before she hit the old woman. She knew the anger was good for her, and welcomed it as a sign that she was coming back to life, and buried her sorrow for Laurence deep, knowing that one day, when all this was over, she would grieve again for her dead daughter.

The priest caught up with her as she turned away.

"Madame Bonneville," he called. "Have you got the death certificate from the doctor – or shall I take care of it for you?"

"I'd be grateful if you could speak to the doctor about it," she said. "He must get the child's name correctly. If you could ask him to come up to the house, I'll find the papers. There was a middle name, I think." Thank God Xavier Guy had remembered, she thought. Paul might have rung the doctor, but there were so many things to think of.

"Perhaps you could both come up tonight," she said for the benefit of any listeners, for it had already been arranged that Father Guy would come. "Bring Dr Jacquot, if he's free and I'll give him the correct names."

Slowly she retraced her steps up the hill, stopping a few times to accept commiseration from the villagers, commiserating herself with others whose children had also died. She passed Robert's cottage, dark and deserted, and then there were no more houses, only her own a few hundred yards further up the hill. As she walked, snow began to fall, pricking her cheeks with sharp cold flakes, already beginning to lay its white blanket on the frost-hard earth. For a moment Marie-Claude wished that she too could be covered with its white softness, could lie down and let herself fall into unconsciousness and forget her misery and worry. Then she shook herself and increased her pace. She belonged with the living, not with the dead.

***

The other memory that Laura was able to tell Miriam Stein about was much more vivid in her mind than the faint memory of the river picnic.

She'd been playing in the garden with Olivier, her youngest brother, though she supposed now that he wasn't her brother at all. It had been very cold, had snowed, she remembered, and they were both wrapped in coats and scarves. Olivier was often naughty and although they had all been trying to be good because it was only a few days since Laurence had died, and Maman looked so pale and still, he had persuaded Laura to come with him and pick one of the wormy old apples still hanging from a branch. But he hadn't been able to persuade her to taste it, though he had tasted one himself and had spat it out with an expression of disgust, and now Laura was glad she hadn't, because Maman looked so strange as she came into the garden, and Laura thought she must have seen them picking the fruit and would be angry. But all she said was "Laura," or rather "*Laure*," for she had never been able to pronounce the "a" on the end, "*Laure*, come into the kitchen, please."

So Laura had followed her into the kitchen and found Maman and Papa and Fernande and the priest, Père Guy, all there, waiting. The memory ended there, but she could still see the stern expressions on their faces and remember the feeling of fear that had overtaken her at the sight of their solemn faces.

"I can't remember any more," she said to Miriam, frowning with concentration, her voice hoarse from having talked so long, and it was only later, when Miriam had talked to Marie-Claude Bonneville, that she could pinpoint the memory for Laura.

"We didn't know how to tell her," Marie-Claude had said. "How do you tell a child that she is going to stop being who she is and become someone else who, as far as she knows, has died?"

She and Paul had talked about how to explain it to her long into the night, after the priest and the doctor had left. Before that the four of them, and Fernande, had gone over and over the details. They thought they'd covered everything, but of course, as the doctor had pointed out, if they couldn't convince Laura to play her part all their planning would be for nothing, and in fact would probably put them all into a German jail.

"Better that than not trying to save Laura from them at all," said Paul firmly and the other four had nodded in agreement. None of them could have lived with just handing Robert's daughter over to his captors.

Now Marie-Claude called Laura into the kitchen. The child stopped at the sight of their solemn faces.

"I didn't eat any," she said to Marie-Claude, glancing sideways at the others in the big, warm room, and then bringing her eyes quickly back to Marie-Claude.

"No, no, we know that, Laure," said Marie-Claude. "Come and sit here on my knee."

She sat down at the big table, and Laura ran to her and jumped on to her knee.

"You're better, Maman," she said. "I'm so glad. But I wish Laurence was here."

"So do we, my pet," Marie-Claude said, "But we have a very good way of remembering her. We're going to play a little game.

We're going to call you Laurence now and you're going to pretend to be Laurence."

"That's a funny game," said Laura, looking puzzled. "Why?"

"Because there are some nasty men looking for a little girl called Laura, and we don't want them to find you. If you pretend to be Laurence, then they won't."

Laura looked frightened. Her lip began to turn down and her chin began to tremble.

"I don't want any nasty men to come," she said.

"Well, that's why we have to play this game. Do you think you can do it?"

"Don't know," said Laura, her lip still quivering a little. Marie-Claude put her finger on Laura's mouth and said. "Let's try. Let's pretend you're Laurence and I'll ask you some questions."

Laura looked doubtful, pursing up her lips so she looked more like a cat than usual, and rubbing at her eyes with a hand still dirty from the orchard and smearing black streaks on to her cheeks. Marie-Claude took out a handkerchief and rubbed the worst of the dirt off.

"All right," said Laura. "I'll try."

"Good girl," said Marie-Claude. "Now, what shall we start with? I know. Now, who is your father?"

Marie-Claude crossed her fingers. It would be so like Laura to say now that Robert was her father, just when they wanted her to forget it. But Laura had denied Robert for too long, and was used to refusing to listen when he arrived and said he was her father. Anyway, it was a long time since he had been to Belay ...

"He's my father," she said triumphantly, pointing to Paul.

"Yes, I am," said Paul. "And where's Maman?"

"Here," replied Laura.

"Who lives in the cottage down the road?" said Paul.

"A man called ... I can't remember. He hasn't been here for a long time."

"And what's your name?" continued Paul.

"Laur ... Laurence," said Laura laughing. Then she suddenly looked grave and turned back to Marie-Claude.

"But what about the real Laurence?" she said. "Aren't you going to bury her?"

"Of course we are," said Marie-Claude. "But just to fool the nasty men, we're going to say that it was Laura who died." This was very difficult, she thought. It would have been too upsetting to an older child; they couldn't possibly have said to Olivier, for instance, that someone was going to be buried in his name, but maybe, maybe, Laura was still so young that she wouldn't quite understand what they were saying. Because to all intents and purposes they were saying that she, Laura, was dead.

"Do you understand?" she said.

"Oh, yes," said Laura. "Laurence will be buried, and then I will pretend to be Laurence to the nasty men. And then, when the nasty men have gone, I can be Laura again?"

"Well, we have to make sure that they've really disappeared for ever, so we're going to go on playing this game for quite a long time. In fact, after a while, we'll probably all forget that it is a game and we'll think you've always been Laurence."

"What about everyone else?" said Laura. "The people in the village. Will they be playing the game too?"

"Yes, they will," said Marie-Claude. And if they forget, and call you Laura *ever*, you must say to them 'Don't be silly, I'm Laurence.'"

Paul, Père Guy and Fernande had been careful to say nothing while Marie-Claude had been talking to Laura, fearful of distracting her. But now Fernande said, "I'm going to start this game now, Madame." She gave a big beaming smile at Laura and said:

"Laurence, would you like some milk?"

Laura laughed and slipped off Marie-Claude's knee.

"Yes, please," she said.

Paul and the priest looked at each other. Had Marie-Claude accomplished it, had she convinced Laura of the seriousness of this so-called game, without frightening her?

"Laurence!" said Paul. "Put down that milk."

Laura looked round, then realised what Paul had said. Quickly she put down her bowl, and looked pleased with herself.

They continued playing this game with Laura for quite some time, drilling it into her that Laura had gone and only the name Laurence was to be used.

Père Guy tried a little test, and went on calling her Laura. Each time, she laughed and said firmly, "Don't be silly. I'm Laurence," giggling at this freedom to call a grown up silly.

After a while, Paul said to Marie-Claude, "I think it's time we told the children."

Marie-Claude nodded. She was looking more herself today. Her short black hair was newly washed and springy, and her face, though still pale and tired-looking with dark circles under the eyes, looked more composed, less anguished than it had. The necessity to deal with this new terror seemed to have pushed the tragedy of Laurence's death away to some place where it would have to wait until there was time to re-examine it in peace; it would have to wait, she thought, until this dreadful war was over.

She went to the kitchen door and called the other children in from the garden. She gave some paper and crayons to Laura, and sat her down in the playroom next to the kitchen. She shut the door firmly behind her – she didn't want Laura to hear the much more frightening and truthful explanation she was going to give to her own children, whom she hoped were old enough to understand and help.

She looked round at them, seeing their dear faces clearly for the first time since Laurence had died, and saw that they were suffering from her withdrawal and from the loss of their sister.

Nathalie, the oldest, was beginning to look like her mother – from being a leggy child not so long ago she was turning into a composed and thoughtful girl, already able to carry responsibility. As she would have to now, thought Marie-Claude. She smoothed Nathalie's dark hair behind her ears and turned to Jean-Claude who as usual was chatting away, to his father, to Fernande and even to Père Guy, who had said more than once that Jean-Claude was too much of a distraction in his catechism class and had asked if there was any way of stopping the flow.

"And, Papa," he was saying, "they're saying in the village that there are lots of Germans in St Didier and that they've captured someone from round here who was in the Resistance. I wish I was old enough to be in the Resistance. I'd show ..."

"Jean-Claude," said his father, "That's enough. Now sit down. We have to talk to you."

Sabine and Olivier, who were very close, both in age and in friendship, looked at each other.

"I told you," Sabine whispered. "Something's happened, something was going on last night. It's not just Laurence. It's something to do with Laura." Her big brown eyes under her straight fair fringe looked wider than ever, and the eyes staring back at her from under Olivier's similar fringe were as wide as her own. They might have been twins, thought Marie-Claude, and wondered yet again where their fair looks had come from.

Paul looked stern.

"You're quite right, Sabine," he said. "It is something to do with Laura. Now, I want you all to listen very carefully. Laura's safety is going to depend on all of us, including you." And he explained what had happened to Robert, how he was in the hands of the Germans and how it was almost certain that the Germans would come to find his daughter.

Nathalie looked stricken. She had known Robert since she was a baby and loved him dearly. This was the first time that the war had touched her, except in the way that it had touched all French families, and it was with fear that she realised that she and her family were not invulnerable.

Jean-Claude opened his mouth to speak, but his father silenced him with a gesture.

"*Tais-toi*, Jean-Claude," he said impatiently, "and listen, for once in your life."

Père Guy couldn't suppress his smile, even in the midst of all this, and Jean-Claude caught his eye and smiled sheepishly back.

It took a long time to explain to the children what must happen, and how they would achieve it. At first, they were horrified at the idea of Laurence not being buried in her own name, being in a sense expunged from her family, not being mourned as herself. But after a while, as Paul explained to them what could happen to Laura, and enlarged a little on the rumours he was now sure were true about the way people disappeared, the children began to see, and soon they were making suggestions themselves.

"What about Laura's brooch?" said Nathalie, frowning. "Didn't it belong to her mother? I mean, if Laura is Laurence, she wouldn't have it, would she?"

"Thanks for reminding me, Nathalie," said her mother. "I thought about that when I saw Robert's photo of Caroline last night. What would I have done if it had really been Laura who died?"

"You would have kept it for Robert, of course," said Jean-Claude. "We've got to think of all those sort of things. Like those books Robert gave Laura, the ones she calls her favourites."

"They can stay," said Paul. "If Laura had died, Laurence would have had them anyway, it would have been natural for them to stay in Laura – I mean Laurence's room. God, this is difficult," he said, clapping a hand to his forehead. "I've just done it, called her Laura …"

"I suppose," said Marie-Claude slowly, "that we might have called Laurence Laure – not Laura, but Laure, the way I say it, without the a – for short. We could say that, anyway, so that if we do make a mistake we might get away with it."

"It's a bit far-fetched," said Paul. "What do you think?" He turned to the priest.

"What's in a name?" said Father Guy. "In this case, everything. Laura, Laure, Laurence – they're all pretty much alike, thank God." He raised his eyes to the ceiling as if personally thanking God. "It's feasible, I suppose, if one of us does make a mistake. We've just got to say to ourselves that the name Laura is forbidden. *'Verboten,'* as our German friends would say." He sighed heavily. "God forgive me, but I hate them. I must go, I've been away long enough." He turned to the children.

"The funeral will be tomorrow, and I want you all to come. When I say the name Laura, I will be thinking of Laurence. Remember that. She is not forgotten." He turned back to Marie-Claude. "It will be quite natural for you not to bring Laura – Laurence – with you. She's much too young, anyway, regardless of whose funeral it is."

"No, no, Père," said Marie-Claude. "That's all arranged. Fernande's sister Marguerite is coming to look after her. We've had to tell her the truth – she knows the children – but she's a good woman and she won't let us down."

"I can vouch for her, Père," said Fernande. "She'll help, too, by chatting about the little Laura dying when she goes back home, and as she's not married she doesn't have anyone to whom she might feel she should tell the truth."

"Very well," said Père Guy, who seemed to have taken over responsibility for Laura and their deceit. He said his goodbyes, and Paul went with him to the door.

"Are we fooling ourselves, Père?" he said. "Can it possibly work?"

"I don't know, Paul," said Père Guy bleakly, shrugging on his thick black overcoat against the winter cold. He opened the door and a blast of freezing air blew in, bringing with it the smell of snow. "All I can tell you is, we've got to try."

He slammed the door behind him, shutting Paul back into the warmth of the house. Paul felt that here was his fortress, his castle, where he could be safe and hidden from his enemies. But he also knew that if the Germans came, nothing would prevent them from storming his fortress if that was what they wanted.

For a few days it seemed as though their precautions had been melodramatic and unnecessary.

The funeral was a sad, bleak occasion. None of them really knew who their tears were for: Laurence herself, whose name was not, of course, mentioned; Robert, of whom there was no news; Caroline, whose daughter could not be told even of her existence until all danger was past; or Laura whose name would now be put on Caroline's gravestone, but who would live on under another name.

The Mass seemed never-ending, thought Marie-Claude, who would not allow her thoughts to dwell on the real child who was being buried, in case she made a mistake when speaking to the women of the village who had come to the Mass.

She looked at Paul and the elder children; they all looked pale, and Nathalie was openly weeping. She longed to get home, to get warm again, to be able to speak to Paul without watching her words.

Finally, the coffin had been lowered into Caroline's re-opened grave, and the sad little convoy made its way back to the house. Only the priest came with them – Marie-Claude had invited none of the few acquaintances and villagers who had come to join them at the church, parrying questions about Robert, saying only that their daughter Laurence was also ill, but recovering, from the same illness which had killed Laura. She found it very difficult to invert the names this way, feeling each time she said Laurence's name that she was denying her real daughter both her life and her death. Laura's – Laurence's – so-called illness was a device which they had worked out to keep her away from anyone who might wonder what was going on, at least until the Germans had come looking for her. Marie-Claude found herself wishing that they *would* come; the waiting was almost unbearable. She felt like an actress whose first night was about to take place without her having had any rehearsals beforehand.

For two more days they waited, and then, on the third morning after the funeral Marie-Claude was in the village buying what few groceries she could for the weekend when she heard the whine of a car making its slow way up the steep road from St Didier. Something told her that this was what they had been waiting for, and dreading. Swiftly she concluded her purchases and started up the road back home.

The car passed her on the way, a black Citroën carrying a German officer and a civilian. She ran over in her mind what they would find. Paul would be in his study. Laura – Laurence – would be up, but pale and tired; the doctor had given Marie-Claude something to put in her night-time milk which would make her sleepy well into the next day. It had worked well – Laura had been white, fractious and tired each day until well past lunchtime, and quiet for the rest of the day. Marie-Claude's own four children were at school, the elder two in St Didier, not returning until evening, and the younger ones, Sabine and Olivier, at the village school. These two would be home at midday for lunch, but they had been well drilled and would play their parts well.

She walked calmly past the Citroën sitting outside the front door, the uniformed German at the wheel watching her curiously, and carried her shopping round to the kitchen door. Fernande was in the kitchen; she put her finger to her lips and Marie-Claude nodded to her to signify that she knew the Germans had arrived. Laura sat at the table, listlessly playing with a rag doll Fernande had made her. She did not look well, and Marie-Claude wondered how long they would have to go on giving her the debilitating pills.

"We have visitors, Madame. They're in the study," Fernande said loudly. "I'm making them some coffee, if you can call it that."

"Give it to me, Fernande, and I'll take it in," said Marie-Claude. She took off her coat and tidied her hair in the mirror on the kitchen wall. She looked pale, she thought, but not overwhelmed, in spite of how she felt. She picked up the tray, walked through into the hall, took a deep breath to steady her nerves, and pushed open the study door.

Paul was behind his desk, looking composed and in control. A fat middle-aged civilian in a tight suit, the trousers of which stretched uncomfortably over his thighs, his braces hauled high over his paunch, occupied one of the armchairs, while in the other lounged a tall, relaxed, good-looking young German, wearing the dreaded grey uniform which Marie-Claude had hoped she would never see in her own house. They both rose politely, though the fat one had some difficulty in levering himself out of the chair.

Paul introduced her and she passed the men cups of the bitter chicory-flavoured brew that passed for coffee. She did not take a cup for herself, much as she would have liked one, knowing that her hand would shake each time she lifted it to her lips.

The interview lasted all morning, the fat man asking most of the questions in a rapid guttural French, the handsome officer playing the conciliatory part, charming and mannered in his apologetic questions, which did not deceive either of them. He might have been a diplomat in another life, thought Marie-Claude, but it was quite clear to her that now he was a servant of Germany and Germany alone.

Did they know Robert Martin; when had they last seen him; where was he living; who lived in his cottage? The questions came at them rapidly, and in different forms. Yes they knew him; no they did not know where he was living now; they had not heard from him for months; no one lived in the cottage. Then at some point Paul volunteered the information that although they had not seen Robert for so long, his daughter had been living with them until the time of her death. In the long night hours, they had agreed that an innocent family would have no reason not to talk about the child, and that if it seemed natural to speak of her, and her death, they should.

"No," Paul said again, "we have not seen Monsieur Martin for some months. In fact, we've been trying to find him for the last two weeks, to tell him about Laura being ill. It's tragic that she died before we could get news to him. The funeral had to go ahead – we buried her last Wednesday, in the same grave as her mother who died when she was born."

The officer straightened his long legs and sat up.

"Is that so, Monsieur Bonneville?" he said in his lazy, charming, almost perfect French. "How very sad. For Monsieur Martin."

"It's sad for all of us," said Marie-Claude. "May I ask why you are inquiring about Monsieur Martin? As you can see, we need to contact him urgently. He must be told of Laura's death."

"Monsieur Martin is an English spy," the civilian spat out and earned himself a cold stare from his companion.

"No, Herr Wippermann, we don't know that for sure," he said. "But we do have our suspicions. And you," he turned to Marie-Claude and Paul, "must have known Monsieur Martin very well. Well enough to take in his daughter for him when he was away. Well enough to know what he was doing when he was away from here?" His voice had become hard and the charming face suddenly seemed skull-like. You can see all his bones, thought Marie-Claude.

Paul spoke, and at the same time the front door banged and the subdued voices of Sabine and Olivier could be heard as they crossed the hall to the kitchen.

"... I have never known that Robert Martin was anything other than a dealer in antiques and pictures," Paul was saying. "Yes, he's often away, but that's quite understandable – his wife died when the child was born, and he's never really settled down here again. That's why Laura lived most of the time with us. But a spy? Robert? Unbelievable."

"But you knew he was English?" said the German.

"Of course," answered Paul knowing that he sounded too frank, too helpful and that that would make the German even more suspicious, but not knowing how else to reply. "Originally. But he took out French nationality years ago. No one ever thought of him as anything but French. I don't quite see how we can help you. We haven't seen him, as I said, for six or seven months."

The German officer got up and walked over to the door.

"I would very much like to meet your children, Madame," he said to Marie-Claude. "I believe I heard them come in?" Marie-Claude wondered if she actually heard the menace in his voice, or if it was just her imagination that led her to think it was there.

She took him into the kitchen, Paul and the civilian following.

"Sabine! Olivier! Laurence!" she heard herself say, and sent a silent prayer to any God who was listening to let Laura respond to her new name. Laura clambered slowly down from the table.

"Yes, Maman," she said, and Marie-Claude let out the breath she had been holding.

"This is Captain Nordhoff, children, and Herr Wippermann. They are asking when we last saw Robert Martin."

She felt sick, and an insistent ache was starting up in her left temple.

Sabine and Olivier had moved to stand behind Laura, and Marie-Claude wished they didn't look so protective. She walked over and took Laura's hand.

"Are you feeling better, Laurence?" she said, pulling the child towards her. "She's had the same fever that killed Monsieur Martin's daughter," she continued *sotto voce* to the Germans, and saw them take an instinctive step back. "I don't think she's infectious any more," she went on, "but she's not well yet."

The fat man had retreated to the door, but Captain Nordhoff was made of stronger stuff.

"I want to know when you last saw the man you know as Robert Martin," he said, looking from Sabine to Olivier. Laura he dismissed as too young to know anything.

"Oh, ages ago," said Olivier and Sabine interrupted him with, "... in the spring, the daffodils were out."

Marie-Claude could remember the occasion. They had sat in the garden for the first time that year, and she had noted the faint greening of the trees and marvelled that the seasons' rhythms continued inexorably however much upheaval and change man wrought. It had been a peaceful interlude, a day or two for Robert away from the concerns that had made his face pinched and wary, his eyes glance round at every unexpected noise. He had been gentle and kind with Laura, but had not insisted that he was her father, almost as if he had no energy to spare for that, and now Marie-Claude was grateful.

"And where had he been, where had he come from?"

"I don't know," said Olivier. "He never said."

"And was his daughter here with him?" continued Nordhoff.

"Of course," said Olivier. "She lived here."

"Describe her to me."

"Well, she was dark, like her father, and she was a bit bigger than Laurence," Marie-Claude heard her son say. She did not dare look at Nordhoff and busied herself tidying Laura's hair.

"She had brown eyes," Olivier continued, "and ..." he shrugged, "... she just looked like a little girl. She was only small," he said dismissively, as if lack of age meant lack of importance.

"Would you agree with your brother's description?" Nordhoff turned to Sabine, who gazed out at him from under her fringe with eyes that looked candid and honest.

"Oh, yes," Marie-Claude heard her lie, and Sabine went on to describe Laurence, the real Laurence, in more detail.

"There's only one thing Olivier's wrong about," she finished. "Her eyes – they were more green than brown."

"No they weren't," said Olivier and Marie-Claude realised that the two of them were trying to confuse Nordhoff, for the only real difference in the two little girls' colouring had been in the eyes. Laurence's had been brown, Laura's were green. If Robert should be forced in some unimaginable way to describe his daughter, the colour of her eyes would not, if Sabine and Olivier could help it, be a giveaway.

"I would like a photograph of her," Nordhoff said to Paul. They were prepared for this, and Paul went to the study and took a somewhat blurred photo of Laurence from the desk, which he gave to Nordhoff. On the back he had written *Laura – photographed for once without Laurence – spring 1940*.

Nordhoff turned it over and looked at the inscription.

"Why photographed for once without Laurence?" he asked.

"They were the same age and were usually together," replied Paul, indicating Laura, and Nordhoff nodded and put the photograph into his pocket. Paul hoped against hope that he would show it to Robert when he quizzed him about his daughter and that Robert would understand the message: Laurence is dead, your daughter has become Laurence.

Nordhoff and the civilian, Wipperman, remained in the house for hours, questioning Paul and Marie-Claude together and separately, then the children, then Fernande. When Nathalie and Jean-Claude came home, they too were subjected to an exhaustive interview. Luckily there was nothing to lie about except Laura, and that Nordhoff did not seem to suspect, though at any moment Marie-Claude expected him to turn on them and produce a picture of the real Laura from his pocket. They were both more thankful than they could say that Robert seemed to have told them nothing. If she had had to conceal anything else, Marie-Claude thought, she would probably have cracked. As it was, she could look Nordhoff in the eye – she had nothing else to hide.

Nordhoff made Paul accompany him to the cottage, which had now obviously been searched, for drawers were pulled open, their contents scattered, cupboards emptied, even mattresses cut open. Any hiding place there they would have found, but as time passed Paul slowly became confident that Robert had hidden nothing of his other life in the cottage. He saw Nordhoff glance at the picture of Marie-Claude's aunt, which Marie-Claude had substituted for that of Robert's mother, and pull out the photo of Laurence.

"Who's that?" he snapped, and Paul replied, "Monsieur Martin's mother," as if he had been lying all his life.

Finally, Paul was allowed home. Nordhoff looked angry, his thin face ugly, without the charm that had given him his good looks. He stared at Paul as he slid his long legs into the back seat of the Citroën.

"If any of you've been lying, God help you," he said quietly, and Paul thought, but did not say: how dare you mention my God to me.

"We have nothing to lie about," he replied, and Nordhoff slammed his door. The engine gunned and the black car disappeared down the hill towards St Didier. Paul took a deep breath. The air smelled cold and clean. There was more snow on the way, and he hoped the road to St Didier would become blocked in the night. He would prefer to remain here, where he would not have to continue lying, than be in St Didier where he could be watched and listened to. He sighed and thought: we must start living the lie today, and every day. They must never find Robert's daughter.

Years later, after the war, they discovered that the Germans had indeed held Robert prisoner. They never knew whether he had seen the photo of Laurence, or indeed if he had been told that his daughter – a daughter – was dead. All trace of him had disappeared, lost forever among the thousands of others who were never found, whose last journeys had been taken anonymously, accompanied only by their memories.

In the meantime, Laura had, in effect, become Laurence. Not by a whisper had any of them disclosed who she really was. She had gone to school as Laurence, taken her First Communion as Laurence, made friends as Laurence. Everyone in the family forgot, as time went by, that she was not in fact Laurence and had once been Laura. Only Marie-Claude thought about it occasionally and pushed the thought away. Not until the war is over, she had said to herself. And then, after France was no longer occupied, she had buried the thought even deeper, for she had grown to love Laura, and the thought of losing her was not to be born.

"It was only after the war was well and truly over," she said to Miriam Stein, "that my conscience became clouded. I remembered, finally, the promise I had made to Laurence, the real Laurence, to have a proper funeral for her. I remembered that Laura had a real grandmother who must have known of her existence. Slowly I realised that we shouldn't deny Laura her true roots, her English heritage.

"Then my duty became clear. Paul was as reluctant as I was, but Père Guy had been prodding us both for a year or more." She shrugged. "Suddenly I knew it wasn't fair to Laura, or to the memory of Robert, and I made myself sit down and write to Robert's mother. It was quite simple. I had always known Robert's mother's address. Robert gave it to me the last time he came to Belay – that spring of 1940 – and when all the business with Laura started I memorised it and destroyed the paper."

Paul looked surprised. "You never told me."

"I'd forgotten I had it until we heard about Robert, and then I thought the less you knew the less you could give away. Luckily, that was one question Nordhoff never asked – why should he care about Robert's mother in England?" She shuddered. "I'll never forget him, Nordhoff. He used to come back, you know, to Belay and just watch. He would just sit in his car and watch the children, staring. He was so thin you could see all the bones of his face – he started to look like a skull. I hated him. Then one day in about 1943, we heard he'd been shot dead, in an alley in St Didier. They never found out who did it, even though they arrested anyone and everyone they suspected, and some never came back."

Marie-Claude stared into space, back into a France Miriam Stein had never known. Miriam liked this woman. No wonder Laura had not wanted to go back to her real self, the self she had been persuaded to forget and had quite forgotten. Now that she'd heard the full story, Miriam thought, she could start to unravel it for Laura.

***

But all that was in the future. Now Miriam looked at the exhausted child who had finally fallen asleep towards dawn, worn out with crying and with forcing herself to remember the life she so longed to go back to, and from which she felt herself barred forever. It was seven o'clock and Miriam had just woken from the uncomfortable sleep she had fallen into on the hard upright chair.

Laura's pinched white face at last looked relaxed and with the lessening of tension some colour had come back into it so that as she slept Miriam could see a faint ghost of the girl she must have been before she was so forcibly removed from everything she knew.

Although Laura had not been able to tell her much, and the scenes had been muddled in time and place, Miriam had been able to work out with the help of what she had learned from her grandmother what had probably happened. It was a horrific story in one way, she thought, and a story of courage and bravery in another. She would have to meet the woman whom Laura had described as her mother, Madame Bonneville, from whom she was determined to learn the whole story in order to help Laura come to terms with who she was. Meanwhile, there was the present to think of. What should she advise Laura's grandmother to do, and how should Edith Morrison be approached? She doubted that it would do much good to Laura to move her to yet another school. She had at least started to find her way around here, and that she had learned quite a lot of English, Miriam had no doubt. She suspected that Laura had thought to herself that the longer she took to learn it, the more chance there would be of them sending her back to France. Which was what she wanted, although at the same time she had decided that the blame for what had happened must lie at Marie-Claude's door.

"I never want to see her again," Laura had wept. "She sent me away. She says she's not my mother. She sent for *Grandmère*. She just wanted to get rid of me."

"Laura, that is not true," Miriam had said. "You have letters from Madame Bonneville which say just the opposite. You've shown them to me." She picked up the pile of tattered envelopes that Laura had produced from her dressing-gown pocket. Some of them had not been opened.

"Why don't you open the others? You'll see. Madame Bonneville is so distressed that you haven't written to her. She loves you like a daughter – she says so, in every letter."

Laura had turned her face to the wall. "But I'm not her daughter and if I'm not her daughter I don't want to know about her," she had said. "I hate her. You don't understand."

Miriam understood only too well what Laura was feeling. She had been rejected, unwanted. She did not know who she was, where her roots were, where she had come from. She felt totally abandoned by everyone she had known, and somewhere, as well, lurked the spectre of guilt, guilt at wanting someone to love her who, in Laura's understanding, did not want to love her any more. Guilt, perhaps, that the real child called Laurence Bonneville had died instead of her, guilt at replacing her in a family which she had just discovered had had to substitute Laura Martin for their own dead daughter because of the exigencies of war, not because they had wanted to.

Miriam sighed. It was going to take a long time to sort out.

Now, as she watched, she came to a decision. What Laura needed was to feel accepted here at Baynes at least; she needed friends, and love. She wondered if Edith Morrison was up to providing them, if they could be found anywhere in this great school full of confident young Englishwomen who had not had to live through the kind of events which had shaped Laura's life. But if Edith could find for Laura just one or two girls who might be able to accept her and help her, it would be a beginning, thought Miriam. She herself could provide some of the love, she thought, even though it might be unprofessional – and wondered why this child seemed to be forcing her way into her life – and her grandmother, who had sounded more puzzled than loving when she spoke of Laura, would surely learn to love her more when she saw the child Laura really was: the Laura to whom Marie-Claude Bonneville had written, over and over again, even though no reply had come back, was clearly someone who had been cherished, the youngest sister in a big, happy family.

She wondered what Laura's grandmother would say if she recommended that she send Laura back to France. But would they want her? Who would she be? Laura or Laurence? No, thought Miriam, whose creed had always been that the truth must be faced up to, however painful; no, if Laura was ever to know who she really was, she must stay here, and discover the other part of her life, the part which had had to disappear with her father's capture. She smoothed the dark hair off the sleeping girl's forehead, her face looking so vulnerable in repose, and went in search of Matron. She would recommend that Laura stay in bed for a day or two, while they sorted out what was to happen to her.

"Only food she likes, Matron," Miriam said. "Eggs and milk, and fresh fruit. A little chicken perhaps."

"I'll see what I can do," Matron said stiffly, her eyes cold and unsympathetic, and picked up the brass bell on the hall table to rouse the sleeping juniors from their slumbers.

Miriam thought again what a barbaric system the English boarding school was, forcibly separating children from their parents for months, sometimes years if their parents lived abroad, letting their lives be ruled by someone like this fat pig of a woman – and yet how spoiled in another way these children were, educated to think themselves special, no pain or money spared to help them emerge as confident, self-elected and elite members of a race of which they would naturally be leaders.

She looked in again on Laura, but Laura had slept even through the penetrating sound of Matron's bell. Miriam left her asleep and crossed the hall again to the front door. As she did so, another door opened quietly and a fair-haired child looked out.

"Are you the person who came to see Laura last night? I could hear you talking through the wall," she said. "Are you French? I guessed you were speaking French?"

Miriam stopped. What an amazingly pretty little girl, she thought, seeing Georgina's fair curls, her heart-shaped face, the startlingly blue eyes fringed with black lashes under dark brows smoothed on her high forehead like birds' wings.

"Yes, I am French," she said. "Your guess was right. Are you the girl who rescued Laura?" she said. The child looked embarrassed and looked down at her feet, encased in rather vulgar pink fur slippers. "Well, I helped," she said. "Is she all right?"

"Yes, she's fine," replied Miriam. "Are you in the same class as she is?"

"Yes," replied Georgina. "Me and Harriet and Laura are all in the same form – Form Three."

"Harriet?"

"The other girl who was with me at the Pond. She ran back to the school and raised the alarm."

"You were both very brave," said Miriam. "And very sensible."

Georgina looked at her feet again. "It was nothing," she murmured and raised her eyes again to Miriam. She looked worried.

"Will they take Laura away?"

"That's what I'm here to see about," replied Miriam. "Do you think they should?"

"I don't know," said Georgina. "She's awfully unhappy. But that's because she doesn't want to be friends with anyone. We did try ... well, a bit ..." She looked down again at the pink slippers. "Well, actually, we didn't try very hard."

An idea was forming in Miriam's mind.

"If I asked you specially," she said, "would you find it very difficult to be nice to Laura, to be her friend?"

"Well, if she could learn a little English it would be easier."

"I'm sure she could do that," said Miriam drily. "She actually understands quite a lot, I think."

Georgina nodded. "Sometimes I've wondered," she said. "When she wants to I think she can. The other day, when Mere ... when a girl in our class was saying something about her getting away with not doing her prep, Laura went very red and looked angry."

Matron could be heard upstairs chivvying the girls to hurry. Suddenly she appeared on the half-landing.

"Georgina Charlton," she said crossly. "If you're well enough to be up, you're well enough to go to school. Come up here immediately and get dressed."

"Yes, Matron," said Georgina meekly. She glanced at Miriam.

"I've got to go. But if you like ..." She stopped.

"Yes?" prompted Miriam softly.

"Well, I was going to say Harriet and me could look after Laura a bit, if she stays here."

"That would be really kind," said Miriam. "You'd better run upstairs now. I hope I'll see you again."

As Georgina disappeared up the stairs, Miriam's eyes followed her. What a nice girl, she thought. But her face continued to look puzzled, and she tucked away a mental reminder to herself to find out a little more about her. There was something there that did not quite gel. Is she too good to be true, she thought?

Later that morning Miriam saw Edith Morrison and told her the whole story.

"What an incredible tale," said Edith thoughtfully. "I wish I'd known all this when I took her on. Why on earth didn't the grandmother tell me?"

Miriam explained that although old Mrs Martin knew the gist of the story, she had been unable to communicate with her granddaughter at all.

"Laura knew no English when she came back here with her grandmother," she said, "and Mrs Martin's French I gather is not very good. Laura says that her grandmother and Madame Bonneville found it very hard to talk to each other. She says that Monsieur Bonneville spoke English quite well, but he and the lawyer were closeted in his study for most of the day, so there was no one there to translate. They arrived totally out of the blue." She thought of the frustration produced by the lack of proper communication – she herself had found it a long hard task to reach a stage where she could express herself fully in English. It's easy enough, she thought, to learn the vocabulary, but to learn to express ideas, thoughts, to hear what is inferred but not spoken, to discern the real meaning behind the words, is incredibly difficult.

"So what do you recommend that we do?" Edith was saying. "I'm loath to keep the child here if it's not going to work. She might be better elsewhere."

Miriam thought, not for the first time, what a hard woman Edith was, and understood that she disliked failure.

"Are you prepared to bend your rules a little?" replied Miriam.

"I can do whatever I think necessary with the rules," said Edith. "Which ones are you suggesting I bend?

"I'm going to suggest that you select two or three girls and let them help Laura to adjust to life here. I think she should probably stay here now – though I would not have recommended a school like this if I had been consulted when her grandmother first brought her back …"

Edith smiled. She knew Miriam Stein's feelings regarding English boarding schools. She had met her a few times socially, sat with her on one or two committees, and had a high regard for Miriam's astute judgement of others.

"That goes without saying. But I'm glad to hear you're recommending that we keep her …"

Miriam looked at Edith searchingly. "I have a great deal of respect for you and your school, Edith," she said. "It's just that in

France, things are done differently. The family is much more important than it seems to be here."

"Don't be fooled by the fact that people here send their children away from home to be educated," replied Edith. "These children come from the kinds of families where family and family name and tradition is all-important. The fact that they're not actually at home for most of the year has nothing to do with it. Their parents exert a tremendous influence. And the richer and more famous the family, the stronger the values and mores it imposes. However ..." she continued, looking at her watch, "we don't have time to go into my views on the importance of family now. We must decide what to do about Laura Martin. Her grandmother will be here at any moment."

"What I was going to suggest was that you involve two or three children of Laura's own age in helping her to settle down. Perhaps they could share a bedroom with her ..."

"We generally keep the ages mixed up," said Edith. "It helps to stop unhealthy friendships forming."

Miriam made a face. "Oh, for God's sake, Edith," she said forcibly, "they're ten years old. Anyway, Laura could do with any kind of friendship, healthy or unhealthy. Don't you see, she has nothing at the moment. No friends. No family that she recognises. And the family she used to belong to she thinks has rejected her. There is a real danger of this child becoming so depressed that she will succeed at what she attempted yesterday." Edith looked sceptical, but worried. "It might be better if she leaves ..." she murmured, but Miriam took no notice.

"What I want you to do," Miriam said, "is to provide a few girls with whom she can make a new relationship, with luck a friendship, who will take it upon themselves to look after her. And of course, the staff must learn the story. No wonder Agnes Becquet could not deal with her."

"Poor Agnes," smiled Edith. "Miles above her head. She's only interested in verbs and vocabulary." She sighed. "I accepted Laura because her grandmother is a friend of one of the school governors and also knows one or two of the parents here. I didn't really go into what had happened to her. We've had one or two girls before who didn't speak much English, you know, and they seemed to learn it pretty quickly."

Miriam nodded. "Most children, if they're young enough, will adjust quickly to a change of language, especially if the home is happy. But that's not Laura's case, is it?"

"No," replied Edith with another sigh. "No, it's not. I must consider what you're suggesting. You think that she might progress more happily if we let her share a dormitory with children of her own age, two or three selected ones?"

"That's one of my suggestions. I'm going to suggest to Mrs Martin that Laura spends some time with me each week too. And that, when it seems the right time, Laura visits her erstwhile family, so that she can see for herself that she was not forcibly rejected as she thinks. She'll be able to accept it once she really understands the reasons for it."

Edith looked doubtful. "Well, all right, Miriam. I'll try it. But I hope you're right. It goes against the grain and I'll have to soft-soap Matron at June's – that's the Junior Boarding House …"

"I've met your Matron," interjected Miriam, "and a less sympathetic woman would be hard to find."

"Perhaps," answered Edith, who had been quite happy with Matron herself; children needed a firm hand. "But I'm not changing Matron for your sake as well. She does a perfectly good job. Anyway, as I was saying, I believe there's a small dormitory in the attic at June's that is unused at present. Now, who do we select to make friends with her? Do you know any of the children here."

"You could start, perhaps, with the girl who rescued her," suggested Miriam. She had liked the bright inquisitive little girl who had been reluctant to claim the glory of saving Laura from the Pond, even though there had been something puzzling, something she couldn't put her finger on.

"You mean Georgina Charlton, " said Edith, nodding her head. "She would be a good choice. She has a very strong character indeed ..." She brought to mind the girl who had come to Baynes two or so years ago, with her grating voice and dreadful table manners, and compared her with the child Georgina now was. She had never known a child observe and copy her peers so quickly. Within weeks of her arrival Georgina's voice had softened and modulated, until now you couldn't tell that she did not come from the same background as the other pupils. Her table manners were perfect, and she had quickly learned the posture and ways of behaving which Edith believed were part of what parents wanted their children to learn at Baynes. A whole way of life was how Edith expressed it to herself. She did not stop to think what these changes might be doing to Georgina's home life. She had almost forgotten what Dotty Brand had told her about the girl's background, and if it had occurred to her to think about it, it would not have struck her as a difficulty that the Charltons' only daughter now seemed a stranger to her father and brothers, although her mother rejoiced at the changes Baynes had wrought. Neither did she question the fact that she had never yet met either of Georgina's parents. The first term Dotty had brought her and since then she had come and gone home on the school train, from which Edith assumed she was met.

"Yes," she repeated. "Georgina Charlton would be a very good choice."

"Wasn't there another girl involved?" asked Miriam.

"Yes. Harriet Bolton. She behaved surprisingly sensibly, all in all. She's not what I would call a sensible child normally. There was an incident with one of the teachers last year ... something to do with what her teacher called her that she violently rejected. She had to be sent to bed without supper."

A picture of Harriet sprang into her mind, the girl's straggly pale ginger hair escaping from her plaits, the hair pulled back unbecomingly from her pale face. Harriet annoyed her, and had particularly annoyed her recently with her outbursts of rage and bad temper, though apparently she was clever. She thought of Harriet as she had sat at her own table at breakfast that morning, pushing to one side the black pudding that Cook had somehow found for breakfast – a perfectly edible, nourishing, if northern dish, Edith thought – and how Harriet, when her more senior neighbour had remonstrated with her, had somehow managed to knock her plate to the floor so that no one could insist on her eating the black pudding. Sly was perhaps the word that suited Harriet best ...

"I don't think Harriet would be the right girl to help Laura," she started to say, when there was a knock on the door and Edith's secretary came in followed by an elderly, delicate-looking woman whom Miriam guessed instantly was Laura's grandmother. The likeness was unmistakable.

"You asked me to bring Mrs Martin in when she arrived," said the secretary, and Edith came round her desk to shake hands with Mrs Martin, and pulled out a chair for her, settling her with more care than she usually bestowed on visitors. She instructed the secretary to bring in coffee. Guilt, thought Miriam, as she was introduced. Edith knows she did not give this woman's granddaughter the time and interest she should have. She was amused to hear the faint obsequiousness in Edith's voice, as she apologised once more for what had happened, and remembered that Edith had said Mrs Martin was a friend of one of the school's governors. I should not be sitting here finding this amusing, she thought to herself, and realised how tired she felt after her night with Laura, so tired that anything anyone said today was going to strike her as sour, wrong. She took a deep breath and pulled herself up in her chair. The coffee had arrived and looked revolting, she thought, guessing that it had been made from the thick coffee essence which the English seemed to think had some relation to the real thing. But she accepted a cup, hoping there might at least be some caffeine in it to give her energy, and brought her attention back to what was being said.

"I should very much like to meet the two girls who, er … helped Laura," Mrs Martin was saying. She can't bring herself to say 'saved', thought Miriam irritably, and wished as she had wished so often before that the English would not always pretend that nothing was serious, would not always use a safe word like 'help' instead of a dramatic word like 'save'.

"Of course," Edith replied. "Georgina Charlton and Harriet Bolton. I'll get Mrs Rodway to bring them in." She got up and went in search of her secretary. A silence fell, awkward and faintly embarrassing. Mrs Martin looked at Miriam.

"What am I going to do?" she said, with a look almost of desperation. "I'm at my wits' end. I feel this is all my fault, and yet I don't know what to do about it. I can't talk to her and she can't or won't talk to me. We're like enemies living the same house. She's my granddaughter. I am her grandmother. And yet we can't, or in her case won't, communicate. Did you find out anything from her, anything at all?" Miriam was touched by the appeal in the old, faded eyes which still held a hint of the greeny, hazelnut colour which gave Laura's eyes such a cat-like look.

"I think you're right to be puzzled by all that has happened," she said gently. "I think I probably know a lot more than you do about what has happened to Laura. It must have been very difficult?"

"It was … is. I feel I can't go on."

"You must not abandon her," said Miriam swiftly. "That would be the final straw."

"No, no, my dear, you misunderstand me," said Mrs Martin, sitting upright in her chair. "I have no intention of abandoning Laura. She's my only grandchild – the only one left of all of us ..." She stared unseeingly out of the window, as if she could see back to a time long past.

"I'll never abandon Laura now," she repeated. "During the war, I had so much time to realise that what my husband, and I by not opposing him, did to Robert, Laura's father, was so stupid, such a waste. And now I'll never see him again."

She looked back at Miriam. "Time goes so quickly and we never appreciate what we have when we have it. My husband did not approve of Robert's chosen career, to work with pictures and antiques, and to work in France, and we, I, allowed ourselves to lose touch with him. My husband was an obstinate man and when Robert defied him he became pompous, idiotic, striking attitudes and saying stupid things like "I won't have him under my roof" – and I allowed him to do it. I went along with him. I've never regretted anything so much. I had all those years of the war, here, on my own, to regret it. I would have given anything to see Robert again. But I knew, I think, that he wouldn't survive. I think I probably knew when he died. It was sometime in 1941 I'm sure, though no one can tell me now. I remember the New Year's Eve. I was alone in the house, my housekeeper out visiting a friend, and I've never felt so bleak, so empty. It was as if darkness would never lift. I had a such a sense of being suddenly quite alone in the world ..." her voice trailed away. "I don't know why I am telling you this," she said. "But I do promise you, I will not abandon Laura now that I've found her."

Miriam smiled. "I'm glad you told me that," she said. "I feel so drawn to Laura, I feel that I too, will not abandon her, if you'll allow me to help her. Perhaps together ...?"

Mrs Martin nodded. "I do feel I need some help with her – that's all I meant, really, that I couldn't deal with it alone ..." She looked at Miriam and saw strength and determination in the dark, almost Eastern, face, black liquid eyes that looked world-weary, as if there were no horrors that they had not seen, and yet optimistic, humorous, at the same time; a wide mouth compressed at the corners so that it looked down-turned, a long slightly curved nose. She wore her fairly ordinary clothes, a grey skirt and jacket over a crimson sweater and white open-necked blouse, with a chicness that could only have been French.

Footsteps could be heard crossing the front hall, and Miriam realised that Edith must have gone to fetch Georgina and Harriet herself. She strode in, looking particularly mannish and in control as the two small girls followed her like acolytes.

"I don't know where that secretary of mine has got to," she apologised to Mrs Martin. "I'm so sorry to have abandoned you ..." (that word again, this whole day is shot through with the word abandon, which is what I will never do to Laura, thought Miriam, surprised at the strength of her feeling) "... I had to fetch Georgina and Harriet myself." Edith settled herself behind her desk again, and the two girls stood near the door, unsure what to do with themselves. Georgina put out a tentative hand and walked towards Mrs Martin.

"This is Georgina Charlton, Mrs Martin," said Edith. "Georgina, this is Laura's grandmother."

Mrs Martin took Georgina's proffered hand and shook it, then held on to it firmly. "Georgina," she said. "I can't thank you enough for helping Laura." She looked across at Harriet, still standing awkwardly at the door.

"This is Harriet Bolton, Mrs Martin," Edith said, nodding at Harriet to shake hands. Harriet shook the old lady's hand awkwardly, a fierce red blush colouring her pale skin. "Thank you Harriet," said Mrs Martin. "I gather it was you who raised the alarm?"

Harriet nodded and Miriam could see her hope that she would not need to elaborate, to speak at all. She guessed that the girl was paralysingly shy. Next to the poised and self-contained Georgina, who managed to wear her green box-pleated tunic and red girdle with some aplomb, Harriet looked untidy and as if her clothes had spent the night on the floor. Her blouse was dirty, with a blue ink stain on the collar, and her yellow girdle hung with one end trailing past her knees, which were themselves grubby and scratched.

Miriam felt a pang of sympathy for her, and saw why Edith had started to say that she did not think Harriet would be the right girl to befriend Laura. Miriam mentally shook herself. How often had she told other people not to make snap judgements on first impressions? She smiled and said to Harriet, "I met Georgina this morning, but I didn't meet you. I'm a doctor. My name's Miriam Stein. I'm going to try to help Laura to stop feeling so miserable."

Harriet smiled, a small, fleeting movement of her lips, and moved her slight weight to the other leg, the blush still brilliant. She wiped a hand across her face, trying to hide it. *She knows Edith doesn't like her*, thought Miriam, and felt a surge of pity for her. It would be very hard to be one of Edith's failures.

"How long have you been here, Harriet?" she said, trying to put the girl at ease.

"Um, a year, I suppose," replied Harriet in a low voice. "Just over a year."

Edith was speaking, her clear voice cutting across and drowning Harriet's reply. "Harriet has been here for over a year, Georgina for a year longer," she said. "They're the same age as Laura. Now Georgina ..." she turned her full attention to Georgina who looked back at her, alert and interested, unquelled by Edith. "Georgina, Dr Stein has proposed that it would be a very good thing if two or three of you, of the same age as Laura, were to take special pains to look after her and become her friend. That way, she will know who to ask when she needs to know something, and she will learn English more quickly in a small group of girls. In order to facilitate this ..." (goodness, she's pompous when she gets going, thought Miriam, watching Edith's expansive, gracious gestures as she spoke) "... in order to facilitate this, I'm going to put you and Laura and perhaps one or two other girls into the small dormitory in the attic at June's. I know it's unusual here to have girls all of the same age sharing, but in this case I feel it is necessary. Will you help us?"

"Of course, Miss Morrisson," said Georgina, her wide blue-eyed gaze serious, her voice concerned. What an actress, thought Miriam, the thought coming unbidden into her mind. She looked across at Harriet and was surprised at the expression on Harriet's face. She looked as though she was holding her breath and Miriam realized she was hoping against hope to be included in this arrangement too. Surely Edith would see it, would not leave this one out who had done as much to save Laura as Georgina had.

But Edith was smiling at Mrs Martin. "I think this might work out very well," she was saying.

Miriam looked at Georgina and saw that a determined look had come into her face. She pushed her chin forward a little and said, "Miss Morrison? You do mean Harriet as well as me, don't you?"

Edith looked at her in surprise. Girls did not usually question her decisions. "Well, I hadn't chosen the other girls yet ..." she started to say, but then Miriam intervened.

"I think Harriet would be equally helpful to Laura," she said, not quite knowing what she was basing her judgement on – fairness perhaps, or just the look of longing on Harriet's face – and as she looked up, she caught Mrs Martin's eye.

"I agree with Dr Stein," the old lady said firmly. "I would like both of them to be Laura's friends, seeing that they've already done so much for her."

Miriam heard Harriet let out the breath that she had been holding, and looking across at Georgina she saw her exchange a look with Harriet. These two are best friends, she thought. Doesn't Edith Morrisson know anything about the girls in her care?

"Very well, then," Edith was saying, "You will both move into the little dormitory with Laura when she comes out of the San. Anyone else you can recommend?" she added to Georgina, sardonically, an imperious eyebrow raised. To Miriam's surprise it was Harriet who answered.

"Alison would be a good choice, Miss Morrisson," she said. "She likes Laura." She turned to Mrs Martin. "Alison Grant – she says that her parents know you, Mrs Martin." Mrs Martin nodded, smiling, and Harriet sat down suddenly on a chair by the door. Miriam saw that her hands were shaking, and the blush, which had subsided a little, had suffused her cheeks again. I think I like Harriet, thought Miriam. And she could probably do with another friend, she thought, glancing at Edith, who was looking angry and put out. Especially if she is going to have Edith as an enemy.

CHAPTER Four

Earlier that day, up in the dormitory, Georgina had whispered to Harriet:

"I've just seen the woman who's been talking to Laura all night. I could hear them. She's a French doctor and she asked if we would be nice to Laura, be her friends. I said we would." She was pulling on her clothes as she spoke, carefully adjusting her knee socks so that the garters didn't show. How does she manage to look so neat all the time, thought Harriet, whose own garters had lost their elasticity long ago and whose knee socks were already in grey concertinas round her ankles. But she knew the answer, really – Georgina took the same care with everything, even making sure that she had elastic in her sewing box to make new garters. I wish I could be like her, Harriet thought, and then brought her thoughts back with a jerk to the present as she heard Georgina say, "You will, won't you, Harry?"

"Will what?"

"Oh, Harry," said Georgina. "You never listen, you're always miles away. Be friends with Laura. You will, won't you?"

"Yes, if you want," Harriet replied. "Come on, George, we'll be late for breakfast."

Snow had fallen again in the night, and Harriet amused herself on the walk over to the main school by walking with one foot on the path, which had been swept clean, and with the other making deep holes in the virgin snow which lined the edge and spread like a white blanket down towards the river. The tennis courts and games huts were all shrouded in white. Like white hulks, thought Harriet, and then realised that snow had got into her wellington somehow, and that her sock was uncomfortably wet. Blast, she thought. Blast, I won't dare get another pair of socks out after breakfast because blasted Matron will know; and she felt angrily once again that Baynes was like a prison, with its endless rules and lists of things that were forbidden, utterly stupid things like not changing your socks when you wanted to.

Her sock was still wet and clammy in her indoor shoe when Miss Morrisson came into the geography lesson. She spoke in an undertone to Miss King, who looked first at Georgina and then at Harriet, and beckoned them out to the front of the class. Harriet was frightened of Miss Morrisson, who was the embodiment of all the rules and embargoes that Harriet so resented, and who towered over the two small girls. She was wearing a tweed coat cut like a man's jacket over a matching tweed skirt, and Harriet, for one irreverent moment, wondered whether she actually *was* a man as she seemed to have no bosoms.

She pushed the thought to the back of her mind and followed Miss Morrisson and Georgina to the Headmistress's study. Harriet had never been in there before, and hardly dared to sneak more than a quick glance at her surroundings, awed by the presence of an old lady whom she guessed to be Laura's grandmother, and another woman who must be the one Georgina had described to her.

As she shook Mrs Martin's hand she felt a blush start up in her face and her whole body feel as if it was pricking with sweat. Why did it have to do it? Why did she always have to go red and fall over things?

She didn't know what it was that gave her the courage to answer Morry's question, which she later realised had been addressed to George and not to her, unless it was the feeling of encouragement which she sensed from the dark woman, and the relief of knowing that she as well as George would share the attic dormitory with Laura. Or was it the fear that Morry would choose Meredith, who would do anything to make George her best friend? Whatever it was, she found herself telling Morry that Alison would be a good choice to make a fourth, and then discovered that her knees were shaking so much that she had to sit down rather suddenly.

When finally they were allowed to go, George was cock-a-hoop.

"Just us and Alison and Laura!" she said gleefully as they dawdled back to their classroom, hoping the bell would ring. "You were brilliant to think of Alison. She's nice to everyone. And Matron can't do anything about it, because Morry's ordered it!"

A few days later, when they arrived back at June's to change into the brown dresses which they all wore after games, they found that their beds had been stripped, and all their clothes had been emptied out of the chests of drawers.

"Upstairs for you two," said the housemaid who was folding a dingy utility-marked blanket into a square.

They went warily up the stairs. Usually, the attic was out of bounds, but now it was to be their territory. They found a long, low room with dormer windows and sloping ceiling. There were four beds, all but one adorned with a woollen animal or doll, all with a tartan rug folded neatly across the bottom. There was a washbasin with flannels draped round it and their toothbrushes in mugs on a shelf above it. The curtains were yellow, giving a look of cheer on yet another grey, cold, cloud-heavy day.

Laura sat on the bed that did not have a toy on it. She was dressed, her brown dress neatly buttoned. She stood up as they came into the room.

"I have to thank you," she said in almost correct English, the first they had ever heard her use. "You saved my life."

Harriet blushed, and picked up her dolls to hide her red cheeks. "This is my bed," she said. "Which one's yours, George?"

Georgina was looking at Laura, ignoring Harry. "We're going to be your friends, Laura," she said in clear, slow unaccented English. "Can you understand?"

Laura gave George a cautious look, then looked at Harriet. She seemed to come to a decision.

"I can understood a lot," she said. "Not the all. But more than *them* know." She nodded her head towards the window, her look conveying her scorn towards her English teachers.

"Did you understand us?" said Harriet. "What about when Meredith said awful things about you?"

"I thought *merde*," said Laura. The others looked puzzled. "It's a wrong word," said Laura. "It's what you do in the *toilette*. Not wet, the other."

"You mean the lav," said Harriet. "You're not allowed to call it toilet here."

She caught George's eye and laughed. "*Merde*," she said, in an execrable accent. "*Merde, merde, merde,*" she sang, swinging Dinah and Dorinda up and down.

Laura smiled for the first time. "You do not say it proper," she said. "Listen", and she repeated the word three times, emphasising the 'r's.

Georgina took up the theme. "Meredith is *merde*, Matron is *merde*, Morry is *merde*," she sang, snatching one of Harriet's dolls and swinging it towards the door.

Suddenly Matron was in the doorway. The doll left George's hand and hit the Bun's stomach.

"What do you think you three are doing?" she hissed, as the doll dropped to the floor. "How dare you make all this noise? Georgina, I'm surprised at you. As for you ..." – she looked at Harriet – "... I told Miss Morrisson I did not think you were a good choice to influence Laura, and you've proved me right in the first five minutes. One more naughtiness from you and you'll be back where you belong with the others. Do you understand?"

"Yes, Matron," said Harriet. She looked at the floor. Georgina and Laura looked at each other, and then Laura said in small voice, "Sorry, Matron."

Matron looked surprised. "Hmm, so you can speak," she said. "Fancy that. And you've had them all fooled ..."

"I do not understood," Laura said, looking puzzled.

"She doesn't understand much," said Georgina quickly. "Sorry, Matron." She put on her most appealing face, her blue eyes wide and innocent. A shame-faced smile hovered about her lips. Harriet, watching Matron, saw her soften under Georgina's gaze.

"Very well, Georgina," Matron replied, "But don't let it happen again. I trust you, if not Harriet."

Rat, thought Harriet, but she said nothing. A new step could be heard on the stairs, and as Matron turned, Alison came into the room. She was a stolid, pleasant girl, old for her age and eminently sensible. Her best friend was a daygirl, and she therefore had no great interest in becoming best friends with anyone else. Over the years that they all shared a dormitory, Alison would be a kind, appreciative audience for the exploits of the others. She never minded not being included in their games and secrets, and helped Laura patiently with her English. More than once she protected them from Matron, covering up for them when they had all three gone down together to the bathrooms, a heinous crime if it was not your bath night, or swiftly making an unmade bed before the going-over bell went when Harriet was reading instead of doing it, or Laura gazing out of the window at an invisible landscape far away.

Now Harriet saw her arrival as a timely release from Matron's wrath.

"Hello," Alison said, her warm face with its friendly smile embracing them all. "Is that my bed? Must be. There's Pongo." She picked up the white bear on the fourth bed and rearranged him on the counterpane. She didn't seem to sense that Matron had been in a bate, thought Harriet, and Matron herself had obviously decided it was over, as with a last baleful glance at Harriet she turned and went down the stairs.

"Hello, Laura," Alison said. "Can you understand me?"

Harriet said, "Laura can speak English ... "

"And she can understand it," put in Georgina "But we'll have to be more careful – I've worked out Matron's room is just below this. She could hear us prancing about."

Alison turned to Laura. "Can you really speak English?" she said.

"A little," replied Laura. "More than them think. It is quite funny, when them think I cannot understood."

"Understand," corrected Alison. "Oh, gosh. Could you understand when Meredith was being foul about you?"

"Some. I did not mind. I did not really care, you see."

George, Harry and Alison looked at each other.

Then Harriet said tentatively: "What did it feel like, walking into the water?"

"I was pleased it was cold. I was wanting to die," replied Laura. "I hated all, *le tout*."

"But you don't now, not any more, do you?" Georgina said.

"Not after Dr Stein – the doctor *français*. I understood why I am here but I do not like."

That night they whispered for hours. Laura told them in her hesitant English a little about her life in France, about the Bonnevilles whom she had thought were her parents, and the four children she had thought were her brothers and sisters, and how awful it had been to find out that this was not true and that she was an English girl with no French blood in her at all. "But I ... I feel still *française*," she said bleakly, to which there was not much anyone could say.

She did not tell them, because she had told no one, of the time the German officer who was called Nordhoff had come to the school yard and gazed at her over the wall, silent and menacing. If she had known then what she knew now, she thought, she would have crumpled on the spot. He would have seen the guilt in her face. They had been right to have wiped out all her knowledge of her father, to have let her believe that she was Laurence, and as usual when she thought about the German, she felt a discomfort in her stomach which she guessed must be fear. He had not come in. Just looked at her. She'd felt cold all over, as if his look had removed her warm coat and the navy sweater knitted by Fernande and her thick woollen socks and all her underclothes, leaving her naked in the raw November wind which whirled the leaves around the playground and whistled through the windows, sending little skittering rolls of dust across the floors. And what happened later she refused to think about at all.

As Laura slowly began to settle into Baynes, learning the language, tentatively making friends with her classmates, cold February became even colder. Coal and coke became scarce and the stoves in those rooms that had them were only lit in the morning, while gas fires were kept at half-mast. Almost every day the electricity was cut off for a period, and when they shivered their way over to breakfast, they usually found the milk left out overnight had blueish ice on it. Helpings of food became smaller. For one long fortnight they were told to keep their outdoor coats on in class. The central heating, lukewarm at the best of times, had broken down. March was not much better, with blizzards and then floods, but at last temperatures rose and sudden showers brought unexpected rainbows to arch over the greening moorlands that they could see from their attic room.

One afternoon Harriet came back to June's from games, to find Laura sitting morosely on her bed. She was allowed off games twice a week to see Dr Stein and this time her eyes were red with wiped away tears.

What's the matter, Laura?" Harriet asked.

"Dr Stein is going to see my French family in the holidays. She thinks I must not – no, should not go."

"Why?"

"Because it's too soon, she say. I have to know who I am – but I don't understand what she meant – means. And she says I have not forgiven Maman, I mean Tante Marie-Claude, because I have not write ... written to her." Her English was becoming more fluent.

"Why not?"

"Because she sent me away."

"I thought you understood all of that – you told us what had happened, the war, the Germans?"

"Yes, I understood – I mean, I can understand it in my head. I can explain it in *français*, but not in England – English. And I suppose she is right, because if I had I would have read the letters and written to her. The letters are still all glueded up. Here." She reached into a drawer and pulled out a large, unwieldy bunch of letters, held together by a rubber band.

"You mean glued, not glueded and the right word is sealed, or sealed up," Harriet said. She leafed through them. Laura turned away, her face screwing up as she tried to prevent herself from crying. She brushed the tears away fiercely.

"You see – even thought about her makes me cry. And I would want to go back, but I do hate her too, for sending me away." She sighed, still scrubbing at her eyes. "It is all such a *confusion*. Anyway, Miriam – I am to call her Miriam – she says *je dois* ..." she searched for the words. "That I must read the letters, and understand why I have to forgive *ma famille*, only they are not *ma famille* any more, not just *say* that I do. And she says I must spend the holidays learning my grandmother and English lessons."

"But your English is much better now, though I think you meant getting to know your grandmother," Harriet said, but as she said it, she realised how much, even in this short, emotional exchange, Laura had stumbled over her words. Her accent was good, she thought, but she didn't know enough words. "And maybe some extra lessons would help."

"They might," Laura said, standing up. "Anyway, it's all, what's the word, arranged. She will go and I will stay. She said I could *probablement* go in the summer. It would be nice to see all my, I do not know what to call them – anyway, see Nathalie and Sabine and Jean-Claude and Olivier. Jean-Claude talks too much. He never stops." Her tears had gone, and a small smile crossed her face as she thought of the Bonneville children. She began pulling off her tunic, blouse, liberty bodice and woollen vest. One of the unbreakable Baynes rules was that vests were changed in the afternoon after games, and even if you had not played games your vest had still to be left on your chair.

"Ugh," Harriet had said when she first saw Matron fingering a still-warm vest, to tell that it had really been changed, and Laura deeply resented the invasion of privacy that life at boarding school presented.

"*Voila*," she said as she draped her vest over her chairback and took her brown dress from the cupboard. "They will laugh when I tell them that. They will not believe it." She sniffed as she made herself cheer up.

"Will you tell them about us, Laura?" said Harriet, wondering what it would really be like to be going back, as Laura would have to, to a foreign country to see people that, all your life, you had thought were your relations and that you now knew were not related at all. She couldn't imagine ever not having Mummy for her mother, though Daddy, now that he lived in London, she had learned to do without.

"I will tell them about you and George, and about Alison and ..." – she made a face – "Meredith, and Matron and Morry and Mademoiselle Becquet..." She broke off and did an imitation of Agnes Becquet, who still found her a total enigma.

George and Alison had come quietly up the stairs, and burst into peals of laughter at the imitation of Mademoiselle Becquet.

"I see why you need a proper English teacher," Harriet laughed.

George and Alison rapidly pulled their clothes off, while Harriet, who was already changed sat silently, enjoying the feeling of belonging that sharing this dormitory had given her. She realised that her life at Baynes had improved a great deal, though she would not admit, even to herself, that she occasionally actually felt happy and the thrill of excitement at the prospect of the end of term was in no way dimmed. Why do I have to be away from Mummy, she thought. If only I could have this and be with Mummy too. The faintest touch of disloyalty fluttered at her subconscious, and swiftly she amended her thoughts to reiterate her hatred of Baynes and her total, undivided, longing for her mother.

The bell rang and Harriet jumped up and said, "Let's race," and they ran down the stairs to race across the grounds to the main school. As they passed a group of older girls from the Senior boarding house, one of them said, "Why it's the little Church Mouse again," as she saw Harriet.

"Why do you always call her that?" said another, watching the four juniors to see if she could catch them breaking a rule.

"Oh, don't you know the story? You wouldn't believe it of her, she looks so meek, but apparently Miss Johnson, who teaches them maths, one day called her a little Church Mouse in fun. I mean, the girl never opens her mouth she's so shy. But this time she was so annoyed that she went charging up with her fists raised and laid into Miss Johnson as if a devil was in her. Miss Johnson said it was really very funny, but of course she couldn't laugh, because you can't have pupils behaving like that. She said she flailed her fists and went bright red in the face, and then started to cry. They had to punish her, of course. They sent her to bed without supper …"

"I should think just having to be in the same house as Matron was punishment enough," laughed the other girl. "I wonder what got into her?"

"Wouldn't you be annoyed if you were called a little church mouse?" replied the first. "She still hates it if you call her that."

"I bet she does," said the second, who remembered her own first days at Baynes and the difficulties of dealing with all the new rules, before she had learned to conform. "But she'll settle down one day, I expect."

But that was one thing Harriet was never going to do. She would never settle down at Baynes, never conform. And as Miriam Stein had guessed, it was not at all nice to be one of Edith Morrisson's failures.

***

It was the summer term.

Georgina, Harriet and Laura watched with awe as the procession of evening-gowned women singing the school song wound past them down the glass-walled conservatory corridor, plants on either side green and lush, and today augmented by jugs of yellow buttercups, the school emblem.

The Old Scholars, as the old girls of Baynes were known, were on their way to the Dining Room which tonight was lit with candles, their soft gleam transforming the magnificent circular room into a hallowed shrine for the gold-engraved names on the boards lining the walls and the portraits of the headmistresses who had led the school since the first, Elizabeth Baynes, had opened it.

Baynes worshipped its ancestors. Old girls of the school were far more important than parents and present girls. Only when a girl had been exposed to the Baynes dictum of excellence, and had come through it successfully, was she considered truly worthy. Then she could wear with pride the invisible laurel wreath bestowed by Baynes on its successes. Its failures were rarely mentioned, and it was not often that a failure came to the yearly Old Scholars Weekend which was a high point of the Baynes school year.

Watching these women, doctors, lawyers, writers, bearers of perfect children who would be sent to Baynes in their time, missionaries, scientists, magistrates, councillors, women who served their country and their fellows as naturally as they breathed, Georgina felt a swell of pride that she would one day be admitted to their lists. This was what being at Baynes was about, she thought. This sense of belonging to a place, being one of a huge family of women whose standards and successes would become your own.

As the singing became fainter, and the last of the old pupils disappeared up the stairs to the Dining Room, a collective sigh went through the groups of girls who had been watching. Georgina turned to Harriet, her face pink and excited, her blue eyes gleaming.

"Gosh, Harry, we'll be there one year," she said.

But Harriet's face was untinged with the excitement that seemed to run like electricity through the school. She looked cross and bored.

"You might," she replied. "I won't."

"Oh, Harry, why not? Don't you think it's wonderful – all those women who were girls here once, just like us."

"What's so exciting about it?" said Harriet, kicking with her sandal at the stone flags, liking the noise it made. "They're just a bunch of boring women."

Laura, who had been watching in amazement as what seemed hundreds of grandly dressed women had marched past her, turned to Harriet.

"Don't you want to be an Old Scholar, Harry?" she said. Her English had improved greatly. "I do. I want to march past all the little girls like us when I'm grown up, and impress them with my dress and my jewels. *Elles sont fières* – what's the word – proud, proud to have been here. You enjoyed this afternoon? Well, the first part, when we picked the flowers ..." her voice trailed away as she remembered what had happened.

Harriet had indeed enjoyed the first part of the afternoon. Breaking the routine, the whole school had gone out into the countryside and picked the thousands of buttercups that would transform the school into a yellow bower in homage to its old girls.

The Junior classes had gone with Miss King to the meadows close to the school, and denuded them of buttercups, filling bucket after bucket. The smell of hay and warm grass had mingled with the sweet, polleny scent of the flowers, and Harriet, feeling for once free and unobserved as she disappeared behind a copse of trees with George and Laura, had thought that this was the best afternoon of the year. She felt the cool tickle of the knee-high grass on her bare legs, and wriggled her toes with pleasure inside the silky white ankle socks that they had at last been permitted to wear. The sun was high and bright in the pale, cloudless sky, and some of the girls had flung off their panama hats. She lifted her hand to take hers off and felt the smooth pale straw warm from the sun. It had a particular smell, sort of malty or floury – a smell which forever after would take her back to that hot sunny June afternoon. Georgina and Laura had brought out their yoyos, and were bouncing them up and down instead of picking flowers. In their green and white checked cotton frocks and cream panama hats they looked like an illustration for a children's book, thought Harriet – *Milly Molly Mandy* perhaps – and she fished her own yoyo out of her pocket and went to join them.

Eventually, Miss King had come in search of them, not angrily, but peacefully and slowly, as if the smell of warm hay and buttercups had made her sleepy and soft. Her arms were full of the yellow flowers, and bits of grass clung to her skirt.

"Come on, you lazy lumps," she said, smiling. "We've got to get back. It's almost teatime. Come and help carry the buckets." She caught Harriet's eye, and smiled and said, "Harriet, the sun suits you. You've got hundreds of lovely freckles."

Harriet felt pleased. She did not, herself, like the way her skin freckled the moment the sun came out, but if Miss King thought it looked nice, perhaps it did. Anyway, nothing was going to spoil today, she decided, and she went over to where the others were lying and sitting round the buckets of flowers.

Slowly they dawdled back to school, hot now and tired. Harriet was carrying two bucketsful, trailing buttercups behind her as the buckets knocked against her legs. Meredith, who seemed to have got out of carrying anything, suddenly appeared beside her. She tugged one of Harriet's plaits and said, "You look very peculiar. What are those marks on your face?"

"They're freckles," said Harriet. "Leave my hair alone." Meredith moved closer to Harriet, and pushed against one of the buckets. The buttercups spilled out.

"Now look what you've done," said Harriet. "You can jolly well help to pick them up."

Meredith looked at her and grinned maliciously. "I wouldn't help you do anything," she said. "Spotty!"

"Buzz off, then," said Harriet. "Leave me alone." George and Laura and the others, led by Miss King, were miles ahead. Now, thanks to Meredith, who, empty-handed, had run to catch the others up, she would be last back. She stooped to pick up the dropped flowers, wondering why Meredith hated her so much, and hating her back. She hated her black curls which framed her boyish face, her tallness, her aptitude for gym and games, the way she seemed to attract everyone else in the form, and she particularly hated the way Meredith seemed determined to draw George into her circle. She looked back at the field, empty now. She wished she could just stay there, watching the shadows lengthen and feeling the heat go out of the sun, instead of having to go back and cope with the intrigues of school life.

She dumped her buckets in the gym, where the seniors were decorating anything and everything, and ran up the stairs to tea. All rules were relaxed as the school's most important weekend began, and today they were allowed to dispense with changing till later. On the tables were loaf-size piles of bread and margarine, and, as a treat, there was raspberry jam instead of the tomato jam, which was in Harriet's opinion disgusting, and iced buns shaped like torpedoes.

Harriet looked around her for George and Laura, and saw with a sinking heart that they were sitting with Meredith. She knew, without quite knowing how, that they were talking about her. She looked down at her sandals, and then suddenly looked up towards Meredith. Sure enough, Meredith was looking at her and saying something; when she caught Harriet's gaze, she looked swiftly away. She said something else to Georgina, and they all laughed. Georgina caught her eye for a moment, but pretended not to have seen her, turning quickly away to Laura. Harriet felt herself grow hot. How could they spoil this afternoon, which was the first she had enjoyed since term had begun? She felt the boiling rage swelling inside her, but tamped it down. She was determined not to lose her temper. Calmly she collected a glass of orange squash, another treat, and carried it to the table. As she approached, Meredith started to laugh.

"I told you," she said. "Harriet's covered in spots. Have you got the measles, Harriet? It looks like it."

George giggled, and even Laura, who was the most loyal of friends, smiled.

Harriet felt as if she had been hit. How could her friends desert her like this? Why didn't they tell Meredith they were freckles, not spots? Why were they all laughing at her? She felt her face going red.

Too late, Georgina saw the warning signs. She started to say, soothingly, "Meredith didn't mean anything ..." but Harriet had boiled over.

"You're a pig, Meredith," she said angrily, and poured the glass of sticky orange over Meredith's black curls. A gasp went up from the other girls at the table. Meredith leapt up, her hair dripping and the front of her dress stained orange.

"I'm going to tell Miss King!" she screamed, "You're for it, Harriet Bolton. They'll probably expel you this time."

"D'you think I'd care?" Harriet yelled back. "I hate it here. It hate it, and I hate you and I wish you were dead."

There was another gasp. You should never ever say you hated someone, and it was inexpressibly wicked to wish them dead.

Meredith looked round, triumphant in her role as victim, but already Miss King was hurrying over.

"What on earth is happening here?" she said. "What's that on your hair, Meredith – and your dress!"

"Harriet poured orange squash over me," said Meredith meekly.

"Is this true, Harriet?" said Miss King.

"It was her fault, Miss King," Harriet started to say. "She said I had spots. I hate her, I hate her ..."

Harriet burst into a torrent of crying. The whole dining room was watching her.

"Go to your classroom, Harriet, and wait for me." Miss King's face was no longer peaceful and sleepy, but angry and long-suffering. As Harriet stumbled towards the door she turned to Meredith.

"What did you say to provoke this?" she said.

She was no fool, and had watched the rivalry for Georgina Charlton's affections between Harriet and Meredith. She herself thought the Church Mouse was much the nicer of the two, but Meredith had the kind of character – years later it would be called *charisma* – that attracted others like pollen attracts bees, and the ability to make others feel honoured if she bestowed her friendship on them. She wondered if Georgina would have the strength to resist.

Meredith said, "Nothing, Miss King. I didn't say anything." She looked round, challenging anyone to correct her. There was silence.

"Very well, Meredith," said Miss King. "Come with me. Someone will have to explain to Matron why you need your hair and your dress washed."

"Yes, Miss King," said Meredith. A triumphant smirk trembled at the corners of her mouth. She turned towards the door through which Harriet had disappeared. Miss King turned to follow her.

Suddenly Georgina stood up.

"It wasn't Harriet's fault, Miss King," she said. "It was mine and Meredith's. Meredith was saying Harry had spots like measles, about her freckles. And I was laughing. We all were."

Meredith turned round. "It was only a joke," she said.

"Not a very funny one, Meredith, if I may say so," said Miss King. "Has no one ever told you that it's rude to make personal remarks? What else did you have to say?"

Meredith looked sulky. "Harriet can't take a joke," she said. "She's so stupid and touchy."

"Perhaps she has reason to be, Meredith, if you insist on teasing her all the time. As I said, it was not very funny and we do not make remarks about other people's looks here. It's extremely ill-mannered."

Meredith looked away and a faint sneer crossed her face. "So's pouring orange juice over someone," she retaliated.

"Harriet will be punished for that, but I think the blame for why it happened must lie on your shoulders, Meredith," said Miss King. "You were both in the wrong. And you, Georgina, should not have laughed at her, though I agree with Meredith that Harriet finds it difficult to take a joke, and I'm afraid that this time we will not be able to make light of what she's done."

As Georgina opened her mouth to reply, Miss King continued firmly. "No, I don't want to hear any more about it. You were all three in the wrong."

She was relieved that Georgina had stood up for Harriet, and realised that she would have despised Georgina if she had not. She found herself thinking, poor Harriet, and smiled to herself as she thought how amazed Harriet would have been to find Miss King championing her. She called a junior mistress over from where she had been supervising the orange juice.

"Miss Hay, would you please take Meredith over to Matron and explain what has happened and tell Matron that her hair needs washing before this evening. I must go and speak to Harriet."

As Meredith, Miss Hay and Miss King disappeared down the stairs, the rest of the class turned silently back to their bread and jam. Laura looked at George.

"What does expel mean?" she said.

Georgina told her, and a look of horror came over Laura's face. She couldn't bear it if her new-found friend were to leave.

"They will not do that, will they?" she said, but Georgina just shrugged, and someone else said: "Harriet's too naughty – she goes too far. You weren't here, Laura, when she hit Miss Johnson, for calling her a Church Mouse."

The others took up the story, delighting in telling Laura of Harriet's previous excesses. Georgina said nothing. She also felt that she could hardly bear it if Harriet were expelled. Harriet was the only girl with whom Georgina felt really safe. She realised that she wouldn't even mind too much if Harriet found out about her family, while if anyone else did she would die of mortification and shame. Everyone here came from a social station to which her parents could never belong. Pictures of her rough, loud brother

Steve lounging outside the pub, cat-calling at anyone who passed, came into her head. The dark cramped house could have been a million miles from here, she thought, it was so alien. She shook herself mentally and pushed the memories away. She would have to face the reality only too soon, for the summer term would be over in a few weeks, and she was determined not to let thoughts of the holidays spoil these last weeks.

The others were still gossiping about Harriet. Her temper was becoming renowned.

"D'you remember the time she threw the blackboard cleaner at you, Mary?" someone said.

"Honestly, how she dares sometimes, I don't know," said Mary, Meredith's downtrodden second-in-command. "Fancy pouring her orange over Meredith, of all people."

Someone giggled, and then, as they pictured Meredith's discomfiture the laughter spread. They enjoyed the idea of their self-elected leader being made a fool of.

"I think Meredith got what she asked for," said Georgina. "And I wish I hadn't laughed." She felt guilty at her disloyalty to Harriet. "I'm going to find Miss King and tell her more about how Meredith's been picking on Harry."

She got up from the table. Laura got up too. "I'll come with you," she said.

"No, Laura," said George. "It'll be better if I go on my own. I'll see you later."

She ran down the stairs, and on to the classroom. The door was shut, and a murmur of voices could be heard. She knocked on the door. Miss King opened it a crack and looked out impatiently. Behind her George could just see Harry, her tear-stained face red and grimy, where she had rubbed at her eyes.

"Not at the moment, Georgina," said Miss King.

"But it's about this afternoon," said Georgina. "It wasn't Harriet's fault. I said. It was mine, and Meredith's."

"It was Harriet who poured orange juice over Meredith," said Miss King. "You're not going to tell me that it was you who did that?"

"No, Miss King," said Georgina, an expression of pleading coming into her blue eyes. "But it was my fault for encouraging Meredith. She's been picking on Harriet for ages, and Harriet's been quite good about it. Meredith's always teasing her. But today I didn't stop her. For some reason I found it funny. If I had made her be quiet this wouldn't have happened."

Miss King thought about the hidden pressures and unexpected reactions that occurred in friendships. Even at this young age they could weigh on people, tempt them into some unthinking disloyalty. She opened the door properly.

"You'd better come in."

She turned to Harriet. "You have a very loyal friend," she said, gesturing towards Georgina. Georgina went to stand beside Harriet, and a small pathetic smile crossed Harriet's lips for a second.

"Now, is this true?" said Miss King. "How long has Meredith been picking on you?"

Harriet told her tearfully about the spilling of the buttercups and other, earlier teasings.

"And then she was talking about me when I came into the dining room, she was laughing and pointing. It's not fair – I can't help having freckles and they don't look like spots." Harriet was getting angry again.

"Harriet, not much in this life is fair," said Miss King. "You'll find that out only too soon. However, we do pride ourselves on being fair here, and perhaps Meredith has gone too far in her teasing of you. I have seen her, you know. We're not blind. Nevertheless, you can't go round throwing things at people and pouring glasses of orange juice over them ..." A faint smile hovered at her lips and Georgina thought, it's going to be all right.

"So there will have to be a punishment, and a firm promise that you will stop letting your temper run away with you. The next time you do, it will be really serious," Miss King continued.

"Yes, Miss King," said Harriet, the red flush subsiding from her cheeks. "I will try. But I don't seem to be able to help it."

"You must help it. We all have to control our tempers. What do you think this world would be like if everyone did exactly what they felt like to everyone else?"

"Like the war," said Harriet. "Hitler did whatever he liked."

"And look at the mess that got everything into," said Miss King. She was pleased at Harriet's astute comparison. "Now – am I going to have to call you Hitler, or Church Mouse?"

A shame-faced look came over Harriet's face and she smiled unwillingly.

"I'd rather be Church Mouse," she said.

"Well-said, Harriet," said Miss King. "I'm glad to see you can take a joke sometimes." She paused. Harriet looked round the classroom, at the old desks, worn and scored by innumerable penknifed initials, but serviceable still, each with its white enamel inkwell; at the blackboard decorated that morning with a design of buttercups; at the worn patch in front of the gas fire where year after year girls had stood to warm their chilblained hands or toast their illicit toast. In the late afternoon sunlight, the dust motes floated and swam like minute pieces of gold. She wondered what punishment she was to get this time? Would she be sent to Morry? She wished she hadn't done it, wished she could remember before she lost her temper the dreadful shame she felt when it was over. She supposed she would be sent to bed again.

Miss King was speaking again.

"Now, as to your punishment. You do see there has to be one, don't you, Harriet?"

"Yes, Miss King," Harriet said dully.

"I could send you to bed once again …"

"Oh, no Miss King!" Georgina couldn't help herself. "It's Old Scholars' Weekend. It's the best weekend of the year. Harriet would miss it."

"Well, yes," said Miss King. "It would be a bit hard to deprive Harriet of it, I suppose. Or to deprive the Old Scholars of Harriet," she added, laughing.

Harriet looked down at her sandals, not liking being teased again. George nudged her. "Come on, Harry," she said. "Miss King's teasing you. You've got to learn to take a joke."

"Oh, all right," said Harry. "I suppose so." She smiled faintly, and took a deep breath.

"I am very sorry, Miss King," she said. "I really will try not to have any more bad tempers, and I'll do whatever you tell me for my punishment, but please don't send me to bed."

"Very well, Harriet," said Miss King slowly. "In view of the teasing you have taken from Meredith this term, and in view of the fact that you have apologised to me, I will not send you to bed. However, you must apologise to Meredith ..."

"But ..." began Harriet.

"You will apologise to Meredith in front of the whole class, as they all saw what happened. As well, you will write out for me, in your best handwriting, the whole of Walter de la Mare's poem, *Three Jolly Farmers*, over the weekend, and you will do double monitor duties next week."

Harriet let out a sigh of relief. She had loved Walter de la Mare's poems ever since Mummy had given her her own copy of *Down A Down Derry*, with the exquisite illustrations by Dorothy Lathrop that gave her a thrill of pleasure every time she looked at them. It would be no hardship to copy out *Three Jolly Farmers*. And monitor duty – well, it just meant tidying up behind the others, both morning and evening.

"Thank you, Miss King," she said gratefully. She looked up at the teacher, and saw, for once, not a remote enforcer of rules but a kind and fair middle-aged woman with a look of concern in her eyes. Quickly, Harriet looked away. She did not want to see any of the Baynes teachers as a friend, and today, as always, she pushed away the invitation to friendship, preferring stubbornly to keep a barrier between those she thought of as The Enemy and those she thought of as Us.

Georgina thought Harriet had got off very lightly, and Harriet concurred later, as they walked across to June's to change into clean cotton dresses. Miss King watched them go and wondered what it was that produced these terrible tempers in Harriet; was something happening at home that made her so vulnerable?

Harriet thought of Mummy as she took out of the cupboard her favourite cotton frock. Just looking at the bright pattern of blue and pink flowers on the snowy white background recalled days at home watching Mummy stitching it, sewing curvy blue braid in two lines round the hem. She pulled it over her head and pushed her thin arms through the puffed sleeves. It sat coolly on her body – it had been announced at breakfast that at last vests need not be worn in view of the hot weather – and she smoothed it down slowly, enjoying the feel of the cotton. She longed and longed for Mummy; even having George and Laura for friends could not make up for not being at home and with her mother, especially on a day like this which she had spoiled by once again losing her temper.

As she went down the stairs from the attic with George and Laura and Alison, Harriet glimpsed Matron waiting outside her sitting room. She hung back, but Matron had seen her.

"Well, Harriet Bolton," she said. "I've heard about your activities this afternoon. I'm surprised you haven't been sent to bed. What do you have to say for yourself?"

George and the others had stopped and it seemed to Harriet that they formed a protective circle around her.

"Nothing, Matron," she said.

"A lot of extra work you've caused me." Matron indicated the open door of her sitting room where Meredith could be seen kneeling in front of the gas fire, drying her hair. As she saw Harriet she put out her tongue and made a rude gesture with her hand. Harriet looked away, pretending not to have seen her. Hatred for Meredith was settling deeper into her.

"I'm sorry, Matron," she said, sounding not at all sorry.

"Sorry! I should think so!" Matron bridled, rolling her fat shoulders. Her heavy bosom shook like a jelly. "I've had to wash Meredith's hair, and her dress, and someone will have to iron it for her. On top of all the work I do for you girls anyway. I don't know who you think you are."

She bent down and put her face close to Harriet's, so that Harriet could see her black button eyes narrowed between the folds of doughy flesh.

"One day you'll go too far," she hissed, and the vehemence in her voice made Harriet physically flinch away. She hadn't realised Matron hated her this much. With a last baleful look, Matron turned back into her sitting room and closed the door. The four girls went down the stairs slowly.

"She hates me," said Harriet. The others couldn't deny it.

"It doesn't matter," said George comfortingly. "We'll protect you. And there's only one more year here. Then we'll be in the Senior School."

But Harriet knew that if the Bun really wanted to hurt her, she would. There were lots of ways that she could punish her – insist on her tidying her drawers when it wasn't necessary; order her to clean the baths in the basement, where spiders lurked; force her to eat huge platefuls of the uneatable macaroni pudding. The opportunities for persecution were endless, and Harriet knew that the Bun would take every one she could. She shivered. Why, oh why, had Mummy let her be sent away like this, when she could have been safely at day school, like her Carruthers cousins? Even the loss of Laura and George would be better than being in this prison, where almost even to breathe you had to ask permission. She sighed, and resignedly took her blazer from its peg. She had thought for a while that life was getting better here, but today had brought back all the misery that her first term had seen. The others, sensing her mood, were silent, and it was a thoughtful foursome that had drifted back to Main School to watch the parade of the Old Scholars and join in the singing of the School Song.

***

Later that night, lying wakefully in bed, Harriet realised suddenly that in three weeks' time she would be home. Usually, she knew to a day how much longer term would last, but this term she had more than once forgotten her usual daily count.

She felt excited at the thought of going home, and then she remembered what had happened. Not only had her father left them and gone to London, and had married Arabella, but now Arabella was going to have a baby. She hated the thought – if anyone should have had a baby it should have been Mummy, Harriet thought, and saw again her mother's stricken face when the news had arrived by post just before she had left home for the summer term.

Harriet had met Daddy's new wife at the beginning of the Easter holidays, and had actually liked her a lot, even though she had been determined not to. But she hadn't thought about babies, and she found the idea repugnant. She didn't really want to know about how or why it happened – she had refused to look at the book Mummy had bought for her but she guessed it was in some way disgusting, especially if it had anything to do with what

Meredith and some of her cronies had been whispering about the other day. She thought back to the day she had met Arabella.

Her father had come up to Newcastle in his impressive new car, stayed the night at the Station Hotel, had a cup of coffee with Mummy, whose face looked sad and tired, and then she and her father had driven off, down the Great North Road to London. It had been very exciting – and although she kept trying to think of her mother, because it was not fair that she was missing all this, it had been hard to remember all the time. They had stopped at a pub for lunch, where Daddy had had beer and had taken a matchstick and dropped a few drops of his beer into her lemonade, as he always used to, and after a long, long time, when they seemed to have been driving for ages, and she had kept falling asleep, they had arrived in London. It was dark, but there had been lights on in the shops, and Daddy kept pointing things out to her.

"There's Madame Tussaud's," he said, and had promised to take her there. And later on he had said, "That shop is Harrods – it's the biggest shop in the world," and the excitement seemed to go on and on, so that by the time Daddy finally stopped the car she had felt full of energy and knew that her cheeks were pink, because she could feel them hot.

Daddy lived in a flat in London, and they had ridden up to it in a lift with a liftman dressed in uniform. All the halls and passages were carpeted in thick red carpet, and the door of Daddy's flat was bright white against it. He had unlocked the door and called, "We're back," and a tall, elegant woman had appeared, holding her arms out to Daddy and saying: "Oh, Alec, I've missed you so much. I'm so glad you're back."

Then she turned to Harriet and put her hands on Harriet's shoulders, as if she was examining her carefully, which Harriet thought afterwards was probably exactly what she had been doing, and said: "So you're Harriet," as if it was the most important thing in the world. She had a high, very clear voice, and Harriet noticed straight away that she said "orf" for off, and "crawse" for cross, which hardly anyone in the North said, except for a few very grand girls at school. She was utterly and completely beautiful, not a bit like her own mother, with very blonde hair done up in a roll at the back. She was tall, almost as tall as her father, and very slim, so that the straight dark blue dress she was wearing looked almost as narrow as Harriet's own dresses. She had dark blue eyes that matched the dress, and on her finger, above the wedding ring, she wore a ring with a stone that flashed with the same blue. Harriet felt stunned by her beauty, as if she came from a different race.

"So you're Harriet," Arabella said, and looked at her for a long moment, as if she was trying to read what Harriet was thinking, and then she took her hands from Harriet's shoulders, and taking her by the hand led her into the flat. She stopped at a door half way along the corridor that stretched ahead, carpeted in the same red as the hall outside.

"This is your room, Harriet," she said. "Every time you come to stay, this will be your room."

She opened the door and pressed the light switch. Instead of a central light, two pink shaded table lamps came on, and Harriet gasped as they lit up a small fourposter bed looped with white material with tiny pink roses printed on it. The bed was covered by a thick white eiderdown, and Daddy put Dorinda and Dinah down carefully on it. The curtains at the window were made of the same stuff as the curtains looping the bed, and the carpet was a thick, rosy pink with a white fur rug beside the bed. There was a little dressing table, with a matching curtain round its base, and a round, gold-framed mirror above. In one corner of the room was a small button-backed chair upholstered in dark green velvet, and beside it was a bookcase, in which Harriet could see some of her favourite books – the E. Nesbitt books, and Christopher Robin, and some Enid Blytons and even *The Wind on the Moon,* which was where Dinah and Dorinda's names came from.

"Do you like it, darling?" said Alec, and Harriet turned round and hugged his legs and said, "Oh, yes, Daddy, it's beautiful." Daddy put one arm round her and the other round Arabella who was standing beside him, and hugged both of them. "I know you two are going to get on," he said. "My two favourite women!"

Arabella smiled at Harriet, but Harriet suddenly remembered her mother, and realised that she hadn't thought about her since they had started driving through London, and felt guilty. All this wasn't fair to Mummy. This lovely room, the lift, the red carpets, Arabella's beauty. So she looked away and easing herself out of Alec's embrace jumped on to the bed and hugged her dolls.

"Harriet! Not on the eiderdown with your shoes on," said Arabella, and Harriet knew at once how to annoy her. But she decided not to, because really she seemed nice and must have done all this room to please Harriet, so she kicked off her shoes compliantly. "OK" she said. She looked at Alec, who had looked slightly worried when she jumped on to the bed, and said, "I'm hungry, Daddy. Can we have supper?"

"Dinner, darling," he said, and turned to Arabella, saying, "She'll soon get out of these northern habits."

Arabella laughed and said, "It doesn't matter a bit, darling. We always had supper at her age, in the nursery," and turning to Harriet, she said, "Come along, then, and wash your hands." She opened another door off the corridor, and Harriet found herself in a marble bathroom, with gold coloured taps and huge peach-coloured fluffy towels, and she suddenly felt lonely, and rather too young to be in this grand flat without her mother.

There was a delicious smell coming from the other end of the flat, however, and Harriet was hungry enough to forget about being lonely. She followed the smell, and came to a large imposing room, set about with sofas and soft cushions, and a number of small polished tables on which silver-framed photographs stood. A fire burned in the grate, and gold-coloured curtains were pulled against the night. Off this room was a smaller, wood panelled room with crimson velvet curtains and crimson upholstered dining chairs. On the walls were two large portraits of people Harriet didn't know, and as she was looking at them Arabella came into the room, carrying a tray laden with food.

"Those are my parents," she said.

"Lord and Lady Canmore," said Alec, coming into the room behind her with a large whisky and soda in his hand. There was a proprietorial note in his voice, which puzzled Harriet, but later she worked out that Lord and Lady Canmore were his parents-in-law now, instead of Granny Carruthers, and she suspected that he liked having a Lord and Lady as relations. She quite liked it herself, and she really liked Arabella, she had decided.

During dinner, which was a delicious dish which Arabella said was a *daube*, but which Harriet would have called stew, although it bore no relation whatsoever to the stew she had at home or at school, Arabella had asked her all about her friends, what she liked reading, what she liked to do, and had planned a wonderful three days, with visits to the zoo, and Madame Tussaud's, and Harrods and Selfridges, the two biggest department stores in the world, she said, and there was even going to be a theatre one evening. Harriet had gone to bed with her head buzzing, probably she thought because Daddy had poured her quarter of a glass of red wine, which Arabella had diluted with water. She hadn't liked it much, but she had drunk it because Daddy liked people to drink, like he did, and it had made her cheeks feel very red.

The next morning, Harriet woke feeling sick. She lay in the beautiful white bed and wondered what to do. She could smell bacon cooking, and the smell made her feel worse. She lay very still, hoping the sick feeling would go away. After a long time, she heard a door bang, and then there was a knock on the door and Arabella came into the room and said, as soon as she saw her: "Do you feel all right, Harriet?" Harriet shook her head, and said she felt sick.

"Come on, into the bathroom," said Arabella, laughing and helping her out of bed. "You're just like my sister. She always feels sick, because she gets too excited. I told Alec he shouldn't have kept you up so late, or given you that wine."

Luckily, Harriet wasn't sick, and after Arabella had brought her some soda water in bed she felt better, and managed to eat some of the thin, dry toast that Arabella had also brought.

She could hear Arabella on the phone. She heard her give a high, bubbly laugh and say: "You're so naughty, Alec. I'll tell you tonight, darling. Can't wait."

She had never heard her mother say anything like that to Daddy, and as she thought of her she realised that now Mummy and Daddy would never, ever get back together, not now Arabella was here and married to her father. Actually, admitted Harriet to herself, she's probably better for Daddy than Mummy was, thinking of how Arabella had joined him glass for glass at dinner, and had teased him in a way that made him less bossy – and then she felt very guilty at having let such a thought escape into her head. She climbed out of bed and shut the door so she couldn't hear any more of Arabella's conversation with Daddy.

When Arabella came back into the room she said: "That was your father. He wanted to know what we were up to today. So I told him we were going to have a quiet morning, because you wanted to read your new books and I have some telephoning to do, and that this afternoon we would go to the Zoo. Is that all right? I thought it would be better not to tell him you felt sick. And I feel the weeniest bit pale this morning, too."

Harriet grinned feebly. "Yes. He doesn't like it when I feel sick. He doesn't like it when anyone feels ill."

"That's what I thought," said Arabella, looking conspiratorial, as though she and Harriet were in league against Alec. She was wearing a pale blue twinset, and a pink skirt, and had a string of pearls round her neck which fastened at the front with a beautiful clasp – another dark blue stone like the ring, set around with tiny pearls. She had on the highest heels Harriet had ever seen, at least three inches she decided, in shiny black leather that matched the shiny black handbag on a gold chain she carried when they went to the Zoo. She was wearing a jacket now to match the skirt, and looked so elegant that Harriet felt even more clumsy than usual in her green Baynes mac, and her boys' black leather houseshoes with elastic sides which up to this moment she had loved precisely because they were boys' shoes.

"We'll have to get you a decent coat," Arabella said firmly, and the next day, when they went to Harrods, she bought for Harriet a navy blue coat with a velvet collar and stitching on the pockets which made her look like the other London children with their mothers buying shoes and cotton dresses. Arabella had picked out a cotton dress too, but Harriet said firmly, "Mummy always makes my dresses," and Arabella had straight away put it back, and said, "Yes, of course," as if she should have known.

On her last night, Daddy took them to the theatre. He wore evening dress, with what he called a cummerbund in emerald green silk round the top of his black trousers, and a white silk scarf tucked into his dark overcoat, and Arabella wore a long dress in dark red, which made her hair look blonder than ever, with diamonds round her neck, and a fur coat. They had puzzled over what Harriet should wear. None of the dresses she had brought were party dresses, and eventually Arabella had rung up a friend who had a girl of Harriet's age, and she had brought the most heavenly dress with a skirt made of layers of different coloured net, and a bodice of turquoise silk, and with it came a pair of plain silver shoes with a strap. Arabella lent her a little shoulder cape in white fur, and although she felt slightly guilty on her mother's behalf, because she hadn't thought to pack a party dress for her, Harriet had enjoyed wearing all this finery. When they got to the theatre, they found Alec had taken a box, which was even better, Harriet thought, than the front row of the Dress Circle at the Theatre Royal in Newcastle, where they always sat when they went to the pantomime with Granny Carruthers.

The theatre wasn't a play at all, but a ballet, and at the end, it seemed to Harriet that the principle dancers bowed specially to their box. She thought she would swoon with the excitement of it. Then they went out to dinner in a restaurant, and ate roast beef with the blood coming out of it, which Harriet thought looked disgusting, although it tasted wonderful, and then she almost fell asleep over the pudding, and Daddy had to carry her out to the car.

The next day she felt extremely tired. She said goodbye to the lovely room, which looked abandoned after she had tidied away the books and taken her things off the dressing table. Alec was to drive her to King's Cross, where she would meet a friend of Granny Carruthers who would take her home on the train. She was looking forward to seeing her mother, but she knew already that she couldn't tell her how much she liked Arabella, or about all the exciting things they had done. She decided she would say nothing about the ballet. She worried slightly about the coat, which she knew Granny Carruthers would say was extravagant, and a foolish waste of money when she already had a green school mac and overcoat, and would make some remark about Daddy always spending money he hadn't got. Too bad, thought Harriet; I'm wearing it, but Arabella said when she saw her, "Why don't you leave the coat here, Harriet. I'm sure you've got a perfectly good one at home ..." so she did and wore instead her green school mac.

Arabella said goodbye to her at the flat. "I've loved having you to stay, Harriet," she said, and looked as though she meant it. Harriet reached up and gave her a kiss. Her hair was hanging loose, held back with an dark blue velvet Alice band, Arabella saying it looked nicer than in the tight plaits she usually wore, and Arabella smoothed it on to her collar, saying to Alec

"Doesn't it look nice like that?"

But Daddy was in a hurry and only grunted, and picked up Harriet's case.

"Come again soon," said Arabella, looking incredibly slim and elegant in the pink housecoat she wore for breakfast.

"I'd like to," said Harriet, and meant it. "Can I come in the summer?"

Arabella frowned for a moment, and then said, "Of course. But we might be quite busy ..." She glanced at Alex, who smiled and nodded. "We might well be" he said.

"Oh," said Harriet. "Oh, well, I'm not sure if I can, after all," she said. "I'll have to ask Mummy."

"Come on, Harriet," said Alec impatiently. "We'll miss the train."

"Goodbye, then," said Harriet, and Arabella hugged her and whispered, "I'll make sure you come in the summer. Don't worry. We'll fix it."

But now it *was* summer, and all Harriet had heard was that Arabella was going to have a baby. The letter had said nothing about the holidays, and Harriet decided angrily that now that a new baby was on the way, they must have forgotten. She decided crossly that even if they did ask her, she would say no, without realising that the underlying emotion which had made her so angry was the subliminal knowledge that from now on she would have to compete for her father's affections.

Although it was late there was still warm summer light coming through the thin yellow curtains. Harriet could hear faint shouts coming from the tennis courts, where some seniors were playing a desultory game now that the heat had lifted. Music was playing a long way away, swelling and fading on the breeze that carried it. Harriet wondered if anyone else were awake, but even as she thought it, she fell asleep, her eyes still faintly swollen from the storm of the afternoon.

***

Georgina too lay awake, her thoughts going round and round. Since the image of her brother had come into her head that afternoon, she had not been able to banish thoughts of home as easily as she usually could.

Georgina had not yet been able to reconcile her two so different worlds, and as she grew older she realised that she never would. So far, she had kept them totally apart, with only Dotty Brand as the link between them. Her mother was pathetically eager for information about this new world she had managed to provide for her only daughter, and at first Georgina had told her everything: how beautiful Baynes was, how clever all the teachers and most of the girls were, what all the strange new rules meant, and the funny words that were part of the Baynes language. She had explained what she was learning in class, why she had a red girdle while others might have yellow or green or blue – it was to do with which House you belonged to – and how you gained or lost House points. But recently she had found it irritating and embarrassing to answer all Edna's eager questions. She didn't want to explain that the way she held her knife was how she had observed it was held at Baynes, or why she had stopped saying toilet and said she was going to the lav. Last holidays, she had made a terrible fuss about the new shoes Edna wanted to buy her – they were black patent with heels a bit too high and with an awful bow on them – and had insisted on going to Newcastle where in

Bainbridge's she had found the boys' house shoes with elastic sides which Harriet always wore.

"Ee, Gloria, you canna wear those – them's lads' shoes," her mother had said, but the sales lady had explained to her mother that quite a lot of young ladies liked these shoes for school, and her mother had reluctantly complied.

The Easter holidays had brought another threat that Georgina had not foreseen. So far, she had successfully prevented her parents, or at least her mother (for her father displayed no interest) from coming to Baynes. She had told them that most girls went to school on the school train, and that it was childish to be seen saying goodbye on the station, so that Edna had left her alone to carry her overnight case from the train from the Coast to the meeting point in the station at Newcastle, and had watched from afar the bottle-green crowd of girls greeting each other. If she had seen that quite a few mothers had, in fact, delivered their daughters into the collecting mistress's hand, she had said nothing. Now, however, Steve had acquired a car, old and decrepit but perfectly capable of covering the miles between North Shields and Baynes, and had proposed driving Georgina back to school.

"Let's see this posh place wor Gloria's at," he said at tea one day, stuffing chips into his mouth and swilling them down with a mouthful of tea. Georgina had looked away disgusted, and had said firmly that she was going back on the school train.

"That's what I always do," she said, horrified at the idea of her family entering the forbidden doorway to her place of escape.

A terrible row had ensued, with Steve insisting that he wanted to see where Gloria disappeared to every term, her father accusing her of being a snob and a stuck-up little miss, and both of them teasing her by imitating her accent, until she burst into tears. Even Geordie, her younger brother, who was usually nice to her, joined in. Her mother remained unusually silent, a strange look on her normally cheerful face. When the row was in full swing, Edna suddenly stood up and banged her fist on the table, so that the chip dish jumped and chips fell onto the floor, and said:

"Shut your gobs, the lot of you. Can you not see that wor Gloria doesn't want you to take her to school? If anyone does, I will. Wilf, you've shown no interest until now in what she's doing, so don't pretend to start now. And you, Steve and Geordie, it's none of your business. Now get out, the lot of you."

Silence fell. Slowly her father got to his feet. He looked round the table, at his two big sons, at his wife, so determined in her efforts to better his daughter that splitting the family didn't worry her, and at his extraordinarily pretty and clever daughter, who was the cause of all the resentment which was seething and rumbling through the house. He rubbed a hand across his forehead, angry and puzzled.

"Right, Gloria," he said. "You've made it plain that you don't want us no more. We're not good enough for you, is that it? Too stuck up to let us see your posh new friends. Well – so be it. You lead your life, and we'll lead ours. You can keep your posh school, and I for one won't come near it. You're lucky it costs me nowt – if it did, I can tell you, you'd not be there." He paused for breath, his face red and sweating, anger showing in the set of his shoulders. He slammed his chair under the table and cocked his head at Steve and Geordie.

"I'll be in the pub," he said, meaning the Percy Arms round the corner. He looked at Georgina, still snuffling into her handkerchief, aghast at the row that had blown up, but even more aghast at the thought of her father or her brothers coming to Baynes.

"As for you, you little snob, you're no daughter of mine while you carry on this way," he said. And you ..." – he nodded his head at Edna, who stood silent after her outburst, a stubborn look on her face – "... you're a fine one. You got her into this, and you'll suffer the consequences. It's not just me and the boys she's ashamed of. It's you too, her own mother. Well, you can deal with it. Ha'way, lads, let's get out of here."

Steve and Geordie swallowed the last of their tea. They looked diminished somehow by the row, Georgina thought, as though something had been taken away from them. She didn't care. They'd always treated her perfectly well, though Steve could be very nasty when he wanted to; but she had always felt different from them, apart somehow, and she guessed that they found her difficult to understand too.

Now Steve turned to her and said viciously, "You're a fool, wor Gloria. They won't accept you, you're not one of them, however much you change your accent and learn to speak posh. And we don't want you neither, so then where'll you be? Come on, Geordie."

Geordie cast a look at his mother, letting her know that much as he didn't want to take sides, he had to choose, and it was simpler to choose his father. He was gentler than Steve, more equable and easy with life, and fond of his sister, who was so unlike the rest of the family and the people who lived around her – although he found it difficult to recognise her now, with her new voice, her new poise, and her unspoken criticism of everything and everyone, even her mother.

"Gloria, you're goin' to find yourself an outcast" he said. "You don't belong with them, you belong here, with us. Mam, take her away from that school. Send her to school in Newcastle if you must, but keep her at home. You'll lose her, else."

Edna was still standing, her arms folded, a determined, stubborn expression on her face. Now she looked from one to another and said, "Gloria's worth ten of you lot, any day. She works hard and she wants to get out of this muck heap. You lot are happy to stay where you are, just drinkin' and spendin' money, when you've got it, and when you haven't you're moaning and grumbling and doing nowt about it. I work, cutting open fish till me fingers are near worn to the bone." She held out a hand, the fingers reddened and sore-looking, the smell of fish tainting her skin, scrub it as hard as she might. "But it'll be worth it, if just one of us gets away from here."

She turned to Georgina, who was still sitting in front of her plate of uneaten meat pie and chips. "Come on, pet, let's you and me clear this up, and then we'll ha'way to see Miss Brand. She'll cheer you up."

"That woman's the cause of all this," muttered Wilf as he turned to leave the house.

Steve looked back at Georgina. "Divvent worry, our Gloria. I'll not take you back this time, but I'm coming one day, to see your secret hidey-hole." He grinned. "There'll be some lovely lasses there, I'll be bound. Might just get me hands on a one."

"You bloody won't," said Georgina, rage blossoming on her usually unrevealing features. "You bloody won't, and you bloody won't come near Baynes. I'd rather die."

She leapt to her feet as her father loomed back towards her, saying, "You watch your language, miss," his hand raised to hit her. She dodged round her mother and out of the back door, across the yard with its line of drying clothes flapping in her face, and snicked up the latch into the back lane as her father lumbered out behind her. She raced up the cobbles, running on and on, until she could run no further. She caught her breath, bending over to get rid of the stitch in her side. When she looked up she found she had taken without thinking the way she and her mother had taken so often when she was at Dotty's school in Tynemouth, up the long hill and out into Front Street. Dotty lived in a flat near here, close to the Priory ruins and the hill which wound down to the long pier that stretched out into the cold grey sea, with its ever-flashing lighthouse directing the ships to and from the great shipbuilding yards on the Tyne.

Georgina knocked on Dotty's door. When it opened Dotty looked surprised.

"Georgina," she said. "What's the matter?" and Georgina realised that her face must still show the tears she had shed earlier. She felt them starting up again.

"Oh, Dotty," she wailed, "I don't know what to do. It's awful."

Dotty led her into her warm, comfortable flat with its shelves of books, its gramophone which played the records Georgina loved and had never heard before she met Dotty, and its radio tuned usually to the Third Programme. On the walls were pictures Dotty had collected on her travels each summer. The room was cheerful with lamplight.

"It's late for you to be out by yourself, Georgina," Dotty remarked, "What's up? What's happened?"

Tearfully Georgina told her about what had happened. "I can't bear it if they come to Baynes," she said. "None of the others have brothers like Steve and Geordie. Or parents that look like mine. They'd know, they'd know I come from, well, you know what I mean ..." her voice trailed away. "It's not that I don't love them," she went on, forcing the words out, her face going red with the difficulty of the emotions she was expressing. "I do. Well, I suppose I do. But I'm ... well... I'm ashamed of them. There. I've said it. I'm ashamed of them."

She looked at Dotty, and then away, feeling a hot sweat on her face at the embarrassment of what she was saying.

"I understand what you're saying, Gloria," said Dotty, reverting on purpose to Georgina's given name.

"Don't call me that," Georgina replied, angrily. "I'm not called that any more."

"No, and that's part of the trouble," said Dotty. "You're trying to live a lie. It would have been far better if you'd never tried to pretend to be something that you are not. No, let me finish ..."

she went on as Georgina opened her mouth to reply. "I feel that this is my fault. I should never have let you start the first lie, over your name."

"I'm not going to go back to being called Gloria," Georgina interrupted forcefully. "It's an awful name, awful. No one at Baynes has a name like that."

"All right, you can't change back now. But you shouldn't deny your parents, and your brothers their right to see where you go to school. After all, whatever he may say, your father must be contributing something to your schooling, even if it's having to pay for more expensive shoes than you might have chosen." Georgina had told her about the shoes Edna had wanted to buy, wrinkling her nose in disgust at her mother's taste. Now she denied what Dotty was saying.

"It's not him, it's Mam who buys them, with the money she makes at the fishquay," she said.

"Gloria, your mother would probably work at the fishquay whether you were at Baynes or any other school," Dotty said. "The point is, if you were not at Baynes that money which now goes on extras for you would go towards the whole family. You know there's a shortage of jobs, and your brothers are having difficulty in finding work ..."

"They don't try," interrupted Georgina bitterly. "They're just lazy. Like Da – he's not working now, had a row at work because he kept skiving off. It's Mam – my mother – she's the only one who's working."

"Well, I'm not going into that," replied Dotty, thinking that Georgina might well be right. Maybe they were all lazy except Edna. "What I'm saying is, no wonder there's resentment towards you and your mother, and it would be much more sensible if you told your friends what kind of background you come from, and let your mother come to Baynes to see for herself what she's managed to achieve for you, and let your friends judge her for themselves.

They'd see she's a good woman." As she said it, she knew she didn't believe her words. Children could be very cruel.

"I'd rather die," repeated Georgina. "I don't want her to come, or any of them. You don't understand, I couldn't tell them at school about home. They wouldn't know what I was talking about."

Dotty understood only too well what Georgina meant, remembering the snobbery that had existed at Baynes in her day, no matter how it was discouraged by the school.

"Do you not feel that your friends are good enough friends to accept you as you are?" she went on, but she knew that Georgina was still much too young to possess the inner confidence that would let her reveal herself truly to others.

"Well, maybe Harry and Laura," said Georgina with a sigh. "But not the others." She thought of Meredith, and what it would feel like to be the subject of her sharp tongue. "No. I couldn't. I can't let them come to Baynes. They mustn't." Tears began to fill her eyes again, and angrily she rubbed them away. "Dotty," she said tentatively. "Could you tell Mam, do you think? She listens to you."

How could I ask her not to visit her own child, thought Dotty, envisaging Edna's determined face? I should never have got involved with this. But she had never regretted the impulse that had made her enter Georgina for the highest reward, and in truth she didn't regret it now, although some way would have to be found round this difficulty. She sighed. "I'll try, Gloria. I won't promise anything, but I'll try."

In the end, however, Dotty had to do nothing. While Georgina was washing her face, and Dotty putting her coat on to take her back through the dark streets, there came a knock on the door. It was Edna.

"I thought I'd find you here," she said to her daughter. "She'll have told you what happened this evening, Dotty?" She and Dotty had become good friends over the years.

"I am sorry, Edna," said Dotty. "I don't know what to say."

"You needn't say anything," replied Edna. She was wearing a tight-fitting coat that looked as if it was made of red felt, and her stocky body looked tough and unbending. Her unmade-up face showed her age and more, the years of bad food and lack of vitamins giving her skin a thick, pasty look. There were patches of red veins on her cheeks and from her headscarf the once-red hair that escaped was faded and greyish, permed into tight curls that turned to frizz in the damp sea air. Her capable hands carried a big handbag and a brown paper carrier, in which Georgina could see her pyjamas.

"You don't have to say anything," repeated Edna, shaking her head. "It's my worry, and I'll deal with it. Gloria," – she had always refused to call Georgina by the name she had picked for herself – "Gloria, you can stop worrying, pet. Nobody's going to come to Baynes with you. I've known all these last few terms that you didn't want us there. I've watched the other mothers bringing their bairns to the teacher at the train – and never worry, I understand how you feel. We're not like them, and we never will be. But *you* will be. That's why you're going there. You'll be my pride."

"Oh, Mam," Georgina flung herself into her mother's arms. "Oh, Mam, I feel awful. I don't want to feel like this."

Her mother hugged her, but her eyes were on Dotty. "There is one thing I'll ask of you, Dotty," she said. "Could she stay here the night? Just while I sort out that lot," she nodded her head in the direction of North Shields. "It'll be better with Gloria out of the way."

Georgina hugged her mother, her arms scarcely meeting round Edna's comfortable bulk, pressing her head into the soft heaviness she knew so well. She couldn't believe that her mother could understand so well, could have seen what the awful thoughts in her head were. And yet, her mother had always understood her. Why would she stop now? She looked up, and a look of love crossed Edna's face as she gazed down into the reddened blue eyes. She nodded her head comfortably, as though to say everything would be all right, and Georgina let go and swung round to face Dotty. "Can I stay?" she said. "Please."

Dotty smiled. "If you want to," she said. "If it would be a help, Edna. I feel this is all my fault, for getting her to Baynes. You wanted the Central High, and it might well have been better."

Edna shook her head. "No. As soon as I saw the book about Baynes, I knew that was where she'd go. And if you hadn't come along, I'd have found some other way." The determined look was back, replacing the soft love which had illuminated her face, and which had showed for a brief moment a likeness between her and her daughter that Dotty had never seen before.

Georgina had stayed for two nights, and when she went back home nothing more was said about Baynes. It had become a taboo subject, for which Georgina was grateful. When the day came to go back, Edna took her with her overnight case on the coastal train to Newcastle, where as usual she had hung back, well away from the green-clad girls gathering on the platform. This time, Georgina had said, "Mam. Do you want to come on the platform?" and for a second Edna had been tempted. But the relief on Georgina's face when she said "No" could not be hidden, and she was glad that she'd refused. She had made up her mind that nothing was to interfere with the betterment of her daughter, and if that meant staying away, stay away she would.

As Georgina lay in bed at Baynes on that summer night, and thought about all this, her mind worrying away at it like a terrier at a bone, a grey depression came over her. How long would she have to live with the deception? How could she keep it up? It had been difficult enough at the beginning to adjust, and each night she had been worn out with her endless observation of the other girls' manners and ways of speaking, although, as Edith Morrisson had observed, she had found it easy to imitate and now would have found it difficult to go back to what she thought of as the years before Baynes. But what she hadn't realised, she thought as she lay in bed, fretful and unable to sleep, was that her home life would one day encroach on her school life. Steve's threatened visit had been near enough, and she guessed that he would still one day carry out his promise, though without telling his mother. Even Mam can't protect me forever, thought Georgina. She remembered how at Dotty's, she had imagined Meredith, for instance, finding out about her background, and at the memory the same cold sweat started pricking at her skin. She could guess only too well what Meredith would say. Far worse than she could say about Harriet, she thought. And then the whole school would know. In her misery, she imagined the school gathered together as it was for the yearly school photo, only this time with her standing in front of them and all of the girls pointing a finger at her. "Fake," they would say. "Fraud." "Who does she think she is?" The words ran round and round, and she thought she would never sleep. It was too bright, too light still. The carefree voices from the tennis courts only served to remind her of what she would miss if she lost Baynes. She buried her head under the blankets and hugged her thin arms round herself, wishing they were Mam's arms, which always brought comfort. As she hugged herself, she made a vow, to herself and to everyone. One day, she determined, I'm going so far away that no one will ever be able to connect me, Georgina, with me, Gloria. And where no one will ever find out that I'm not what I seem.

She heard a sigh from Harriet's bed, and lifted her head from under the blankets. Looking across at Harriet, she wondered if she was asleep, or lying wakeful like she was. But Harriet's eyes were shut, and as Georgina looked she turned over in her sleep. Lucky Harriet, thought Georgina.

***

Although she lay so still that no one would have guessed she was awake, Laura too was unable to sleep on that hot June night, with the late sun still filtering through the curtains, and the faint voices of the tennis players.

But it was neither the sun, nor the voices, which were keeping Laura awake; rather, it was the thought which had come to her earlier that evening, when flushed with the pride of belonging, she had watched the evening-gowned Old Scholars making their stately way to the dining room, their deeper voices swelling the rousing harmonies of the school song which rang out around them. As she had listened, not yet knowing the words, Laura had suddenly realised that she no longer wished only to return to France, as secretly she had been determined to do. Instead, a creeping doubt was troubling her, causing the determination which had until now been so strong to tremble, to crumble a little at the edges, as she admitted to herself, for the first time, that perhaps to stay here in England, at Baynes, would not be so bad after all.

Now as she lay in bed, she tried to examine the thoughts which had been twisting and turning in her head since the excitement of the ceremony. In the light-filled silence she made her thoughts be still, so that she could look at what it was that was threatening the calm determination which up to now she had hugged secretly to herself, like a talisman: the determination to demand and insist that she be allowed to go back to France, and back to the Bonnevilles, who were her parents still in everything but name.

Since the never-to-be-forgotten February day when Miriam, and hope, had come into her life, and after she had made her peace with Tante Marie-Claude, had read the letters and written to the Bonnevilles, Laura had seemed to accept what her learning of the facts had told her: that she was not the child of Marie-Claude and Paul Bonneville, but of two people who were still strangers to her, Caroline and Robert Martin; that her true home was not in France, but in the damp dark north of England, so different from the French countryside which was all she had known since she was born; and that she was not French at all and only English blood flowed in her veins.

However, her knowledge of the facts, and her acceptance of them were two different things, and silently and secretly, after the first relief of talking to Miriam and understanding what had happened had passed, a passionate determination had lodged in her mind to persuade Marie-Claude and Paul to let her come back. She had never voiced this to Miriam, or to her grandmother, with whom she was beginning to make a relationship, saving it for when she saw the woman she had called Maman for so long. She knew that Marie-Claude would eventually say yes, that she could persuade her that only this would be the true solution to the problem of what was to become of her. She knew, too, that her grandmother, old and tired and finding it difficult to understand this unexpected grandchild, could be coerced into agreeing with her. There would be no need for Laura never to see her grandmother again – why could she not just visit her occasionally? Laura's solution to the problem had seemed to her childish mind sweet and certain – until today. Today, doubt had crept in. Today, for the first time, she had found herself thinking with something like envy of those who would be staying on at Baynes. She had so convinced herself that she would not be there, that never before had she visualised herself being one of them.

In the quiet of the slowly darkening room, she made herself picture next term here at Baynes, seeing herself with George and Harry continuing up into the next class, leaving Miss King's domain for that of Miss Brown, and then, later on, braving the rigours of the senior school. No longer under Matron's leaden rule, but freer and older, and still together, in the senior boarding house where, she had heard, different and lesser rules governed a less constrained existence.

Reluctantly, she pushed the picture away and tried to see herself as she would be if she succeeded in going back to Belay. To her distress, she could no longer remember the faces of the children she had been at school with, although it was less than two years since twice daily she had run through the village to the school down the hill, coming back home for lunch, first with Sabine and Olivier, and later alone, where Fernande and Maman would be waiting to greet her, her lunch ready on the table, then rushing back for the afternoon and then home again with her *devoir* to do in the evening,

She shut her eyes, and involuntarily slow tears started to run down her cheeks. She could hardly bear to think of life in Belay going on without her — and yet, as she tried and tried to see the faces of her friends, she knew, with a leaden sinking of her heart, a desperate giving up of her secret wish, that she could never go back.

The wish that she had hugged to herself all these months suddenly seemed what it had really always been: just a way of getting through the days, something to think about, to promise herself, when reality got too uncomfortable, in the same way as the possibility of killing herself had helped her through the awful dark months after she had been brought back from France. The memory of them still haunted her.

She thought of the terrible day when Marie-Claude had told her the truth, that she was not her daughter, not even French. Although she had listened, she had not understood — had refused to understand. She remembered how she had run upstairs and shut herself into the room which she had always regarded as hers, and which now turned out really to have belonged to someone else called Laurence, while her real name was not Laurence at all, but Laura. Laura Martin.

She shivered under the blankets, though the attic room was still hot from the day's sun. She never wanted to experience days like those again. The nightmare of her grandmother appearing, old, unfamiliar, foreign, unable to speak much French, accompanied by an English lawyer. The day-long discussion that had gone on between Paul Bonneville and the English lawyer, between the grandmother and Marie-Claude Bonneville, no one entirely understanding the other, then the next morning the terrible inevitability of being taken away, although she had cried and shouted, refused to eat, even refused to move until Paul had bodily carried her to the taxi which was to take her and this strange old woman and her lawyer to St Didier to catch the train. It had been a dreadful journey, on trains which had been slow and crowded, her grandmother becoming paler and less patient as the hours passed, the lawyer sleeping throughout much of the journey, her grandmother speaking to her in a low angry voice in a language she didn't understand, then finally giving up and not speaking to her at all, just sitting in silence as the trains made their ponderous way through unfamiliar countryside. There had been a stop and a hotel somewhere, where she had gone to bed unable to eat and had slept solidly as an escape from what was happening, and then being woken by her grandmother and feeling hungry for breakfast even though it seemed to mean a surrender to what had happened. She couldn't remember much about finally getting to England, exhausted with crying and travelling, afraid, desolate, abandoned, but she could remember the feeling of utter misery, and the total hopelessness which had engulfed her.

She put out her tongue and tasted the salty tears that still flowed quietly down her cheeks. Her face felt wet and she turned into the pillow to dry it and try to stem the flow, but the tears would not stop coming. They were not the harsh sobs which had racked her on the night she had first met Miriam, and which had accompanied her first weeks in England, but more a silent requiem for something which had died; and slowly she realised she was crying for what was no longer to be. She would not be going back to the Bonnevilles and Belay, except for holidays. She would never be the French girl she had thought she was, to follow Nathalie and Jean-Claude and Sabine and Olivier to the Lycée in St Didier. Instead, she would have to accept what she really was, an English girl of English parents, and grow up into an Englishwoman like the ones she had seen this evening, and one day come back here as an Old Scholar, perhaps even send her own children here.

As she thought this, an unexpected feeling of relief came over her, and she understood that she was making the right choice, that she could give up the secret wish that had buoyed her up over the last months, that she no longer needed it. She would no longer have to pretend to Miriam, whom she suspected might well have seen through her pretences anyway, and could settle down to learning the things she had to learn about her new life. She thought with something akin to pleasure that she would not have to give up her friendship with Harriet and Georgina, and realised with a slow lifting of her spirits that she could now envisage the future, know where she would be and what she would be doing for the years she would be at Baynes at least.

She thought of Marie-Claude and Paul, and realised that gradually, over the months, she had started thinking of them a lot of the time not as her parents, but as people she had once known. She thought again of the life going on in Belay without her and this time there was only a small pang of regret. She would never forget it, of course, nor her erstwhile brothers and sisters, and the excitement of seeing them again in August had not left her, but now she could look forward to it properly, not see it tinged with what she had been determined to achieve while she was there.

Darkness had gathered in the corners of the room, and the noises from the tennis courts had long ceased. A profound silence seemed to hang over everything. Laura sat up and quietly got out of bed, making sure she woke none of the others. She crept to the window and lifted a corner of the curtain. Instead of sunlight, silver moonlight bathed everything in its odd two-dimensional light, making strange shadows of the trees and seeming to cast a hazy mist over the lawns and fields. The window was wide open and Laura leant out and breathed in the warm, grassy air. She felt as though a great weight had been lifted from her; she was as light as featherdown and free. Across the field she saw a shape detach itself from a tree and wing its way towards her, its owl's eyes sharp for mice or moles, its great wings floating and lifting on the warm air currents. She watched it swoop and pounce, then spiral away back to its nest. As she watched, entranced, the peacefulness of the scene gradually made her feel drowsy, and she realised it was very late. Behind her, someone turned over in sleep and murmured a word, and slowly Laura withdrew her head from the window and tiptoed back to bed. She felt sleep coming over her and for the first time since she had come to England, she slept without first praying to God to allow her to be taken back to France.

CHAPTER Five

Summer, 1947

The ceremonies the next day started early. At breakfast, Miss Morrisson ran through what was to happen during the day. In the morning the old girls would inspect the classrooms, all of which had been decorated in some way with the ubiquitous buttercups, real or drawn. After lunch, there would be the Shakespeare play, performed by the girls, and after tea there would be Prizegiving.

The Shakespeare play was always performed in the natural outdoor theatre formed by a serendipitous growth of hazel trees round a wide patch of lawn, with exits and entrances through the trees, and this year, it was to be *A Midsummer Night's Dream*. Georgina, whose scholarship included elocution and music lessons, was to play Mustard Seed.

"It's magic, Laura," Harriet told Laura, remembering the previous year when she and George, who was too young then to have a part, had watched the unfolding of *The Tempest*.

Laura, who was in good spirits that morning, which surprised the others as she had been morose and silent the previous night, stood on her desk chair and imitated the Midsummer Night's Dream fairies, quoting: *"Ready. And I. And I. And I. Where shall we go?"* in a ridiculous hammy French accent. Meredith, who was playing Cobweb, but who had been secretly learning the part of Puck and praying for the demise of the older girl who was to play the part, looked annoyed.

"Really, Laura," she said. "You sound ridiculous. You'll never be able to speak English properly."

"Shut up," said Laura, in an almost perfect accent. "You can't even take a joke. It's you who's ridi ..." The word defeated her and she reverted to French: "*C'est toi qui es complètement ridicule.*"

"Ridicule, ridicule," taunted Harriet, who knew that only a few minutes later, when Miss King arrived, she was going to have to apologise to Meredith for yesterday's debacle.

"*You* shut up, Harriet," said Mary. "You're one to talk, after yesterday." She went to the desk she shared with Meredith and sat down, sticking her chin out and tilting her head in a goody-goody way which Harriet hated. She had often secretly copied this face of Mary's and knew that by doing it Mary was feeling superior. She opened her desk lid and holding it up between herself and the door with her elbow, in case Miss King should come in early, made a face at Mary, pulling down her eyes and pushing up her nose. Mary looked away. Footsteps could be heard coming down the corridor, and Laura jumped down from her chair quickly.

As the door opened, the girls all stood up.

"Good morning, Miss King," they intoned before sitting down again.

Miss King took the register, necessary as by now the boarders had been joined by the daygirls. When she had finished she looked sternly at Harriet.

"Now Harriet," she said. "I think you have something to say to Meredith."

Harriet stood up once more, the angry red coming into her cheeks no matter how she determined it wouldn't. She looked towards, but not quite at Meredith, who was smiling slightly. Harriet thought of her mother and how she had apologised when she had knocked over her mother's sewing box and all the threads had unrolled, and pins and needles had been lost in the shaggy hearth rug so that she dared not walk on it with bare feet. She visualised Mummy's cross face, and said:

"I'm very very sorry, Mu ... Meredith. I'm sorry I spoiled your dress and your hair and I won't do it again." She looked appealingly at Miss King, to see if she had said enough.

"Do you accept Harriet's apology, Meredith?" asked Miss King.

"I suppose so," said Meredith grudgingly. "But she should have had a punishment ..."

"That is not for you to decide, Meredith," Miss King interrupted. "Harriet's punishment is my concern, and mine alone. Now Harriet, come over here and shake hands with Meredith."

Harriet got up and walked over to Meredith's desk. She put out her hand, her face expressionless. Meredith took it and squeezed as hard as she could without it being obvious what she was doing. It hurt, but Harriet refused to give her the satisfaction of knowing that it did. She went on staring implacably over Meredith's head.

"Right," said Miss King. "Now let's hear no more about this unfortunate episode. Go back to your desk, Harriet."

Harriet sat down, surreptitiously rubbing her hand. She felt hot, as though she were in a bathroom full of steam. She looked over at Meredith again. Meredith had a triumphant look on her face, which Harriet copied. They stared at each other for a moment, like two cats trying to outstare each other, and then Miss King, who had been arranging her books looked up, and Harriet looked quickly away, knowing that Miss King would have spotted the hostility towards Meredith in her face.

"Now, girls," the mistress said, picking up a reading book. "We have only the one lesson period this morning, before the Old Scholars come round. We're just going to do a little reading. Susan, will you start, please, on page fifty."

Before the lesson had even ended, there was a knock on the door and the first bunch of old girls was crowding into the room, admiring the buttercup design on the blackboard, and looking through the exercise books put out by the window to show the girls' good work.

"D'you remember the time we tricked old Pegleg into letting us off gym," Harriet heard one smartly-dressed woman say to another, and marvelled that these women, perhaps the same age as her mother, had once been ten-year-olds in this very classroom. The woman's companion laughed.

"Those spots!" she laughed. "Honestly, you'd think she would have guessed we'd used pink crayons!"

Miss King was smiling to herself, and as the bell rang she gathered up her books and stood up, saying, "Now, don't get over-excited today, girls. Georgina, Meredith, you will be going to lunch early, don't forget. I want you in the dining room at twelve o'clock sharp."

"Yes, Miss King," Georgina and Meredith said together, not looking at each other, and then Miss King had gone, and the girls had the rest of the morning free.

"Let's go round the other classrooms," said Harriet excitedly. Normally, they were not allowed into other classrooms, especially those of the more senior girls. "I want to see the sixth form."

Together, the three of them walked round the rooms, Laura in particular looking at these new rooms carefully, knowing now that one day she would be a pupil in them, the sense of guilt that had begun to build up inside her about Baynes, because of her plans to leave it, gone. The relief was intense.

That afternoon, she and Harriet squeezed themselves on to the end of one of the back rows of Old Scholars seated in the tiers of seats erected for the Shakespeare performance. The weather had held, luckily, because if it hadn't the performance would have had to be in the gym, where it would have lost some of its magic, and most of the Old Scholars wore hats to shade their eyes. Their smart brightly coloured frocks glowed and shone under the hot sun like a garden of exotic flowers, and a heady scent of perfume rose in the warm air. Their chatter sounded like a pack of starlings gathering, and then, suddenly, as if a signal had been given, everyone fell silent and the thin strains of a harpsichord could be heard, its tinkling sound loud in the waiting quiet. A figure wearing a brown velvet doublet and green hose, the crimson feather of a velvet hat falling over one eye, appeared through one of the tree tunnels, followed by a woman in regal costume and another man in similar clothes to the first one.

"Now, fair Hippolyta, our nuptial hour draws on apace..." the first man said, and as he spoke it was clear that the voice was that of a girl, although the make-up and costume was so cleverly done that Theseus could well have been the male Duke of Athens.

Harriet gazed, entranced. It was going to be magical again, and as the play went on she became lost in it, hardly realizing that Georgina and Meredith and other girls she knew were the fairies, or that Puck was the beautiful Alexandra Hardie, three forms ahead. At the interval, she was still in Athens' wood, and Laura had to nudge her twice before she clambered down from her seat to let others out.

As usual, the play had amazed everyone, even though each year it was equally good.

"It's just as good as when you and I were Puck and Oberon," Harriet heard one thin, dark-haired young woman say to another, and realised that she was looking at an actress whose face had been on every cinema screen last holidays. Gosh, thought Harriet. Did she go here? She turned to Laura.

"That's Elizabeth Hunter," she said, "The film star." Laura looked blank, and Harriet remembered that of course Laura wouldn't know. Her English was getting so good that Harriet had almost forgotten that she was French. Well, sort of French. She explained.

"Who else is famous here?" Laura whispered as they made their way back to their seats, but Harriet didn't hear. Already she was absorbed in the play, laughing at Bottom, yearning for Oberon, leaping and flying with Puck as he made his mischievous way around the stage, Alexandra Hardie's long muscled legs seeming to leave the ground as often as they were on it.

When it was over Harriet sighed with the rare pleasure of the afternoon. Now it would be back to being at Baynes, which, no matter what pleased her, she was determined not to enjoy. Things like the Shakespeare play she would allow herself to admire. But she still despised the whole.

As she and Laura waited for Georgina to come out of the bootroom where the cast had been changing, a woman came round the corner, head bent in conversation with a companion, and Harriet's heart turned over. It was Mummy. Then the woman raised her head, and of course it wasn't. Suddenly the afternoon seemed flat, the Shakespeare pointless. If only Mummy had been there. If only she could go home to her tonight, like the daygirls could. Harriet wondered if all the boarders felt as she did about her mother and home, but she suspected that they did not. Other girls seemed to be able to enjoy themselves here, and seemed not to long all the time to be at home. She wished in a way that she didn't long for her mother all the time, but she couldn't imagine how it would feel. For a moment, she felt she couldn't face the rest of the weekend, with all these women here who reminded her of the world outside of Baynes. Why, why had she been sent to this prison?

A terrible impatience was rising up in her, which she realised she must control. After yesterday's episode, there would be no forgiveness. She suddenly thought, this is how Daddy feels when he says he must have a drink. She wished there was something she could drink to help the feeling pass, but only tea would be on offer. She peered round the door to see if George was nearly ready, and saw her deep in conversation with Meredith. Oh, blast Meredith, she thought. I can't stand her, I can't stand being here, I hate it all. She wanted to shout and scream, kick Meredith, kick Georgina for her desertion, blast all these stupid Old Scholars to Hell.

Laura, who had been talking to Mary and Alison, heard Harriet mutter something to herself under her breath, and turned round. Harriet had gone red in the face again, and with horror Laura saw that another temper was about to erupt. She mustn't, she thought, she absolutely must not have another temper. She grabbed Harriet's arm, and pulling her away, said to Alison over her shoulder, "Tell George we've gone to the Pond."

Half running, half being dragged, Harriet found herself under the dark trees lining the path that led to the Pond. There was a smell of mould and rotting leaves. Laura was pulling on her arm. Harriet stumbled and half-fell, her feet dragging through the rich loamy damp soil.

"What are you doing, where are we going?" she demanded angrily, pulling her arm away.

"We're going away from everyone until you calm down," replied Laura. "I know you're in a temper again, and honestly, Harry, they might expel you if you do anything like yesterday again."

"I'm not in a temper," Harriet said crossly. "And I wish they would expel me."

"Yes you are in a temper," Laura replied. They had reached the end of the path, and the Pond lay before them, its dark still water green with algae, a damp stench rising in the heat. There was no one there, as the tea bell had rung, and girls and Old Scholars were all crowding into the dining room for strawberries and cream.

"Oh, Laura, how did you know?" Harriet sighed, giving in. "You're right. I am angry. I want to go home."

"So do I," Laura said bleakly. For a moment the exhilaration she had been feeling left her, and she felt tired and abandoned. "If I knew where to go."

Harriet looked remorseful. "I'd forgotten, Laura," she said, tentatively touching Laura's hand. "It must be awful for you."

"It's not too bad. Anyway, I've decided. I'm going to stay here at Baynes. Until yesterday, I was going to persuade them to let me go back to France, but now I've decided not to."

"Why?" Harriet had forgotten her temper for the time being.

"Because I am English, and my family, what's left of it, is here, and I'm not really related to Tante Marie-Claude and Oncle Paul. Not really."

As she said it, the reality of what she was saying struck Laura, and the earlier bleakness became an all-enveloping sadness. She stopped speaking, and in silence the two girls stared at the dank dark water, both of them lost in their thoughts. Harriet wondered why she felt so angry, when she was so lucky compared to Laura. Her mother wasn't dead, nor the people whom she thought of as family miles away across the sea. But none of that made her feel any less bad-tempered.

There was a noise behind them, and Georgina appeared through the trees.

"Why've you come down here?" she said. "It's teatime."

"Harry was going to have a temper again, so I dragged her down here so that no one would see," said Laura.

"Yes, I was angry," said Harriet. "But I can't remember why," she lied. She wasn't going to admit to George that she was jealous of Meredith. "I just wanted to go home," she added, which was the truth.

"You're just tired," said George. "I am, after the play, and that blasted Meredith" – they all used Harriet's father's adjective now as a matter of course – "that blasted Meredith would go on and on about how good I was, and how she wants to be an actress, and why don't we do a piece together in elocution next term. As if I would!" George said eloquently. "Doesn't she realise she nearly got you expelled yesterday?"

Harriet shrugged her shoulders, but inside she was pleased. George had not let her down after all.

"Probably wishes she had," Harriet said. "Maybe she will one day. Anyway, I wish she had."

"Oh, Harriet, don't say that," wailed Laura. "Baynes would be horrible without you, you and George."

"Yes, it would, Harry," George agreed. "It wouldn't be the same. Or if you left, Laura. You're not going to, are you?"

"She's not going to leave now, but she did want to," said Harriet. "Tell her, Laura."

Laura told Georgina of her decision. As she talked, the momentary bleak desolation faded, and she knew she had made the right choice, hard though it might have been.

"It would be quite hard to go back to an ordinary school after being here," Georgina said, thinking of her own first school under Dotty.

"I know," replied Laura. "And the school in Belay is very small. And after that, you have to go to the Lycée in St Didier and that's not a bit like this. It's a horrible big building right in the middle of the town, and they never play any games, or have any fun that I could see." She remembered Nathalie and Jean-Claude coming home night after night with endless *devoir* to do. But it's not because of that, really, that I decided. It's because I am English, and my grandmother is my only real relation, even though Tante Marie-Claude and Oncle Paul seem a hundred times more real to me. I don't really understand my Grandmother." She stared across the black water to the dark trees at the other side, and said with seeming disconnection, "I haven't been down here since – you know – the day when I tried …" she stopped, embarrassed.

"The day Georgina rescued you." Harriet said bluntly.

"Yes. That day."

"You don't feel like that any more, Laura, do you?" Harriet asked.

"No. I can't really remember how I did feel then, except that I was miserable."

"And then we became friends, and everything was all right!" teased Georgina.

Harriet was kneeling on the ground, absently scraping out a hole with a piece of blunt wood. She went on digging and said, without looking up, "Are we your best friends now, Laura?"

"Of course," said Laura, surprised that Harriet had to ask.

"And are Laura and I yours, George?" continued Harriet.

"Yes," said Georgina. What on earth was bugging Harriet now? "Of course I am. Who else would I be best friends with?"

"Meredith," Harriet muttered. "She's always trying to get you into her gang."

"Well, she's not going to," said Georgina, who, although flattered by Meredith's attentions, knew that her credibility might collapse under Meredith's close scrutiny.

"You and Laura are my best friends," she repeated. She thought for a moment, while Harriet went on digging.

"I know," she said. "Why don't we make a pledge, to be best friends for ever and ever, and not let anyone else join?"

"What's a pledge?" said Laura, puzzled.

"It's a sort of promise, that commits you to something. Like in marriage, when they say 'I pledge thee my troth'," said Harriet.

"How do you know that?" asked Georgina. She had no idea of what the marriage ceremony said.

Harriet looked secretive for a moment, and then she said, "Well, I might as well tell you, seeing we're going to be friends for ever and ever. My father's not married to my mother any more. He's married to someone called Arabella, and when he told me, I looked the service up in my prayer book to see what it said. But they got married in a Registry Office instead. That's a place where you can get married instead of in a church," she said, turning to Laura.

"In my religion, you can't get divorced," said Laura. "It's not allowed. If you get married, it's forever."

"Well, I wish we were Catholics then," said Harriet. "It's awful. Mummy's all alone now."

Georgina looked at Harriet sympathetically. She wondered if this had anything to do with Harriet's awful temper.

"She's got you," she said.

"That's not the same," replied Harriet scathingly. "Anyway, I'm not at home, I'm here. And I hate it," she added.

"Oh Harry, you don't really," said George, who couldn't imagine anyone not liking being at Baynes, with its huge grounds, its sense of solidity, its promise of golden opportunities. "I love it here."

"You never want to go home," stated Harriet. "I know you don't. You always look sad at the end of term, while everyone else is dying to go. Why?"

"Oh, I can't tell you," Georgina looked embarrassed.

"Oh, go on George. I told you about my father." Harriet insisted, and Laura said, "Yes, tell us George. If you tell us, I'll tell you a secret about me. We should all tell a secret, for the ... what was that word ... pledge."

Georgina shrugged. "You wouldn't understand," she said. "It's just that my family ... well ... it's not like your sort of family." She thought, frowning with concentration. She was not going to tell them the whole truth about her background, but she'd have to tell them something, she decided.

"It's just that they're very ... poor," she said. "We have to live in a horrid little house, in a horrible town called North Shields. Not Tynemouth, as I always say."

"I've been to North Shields," said Harriet. "There's an awful smell there, from the fish quay. Ugh!" She wrinkled up her nose at the remembered fishy stench, and Georgina thought, I'm not telling them that my mother has to work there.

"That's because its main industry is fishing," she said pompously.

"You sound like a geography lesson," said Harriet. "Anyway, it can't be that bad. North Shields, I mean."

"Well, it's not nice if you're poor," replied Georgina. She badly wanted to change the conversation. "Come on, Laura. What's your secret?" she said.

Laura blushed. She looked down at the ground and said, "I've never told anyone this. D'you remember, I told you about the German officer, Nordhoff, the reason why everyone had to pretend I was Laurence?"

"The one who had your father killed?" stated Harriet.

"Yes. Him. Well, one day he came to the village and just sat in his car outside the school playground watching me. I didn't know what he wanted, and it was funny, odd. I couldn't take my eyes away from his. It felt as though I was hypno... what's the word?"

"Hypnotised," said Georgina and Harriet together.

"Yes. Hypnotised. Well, after school was over, I was going home, and Olivier and Sabine had gone on ahead, and suddenly he was there again. He was so tall ..."

She broke off, remembering his long thin form looming over her as the German had emerged from a doorway. He had been waiting for her, she realised afterwards, but at the time it seemed as though he'd just bumped into her by accident.

"Go on," demanded Harriet.

"Well, he pulled me into a yard, behind one of the houses, up an alleyway. And he said not to be frightened, he just wanted to look at me. And then he ..."

She stopped. "I don't think I can tell you this bit," she said. "I don't even want to think about it."

She had gone quite pale.

"You don't have to," said Georgina.

"No, I know, but you've both told a secret." She paused, and then said, "Well, it might make it a bit better. To tell someone."

She turned her back on Harriet and Georgina, and started to walk slowly round the pond. They looked at each other and Harriet scrambled to her feet. They couldn't imagine what it could be that Laura could not talk about, but they followed her. Eventually, she stopped and turned round.

"I'm going to tell you," she said. "He ..." she wriggled, looking uncomfortable. "He ... told me to pull my knickers down ..."

"What for?" said Harriet, still innocent. But Georgina said nothing, thinking of the men she had seen at home, who had eyed her more than once, and one in particular, sitting on a park bench, who had said, "Come and sit on me knee, and I'll show yer somethin' nice," fumbling in his trousers. She had run off as fast as she could, but she could still feel the inexplicable blush and guilty excitement, and remembered the horrible, knowing look in his eye.

"To look. That's all. To look," Laura was saying. "He made me hold up my dress, and he just looked. And then there was a noise and he said, 'Get out. Go. And if you tell anyone, I'll kill you.' I believed him. You're the first people I've ever told."

"How awful," breathed Harriet. "What did you do?"

"I just pulled up my knickers and ran. I was only six. I never told anyone, not even Sabine or Olivier. They had come back and were looking for me, so I just said I'd heard a cat yowling and I'd gone to see if it was all right."

"Did they believe you?" said Georgina, wondering if Laura was as adept a liar as she herself was.

"Oh yes, why shouldn't they? They hadn't been in the playground when Nordhoff was there in his car, and they had no reason to be suspicious of anything. Ugh! It makes me feel sick to even think of it."

"Me too," said Harriet. "What a horrible man."

Georgina suddenly looked at her watch.

"Oh, blast," she said. "It's five to five. The prize-giving will be beginning. Come on!"

The path back up the slope from the pond seemed to go on forever. No one was on the terrace, and the sun-filled garden, the blue-green shadow of the cedar tree just beginning to lengthen, was still and silent, the bright roses on the pergola with their sweet powdery scent almost overwhelming in their heavy beauty. Georgina thought Baynes had never looked more beautiful than it did this evening, waiting in stillness to hear which of its daughters had won a prize.

She pushed open the heavy front door, forbidden to them but much nearer to the dining room, where the prize-giving was held. Silently they tiptoed up the stairs. They could hear a rustle of people and of chairs being moved. They were almost too late – everyone was in place for the ceremony.

As they slid round the door, Miss Morrisson must have given a signal, for the piano started and the whole room rose to sing *Jerusalem*. Under cover of the singing, they slipped into their places with the rest of the juniors. Miss King, in her place on the platform with the rest of the staff, had been looking worried, Georgina saw; when she saw Georgina she heaved an almost audible sigh of relief and Georgina saw her mouth, "Where have you been?" and indicate to her to tidy her blazer and comb her hair. She nudged Mary. "Lend me your comb," she demanded, and meekly Mary pulled a comb from her top blazer pocket, and handed it to her. She pulled it roughly though her fair curls. She passed it to Harriet, whose sandy plaits were fluffy with escaping hair. All she could do was comb the top. Laura's straight black hair was sticking up where she had pushed her hand through it. She took the comb and smoothed it down, and brushed the shoulders of her blazer. The triumphant hymn was ending, and girls and Old Scholars were settling back into their chairs.

Miss Morrisson was at her grandest. She was wearing an extremely smart black suit and a mannish white shirt, with her black Oxford gown over the top. This was her moment of triumph, when not only could she award Baynes's internal prizes, but would also announce the successes of her pupils in the outside world, listing those who had gained Oxford or Cambridge, Durham or St Andrews last year, those who had made their mark in public during the year, those who had had private triumphs which they wished to share with Baynes, and finally listing those who had died – "gone to a better Baynes in the sky," as one cynical ex-Baynes girl had muttered once.

There were countless prizes to be won by girls varying in age from five to eighteen. Each girl had to be clapped as she came back from collecting her cup, and the ceremony took a long time. Georgina won the Junior Cup for all-round excellence again, and Harriet was wishing she had had time to go to the lav, and was not paying much attention, when suddenly she heard her own name being called.

"To Harriet Bolton, the Junior Cup for English," Miss Morrisson was saying. Harriet could hardly believe her ears. Her knees were shaking almost as badly as they had when she had told Miss Morrisson that Alison would be a good choice for the dormitory. She felt an inane grin starting involuntarily on her face as she squeezed her way out past George and Laura. It seemed a very long way to the platform, and when she got there Miss Morrisson looked forbiddingly tall. As she handed Harriet the Cup, the smile which had seemed fixed on her face faded, and she said in the low voice she used to speak to each winner: "Miss King was insistent that this Cup went to you, though there were others who were almost as good. I hope you will not let her down, Harriet."

"Thank you Miss Morrisson," Harriet said as she had heard others say, and took the Cup, but as she made her way back all she could think was, why did she have to spoil it? She knew she was good at English, but Miss Morrisson had made it clear that she wasn't *the* best, just one of the best, and the joy of winning was tainted by wondering who else had been in the running. Meredith was very good at English, too, thought Harriet, but she had won one cup already, for gym, and they probably thought it would be bad for her to win another, so they gave it to me. These sour thoughts coloured the rest of the prize-giving for her, and she hardly noticed when they sang *To Be a Pilgrim,* one of her favourite hymns, and then the school song, which roused such fervour in others, but not in her.

She took the Cup back to the form room, where it was to be handed over to Miss King to have her name engraved on it and be safely locked away in the glass-fronted cupboards in the dining room.

"You don't look very pleased, Harriet," Miss King remarked as she saw Harriet's unsmiling face. "I thought you would be delighted. You deserve it, you know."

"That's not what Miss Morrisson said," replied Harriet. She was alone with Miss King, the rest of the class having handed over their various Cups and started on their way over to supper and bed.

"I didn't hear what she said?"

"She said that others were equally good and that only you wanted me to win," exaggerated Harriet.

"That's not true, Harriet. Others *were* good, but you were the best," insisted Miss King, thinking damn Edith Morrisson, can't she see the damage she does?

"You must learn, Harriet, to see the bright side of things, and not always to read something that is not intended into people's remarks. Life is going to be very uncomfortable for you if you won't take things at face value. Do you understand what I mean?"

Harriet nodded. She understood only too well what Miss King was saying, but to understand and to believe were two different things. She still felt that Miss Morrisson had meant exactly what she said.

"Of course," Miss King was saying, "If you had bothered to make yourself look tidy before prize-giving it might have helped. Just look at yourself, Harriet. Your socks are filthy, and your knees ..."

Harriet looked in surprise at her once-white ankle socks. They were streaked with black mud from the path to the Pond, and her knees were grey where she had knelt down.

"And your hair! You could at least have redone your plaits! It's no wonder that Miss Morrisson was irritated and that, no doubt, made her speak more harshly to you than she might have. It lets down the school, you know, in front of the Old Scholars if someone comes up to collect a valued Cup looking as scruffy as you do. It's as if you don't value what you've won."

"Well, I didn't know I was going to win it," said Harriet with perfect logic but far from perfect tact.

"That is not the point, Harriet." Miss King was exasperated with her. "The point is, everyone should have been clean and tidy for prize-giving. You know that."

"Yes, Miss King." Harriet looked at the floor and at her dirty socks. Miss King was right. She did look scruffy, but there had been no time to go to the bootroom ...

As if reading her thoughts, Miss King said, "Anyway, where were you? I saw you three come in late. It really is too bad, Harriet."

"We were down at ..." she remembered in time that the Pond was out of bounds for juniors. "We forgot the time."

"Well, don't do it again. Try to be on time and to look reasonably tidy till term ends. And Harriet ..." Miss King had noticed Harriet's downcast face ... "You really did deserve to win that Cup. You must believe me. Your English is excellent."

Harriet felt her spirits lift a little. Perhaps Miss King was right, and Morry had only been sour because she, Harriet, had looked such a mess?

Harriet smiled, her plain face suddenly attractive. Miss King could see her deciding to believe what she had been told, but as Harriet disappeared, running to catch up with the others, she shook her head. Harriet would never fit in, she thought, with her touchiness and bad temper. I wonder if this is the right school for her, and realised that although Baynes was one of the best schools in the country, where she was proud to be a teacher, for Harriet it was probably a choice that should never have been made. She's the sort of child who needs constant boosting from someone, probably her mother, thought Miss King. The sort of toughening experience we put them through here won't do her any good.

She picked up the four Cups that had been won and shut the door on the classroom, glad that prize-giving, with its surprises and disappointments, was over for another year.

After their various sleepless nights the day before, Georgina, Harriet and Laura all fell asleep instantly, not even the thunderstorm which broke in the night, and which signalled the end of the good weather, waking them.

In the morning, Alison, who had woken and had watched the cracking skies and streaming rain from the window, could not believe that all three of them could have slept through it.

"It was super," she said. "I leaned out of the window and these huge drops of rain were falling, as big as spoonfuls."

"You did *what?*" hissed Matron, who had crept silently up the stairs on her crepe-soled shoes and had heard Alison's description. "You know perfectly well that no one is allowed to lean out of the window, and especially not during a thunderstorm. You might have been struck by lightning."

"Sorry, Matron," said Alison, her stolid good-natured face looking alarmed. "I didn't think."

"Thinking is what your parents are paying for you to learn here," retorted Matron. "Now get a move on, the lot of you."

She crossed to Harriet's chair and picked up the green artificial silk frock that was obligatory on Sundays.

"Do you call this collar clean, Harriet Bolton?" she said, ripping the spotless cream collar from its press-studs. "Get a clean one immediately."

"Yes, Matron," said Harriet meekly. She guessed that Matron was starting to have her revenge for having to deal with Meredith's hair and dress on Friday. She opened her drawer and took out another collar and methodically press-studded it on to her dress, noting automatically Mummy's neat, tiny stitching.

"Everyone will wear mackintoshes today," said Matron, turning to go down the stairs.

They groaned theatrically, for although it had rained, it was still hot and sultry. Huge black clouds hung in the sky, motionless, as if waiting for something to happen. Looking out of the window, Harriet saw the cows, which had been allowed by the farmer back into the field where they had picked buttercups, lying in solid black and white heaps.

"The cows are lying down," she said. "That means it's going to rain."

"That's not what it means in France," said Laura.

"Well, what does it mean?"

"It means they're tired," said Laura, straight-faced.

Harriet groaned again at Laura's bad joke, and now dressed in their pale green dresses and blazers they went down the stairs to the basement to fetch their macs.

Today, the last day of the Old Scholars weekend, was the most formal day. After breakfast there would be Church, which all girls would attend, even if they usually went to a different service, as Laura did. This had been engineered by Miriam, who had insisted that she go to Mass on Sundays with Agnes Becquet and a few others as soon as she had realised that Laura had been brought up as a Catholic, for which Laura had been grateful, the familiar words of the Latin Mass making her feel more at home in this alien country.

But today the whole school, with those Old Scholars who had stayed, would attend the huge spired church in town, the official school church, filling its pews with row upon row of green-clad girls.

Two by two they lined up, each girl clasping her prayer book, a sixpence for the Collection tucked into her palm inside her white glove. Cream panama hats looked odd today with their dark green macs over their blazers, but the weather boded no good, thunder still grumbling behind the dark clouds, and a few spots of rain heralding the downpour which was sure to come.

Harriet walked with Laura, with Alison and Georgina behind them. The long crocodile of girls, accompanied every ten pairs or so by a guardian mistress, snaked its way into the town and towards the church.

"You'd better share my book," said Harriet to Laura. "Yours won't be any good." Laura was clutching her black missal.

"I know it won't," she said. "I thought I'd read it in the church. You know, Catholics aren't really allowed to go into a different church."

"Try telling that to Morry," said Harriet. "Anyway, you came to our church for quite a long time when you first came here."

Laura nodded. No one had told her, when she had come to Baynes, that the church the school went to was not a Catholic one. She had been horrified, on the first Sunday, to find that the service was in English and bore no resemblance to the Latin Mass she knew. To all the other muddled feelings she had had, this had added a sense of irredeemable guilt, for she thought she recalled from some half-remembered Catechism lesson that it was a sin for a Catholic to enter a church that was not Catholic. Miriam had tried to put an end to this misconception, but a remnant of it lingered on, and today Laura had decided that she would not listen to one word of the alien service but read the lessons and gospel for today in her Missal.

The Church of St Cuthbert was a monument to the perpendicular style. Its cavernous interior could have held most of the town, if they had bothered to come, and the addition every Sunday of the Baynes girls to the congregation was a welcome supplement. A Bach voluntary sounded on its magnificent organ as the green crocodile filed into place. How different this church smelled, Laura thought as she took her place, feeling odd at not genuflecting towards the altar. She supposed it was because there was no smell of incense, but instead a smell of damp, of cold stone, of mothballs. Quite nice, she thought, taking another sniff. But not church, not *The Church*.

The voluntary had stopped, and everyone rose to sing the first hymn. Harriet had pointed to the board with the hymn numbers on it, and had shown Laura the copy of *Hymns Ancient and Modern* she could use. Harriet herself did not need it, as her prayer book had all the Ancient and Modern hymns in the back. Laura thought it strange to sing standing up in church; in her experience, if you ever did sing, which was rare, you sang sitting down. You stood up to pray, but here you knelt down. It was all very puzzling.

She opened her hymnbook at the right number and found that the tune was so simple that she could join in easily, although she had never heard it before.

"*New every morning is the love ...*" she sang, rather enjoying the feeling of being in an immense choir. She could see the Old Scholars, who sat in front of the school, throwing themselves heartily into the singing, some, especially the ones who wore no make-up, with an expression of such piety on their faces that she wanted to smile.

"Don't they look silly," Harriet whispered, as if she had been mind-reading, though really she had only been watching where Laura was looking, but before Laura could whisper back Miss King leant forward from her place on the aisle with a look that sent them back to their hymnbooks.

The service seemed to go on forever. Much longer than Mass, Laura thought, sighing as the long sermon droned on, the vicar, as Harriet called him, using a dreary sing-song voice like the one he used when he said: "Let us Pray." Laura had quite enjoyed bits of the service – the Magnificat had a lovely tune, she thought – but this bit was awful. She remembered that she had been going to read her Missal, and opened it, but it was difficult to keep her mind on it. Harriet kept sighing beside her, her boredom threshold having been reached long ago. She was leafing through her prayer book, counting something.

At last, the droning voice droned to a stop. The sticky sixpences were retrieved from the gloves and dropped into the collecting plates. That at least, thought Laura, was the same as Mass, though she was surprised to see the plate being passed along the rows – in her church, the person who brought the plate round never let go of it; perhaps they thought someone would take something out of it instead of putting something into it, Laura thought, never guessing that for years to come now that particular manoeuvre would annoy her every time she saw it. Just pass it along the row, she would think, as she saw the holder desperately clinging on to it, leaning further and further over in the effort to pass it to everyone.

At last the final hymn was reached. The congregation got to its feet swiftly, and a half-heard sigh of relief seemed to percolate through the church. Even the organist seemed to quicken his tempo, as the congregation launched with enthusiasm into *Immortal, Invisible, God only Wise* ...

"God, wasn't that boring," said Harriet loudly as soon as they were outside the church, lining up for the walk back.

"Sssh, Harry," said Georgina behind her, "Morry will hear you," and indeed Edith Morrisson had turned her elegant, Eton-cropped head away for a second from the very old Old Scholar she was talking to. Briefly, her eyes fell on Harriet, and an infinitesimal raise of her eyebrows told Harriet that her remark had been registered before Edith turned her attention back to the Old Scholar.

"You never think before you speak, Harriet." Miss King was beside her. She was about to order Harriet to lose a house point, when she saw Meredith watching with a hungry look, and changed her mind.

"Well, it was ..." Harriet was beginning.

"Harriet." Miss King silenced her. "Please keep your views to yourself on the merits or not of the church service. No one is interested in what you think."

"Yes, Miss King," said Harriet. Two of the Old Scholars were watching, suppressing smiles.

On the way back to school, Laura said, "What were you counting?"

"I was so bored I could have died," Harriet said. "I was counting how many times it said 'Oh Lord' in the prayer book to keep myself awake."

Laura, who went to Mass without question, as she had always done with the Bonnevilles in Belay, was shocked at Harriet's attitude.

"But, Harry," she started to say, and then shrugged. "It's because there's no proper Mass in your church," she stated. "You don't take communion."

"I couldn't anyway," said Harriet. "None of us could. We haven't been confirmed yet. You don't get confirmed until you're fourteen or fifteen."

Laura found this even more confusing. She had taken her own first communion at the age of seven, and the word confirmed was new to her.

"I give up," she said. "It's so different. I'm glad I go to Mass. It's all a lot simpler there. And you can understand it wherever you go – it's always in Latin."

"Latin!" said Harriet. "How can you understand it? We haven't done Latin yet."

"You just do," replied Laura. "You know what it means, because you've been taught."

The school gates were coming into sight.

"I'm starving," said Harriet, changing the subject. She felt awkward, talking to Laura about church. Laura was obviously much more religious than she was, or any of the girls she knew. "I wonder what's for lunch?"

"Roast brown something in brown gravy," said Georgina from behind her. "It always is."

"With cabbage boiled with snails."

"And Dead Man's Leg for pudding."

"With lump-laden custard."

"A suitable menu for young ladies."

Laura laughed. "You two are so silly," she said, though she agreed that the food was bound to be awful. It always was, and she always imagined what Fernande would have done with it. She remembered the times during the war when there had been no food, or very little, and they had had to supplement their diet with things caught in the fields. They had eaten anything then – rabbit, hare and pigeon were luxuries, and one didn't always ask what animal or bird had gone to make the evening's meal. But Fernande had always been able to make whatever she was cooking taste delicious; herbs and garlic flavoured most things and every bit of every vegetable was eaten. Anything leftover went into the soup pot.

She remembered, too, the thin, tired people who would come from the towns, illegally, to forage for anything that might help the meagre diet they had to live on. If possible, they gave them apples from the orchard and sometimes a rabbit, but it was risky; the Germans would punish anyone they caught.

She imagined the dishes Fernande could have created with the food that was so abundant and yet so unappetising here at Baynes. Not tomato jam, she thought, or bread-and-butter pudding – her own particular hate; she loathed it as much as Harriet loathed the macaroni pudding. And how could they cook cabbage for three hours, for that was what it tasted like, and there was always a suspicious crunch, reminding one that cabbage often had snails in it.

She suddenly realised that although thinking about France usually made her sad, today it didn't. She found she was able to let the thoughts of Fernande and Belay, and the big kitchen filled with cooking smells come into her mind at last without wanting to burst into tears.

Surprisingly, she also found that she was looking forward to seeing Belay again, much more than when she was going to try to persuade Paul and Marie-Claude to let her come back. Now, she would just be able to enjoy being there. A sudden thrill at the nearness of the visit ran through her, and she wanted to laugh out loud.

"Cat got your tongue?"

The voice was Meredith's and Laura suddenly realised that they were back at school, almost at the junior boot rooms, and that she had not noticed anything on the walk since Harriet and Georgina had been joking about the food. Now the neat crocodile was breaking up, and Meredith was jumping and scuffling about in front of her.

"What do you mean, cat got my tongue?" she said puzzled.

"Oh, I forgot, you don't speak English properly, do you? It means why aren't you replying to my question?"

"Because I didn't hear it," Laura riposted back. "What do you want?"

"I want to know if you'll come down to the summerhouse with us."

"What for?" Laura looked round, but Harriet and Georgina seemed to have disappeared and most of the rest of the class was milling round Meredith.

"We just want to talk to you," said Meredith, taking Laura's arm. She started to pull her towards the terrace and the summerhouse, which was where Meredith's gang usually congregated.

"No," said Laura. "I don't want to come with you." She looked over her shoulder, willing George or Harry to appear.

"Well, you are," replied Meredith, tightening her grip.

Suddenly an unreasoned panic filled her, a faint memory of something hovering just out of sight in her mind, and she wrenched her arm away and shouted "NO, NO, GO AWAY, LEAVE ME ALONE!" at the top of her voice. A mistress who had been supervising the crocodile looked over in surprise, and

Meredith, taken unawares by Laura's panic, dropped her grip on Laura's arm.

"OK, OK," she said. "Keep your hair on. Don't come if you don't want to."

Laura found that her hands were shaking. She made herself walk calmly back to the boot room, hoping that George and Harriet were there. George appeared in the doorway.

"Laura," she said, a worried expression on her face. "We heard you shouting. What happened?"

"Oh, nothing, really," Laura replied, but her voice was shaking. "It was just Meredith, trying to get me to go with her to the summerhouse, and suddenly it felt like it did ... before ... something to do with that German I told you about, I think. I felt trapped. It was horrible ..."

Harriet appeared behind Georgina. "We'll protect you," she said. "She probably wanted you to join her gang, now that she knows George won't."

"Well, I'm not going to either," said Laura shakily. She sniffed, and pulled out her handkerchief. She turned away, and scrubbed at her eyes, where tears had suddenly appeared. Harriet put a tentative hand on her arm.

"Come on, Laura," she said. "We'll go down to the Pond, and make our pledge. Then we'll be best friends, and Meredith won't be able to do anything."

"Harry's right," said Georgina. "Come on, we'll go now, before lunch."

Down at the Pond, it was as dark and gloomy as winter, and the heavy summer leaves made even more dark shade. The water looked still and black. It was very hot, and thunder still rumbled behind the clouds. A bird's call seemed unnaturally loud as the three of them disturbed it.

"What shall we do?" said Harriet.

"You're good at English," said Georgina. "You make up a pledge."

"All right." Harriet thought for a few minutes. "This is what we'll say. '*We solemnly promise and pledge that from this day forward we three will be best friends, only unto us, forever and ever, Amen.*'"

"That sounds good," said Georgina. "Does it come from the Bible?"

"Not exactly. Bits come from the marriage service. But it makes it sound really solemn."

"It sounds funny to me," said Laura. "What does '*this day forward*' mean, and '*only unto us?*'"

"It just means from now on, and only us, no one else." Harriet explained. "Now what we should do, is all join left hands …"

They each put out a hand, one on top of another.

"Now put your right hand up, like in Brownies."

Solemnly they complied.

"And now repeat it after me."

Harriet made her voice sound like the vicar's in church that morning, and intoned the words like a dirge. The other two repeated it, somewhat spoiling the effect by giggling. Harriet dropped her hand and laughed too.

"Well, we've done it," she said. "You can't go back on a pledge. Now we have to be best friends."

"Forever," said Georgina.

"From this day forward," said Laura who liked the biblical sound of the phrase.

"Only unto us," continued Harriet. "That means no one else can join, however much we like them."

George and Laura nodded. "No one," said George.

"Ever," said Laura.

A raindrop plopped into the pond with a splash. The air was darker and stiller than ever.

"Oh, blast," said Harriet. "It's going to rain. We'd better run." As she spoke, rain could be heard dropping on to the ceiling of leaves over their heads, and tiny rivulets were already darkening the mud of the path. In the distance, the bell for lunch could be heard. The three girls ran as fast as they could, but by the time they reached the boot rooms, they were soaked. Luckily, they had kept their macs on, but their hair dripped into their eyes, and their shoes were caked in mud.

"Blast, blast, blast," said Harriet, pulling a comb through the top of her hair and wiping the mud as best she could off her shoes. Her feet felt wet inside them.

"You'd better redo your plaits," said Meredith. "You look a mess. Where've you been?"

"Mind your own beeswax," retorted Harriet, but nevertheless she went over to the mirror by the washbasins. The face that looked back at her was not reassuring. A streak of mud coloured one cheek, and the bottle green ribbons tying her plaits looked like wet black bootlaces. The plaits themselves were half undone. She pulled off the ribbons and swiftly undid the plaits, but as she did so, the second bell rang, and the boot room was suddenly empty as the girls raced to queue up to go in to lunch. Only Laura and George remained.

"What're you going to do?" said Georgina, aghast at Harriet's long hair. One of the sillier Baynes' rules was that hair longer than your earlobes had to be in bunches or plaits.

"What *can* I do?" said Harriet. "Leave it and get a row for that, or be late and lose a house point?" She shrugged. "We'd better go." She yanked the comb one last time through the damp, tangled hair and scrubbed with the towel at her face. "Come on."

As luck would have it, Harriet was at Edith Morrisson's table that day. In the silence that took the place of grace at Baynes before meals, each girl standing silently behind her chair, she felt Morry's eyes turn towards her. Studiously, she gazed at the table. Even when the tinkle of the silvery bell sounded and chairs were pulled out she endeavoured not to raise her head. Her neighbour, a solid senior school girl with a large bosom which stretched the thin artificial silk of her dress to a fat green point which would normally have fascinated Harriet, silently passed her the plates of brown meat, mashed potato, cabbage and gravy. Usually, Harriet would have asked for a small helping, but she had no wish to draw attention to herself today. Surreptitiously, between handing plates on to her other neighbour, she pushed her hair behind her ears.

"It won't do any good," whispered the girl on her right, as Harriet passed her a plate. She was only one form ahead of Harriet and just into the senior school herself. "Morry's already seen."

"Maybe if I just don't look at her she won't do anything – especially not with all the Old Scholars around?" Harriet whispered back hopefully. There were two particularly old, and therefore special, Old Scholars sitting one on each side of Morry. The rest were gathered at the spare tables the daygirls filled at weekday lunchtimes. Their cheerful chatter could be heard above the usual hum of conversation.

"I shouldn't count on it," her neighbour said. "What on earth were you doing? I mean, today of all days, when Morry wants everything perfect."

"Oh, I don't know," said Harriet morosely. "Everything's gone wrong this weekend."

She bent in silence over the thick slab of indeterminate meat on her plate, forcing herself to eat it. She heard a crunch as her teeth met on a questionable bite of dark green cabbage and steeled herself to swallow whatever it was. She still had not raised her eyes from the table, and did not, therefore, see Edith Morrison gazing thoughtfully at her, before turning her attention back to the Old Scholars.

Pudding came, not Dead Man's Leg but tinned fruit salad with evaporated milk, and finally, the tinkle of Morry's bell for another silence before chairs were scraped back. Harriet pushed her chair in, thankful that she had been sitting in the middle of the long table which sat twelve on each side, and had not therefore been called upon to carry plates to the kitchen, when her long hair would have been sure to have been noticed. She was about to turn and make for the door, when a hand descended on her shoulder.

"One moment, Harriet," said Edith Morrisson. "I would like you to wait until everyone has gone."

"Yes, Miss Morrisson," said Harriet despondently. She saw Georgina stop in the doorway and look back at her, and raised her shoulders in a hopeless gesture. Miss Morrisson had turned away and was speaking to a group of old girls who were saying their goodbyes. One of them caught Harriet's eye as she turned to wait for Morry, and touched her hair and smiled sympathetically, knowing what Harriet's crime had been. Nothing ever changes here, thought Harriet, and felt the tears, which this weekend seemed to be there all the time, tightening her throat.

"Now, Harriet," said Edith, when the dining room was empty. She had her more in sorrow than in anger face on.

"Tell me. Are you happy here?"

Harriet was surprised. This was not what she had expected to hear.

"Yes, Miss Morrisson," she lied. Her eyes did not meet Edith's.

"Because if you are not, perhaps I should have a chat with your mother. I don't want girls who are unhappy in my school."

Harriet's heart lurched. Oh Lord, she's going to expel me, she thought, and was surprised to feel not joy at being able to go home and never come back, but horror, comprised of a mixture of shame at being asked to leave, fear of what her father would say, dread of the sorrow that would cloud Mummy's face, and the knowledge that she might never see George or Laura again.

"No, no Miss Morrisson," she said quickly. "I am happy. I really am. I don't want to leave Baynes."

"If it came to that, Harriet, it would not be a question of what *you* wanted, but what I or your parents would decide," said Edith. Having to ask a girl to leave was not something she liked doing, for many reasons, not the least being the bad publicity an unpleasant episode brought to a school, especially one where many of the parents moved in the same social circles. But Harriet Bolton was being, if not actively disruptive, then passively disturbing. This was the third or fourth time, thought Edith, that she had seen or heard about Harriet being out of order in just one short weekend. A warning given now might give the child enough of a fright to make her conform.

"However, Harriet," she continued, "it has not come to that yet. Yet," she repeated. She lifted a lock of Harriet's damp hair with an elegantly groomed finger, the perfect pale pink nail polish on the smooth white hand an unspoken comment on the difference between the unkempt small girl and the poised, successful headmistress. "But we cannot have you coming to meals looking like this. You know the rules about hair?"

Harriet hung her head. "Yes Miss Morrisson," she said in a low voice.

"And yesterday I was ashamed to see a girl coming up to collect a Cup looking as messy as you did. And I gather there was some kind of..." – she hesitated, searching for the word – "... scene ... in here on Friday?"

"Yes, Miss Morrisson," repeated Harriet." But it won't happen again. I promise, Miss Morrisson." She tried to sound as convincing as possible, but to herself Harriet felt she could detect the lack of conviction in her voice. It was no use her promising that her tempers would not happen again, she thought. They just came, and took over. Morry also seemed to detect a note of falsehood.

"I hope I can believe you, Harriet," she said. "A promise is not something to give lightly. Can I believe you?"

"You can, you can, Miss Morrisson," Harriet said quickly, the words tumbling over each other. "It's just that, well, I don't seem to be able to get anything right this weekend. I didn't mean to be late yesterday, and then again today, it was the rain, well I didn't know it was going to rain, and my hair got soaked, and I undid it to comb it and then the bell went ..."

"Yes, yes, Harriet," said Edith, a faint smile lightening her severe, handsome features. "I don't want to hear your excuses. I just want to be sure that Baynes is the right school for you. As I said, I don't want girls here who are going to be unhappy, and lately it has seemed to me that you don't look, well, as if you fitted in properly. Am I wrong?"

"Yes, Miss Morrisson," Harriet said once more. How was she going to convince Morry that she must not expel her? "I really am happy here," she said.

"Very well," said Morry. "I won't speak to your mother this time, but we will have to see an improvement in your behaviour. I want to hear no more about tempers and scenes. And I do not want to see you looking like this ever again." Her gaze swept over Harriet's lank hair, untidy blazer and mud-covered shoes. "Do you understand?"

Harriet pushed the embarrassing hair behind her ears once more.

"Yes, Miss Morrisson." she said, letting her gaze rest at last on Morry's face. "I promise. And I really will try."

As she made her way back to the classroom Harriet didn't know whether to be happy or sad. She couldn't understand her reaction to Morry's threat; up to now she had thought firmly that to escape from Baynes was all she wanted. But, when Morry had handed her the possibility on a plate, why had she so firmly rejected it? Her head felt tired from all the tears, tempers and thinking this weekend had entailed. She would be glad, she thought, when all the Old Scholars had gone, and life could get back to normal which, she realised with a sigh, meant life here at Baynes, not some imagined existence at home.

CHAPTER Six

Harriet felt sick when she woke up the next morning, which came as no surprise as she had felt so tired and ill after her unpleasant heart-to-heart with Morry the day before that she had hardly been able to write her letter home. The afternoon had passed in a shivery trance. The rain had poured down relentlessly, so that the lights had had to be switched on, and the temperature had dropped so low that, against the rules, they had lit the gas fire. Having written her short and perfunctory letter, Harriet had huddled near it all afternoon, unable to get warm.

The fright she had had from Morry had left her feeling uncertain and threatened. She couldn't understand why she had not been delighted at the prospect of leaving Baynes, and she decided that it must be because she knew she would not be able to deal with Mummy's disappointment, while Daddy's anger would be even worse and she would feel ashamed and useless. She admitted reluctantly that although she never would like Baynes, she would have to do her best to stay. The thought filled her with dreary horror. She counted the years ahead. Probably at least six, she calculated, maybe more. Even the prospect of staying with George and Laura seemed hollow, and as cold shivers overtook her body, she realised she was beginning to feel ill. This morning's nausea confirmed it.

Matron arrived, summoned by Georgina, her fat face creased with annoyance.

"It would be you feeling ill this morning, Harriet Bolton," she said crossly, shoving a thermometer with unnecessary force under Harriet's tongue, and pulling up her wrist to feel her pulse. "I expect you ate too much this weekend."

The mention of food made Harriet feel a lot worse. A vision of the strawberries and cream she had missed on Saturday afternoon floated into her mind. She sat up quickly, pulled the thermometer out of her mouth and rushed to the lavatory next door, where she heaved and retched until her stomach was empty. The little room seemed to swing up and down, round and round.

When she returned the others had gone to breakfast and Matron was gathering up her dressing gown and slippers.

"Well, you're not faking this time," she said. "Your temperature's a hundred and one. Put these on and come down to the San." Harriet put them on, still shaky and sick, her knees trembling, and picked up Dinah and Dorinda, the book she had been reading, and the tiny bedside clock Daddy had given her for Christmas. She followed Matron down to the ground floor, and climbed into the high hospital bed with its plain white bedspread.

"You won't need this," Matron said, taking her book and putting it out of reach. "Sleep is what you need. Did you get wet yesterday?"

Harriet nodded. Her socks had still been damp when she had taken them off the night before.

"I thought so. You're a naughty and thoughtless girl. This serves you right." Matron went over to the window and drew the curtains, so that the room was in half-darkness. It seemed wonderfully restful to Harriet, who lay back on her pillow and stretched her legs down between the cool, stretched sheets. Matron brought a glass of water over to the bed.

"This is all you'll have today, my girl," she said. "You've got a chill on your stomach. Now try to sleep."

"Yes, Matron," Harriet murmured. Already she felt calmed by the quiet of the sickroom atmosphere, and the memory of the restless dreams that had threatened her all night was receding. She closed her eyes and heard Matron go out. She lay very still, knowing from experience that the least movement would make her feel sick again. It was quiet, and she could hear the rain dripping monotonously on to the gravel outside. Half asleep, she heard the maids coming and going, and the faint hum of a vacuum cleaner upstairs. Slowly she drifted into sleep, still nauseous, still lying unmoving.

Suddenly she heard Laura's voice from Saturday saying, "He told me to pull my knickers down. Knickers down. Knickers down."

The voice seemed to come from a long way away and she could see a man dressed in uniform standing in the room, enormously tall, bending towards her. He stretched out his hands, which grew bigger and bigger as they got nearer, till they were scrabbling at the bedclothes. Harriet screamed, and a door banged and she could hear a voice saying, "She's having a nightmare."

She tried to open her eyes, but she felt as if she could not fight against the waves of sleep that were overpowering her, taking her back into the room where Nordhoff was waiting. She forced her eyes open, and thought she was awake, and then the door opened and Nordhoff came into the room. He put a hand on her shoulder and started to shake her, and although she tried to scream she couldn't.

Matron's voice was saying loudly, "Wake up, Harriet, wake up. It's only a dream."

She opened her eyes, properly this time, and instantly the waves of nausea were back. She sat up, her hand over her mouth. Matron thrust an enamel basin at her, and the retching and heaving started again. She lay back, not daring to shut her eyes; when she did so the room started going round and round, and the image of Nordhoff kept looming up.

Matron came back into the room, with a damp towel that she placed on Harriet's forehead, and put the thermometer back in her mouth. She looked at it with a serious face.

"Hhmm," she said, "even higher. I'll have to get Doctor Maxwell. You've really gone to town this time, Harriet Bolton."

Harriet was ill for more than a week. Her throat hurt, her head ached. Dr Maxwell came, and prescribed M&B tablets. They made her feel terribly unhappy, though Dr Maxwell said not to worry, that was one of their side effects. Nevertheless, she could hardly summon a smile when he told her "worse things happen at sea". The nightmare she had had on the first morning was still in the forefront of her mind, although she had not actually dreamed of Nordhoff again, and when she thought of it a kind of nameless horror came over her. She deliberately did not think of what Laura had told them, but one day, towards the end of the week, when she felt slightly better and had been able to eat a boiled egg without feeling sick, she let herself hear Laura's words again. This time, there was no nightmare, and she lay quietly, thinking about what Laura had said.

Harriet had always hated that part of herself. She wished that whoever had designed the human body had just put a simple hole there to urinate through. She didn't want to know about the rest, and when she thought of what Nordhoff had said it made her feel disgusted, and squirm involuntarily. She wondered what men looked like. She knew they were different, but not exactly how. When Mummy had shown her the book about babies, she had tried not to look, but she hadn't been able to help seeing the funny looking thing that men had. She felt her smooth body, and wished that it could stay that way forever, although she knew it couldn't. Already, one of the daygirls in the class was claiming to wear a bra, and had shown it to one or two privileged girls. Certainly, in the form above, some girls were looking quite fat in the front, and those in the senior school often had an air of mystery about them, and whispered things to each other about not being able to do games. Harriet thought again that she didn't want to know and then, resignedly, that she would eventually *have* to know. She thought again of Nordhoff and Laura, and again she felt the involuntary squirming feeling between her legs, and knew it had something to do with growing up.

Georgina had brought her letters over and Matron had brought them in, though she had felt too ill to read them properly. Now she reached out to the bedside table and picked up Mummy's letter again.

Among the news about home, and Granny and the Carruthers cousins, was the longed for invitation to London to say with Daddy and Arabella.

"Your father would like you to go for a week at the beginning of September," her mother had written, "and I see no reason why you shouldn't, although I think you should realise that as Arabella is expecting a baby she will not be able to do as much with you as she could at Easter."

Mummy writes as if it's my fault, thought Harriet, and felt torn again between staying at home with Mummy and tasting once more the treats of London. I hope we go to the ballet again, she thought, and then, depression taking over, I suppose that's one of the things Arabella won't be able to do.

There had been a letter from Daddy, too, that week, which was rare, and she re-read it now. It was short and sentimental, and also contained the invitation to stay.

"I hope you know you will always be my wonderful eldest daughter," Alec had written, "of whom I am so proud. No matter what other children I have, you will always come first." Harriet wished he wouldn't say things like that. It was embarrassing. Especially as she thought it wasn't entirely true. Daddy could be very off-hand at times, and then he would try to make it up by being over-affectionate and saying silly things like that, she thought sourly. She wished he could just have stayed at home with her and her mother and not gone to London and married the Honourable Arabella, with whom he would now have more children who, she was quite certain, he would love as much if not more than her, and who, she knew, would displace her in his affections, no matter how much he might pretend they hadn't.

There was also a postscript in the letter from Arabella that was worrying her. Arabella had written that the younger sister she had talked about at Easter would be staying there too, and she hoped she and Harriet would be friends. Harriet thought grumpily that she wanted to be on her own with her father and decided that Arabella's sister, who was called Ariadne, of all stupid names, would probably also be annoyed that someone else had to be there.

She felt exhausted after reading the letters and thinking about Mummy and Arabella and Daddy, and lay back luxuriously on her pillows. She looked at the little clock. It was almost four o'clock, and soon she would hear everyone coming back to get changed. For the first time during that long week of sickness she hoped that George or Laura might look round the door. It seemed a long time since she had seen any of her friends. I must be getting better, she thought. She heard voices getting nearer, receding down to the basement, and then outside her door as the juniors came up again to get changed. She strained her ears, and after a while the door opened a crack and she heard George whisper, "Harry. Can you hear me?"

"George," she whispered back, as loudly as she dared. "Come in!"

The door opened and Georgina slipped into the room, shutting it quietly behind her.

"Harry! Are you all right? When are you coming out?" George's face was flushed with the game of rounders she had come from, and her hair was damp with exertion. She smelled of outside, of grass and sweat and dust.

"Dr Maxwell said I can probably come out on Monday. What's been happening?"

"Oh, nothing much. It's been boring without you. Laura's been off games three times this week, to see that woman, Dr Stein. I wonder what they talk about?"

Harriet shrugged, and said, "I dunno. D'you think she's told her about the German, the one who asked her to ..." she couldn't say the words. "To undress."

"She said she hadn't told anyone. Perhaps telling it to us made her able to tell it to Dr Stein. It must have been horrible."

"Vile," said Harriet. "Absolutely vile. I don't understand what he was going to do to her – do you?" She threw this last remark off lightly, looking out of the window as though she wasn't really interested in the answer.

"I can guess," said Georgina. "You know, what men always want to do."

"Oh," said Harriet, unenlightened. "I suppose so."

It was Georgina's turn to look out of the window. "It happened to me once," she said. "It was horrible. A man in the park. He'd got his thing out, and it was sticking up. It was revolting."

"What did you do?" said Harriet, hoping she would glean more from Georgina's answer. She wondered what thing the man had got out.

"I ran away," said George. "It made me feel really ... well, peculiar. And frightened," she added. Suddenly she stopped and listened.

"I can hear the Bun," she whispered, and indeed the sound of Matron's voice was getting louder, as she descended the stairs.

"Has anyone seen Georgina Charlton?" they heard her say, her feet silent in her crepe soles, but undoubtedly getting nearer.

"Quick, hide," said Harriet, pointing to the other bed in the room whose white counterpane hung down enough to hide the space beneath. George disappeared under the bed, pushing herself into the corner. The door opened and Matron came in. She looked round the room suspiciously. Harriet was lying flat, reading her Enid Blyton.

"Has Georgina Charlton been in here?" Matron said, sniffing as if she could scent out George like a bloodhound.

"No, Matron," lied Harriet smugly. "It's against the rules."

"That has never been a reason for you not doing something," replied Matron. "I hope you're not starting your old tricks, Harriet, though I suppose I can't expect anything else from you now you're almost well. The sooner you're back to school the better." She stared at Harriet, dislike apparent in her deceptively comfortable-looking fat face. I wonder why she hates me so much, thought Harriet, staring back silently. Matron looked away first, and gathering her white skirts around her moved towards the door on her silent shoes.

"If I find Georgina has been in here there'll be trouble," she said, opening the door and banging it behind her.

Georgina emerged, giggling. She opened the door a crack and looked through. Matron's back was disappearing down the stairs to the basement. With a finger to her lips she slipped out and ran silently upstairs. She won't get caught, thought Harriet, and mused on the fact that some people were undoubtedly lucky like that, though not her. The visit had done her good, and she felt almost strong enough to get up. She thought about what George had said about men, and felt even more puzzled. If the thing George had spoken of was what she suspected it was, how could it be sticking up? She made up her mind to find out from Mummy's book. She had a good idea where Mummy had put it, and she could just pretend that she wanted to know about Arabella being pregnant. Thinking of Arabella made her think of the other thing that was worrying her, Ariadne. Arabella's sister. She knew she was going to dislike her. She hated people who had strange names, like Meredith or Ariadne. What a stupid name. Why couldn't she be called Jane or Anne? Irritated, she picked up her book again, but the story had palled. She realised suddenly that she was bored – and hungry, for the first time that week. And since George's visit, no longer depressed.

The maid came in with her tea, bread and butter and a piece of sponge cake. Harriet said quickly, before she disappeared again, "Ruby. Can you bring me some more bread. I'm starving."

"You mun' be better, Miss," said Ruby in her thick accent. "Matron, she's that fed up, she'll be glad to see the back o' you."

"Well, I'll be glad to see the back of her, too, Ruby," said Harriet. "Only I never will, as long as I'm in this house."

"Won't be long, now, Miss. I've seen all sorts cum an' go, an' they all go in t'end. What've you got, one more year here?"

"Mmmhmm," said Harriet, stuffing a piece of bread into her mouth.

"Ee, you are hungry an' all," said Ruby, an admiring glance watching the speed with which Harriet was eating. "If ye' say nowt, I'll bring you another piece o' cake too."

Harriet lay back on her pillows while Ruby was gone. She wondered what sort of life Ruby had, being a maid here, and thought, at least I won't end up like that, if I stay at Baynes.

***

On the wet Monday afternoon following the Old Scholars weekend Laura was waiting for Miriam, in Miriam's study which Laura never tired of examining. She had been delivered by taxi and Miriam would drive her back.

Everything in this room had a story, a history, a meaning. Packed with objects – books, pictures, papers, photographs, newspaper cuttings – it exuded a passion for life which also apparently included looking at the dead, their works, their memorabilia and their images. Not one thing is here by mistake, thought Laura, as once again she felt as if she were in an Aladdin's cave of precious possessions collected by Miriam over the years of unsettled existence.

Laura knew quite a lot about Miriam's life and history now, though not as much as Miriam knew about hers. Miriam never told you something by mistake, she thought; everything she told you was for a reason, as an explanation perhaps for the way you felt, or as an example of something she had been talking about. Miriam's life fascinated Laura, particularly, she thought, because Miriam only told you some of the story.

She picked up the round, clear glass ball that lay on a wooden stand on Miriam's desk. She loved the way it felt, heavy and solid in her hand, transparent and yet opaque, as if it could tell you the secret of life. It couldn't, of course, she knew, and remembered Miriam saying once,
"I keep that crystal ball here to remind myself that we actually have *no* way of foreseeing the future. No crystal ball can foretell it. We can only make educated guesses at what might happen. We should never say that we know what will happen if a given set of circumstances, or actions, takes place. We don't, because we can't see a wide enough picture. We can't see what accidental happening, what contingency, might affect the picture we have imagined. Never think, Laura, that you know what the future holds for you, no matter how certain you are, because you can't know."

She had gone on to talk about Laura's attempted suicide, the reasons for which had been based on false knowledge.

"What you thought, Laura, and what was actually so, were quite different. You thought you had been abandoned by the Bonnevilles, while the facts are, as you now know, that for a whole year they battled with their consciences because they didn't want to give you up. They wanted desperately to keep you as their daughter, but they also believed in the truth, as all good human beings do, and in the end they had to do what the truth dictated.

But you were never abandoned. Never not loved. You can see that now?" And her head had bent to one side in the gesture that Laura now knew so well, her black eyes glinting with the question to which she wanted an answer.

"Yes. Yes. I see that now," Laura had said slowly. "But it still doesn't stop me feeling unhappy about it."

"I didn't say it would," replied Miriam. "I never said that the truth would make you happy. Only that you should not act when you don't understand the facts. The truth might satisfy you, as it does me, but it doesn't necessarily make you happy."

Over the weeks of seeing Miriam, which had turned into months in which Miriam had grown from healer into friend, they had explored what had happened to Laura, how she felt and how she should perhaps feel, and how she could deal with the mixture of strong emotions which she had not been able to express earlier, and not just because of the language problem.

"It didn't really have much to do with your not being able to speak English," Miriam said. "You could have written to Marie-Claude with your problems. You could have tried to communicate with your grandmother, who gave you every opportunity. But no. You decided right at the beginning to hide your emotions away, to refuse to speak of them. You did yourself a lot of damage, doing that."

Laura had been silent. Miriam did not understand what it was like to be taken away as she had been, and put down in a strange, alien land where no one could understand you and you could understand no one. She said as much.

"Oh, you think that, Laure, do you?" Miriam had replied cryptically, her black eyes gleaming again, but she had not at that time enlarged on what she meant, only going on to ask Laura to try to remember back to the weeks before she had been sent to Baynes.

"Did your grandmother not show you great love and compassion?" she said. "Think back, Laura, with honesty."

Laura had thought back, reluctant at first to admit that there was any truth in what Miriam was saying, but slowly beginning to understand that there was. She remembered how her grandmother had sat with her while she cried uncontrollably, stroking her hair and saying in her bad, half-forgotten French, "It will be all right, Laura. We will soon be able to understand each other. You're a miracle to me, a grandchild I never expected to see, a gift from my dear son, Robert, your father. A bridge into the future …"

Laura had not understood all of what her grandmother was saying, but she had understood enough to realise that her grandmother was offering her love and comfort. She had turned her face away from it, both figuratively and actually, turning her face into the wall, pushing her grandmother's gentle hand away. She remembered the steely determination with which she had refused to learn anything. She had refused to speak. She had tried to refuse to eat, though without much success as hunger had got the better of her, but even then she had only eaten enough to stop feeling hungry, so she'd become thinner and thinner. She had refused to go out, shutting herself away in the bedroom that she did not regard as hers, and she had refused to respond in any way to any advances.

Now she remembered the people Grandmother had brought to see her, people who had spoken French to her, which she had pretended not to understand. Her grandmother had brought in the big English/French dictionary that had been mouldering away in the study; Laura had never opened it. Her grandmother had invited children of Laura's own age, children that her grandmother herself hardly knew, Laura had guessed, and with whom Grandmother had felt highly embarrassed, as Laura had turned her back on them. She had refused to eat the tea which had been prepared by her grandmother's housekeeper, Hilda, taking a sandwich from the plate held out to her and dropping it on the floor, deliberately spilling her lemonade over her skirt, and finally picking up a jelly and emptying it on to the starched white cloth, squashing its paper holder flat onto the table, watching the green jelly ooze out from underneath. After that, as the other children sat in stunned silence, her grandmother had opened the dining room door and pushed her out, even her long-suffering patience giving out.

That had been the beginning, Laura now thought, of the real coldness that had developed between her and her grandmother, so that by September her grandmother had stopped trying to comfort her, hardly even spoke to her. Then one day a lady had arrived with school uniforms. Her grandmother had sat silently while Laura had tried on the clothes, turning her round with stiff little gestures, her face grave and sad. The pile of selected clothes grew, and eventually the shop assistant had taken away the discarded sizes with an order for more blouses, socks, Chilprufe vests and liberty bodices. Her grandmother had told her, in careful French, obviously rehearsed and worked out beforehand, that she was to be sent away to school where perhaps she would progress better than she had up to now.

"I have written of my decision to your ... to Monsieur and Madame Bonneville," Grandmother had said. "This situation cannot go on."

Laura had registered this as further evidence of abandonment by the Bonnevilles, who should surely have come and saved her, and stored it away with all the other painful thoughts which would one day drive her down the dark path to the Pond. But she said nothing, just shrugged and took off the strange boarding-school clothes and climbed silently into the flannel skirt, woollen jumper and cardigan she had been wearing against the cold of the English summer.

Miriam had said, when told about this particular scene, made even more awful for Laura by the added evidence of Marie-Claude's abandonment, "But what did you expect, Laure? You were testing your grandmother to the furthest possible limit. What else could she do? She was worried enough to write to Madame Bonneville and get her approval, and Madame Bonneville probably felt that she had no right, any longer, to have a say in what should happen to you. She must have felt doubly guilty, firstly for not having told you the truth herself long before, though that was through circumstances which were beyond her control, and secondly for hiding the fact of your existence for almost a year from your true family. She may have longed to have you back; in fact we know she did, but she had no right to say so. But in no way was she abandoning you. If you had read her letters when they came, you would have seen how much she cared for you, and how worried she was at hearing from your grandmother how difficult you were being."

This was early in the long weeks of treatment by Miriam, and Laura had burst into floods of tears as the memory of those bleak, strange first weeks came back to her, the feeling of being lost, abandoned and forgotten by everyone she knew and loved. Now thinking back on them, she knew that much of the horror had been her own fault; her stubbornness had engineered what had happened to her. How much happier she would have been if she had listened to what her grandmother had been trying to tell her, and had read Marie-Claude's letters when they came instead of stuffing them unread into a drawer.

"Of course," Miriam had said, "you meant to read them one day. Otherwise you would have torn them up."

Hearing a step in the hall, Laura put down the glass ball into which she had been staring, unseeing. She had something to tell Miriam, something she felt she had to tell her immediately, though she half-expected that Miriam, who seemed to possess extraordinary powers of being able to see what you were thinking, might already know what she was going to say.

Miriam, who had been on the telephone when Laura arrived, came into the room with a firm step, briskly shutting the door behind her.

"Bonjour, Laure," she said, stooping to give her a kiss on either cheek in the familiar French way. "You look ... expectant. And better. Do you have anything special you want to talk about today?" Her black eyes, twinkling and glittering, fixed themselves on Laura's. Laura took a deep breath.

"Yes, I've made a decision. I've decided ..." she said, "I mean, you probably thought I'd agreed before this ... to stay here ... but I hadn't. I was going to make the Bonnevilles take me back, let me stay there after the summer. But now I've decided not to. I've decided to stay with my grandmother and go on going to Baynes." She spoke with a kind of challenge in her voice, as if she was daring Miriam to contradict her, not looking straight at Miriam but at a picture to the right of Miriam's head. Now she looked at her and saw that Miriam was smiling a crooked little smile.

"I've been waiting for this, Laure," she said, "Waiting for you to make this decision."

"But how ... how did you know?"

Although she had half-expected Miriam to know, because she seemed to know everything, Laura was still surprised to have her guess confirmed. Miriam put her hands together under her chin, a gesture which Laura knew usually meant that Miriam was going to impart some part of her own mysterious story. She was looking very French today, dressed in a flowing black skirt and a grey silk blouse fastened at the neck with a brooch set with pale colourless stones that reminded Laura of the moonlight she had seen two nights ago. Her short black jacket she wore loosely over her shoulders against the unseasonal cold of the June day. Outside, the grey rain still fell in sheets, beating down the roses, flattening the bright blooms of the herbaceous borders.

"I knew, Laure," she began, her eyes looking down at and through the papers on her desk, "because many years ago a little girl, who was very similar to you, had a dream which she used to get her through a time which she found heart-breakingly difficult." She raised her eyes and looked at Laura, a gaze that seemed to hold all the sorrows of the world. Laura nodded, understanding what she was saying, and knowing also that Miriam was speaking of herself.

"This girl lived with her parents and her brothers and sisters in a small town in Russia, near Odessa. It was not a particularly beautiful place, but it was where her family had lived for as long as anyone could remember. Then one day, soldiers rode into the town, and started burning the houses and chasing out all the people. The girl and her family had to flee for their lives. They all escaped, except for two – the littlest boy, and the mother. The father and the eldest children ran and ran, carrying the smaller ones, or dragging them, and as they ran they could smell the houses burning and hear the screams of the people who were dying in them. And when they finally stopped, the little girl's mother and her smallest brother were no longer with them. But they couldn't go back to look for them, or the soldiers would have killed them all."

"It was you, Miriam, the little girl, wasn't it," interrupted Laura. Miriam's eyes came back from where she had been looking, not seeing dripping trees and grey English sky, but rearing horses and yelling soldiers whirling firebrands in the air before chucking them at the houses, and screaming people running from them, like black ants from a burning anthill.

"Yes, it was, Laure. I was that girl."

"But why, Miriam? Why were you chased out and your house burned? I don't understand."

Miriam shook her head as if she could shake away the memories, and her voice became brisk. "I don't imagine you know much about Jewish people, Laura?" Laura shook her head. "No matter. I'm Jewish, and soon you'll learn of the terrible things that were done to the Jews in this war. But terrible things have always been done to Jews, though perhaps not on the scale that Hitler attempted. And this was something that happened to Jews who lived in Russia or Poland. The soldiers would come, to a village or a town, the houses would be burned, and the families forced to flee to anywhere that would accept them. Some went to England, some to America. Many of them died. We went to France, where my father's brother had settled in his youth, so we had a family there to take us in. I won't go into how we got there – it was a long journey, and frightening, and all the time I was thinking of my mother who had disappeared that dreadful night with my brother, Daniel – he was only three years old ..." She stopped suddenly, and looked at Laura.

"I'm sorry, Laura," she said. "I didn't mean to tell you all this." She smiled apologetically. "Promise me you won't think about it."

Laura nodded, although she knew that she would visualize many times a dark-haired woman and a little boy burning to death, or being chased by soldiers.

"Did your mother ... I mean, did you ever find ...?"

"No. We never saw them again." said Miriam calmly. "But the point I wanted to make – and I'm sorry if I have upset you with the story – was that I got through that first year in a strange new country by spending every moment thinking about going back to Russia to find them. One tiny part of me knew it was an impossible dream, but my conscious mind rejected that, and everything I did, I did with this journey in view. Do you understand?"

Laura nodded. How well Miriam understood. There was nothing you could tell her that she couldn't explain. Perhaps one day she would tell her about her experience with Nordhoff. But not today.

"It's exactly the same," she said, her sallow face made prettier by the flush that had come into her cheeks. "Until Friday, I was so sure of what I was going to do. It seemed so clear, and by always having it in my mind I was able to endure – no that's not the right word, it's too strong – I was able to ... I can't get the word ..."

"Tolerate?" said Miriam.

"Yes, tolerate, tolerate all the things I was being asked to do. And then, suddenly, it was no longer at all clear and I realised that it had just been a dream."

"Dreams are what make people able to go on living under the most intolerable conditions," said Miriam. "Most people have some dream, some plan for the future which colours the present, gives them hope."

"What happened to your dream, Miriam?" asked Laura.

"My dream, my plan to go back, remained strong as the year passed, as I became six and then seven, Then one night, I got out of bed, because it was so hot and there were eight of us in a room, me and my three brothers and my sister and three cousins" ... she saw again the cramped, airless room laid out with thin mattresses, and smelt the smell of eight bodies varying in age from five to fifteen, girls screened from boys by a rough curtain down the middle of the room...

"Anyway," she continued, " I went to sit on the stairs, where it was a bit cooler, and I heard my aunt and uncle and my father talking ..." – she heard again the guttural Yiddish which was the common language – " ... and I heard my father say that he had had news that morning from someone that the bodies of my mother and Daniel had been seen by someone on that fateful night and that there was no doubt any longer that they were dead. And as he said this, I realised that I had really known this all along, that the chances of my mother being alive were so small that they really didn't exist, and that my plan had only been a dream, a way to get through the days and weeks and months without her. So I went back to bed, and lay awake for a long time ..."

"So did I," interrupted Laura. "Ages."

"It's the best time to think," said Miriam with a smile. "Often the only time."

"Go on," said Laura. "What did you decide?"

"I decided that I had to make the best of what I had. That I was lucky to be alive, and lucky that I still had my father and my brothers and sister even though I would never see my mother again, and that it was stupid to go on yearning for what I couldn't have."

"So you never did go back?" said Laura.

"Never. Not even when I could have, after the Revolution, before the war. I don't know why. Perhaps I thought it would be pointless to churn up old memories, that they were better left alone. Sometimes I wish I had – I can still see the river, and the cobbled streets, and the places where we used to go and play. But there would probably have been nothing left, and that might have been worse. Anyway, I never did go." She stopped, suddenly aware that she had told Laura, who seemed somehow to have slipped under the professional barrier she put up against most people, more than she had meant to.

"Your story is much worse than mine," Laura said. "You make me feel bad, making such a fuss."

Miriam looked contrite. She shook her head. "No, Laure," she said, picking up the crystal ball and cradling it in her hands, "you must not feel bad because of what I've told you. I told you only to make you understand how I knew how you were reacting, why I can understand so well what has happened to you. Though of course it is my job to understand, as well. But, Laure, your story is just as important as mine. Don't under-estimate what's happened to you. You're right to feel so strongly. You've been torn up by your roots, forcibly taken away from everything you knew, and you were on your own. I at least had brothers and a sister. But now, at last, you're realizing that the only way to survive is to grow new roots, ones that are planted in reality, not dreams. One cannot go back, Laure. You couldn't go back, not now that you know the truth about where you come from, who your parents were. And in one way you *are* much luckier that I was – you can go on knowing what you've left behind, you can absorb it into your present life."

"We can still go to France in the summer then?" said Laura, an anxious expression on her face.

"Of course. It's what we've planned, and there's no reason to change it. You know ..." Miriam hesitated.

"I know what you're going to say," said Laura. "You're going to say that the Bonnevilles would have had to say 'No' to me."

Miriam nodded. "They would have been in an impossible position. They wouldn't have known what to do, with you pressuring them on one side, and your grandmother and their own knowledge of the truth on the other. I want you to promise me you'll tell them that you have accepted the change in your life. That although you don't necessarily like it, you will stop fighting against it." She got up. "I need some coffee. Would you like some?"

Laura loved the strong black coffee that Miriam let her have. The smell reminded her of France, and she wondered again how the English could drink the disgusting brown liquid such as was served at Baynes and call it coffee.

She stood up and wandered restlessly round the room, looking at the photographs that were displayed on every possible surface. Many of them looked old, yellowed, and one or two were in a brownish tone instead of the usual black and white. Laura peered carefully at them, trying now to work out which were Miriam's brothers and sisters. There was one group of about ten children and three adults. They could be Miriam's father and her aunt and uncle. She picked up the photograph and carried it to the light. The men both had heavy, bushy beards, one with dark hair, one with greying hair and more unkempt than the other, while the woman looked thin and worn, though her smile was bright enough. She wore a dark shawl pulled tight across her floor-length dress and her hands caressed a small, dark-haired girl standing in front of her. On either side, and in front of the adults stood children of various ages. Their dark eyes looked solemnly at the camera. There, thought Laura, her eyes focusing on a thin girl of about ten, that's Miriam. The eyes had the same long, hooded look that Laura knew so well, and the patrician lines of the nose were unmistakeable. The gaze that met Laura's was profoundly melancholy.

The smell of coffee wafted deliciously from the kitchen and Laura put back the photograph, embarrassed that Miriam might catch her looking at it. She wondered if Miriam had said more than she meant to about her background, and felt glad that she had, because it must mean that Miriam didn't just think of her as a patient. When Miriam came back into the room, carrying a tray, Laura was gazing out of the window, watching the cars splashing through the still heavy rain. Miriam put down the tray and joined her at the window.

"It's so English, isn't it?" she said, and Laura nodded, thinking of the hot, hot summers in Belay when even the thinnest cotton dress had seemed too warm.

"Does it always rain here?" she said.

"Yes," replied Miriam. "Always." She turned away to pour out the coffee. Laura's bowl was a smaller replica of the blue-rimmed breakfast bowl which Miriam used throughout the day, an affectation which Laura recognised, without quite being able to put it into words, as being a way in which Miriam could remind herself of something which had gone from her life. The coffee was black and bitter and Laura put three sugar lumps into her bowl and used a fourth to make a *canard* to dip into the coffee and suck until the melting grains of coffee-flavoured sugar broke off in her mouth.

"What happened to your brothers and sisters?" she said as Miriam resettled herself behind her desk.

"We're here to talk about you, not me," replied Miriam. "But to satisfy your curiosity, they all survived and made a success of their lives. Three of them are in America, and one of them is still in France." I hope, she added silently to herself, for nothing had been heard of Nathan since the first year of the war. His name had been given to the International Red Cross tracing service but they had had no more luck than she had had on her own. She was not, however, going to burden Laura with that.

"And I am here, waiting to talk to you. Tell me how you came to this decision of yours?" She sipped her coffee, her black eyes intent once more on Laura, no longer gazing inwardly back to her own troubled childhood.

Laura told her of the little nagging doubt which had crept so insidiously into her mind, undermining the plan which she had thought so certain; of how she had never properly envisaged her future until the long sleepless hours two nights ago; of how she could no longer remember clearly the faces of her old Belay friends. Miriam listened intently, making an occasional note, her dark head supported on one long-fingered hand. In the rain-sodden, darkening afternoon the room was a warm cocoon of light. The tall, tapering grandfather clock, which reminded Laura of the one in the salon at Belay, steadily ticked the minutes away.

As she talked, Laura felt more and more how impossible it would have been to try to go back to Belay as if nothing had happened. How could she forget, now, the truth of her existence? How could she deny the reality of her grandmother, or pretend that she had not had a mother called Caroline and father called

Robert. She realised, sadly, that she was finding it easier every day to refer to those whom she had thought her parents as Tante Marie-Claude and Oncle Paul, though she still longed unbearably for the familiar touch of Marie-Claude's soothing hand, and the deep gravelly tones of Paul's voice as he checked her *devoir* or played some boisterous game.

As she finished talking, the clock struck five, and she clapped a hand in horror over her mouth.

"I've got to go," she said, springing up from her chair. "I've missed changing, and tea, and Matron will be livid, and at six we have to go back to June's to have supper and go to bed. They make you go to bed terribly early ..." She caught Miriam's eyes raised in a glance to heaven which once again said that she could not understand the ways of England and their boarding schools, and together they laughed, united in scorn.

"Don't worry," said Miriam. "Sit down. I'll drive you back soon."

"But they'll be cross that I've missed tea – they have to know where you are all the time."

"Not when I've talked to Edith Morrisson," said Miriam, picking up the telephone. "Are you hungry? I never have tea. Here." She pushed a box of rich, chocolaty florentines across the desk and Laura took one and delicately bit into the nutty sweetness. Miriam was speaking to Edith Morrisson, saying, "Yes, I know, Edith. She'll be back, I forgot the time, it's my fault. I'll drive her straight to, what is it you call it? Jean's? ... Oh, June's." Miriam listened, her eyebrows rising higher and higher until Laura thought they might disappear into her black hair.

"No, Edith, I disagree with you totally. There must be no more changes. She is not coming under a bad influence. Quite the contrary, in fact ..."

Laura could hear Miss Morrisson's clear, rather harsh voice saying something in which she distinctly heard the words "Harriet" and "incorrigible."

"Oh, really, Edith," Miriam interrupted. "It can hardly be called a crime not to plait your hair ... yes, I know rules should not be broken ... well I think it would be a great pity to separate them. Laura has become very good friends with Harriet and Georgina. They give her a great deal of support." She looked over at Laura, who nodded vigorously. "A great deal, Edith. I'd be grateful if you would make *no* changes to the arrangement we agreed on ... yes, I would say it was very important ... Thank you, Edith. I'll see she's back in Matron's clutches by six o'clock." She put down the phone.

"Well, I seem to have saved your friend Harriet from a fate worse than Baynes," she said in English, though up to now she and Laura had been talking in French, and her face widened into the creases of laughter which always followed one of the word-plays which she loved to make in any language. "What on earth has she done to incur such anger from your respected headmistress?"

Laura explained how Harriet seemed to be unable to keep out of trouble. "And she's got a terrible temper, too. She poured orange juice over someone's hair on Friday."

"Really?" said Miriam, her mouth trembling with laughter. "I like her style. Though I can see it wouldn't go down too well at Baynes. But I thought she was terribly timid and shy?"

"Oh, she is," said Laura. "Harriet's very shy. Only sometimes, something seems to come over her and she can't help doing these awful things. And she's unlucky, too," she added. "She always gets caught while other people, like the girl she poured the orange juice over, always seem to get away with things."

Miriam sighed. "I've met people like that. It's something to do with lack of confidence, I think. They hesitate, and then they're lost. That's what the English proverb says – he who hesitates is lost.

And there are some people who just seem to be unlucky – the one the bird-dirt falls on, the one who always gets someone taller in front of them at the theatre, the one who reaches the front of the queue when everything's sold out."

"She's not always like that," said Laura, determined to protect her friend from this unflattering picture, though in fact she thought Harriet probably was unlucky in precisely that sort of way. "And she did win the English Cup. I didn't win anything."

"You will, Laura, you will," said Miriam. "Now that you've made up your mind to stay." She stood up. "Come on, we'd better get you back." She picked up the box of florentines. "Here. Take these. You can have a midnight feast, or whatever it's called."

As she watched Laura disappear up the steps of June's, the box of biscuits hidden under her blazer, Miriam wondered how this little French-speaking waif, with her cat's eyes and sallow face, had managed to get through her barriers. I like spending time with her she thought; it's like therapy for me, as well as for her, and realised that she had not spoken to anyone for many years about the events which had shaped and formed her so long ago. I'm the same age as the century, she thought, and a scene which she had not consciously thought of for decades flooded her memory: of herself on her fifth birthday in the primitive, hardly-remembered kitchen of the house in Russia, her mother preparing the chicken for the Friday night dinner – probably an old hen, thought Miriam now, but her taste buds could still remember the fragrant broth – while Miriam looked on. Her mother had wiped her hands on her apron, and pushed a strand of hair back off her brow, saying: "You're as old as the century, Miriam. Five years of this century, and you're five years old today." And she had taken a still-warm cake from the batch she had just baked and given it to Miriam before pushing her out of the kitchen to play with her friends.

A feeling of utmost loneliness and longing swept over Miriam, a feeling which she thought she had buried long ago when she had, in her twenties, come finally to terms with her history, and had put the past behind her. Now she wondered bleakly what she was doing in this cold English town, where there was no culture, no life, no *joie de vivre*. Only a famous hospital, which had welcomed her warmly when she had run once more from persecution, this time managing to escape before her life was literally threatened, but feeling the spectres of those earlier soldiers always at her back. For a moment she was tempted to lay her head on the steering wheel and weep but then thought, what's the point, and, resolutely switched on the engine and turned the car in the direction of the hospital. This was the reason why she was here. To give succour and support to those wrecks of humanity who could go on no longer, who had called for help by cutting their wrists, or swallowing pills, or by just refusing to get up, or go out. And, she added, to help one little girl whom she vowed would not go through the torments she herself had suffered. Her thoughts brightened again as she thought of Laura, and when she drew up in front of the hospital she was vital with energy once more.

***

The last Saturday of the summer term was a perfect July day, the air warm and balmy, the sky a luminous blue. At Baynes, there was a feeling of regret in the soft air, a suggestion of things coming to an end. Girls who were leaving in a few days to make their way in a bigger, less safe world than they had become accustomed to, found themselves unexpectedly sad, the excitement of graduating overwhelmed by the knowledge that this was the last weekend they would ever spend as schoolgirls here at Baynes. Some of them spent the day frantically making sure that they had all the addresses, contacts, and assurances of friendship that they needed to carry them into their new lives. Others went quietly, alone, to visit their favourite places, saying sad farewells to the gardens and buildings that had seen them grow from untutored juniors to self-confident young women. A few, whom Baynes had not blessed and who had not conformed to Edith's patterns, were honestly glad to go, and said so, jubilant that at last they would be able to move without the constraints of Baynes rules, Baynes customs, Baynes expectations.

Younger girls spent this last Saturday building on this year's friendships, subconsciously laying foundations for next year's successes. Addresses were swopped, visits arranged. Some friendships were ended, some enmities forgiven.

In the Junior classes, excitement bubbled. Everyone wanted to go home. Only Georgina dreaded the end of term, though warned by Harriet she kept it hidden. Later that afternoon they were to go with Laura to tea with Miriam, a visit that seemed to put a gloss even on this last Saturday's shining perfection. Meredith danced around them.

"Where are you three going to?" she said. "No one goes out on the last weekend."

"Well, we are," replied Harriet, "so boo sucks to you."

"Where to?" insisted Meredith, practising ballet steps around them, pointing her long legs and making the muscles which Harriet often tried to draw swell in neat tight bunches, so that her legs looked sinewy and strong.

"Mind your own beeswax," said Harriet.

But Georgina, not wanting an argument, said, "We're going to see a friend of Laura's." She glanced at the big clock over the mantelpiece. "Come on, it's time we got ready. She'll be here soon."

In the dark boot room, with its smell of leather, dampness and drains, they shrugged their blazers on over their cotton frocks. Their panama hats shaded their faces, so that Miriam, when she arrived to collect them, could hardly tell which girl was which.

Laura stepped forward and said shyly, "This is Dr Stein," and Harriet and Georgina put out their hands politely. "Miriam, please," said Miriam, smiling, her black eyes missing nothing as she observed the girl whom she had protected so vigorously from Edith's condemnation, and the other whom Edith so obviously favoured, but from whom Miriam now felt a strange coolness, withdrawal, awkwardness, a loss of the open sunniness she had observed a few months ago outside the sickbay. She couldn't quite put her finger on what it was.

"You must call me Miriam, as Laura does," she repeated. "I hate being called Dr Stein."

Georgina and Harriet looked at each other. They had rarely before been invited to call an adult who stood in such a position of authority by her first name.

"How do you do ... Miriam," said Georgina, less shy than Harriet, and Harriet followed suit, muttering "Miriam" into her chest, her face once again going the unflattering shade of pink which she was unable to control. Miriam shook hands with each of them, looking carefully at each face as if she were planting it in her memory. Harriet smiled, but Georgina, who could normally stare anyone out, looked away.

It was an unforgettable afternoon. Laura, who had been reluctant at first to admit her friends into the hallowed sanctum of Miriam's flat, subconsciously jealous of anyone else knowing the pleasure she took in having the entrée to such a kingdom, found herself in the pleasant position of intimate, allowed to show off Miriam's possessions as if they were her own. She enjoyed watching her friends' faces as Miriam opened the door to her study and they took in the red walls covered with the myriad pictures, photographs and hangings which had first bewitched Laura, and looked in amazement at the shelves crammed with books, chairs piled with books, and corners untidy with books. Papers were flowing off the big desk, and on the mantelpiece cards and pieces of paper were stuck behind vases and ornaments and into the corners of the great gilded mirror that reflected their astonished faces.

"This is where I do my work," said Miriam. "But I'm not working today, so let's go into the salon." She shut the door and led the way into the room which reminded Laura most of France. It was not a sitting room in the usual English sense. The chairs were formal and hard, covered in green and gold striped brocade. The sofa, similarly upholstered, looked wide and slippery. On the floor was an intricately patterned carpet, its once-rich colours faded into delicate, subtle shades of red and blue, which Miriam had told Laura was centuries old. Two paintings dominated the room, one a shimmer of dotted colours which seemed to flood out into the room, the other of a woman standing in a pattern of light and shade so pleasing to the eye that one could not avoid looking at it. A complicated piece of furniture filled almost one wall, carved into many small drawers and doors in a heavy, almost black wood. Laura had once opened one of the little drawers but had started back in dismay as its parallel on the other side had opened too, and had quickly closed it.

The three girls stood at the door of this room, two of them struck silent by its formality, the third feeling once again the strange thrill of recognition this room produced in her, its atmosphere, its sense of having been undisturbed for days so like that of the salon at Belay that she half-expected to hear Marie-Claude's well-remembered step in the passage behind her. She turned away, tears welling unexpectedly. Harriet and Georgina remained in the doorway. Their eyes ranged over the rich furnishings, but they were reluctant to go in, feeling that by their very presence they would damage something, and Miriam, laughing, shut the door again, and said, "On second thoughts, perhaps not. We'll have tea in the study after all."

"Everything in that room is precious," said Laura, proprietarily, recovered from the moment of sadness, as she led the way back to the study. Miriam had turned away to the kitchen to bring in the tea.

"It's beautiful," said Harriet. "But a bit uncomfortable, do you think?"

"The French always have salons like that," said Laura. "They don't have comfortable sitting rooms, like you do here."

"Our drawing room has a big soft sofa and chairs," said Harriet, "and so does Granny's."

Georgina said nothing, as she thought of the room at home that was never used, furnished with a table covered with a chenille cloth, some unmatched dining chairs and two uncomfortable armchairs facing the cold fireplace. There were no pictures, no books, and no comfort. A faint, painful emotion went through her composed of jealousy, disloyalty to her mother, and the beginnings of anger, and she realised that she had been feeling odd, cross and uncomfortable, since they had got into Miriam's car.

Harriet and Laura were looking at the pictures and photographs, but Georgina sat down at a chair at the table by the window, and gazed unseeingly at her shoes. Soon, too soon, she would be back at home and once again unable to fit in. I don't fit anywhere, she thought, not here, not at home, and the almost palpable feeling of irritation grew stronger.

Miriam came in, carrying a tray. She put it on the table, and reluctantly Georgina made herself help to put out the delicate cups and saucers and plates of sandwiches, scones and cakes. One plate held slices of something which looked like bread but which was almost black in colour.

"What's that?" she said, forcing herself to sound interested. Miriam shot a glance at the beautiful but brooding little face that almost, but not quite, hid the smouldering anger Georgina was trying to control. She wondered again about Georgina.

"That? That's black bread, pumpernickel, a kind of German bread. I thought you might like to try it," she said.

"It looks horrible," said Georgina rudely, surprising herself as she found herself unable to hide the anger in her voice.

"Not if you're hungry," said Miriam. "In fact, it's delicious. Come and sit down," she said to the others. "Tea's ready."

She poured tea into four cups, and put a slice of lemon into each. Harriet looked puzzled.

"Excuse me," she said, "but may I have some milk in my tea?"

Miriam laughed. "I'm sorry," she said. "I don't understand English tea. This is the nearest I can get. It's China tea, and you drink it with lemon and without milk, but with sugar if you like."

Harriet took a sip. "It's strange," she pronounced, "but quite nice. I'll try some sugar."

"That's how I like it, with sugar," said Laura, passing the sugar bowl. "What about you, George, do you want sugar?"

Georgina looked defiantly at Miriam. "I'd rather not have any tea," she said.

"Oh go on, George," said Harriet. "Try it. It's nice."

"Don't force her," said Miriam quietly. "Though I'm surprised that someone who has the enquiring mind which I've heard that Georgina has isn't willing to learn a new taste."

Georgina looked out of the window. She didn't know why she was being so rude and stubborn, and what had caused the quiet anger to simmer away inside her. Was it envy? She wondered if she was about to lose her temper, like Harriet, but knew instinctively that she wouldn't. Miriam was looking at her, waiting for a reply. I mustn't go on being so rude, Georgina thought. Why am I behaving like this? I've got to stop it. She forced the anger down, promising herself that she would think about it later on, but not now, not now. Harriet was looking at her, a troubled look on her face coupled with surprise that Georgina, who was always equable and calm, who always knew what to do, should be so strangely out of step here.

Although it was only a second since Miriam had spoken, the room seemed as though it were waiting until Georgina replied. I will stop being cross, I will answer politely, she willed herself, and suddenly felt capable again of being herself, not this strange prickly creature whom she hardly recognised.

She lifted her head towards Miriam. Her brooding face cleared and the striking looks that had astonished Miriam the first time she had seen Georgina, on the morning after Laura's immersion in the Pond, came back.

"All right ... Miriam ..." she said, a smile blooming on her perfect features, "You're right. I will try it. It's silly not to try new things. May I have a piece of that funny black bread, too? I'm sorry I was rude about it."

Miriam passed the bread, and they all took a piece. Laura and Harriet declared it all right, not wonderful, but Georgina ate her piece with curiosity, savouring each bite, and said, when she had finished, "Well, it was ... different." Everyone laughed and some of the tension lifted from the room.

Miriam thought to herself, I don't seem to be handling this properly. I feel as though Georgina is an adversary, though for what reason I don't know. She passed the scones and the cakes, but ate nothing herself, not used to the heaviness of an English tea. As they ate, Laura and Harriet told her about Baynes, Harriet backing up Laura's ever wilder claims about the silliness of some of the rules, and about the way everything always had to be done in the Baynes way. Georgina said little, though she laughed with the others when they laughed, and agreed with remarks put to her, while she delicately ate her way through the strange new biscuits and bread that had arrived in a very welcome food parcel from David and Leah in New York. Most of all, she liked the florentines, recognising them from the box they had shared with Laura a week or two ago. Laura was talking about all the clothes they had to have at Baynes.

"Seven pairs of knickers and seven pairs of linings," she said. "And three Liberty bodices ..."

"What on earth is a Liberty bodice?" asked Miriam. "What is it in French?"

"I don't know," said Laura. "I've never seen one in France. And I thought liberty meant freedom, but it actually does the opposite. One more layer of clothes to put on."

"It's got rubber buttons all over it," said Harriet. "We'll show you, next term. We don't wear them in the summer." She was feeling wonderfully at home with this exotic woman who seemed to be interested in everything they said.

"That's a date," said Miriam. "Go on, what other funny rules are there?"

"Well," said Laura, "you're not allowed to sit with your friends at meals ..."

"... and you're not allowed to link arms with another girl ..."

"... and you're not allowed to lock the bathroom door ..."

"... and you have to put hospital corners on your bed ... and fold your rug in a special way ..."

Miriam looked puzzled, and was about to ask what hospital corners were, when Georgina said quietly, "And you get the best education you could find anywhere. If you don't like it, you should go somewhere else." The smile had faded from her face again and she looked defiantly at her two friends.

Laura looked surprised, but Harriet, who had known Georgina longer, said, "It's OK, George. I know you like it. I just think some of the rules are silly."

"Maybe," replied George. "But it's still probably the best school in England. I think I'm very lucky to be there."

Is that what this could be about, wondered Miriam suddenly. Could it be that Georgina was at Baynes on a scholarship? That might explain the resentment she felt from Georgina towards her possession of so many old, beautiful, and valuable objects, and to her proffering of new tastes and ideas. If she came from a poor or deprived background, she might feel that Miriam was testing her to see if she could fit in, or was watching her to see if she made a mistake. Miriam wished now that she had not produced the strange bread and cakes – if she were right, it would explain the peculiar rudeness about the black bread, and the initial refusal to try the China tea. But the last thing Miriam wanted was to be seen by Georgina as someone who was trying to catch her out, or dig secrets out of her which she did not want to divulge. And perhaps, thought Miriam, because of what Laura has said of me, Georgina thinks I am capable of seeing these secrets by some kind of magic. And then she thought, well, of course, I am, though not by magic, but by observation, deduction, knowledge of human nature. But if I'm right about Georgina, it will seem to her like magic. I must be very careful.

She determined to ask Edith to see if she was right, but remembering the strict rules that Baynes, and Edith, enforced on the anonymity of scholarships, thereby ensuring that no girl felt different from the rest, she doubted whether she would tell her. She wondered whether Georgina had told anyone she was on a scholarship, if, in fact, she was – would she have told Harriet or Laura?

"I think you're right," she said to Georgina, who was still wearing the defiant look on her face. "Baynes is renowned. I just think the rules are a bit odd, but that's probably because I'm not English. Now tell me what you're all going to do in the holidays," she continued, looking from one girl to another, and firmly changing the subject.

"I'm going to London to see my father," Harriet answered, wriggling slightly in her chair. "He's … he's divorced. And

Arabella, that's his new wife, is going to have a baby quite soon," she finished, looking slightly embarrassed.

"That will be nice," said Miriam, suspecting that it would not be. "Do you want a brother or a sister?"

"I don't mind," said Harriet, who had not really thought about the actual fact of a living brother or sister, as opposed to an anonymous baby.

"I'd like a brother," said Laura, "a real brother I mean."

"I've got two, and they're awful," said Georgina, and they all laughed.

"Why?" asked Harriet, and Georgina told them how noisy they were and how big and how they were always arguing with each other. She's not quite telling the truth. Miriam thought, she's not giving anything away about her family; just making amusing, funny remarks that could be about anyone. She got up from the table.

"Well, you'd certainly eat me out of house and home," she said. She looked at the clock ticking away in the corner. "I'd better drive you back, or I'll be in Edith's bad books once again."

They groaned theatrically, pushing back their chairs. Then Harriet said, "Edith," pronouncing it as Miriam had, in the French way, Aydeet, and they all giggled. The tension had quite gone suddenly, and Miriam realised she had enjoyed having these three so different children in the flat, which would feel empty when they had gone.

"You must all come again next term," she said. "Laure will arrange it."

"Why do you call her Laure," asked Harriet. " Her name's Laur – aa."

"It just slips out," said Miriam, remembering that Laura had been called Laure by the Bonnevilles, as well as Laurence, and glancing at Laura to see if it hurt. "In France Laura is Laure. You don't mind, do you, Laura?"

Laura shook her head and shrugged. "It's just another name, Laura, Laure, Laurence ... what does it matter?"

Miriam was about to say that of course it mattered, it was part of someone's identity when Harriet defused the moment by saying, "In England Laurence is a boy's name, so no wonder we all got confused when you said Laurence was your name. It must be funny to have so many names," said Harriet. "Laura, Laure, Laurence. I'm just called Harriet."

"Or Harry," countered Laura.

Georgina said nothing, burying her knowledge of the name Gloria as deep as it would go.

"Have you got any nicknames, besides George?" Harriet asked, turning towards her. Georgina smiled her wide innocent smile.

"No," she said, " not really. Just George."

***

Once again Georgina lay awake, her thoughts chasing themselves round and round. She felt hot as she thought of the rude way she had behaved at Miriam's tea party. Harriet had said to her, as soon as Miriam had dropped them at school, "What got into you, George? Didn't you like going there?" and Laura had waited, worried, for George's answer.

"No, no, it wasn't that," said Georgina swiftly, making up the lie as she spoke. "I just had a headache, a bit, and I wasn't very hungry. But then, when I started eating, I felt much better and the headache's gone now. It was probably just the flap of going home. I wonder if our trunks will be there?"

The trunks would be packed and on Monday sent on their way 'Luggage in Advance' and their appearance in the dormitory was the signal that term was truly almost at an end.

Sure enough, when they reached their attic room, the trunks were there, waiting for Matron's swift packing and the final addition, tomorrow, of the things which would be brought over from the Main School. On Monday morning, the last books and the leather photo frames which usually garnished the white chests of drawers, bringing a breath of home to the room, would be laid on the top, and that night the dormitories would appear empty, like ghost rooms, only the clothes for the last two days left in the cupboards and drawers, and by each bed would be a small overnight case waiting to be filled on the last morning. Excitement hung in the air, and there had been murmurings higher up the school about midnight feasts and other festivities to mark the end of the year, but at June's Matron's ears were too sharp and the only celebration would be louder than usual talking after lights-out on the last night.

But now there were still three more days, precious to Georgina, until Wednesday morning. She turned restlessly in her bed once more. The house was silent and almost no light came in through the yellow curtains. It must be very late, she thought. The anger that had come to her that afternoon was still there, rumbling and spitting like a dormant volcano. It was so unfair, she thought, so unfair. Why had she been born into the mean threadbare family that was hers, instead of, like Harriet and Laura, into a comfortable upper-middle-class heritage that accepted education and learning as natural? Their houses were filled with the kind of books she had seen at Dotty's; their way of life did not include most of the things that hers did. She must be the only girl in the school, she thought, whose mother came home every night smelling of fish, tired, harassed, unable to provide the smallest companionship for her precocious daughter, who in the holidays spent a great deal of her time by herself, reading or drawing, mooching round the Public Library, and going to see Dotty.

Other girls in the street thought her odd, she realised, and any with whom she used to be friends she had grown away from. Her voice and her manners made them think she was 'stuck up', which Georgina quite liked because it meant that she had moved up from their level; and she would lift her head and walk away with her nose in the air as if there were a bad smell around, her very manner showing that she didn't care.

Sometimes she went to Edna's sister's house, where Auntie Vi did not have to go out to work, but Georgina hated the unspoken criticism from her aunt and her two older girl cousins, who asked endless questions about her 'posh' school, and imitated her voice. "Go on, wor Gloria," they would say, "let's hear you speak posh." They were both at the local secondary modern and spent their holidays doing each other's hair, painting their nails, and making eyes at boys when their mother wasn't looking. Their only reading matter was magazines, which they called 'books', and their favourite outing was to the Spanish City in Whitley Bay, a garish amusement park near the seafront where the big dipper, the swingboats, the roundabout, the dodgems and the ghost train would swiftly swallow your money, leaving just enough to buy fish and chips to eat from the newspaper wrapping, while you lounged invitingly against a smeared wall, eyeing the boys. Georgina had been there a few times with them, but they thought her too young, and too much of an embarrassment, to suggest that she came with them often.

"Keep your mouth shut, kiddo," her elder cousin had advised her kindly when Georgina's clear tones had attracted a sneer from the gang of boys playing the pinball machines in the entrance.

Her spirits drooped even lower as she thought about this. How her cousins would despise Baynes, she thought; and how Baynes would despise them. Once again, she wondered how long she would be able to keep up the pretences. She distrusted Miriam, whom she felt had been able to pierce her secret self with her black, all-seeing eyes. She wished she could sleep, but her worries about what she might have given away that afternoon were too great.

I must look at it calmly, she told herself, and, thinking back, decided that she had exaggerated what had happened. She had said nothing that might give away her background, although she had been rude and ungracious. She had no way of knowing whether Miriam had guessed that something was not as it seemed, and all she could do, if she ever saw her again, which she would avoid if she could, was to behave as carefully as she usually did. Care was what mattered. Care in everything she did. And that meant not letting herself go as she had this afternoon. Anger was dangerous, and so was jealousy. She would refuse to recognise those emotions, she decided. Never, ever again would she speak in anger. It shouldn't be too difficult, she thought. Calmness and confidence came to her easily, and she naturally tended to deal with any kind of crisis coolly, with thought beforehand. It was rare, she realised, for her emotions to run away with her as they had this afternoon. She wondered why they had, and decided it must have been because of the unwelcome end of term. And perhaps, also something to do with Miriam, who somehow made her feel transparent, exposed. Another good reason for avoiding her as much as possible. Was there anything else she must do, she wondered. Was anyone else a danger? She didn't know how she would do it, but she must prevent Steve from coming here, no matter what it cost. And Mam.

At the thought of Edna, a great longing came over her to be enclosed by Edna's strong red arms. She missed Mam more than she usually admitted to herself, instinctively burying the insidious, weakening emotion before it had time to overcome her. But tonight, it didn't matter. Term would be over in three days, and she could admit to herself how much she longed to see Edna again, longed to hear the sound of her mother's key turning in the door.

She thought how shocked everyone at Baynes would be to know that she had her own latchkey and spent most of the day doing whatever she wanted, going wherever she wanted. Sometimes she went to the cinema, if Edna had given her enough money. Other times she might wander along the sea front as far as Monkseaton, and then be so tired she had to take a bus back. Sometimes, on these expeditions, she would see girls of her own age out with their mothers, being shepherded into a car, or having their hands held across a road, wearing what she recognized as expensive, cared-for clothes, and a stab of jealousy would shoot through her, sharp as a knife. The pain would go back home with her, making her short with Edna, monosyllabic in her answers, as the hatred for her own mean circumstances filled her. She would imagine those children going to riding lessons, and ballet lessons, being invited to birthday parties by similar children, whose mothers all knew each other. They would go to schools like Baynes, would speak with the clear, concise voices she had become used to at Baynes. They would never know what it was like to live in a sordid street in a mean part of town, where every evening the men lurched drunkenly out of the pubs, their coarse voices jeering and cursing, spitting into the gutters. They didn't frighten Georgina, but she sometimes imagined what her friends at Baynes would say if they found themselves put down in her place. She shuddered. It was not to be imagined, not dreamed of.

For a split second, she wished that she were back as she had been, not knowing about Baynes, friends with the girls in her street, the same as them, unaware that a different kind of life was available. Then the wish was gone, replaced with the burning ambition that had become her customary state of mind. She stared up into the dark, not seeing it, but seeing instead the road she was going to follow. The road which led away from home, Edna, her father and brothers, Marlene and Deanna, fish markets and corner pubs. The road which would take her into the world of Harriet and Laura and further, to London and abroad, to worlds which she did not yet know, but which she knew were waiting for her. She was going to get there, and if it meant lying and deceiving, weaselling her way round interfering know-alls like Miriam, well so be it. In the dark, her small, dimpled chin jutted forward. The important thing was, she thought, never to forget what she was determined to achieve; never to give in to anger, or jealousy, or homesickness, or even, perhaps, love. Emotions like those made you vulnerable, made you give things away. And that, Georgina vowed, she would never do.

Relaxed suddenly, clear now about what she wanted to do, she turned over, and the dreamless sleep of the innocent, or those who think they are innocent, wrapped her gently in its arms.

CHAPTER Seven

The summer holidays of 1947 seemed long and sweet to Harriet, back in the security of home in the house Isabel had bought in Newcastle, near to, but not too near, her grandmother's house. She loved being alone with her mother, waking up with the day spread out before her, not run by Baynes rules, nor measured by Baynes timetables. The freedom of being able to get up when she wanted to, being allowed to eat what she liked, being able to put on the clothes she chose, seemed to Harriet the purest freedom in the world – a feeling she was to carry with her all her life, as if Baynes had marked her forever with its insistent disciplines.

She also loved having her mother to herself, though Isabel sometimes seemed preoccupied, lost in her thoughts for minutes on end, and Harriet's chatter sometimes seemed as if it were interrupting a conversation which Isabel was conducting silently with someone out of sight. But these preoccupations did not last long enough to worry Harriet, and the days passed in pleasant nothingnesses: some days they might go to the big library in town or they might go shopping in one of the department stores, treating themselves to coffee in the restaurant. She liked watching the ladies in their smart hats, the ritual of pouring out the coffee, the sampling of the biscuits. Sometimes Isabel would be greeted by someone she knew, and then Harriet was subjected to questions about school, usually followed by puzzlement as to why she was not at her mother's old school, as the friend's children, if she had any, were. Isabel would say vaguely something about Alec having insisted on Baynes, and turn the conversation, and Harriet herself would wonder why Isabel didn't insist that she came home now. But when she pressed her, Isabel's face would take on the vague but stubborn look that Harriet was getting used to, and Harriet knew that it would be no use losing her temper or shouting; Isabel would not change her mind.

There were walks in parks and visits to the Coast, where they would sit on the sands, eating their lunch of hard-boiled eggs and bread and butter wrapped in grease proof paper, with a thermos of tea for Isabel and some orange squash for Harriet. Sand would get into everything, crunching in your mouth as you ate, but in the magic of the vastness of the sea it didn't matter. She would construct elaborate sandcastles, then watch the tide run in and fill the moat until suddenly everything melted away. She would paddle cautiously at the edge of the sea – the water frightened her and she would never go in more than leg deep. She would search for shells in the rockpools, and climb the cliffs while Isabel looked on half-worried, half-admiring. Once, having walked further along the sea front than usual, they had found a big white arch with the words Spanish City written on it in garish lights. Harriet wanted to go in. She could see swing boats and roundabouts, and could hear tinny, jazzy music, but Isabel laughed, and pulled her away.

"It's full of horrible people," she said. "Rough boys. You won't like it," and reluctantly Harriet had followed her mother back to the sea front. On the way home, Isabel bought her an iced lolly, a new treat. It tasted blissful to Harriet, the cold melting orange filling her mouth with sweetness, much better than sickly Eldorado ice cream. It was while she was sucking this lolly that she thought for a moment that she saw Georgina in the distance, walking by herself, but the figure disappeared rapidly along the promenade, and Harriet decided she must have been mistaken. George would not have been alone, she thought. She was too young, as she herself was.

Then, at last it was time for the promised visit to Alec and Arabella. She was apprehensive about this. It seemed a long time since the Easter holidays, and although she had happy memories of Arabella then, this time would not be the same. Arabella was expecting a baby for one thing – although Isabel had pointed out that Arabella must have already been expecting in the Easter holidays, that was different because Harriet hadn't known about it – and for another, Arabella's younger sister would also be there. What if they didn't like each other? And what was someone like when they were about to have a baby? Would her father have time for her? Isabel had told her that he was very busy at the moment, making money. "Making money is what he's really interested in – that and pretty women," she had said in an uncharacteristically bitter voice, and Harriet had seen a look of hatred come momentarily into her mother' face.

"What did you mean about the pretty women?" Harriet asked but Isabel had just smiled and said, "Well, Arabella's pretty, isn't she? That's all I meant." And Harriet had had to be satisfied, as Isabel had picked up her book and immersed herself in it, not hearing Harriet when she spoke – or pretending not to, thought Harriet crossly, though she knew it was no use trying to interrupt her mother when she was reading.

The visit was not totally successful. The flat seemed the same at first, when Harriet arrived, her room waiting for her with its pretty bed and chair, but another bed had been put into it, making the room look smaller, with alien clothes lying on it, including a pair of jodhpurs. Neither Arabella nor her unknown sister was there.

"Ariadne's gone riding in Rotten Row, and Arabella's gone to watch her," said her father puzzlingly. He had been silent in the car on the way from King's Cross, where she had been deposited by one of Granny Carruthers' friends, although he had seemed pleased to see her, but Harriet had been busy looking out of the window. Now she frowned.

"What's Rotten Row?" she asked.

"It's part of Hyde Park," Alec said, "Where rich people go to ride. You can hire horses in Knightsbridge."

This was not much clearer, and the reference to rich people worried Harriet. Was Ariadne rich? Was Arabella rich, too? Would it matter that she, Harriet, couldn't ride?

"Unpack your suitcase, Harriet," said Alec. "You must be helpful to Arabella. She gets very tired."

"Because of ... because of the baby?" Harriet said hesitantly, embarrassed.

"Yes. Because of the baby." Alec looked equally embarrassed, his big, well-fed face flushing red. It was the first time he had actually spoken to Harriet about the baby. He cleared his throat and looking out of the window said, "I hope you're, well, pleased about the baby, Harriet. It will be a new brother or sister for you."

"It won't be the same – it's not Mummy's," said Harriet. "Like I am."

"Well, of course not, not quite the same. But it will be a half-brother or sister," Alec said. Harriet guessed that he didn't particularly want to talk about it. She wondered whether it would be prudent to change the subject, and then decided stubbornly that she wouldn't.

"It won't be the same as having a proper brother or sister, and now I'll never have one," she said sulkily. "So I'm not really interested."

Alec looked put out. "That's enough, Harriet," he said. "What can't be changed can't be changed. Arabella is my wife now and I don't want to hear any more about proper brothers or sisters. This new baby will be your brother or sister."

Harriet looked at the floor, scraping her sandal along the edge of the fur rug. It rucked up and Alec said crossly, "Put the rug straight, Harriet. I don't want Arabella to trip over it, not in her condition."

Harriet bent over and straightened the rug, the sulky look still on her face. As she looked up, Alec touched her shoulder.

"Come on, now, Harriet," he said. "You mustn't worry about it. You'll always be my wonderful first child. Remember all the things we used to do. Remember the first time I took you to the sea?"

This was one of Harriet's earliest memories, the faintest remembrance of the sensation of wonder on beholding the immense blue-grey water spread out in front of her, seen from her father's shoulder.

She nodded, and forced a faint smile. It would be foolish, she thought, to let the anger she was beginning to feel towards this new baby get out of hand. Anyway, she didn't want to spoil this visit, and she suspected that Arabella would not be forgiving about making a scene.

"It's my first memory," she said.

"Right, then," said Alec, looking relieved. "I remember that day as if it were yesterday. You were only two. And nothing is going to change that, is it, Harriet?"

"I suppose not," she said grudgingly. "But you're bound to like the new baby. You'll be with it all the time."

"Of course I'll like it Harriet," Alec said. "We'll all like it. But as to being with it all the time, I don't think so. Not like I was with you. Arabella wants a Nanny, and so do I. I'm much too busy to deal with a baby crying in the night. Now with you, I used to get up in the night often, when Mummy was tired. So that makes you special, doesn't it? The new baby won't get that."

But it will get all sorts of other things, thought Harriet silently. She forced herself to sound cheerful.

"Are we going to the theatre this time?" she said.

Alec looked relieved at this change of subject.

"Of course," he said. "We're going to a show. Not the ballet – a musical. All four of us."

"How long is Ariadne staying?" said Harriet.

"As long as you are, a week," replied Alec, his big hand rubbing his cheek, a habit which Harriet had forgotten but which she remembered he tended to do when he was pleased with something.

"You'll like her," he said. "She's only two or three years or older than you, though she's growing up fast. Grown out of her jodhpurs. Had to borrow a pair of Arabella's." He indicated the pair lying on the bed. "Wouldn't you like to learn to ride, Harriet? I'm sure we could arrange it."

It was the last thing Harriet wanted to do. She found the girls who rode at school boring – they tended to talk about and draw horses all the time. And horses were terrifying, with their huge eyes and huge nostrils, their ears flicking and their legs pawing the ground.

"No I wouldn't, Daddy. I hate horses," she said.

Alec looked disappointed. "Well, that's a very stupid reaction," he said. "We'll see later on. It's a useful accomplishment to have. I ride, when I get the chance."

Harriet looked surprised. Daddy had never ridden when they lived in the country.

"Used to when I was young. Of course, your mother never liked it, so I gave it up. But now ..." He stretched himself, and yawned, running his hands down his body, which Harriet thought looked heavier than it used to. "Keeps me fit. And of course, Arabella's a first-rate rider, used to win all the prizes when she was younger." He smiled with pride. "Now get that suitcase unpacked, Harriet. They'll be back soon."

He rubbed his big hands together, as if satisfied at the thought of Arabella and his young sister-in-law coming back to the provision he had made for them in his warm, comfortable flat, with its daily housekeeper, its portered lift and its newly furnished nursery suite, accomplished by buying the smaller vacant flat next door, and converting the two into one. There's nothing he can't organise, thought Harriet, as he went off to the kitchen to warn Mrs Thing, as he called her, to prepare tea. Except Mummy, he couldn't organise her to his satisfaction, she thought. He had failed with her, and of course, Mummy had failed him in return. She could remember them arguing about people coming to dinner, or about Mummy not wanting to go somewhere with him ... He can't tolerate failure, she thought, and wondered why she hadn't seen it before. That was why she could not risk being asked to leave Baynes. She felt a hot flush of shame and fear come over her as she remembered how close she had come to it, and hoped that Daddy would never hear about it. Her report hadn't said anything directly. Only she had known exactly what Morry meant with her comment about Harriet "not always conforming to Baynes standards", and had promised Mummy that she would try harder next year.

Soon they heard the sound of Arabella's key in the lock, and she came into the drawing room with a quick, light step, carrying the bulk of the baby proudly before her. Her face looked fatter, and younger, thought Harriet, but the hug she gave her was the same – warm, welcoming and as if Harriet was the person she had been longing to see most. Harriet hugged her back, though the bump was embarrassingly rather in the way, and then Arabella pushed her away, saying, "Let me see how you've grown, Harriet. Oh, you've still got your hair in plaits. Didn't your mother like it loose?"

Harriet shook her head, not knowing why Isabel had not liked her hair hanging loosely down her back, held in place with the navy-blue velvet alice band. "It'll get too untidy for you," her mother had said, swiftly plaiting it up again.

"No," she said, "But I did. So I'll do it that way tomorrow." A whisper of disloyalty touched her but she ignored it.

"It looks really pretty loose," said Arabella, and turning round pulled the tall, fair-haired girl who had followed her into the room towards Harriet. "Harriet, this is Ariadne," she said.

The girl held out her hand. She was very like Arabella, thought Harriet, but with something added, something Harriet couldn't put her finger on. Her face was the same perfect oval, her eyes the same deep grey, but the nose was tilted more, and the lips had a little, fleeting, crooked smile which seemed to hover there all the time, as if she were secretly laughing about something. A few years on, when Harriet saw the Mona Lisa, she recognised Ariadne's enigmatic smile. Her long blonde hair was pulled back into one thick, straw-coloured plait.

She was wearing jodhpurs, a brown tweed jacket and a yellow aertex shirt. She looked like a boyish version of her sister, and she also looked unquestionably more adult than any of the Baynes girls, even those in the sixth form.

"Hello, Harriet" she said. Harriet took her hand and shook it. The little smile on Ariadne's face widened.

"I'm awfully glad you've come," she said. "We'll have some fun."

Harriet felt a surge of relief. This might be all right. She smiled back.

Ariadne flung herself into one of the yellow silk sofas and looped her long legs over the arm.

"Ari, take your boots off," said Arabella, glancing over her shoulder from where she was leafing through a pile of letters at the desk in the window. "I've told you before. No boots in here. You'll put mud on the sofa."

"Oh, don't be so middle-class, Ari," said Ariadne. "You won't make me, will you, Alec?" She removed her legs from the sofa arm nevertheless, and getting up moved towards Alec.

Harriet looked in amazement at her father. Surely he didn't allow Ariadne, who was only a year or two older than she was, to call him Alec? Alec, however, only smiled deprecatingly, and put his arm round Ariadne's shoulder.

"You can do no wrong, as far as I'm concerned," he said laughing. "I'm your champion, Ariadne." Ariadne looked up at him as he hugged her close, and then catching sight of Harriet's surprised face, Alec put out his other arm and pulled her to him. "Two little girls I've got now," he said, "though you're not so little any more, Ariadne." Harriet saw a secretive glance pass between him and Ariadne. She looked at Arabella, who was plumping up the cushions now, one hand pushing downwards on her back. As she straightened up, she groaned theatrically. Alec instantly dropped his arms from the girls' shoulders and going over to Arabella said firmly, "You've been overdoing it again, darling. Sit down here." He levered her on to the other sofa and placed a cushion behind her. "Bring me that stool, Harriet," he ordered, and lifted Arabella's feet carefully on to it.

"There now, darling. You sit there. Mrs Thing's got the tea all ready. I'll just call her."

"Alec, you are the limit," laughed Arabella as he opened the door. "Her name's Mrs Mason. You mustn't call people Mrs Thing. Now go and organize the tea, and let me talk to Harriet. Come and sit here beside me."

She patted the seat next to her on the sofa, and Harriet placed herself carefully there, determined not to do anything clumsy that could upset Arabella. Obviously, pregnant women had to be treated with great care. She let her eyes stray to the huge bump. It was hideous really, like a monstrous balloon. She thought of the book about babies and how they were made. It sounded ridiculous, she had thought as she read it, and disgusting, impossible, really, and now thoughts of Daddy and Arabella doing what the book said they had to have done flashed with horrible clarity through her mind. Involuntarily she drew back a little from Arabella, and hoped she would not notice. But Arabella was laughing with Ariadne about some incident in the park with the horse.

"You looked so funny, Ari," she said, "riding along with that chap with the huge moustache. Did he talk to you through it."

"A bit," replied Ariadne, who had compromised by removing her riding boots and throwing them into a corner. She was stretched out on the other sofa again, her hands behind her head. "He's Lord Glendiven's son – the On Rollo."

"Of course," said Arabella. "I thought I'd seen him somewhere before. When I was a deb he was supposed to be a great catch. He was on Ma's list of 'not safe in taxis' men." She laughed. "I wonder what being kissed by that moustache would be like?"

"Ghastly," said Ariadne, knowledgably. How could she possibly know, thought Harriet. She's only thirteen. And who was this On Rollo? Ariadne was still speaking. "Anyway, you ought to know, Ari," she was saying. "Alec's got a moustache."

"Nothing like the On Rollo's," countered Arabella. "Alec's is lovely. Just a bit scratchy."

Harriet felt herself going red at this reference to kissing Alec. She couldn't get the pictures in the book out of her head. She looked at the bump again and to her horror she saw it move in an undulating sort of way under Arabella's dress. Arabella didn't seem to notice, and at that moment Mrs Mason, followed by Alec, came in with a tray.

"Mrs Mason, you're a treasure," said Arabella as the housekeeper put the tray down before her. "What would I do without you?"

The thin, middle-aged woman, wearing a flowered pinny tied round the back, and a scarf tied like a turban over her hair, smiled at Arabella. "It's nothin', mum," she said. "I'm pleased to 'elp out."

"Have you met my step-daughter, Harriet? This is Mrs Mason who keeps your father and me in order," she said, turning towards Harriet.

"How do you do, Mrs Mason," said Harriet getting up from the sofa.

"Pleased to meet you," Mrs Mason said, looking her up and down, her voice twangy with the thin cockney accent that Harriet found not as friendly as the north-country voices she was used to. But Mrs Mason's smile was wide as she said, "You'll be lookin' forward to the little 'un comin'?"

For a moment Harriet didn't understand, then she saw Mrs Mason's eyes had moved to Arabella's bump, and she said quickly, "Oh yes, I suppose I am." The lie came out smoothly and sincerely, and Alec smiled approvingly at her over Mrs Mason's head.

"That'll be all, Mrs Mason, thank you," he said, rubbing his hands together again.

"I'll be off then, Mrs Bolton, Mr Bolton. There's a casserole in the oven, and you just need to put a light under the potatoes."

They could hear Mrs Mason gathering her bits and pieces together, and then the closing of the front door. Arabella was pouring tea, Alec watching her, with a pleased, possessive look on his face. He surveyed his females.

"This is what I like," he said, smiling. "All my women together. Thank you, darling." He took a cup of tea from Arabella and stood sipping it, balancing on his heels.

"Oh, for goodness sake, Alec! We're not your *women*. You sound like a Sheikh with his harem," Arabella said, then turning back to Harriet and smiling her wide, gentle smile, said again, "Now tell me what's been happening to you, Harriet," and Harriet felt herself gathered up in the warmth of Arabella's interest once again, and remembered why she had wanted to come back.

***

The sun was still streaming in from the west, filling Harriet's bedroom with yellow light, when she and Ariadne came in to fling themselves on their beds. They were supposed to be having baths and getting changed for dinner. Harriet had forgotten how formally Arabella and Alec ran their lives, and for a moment she hankered for scrambled eggs on toast on her knee with Mummy.

Ariadne stretched her full long length on her bed, her hands behind her head, her blonde hair, which she had undone from its plait, fanning out on the counterpane. One leg was casually resting on the other bent knee as she gazed with apparent interest at her foot, pointing and turning it.

"Your Dad's not short of a bob or two, is he?" she said.

It had not struck Harriet before that her father was rich.

"No, I suppose he's not," she replied, hesitantly. "But ... well, I've never thought about it."

"You would have if you lived with my parents," said Ariadne cryptically. "They're always on about being broke."

"But your father's a Lord," said Harriet, knowing it sounded stupid as she said it.

"And I'm an On," said Ariadne. "It doesn't stop us having no money."

"What do you mean, an On?"

The answer came to Harriet in the instant that she spoke. Blast, she said to herself, blast, blast, blast, I'll sound stupid again. Ariadne was already speaking.

"An honourable, stupid. You know, daughter of a Lord. We're all Hons."

"Oh, yes, I'd forgotten," replied Harriet, trying to look as if she'd known all along. "Who's all?"

"Me and Arabella, and Piers and Tristram. They're both at Eton."

She gave Harriet a long, cool look.

"Your family's not nearly as grand as mine, is it?" she said. "But it doesn't matter, because your father is rich. My father said a bit of new blood was no bad thing, either. He didn't want Ari to marry anyone we're related to, and as we're related to hundreds of people it was going to be difficult for her not to. Then Alec came along. I think he's super." She stretched out her leg again and inspected it, then leapt off the bed in one smooth, athletic move.

Harriet blinked. She was not used to hearing her father described as super, especially not by someone who had smiled as Ariadne had smiled when she said his name.

Ariadne twirled around once in the middle of the room and was now practising a ballet step, going up on her toes and down again, the leg muscles flexing. She reminded Harriet of Meredith.

"I suppose you're too young to have a crush on anyone?" said Ariadne. Harriet smiled weakly.

"Well, yes, I suppose so," she said, not looking at Ariadne.

"Well, I've got a crush on your father. It probably sounds stupid to you. But he's so attractive. Sexy."

Harriet felt a blush rushing up her face like the tide. She turned away, but not before Ariadne had seen.

"Oh," she said her hand flying to her mouth. "Oh, I say. I'm sorry. I've embarrassed you. That was unforgiveable. Please, Harry, I can call you Harry, can't I? Please Harry, that was so stupid. I'll never mention it again. You must think me a complete idiot. I am, I admit it, I am."

As Ariadne spoke Harriet felt the beginning of laughter. It was really terribly funny, someone having a crush on her father. The laugh reached her lips, and her shoulders began to shake.

"You're not crying, are you?" asked Ariadne, a horrified look on her face.

"I'm sorry," said Harriet, unable to stop laughing. "I'm sorry, it's just so ... so ... so funny. I mean, Daddy ..."

Ariadne's lips twitched and then, in an instant, they were both laughing uncontrollably, lying on their beds.

"You said he was … sexy …" giggled Harriet, and a new wave of mirth overtook her.

"Well he is …" replied Ariadne, forcing each word out between gusts of laughter.

Harriet's stomach hurt, and she felt as if she would never stop laughing. Ariadne had her face buried in her eiderdown.

There was a rap on the door." Hey, you two," Alec's deep voice said outside. "Stop that noise and get a move on." He opened the door a crack. "May I come in?"

Harriet and Ariadne looked at each other, trying to keep their faces straight.

"Yes, you can come in, Daddy," said Harriet, her voice breaking on the Daddy.

Alec opened the door. "Well, what are you two laughing at? Can I share the joke?" He had changed from his city suit into cavalry twills and a blazer, with a dark red paisley patterned silk scarf tucked into his shirt collar. His face was newly shaved and his fair hair brushed neatly back. Harriet could visualize him using his two hairbrushes. The faintest waft of a pleasant, woody scent came into the room with him. At that moment, Harriet saw why Ariadne had what she called a crush on him, and why Arabella had married him. For a moment, she hated him, for being attractive, for leaving her mother, for being his cocksure, successful self.

"You wouldn't understand, Daddy," she said. "It's a private joke."

Alec looked again at Ariadne and back at Harriet. He beamed, his big face shining with good health and the knowledge of his own prosperity.

"I'm glad you're getting on so well. But get a move on. I thought I'd open a bottle of champagne – would you like that?"

"I love champagne," said Ariadne. She had composed her face again. "You are a brick, Alec. A super, super brick," she added teasingly.

Alec looked pleased. "Right then. You two have your baths and put on your prettiest frocks." He shut the door and they could hear his feet going down the corridor towards the kitchen.

"I've never had champagne," said Harriet. The conversation they had had about Alec seemed to have made them intimate friends.

"Oh, it's lovely," said Ariadne. "It tickles, the bubbles get up your nose. And you can get marvellously drunk on it."

"Drunk?" said Harriet disbelievingly. "You haven't been drunk?"

"Yes, I have. Twice." retorted Ariadne. She was stripping her clothes off quickly, flinging them on to the bed in a way that would have made the Bun storm.

"It's great. You don't care what you do. We did it last hols, when Ma and Pa were out. Piers and Tris and I. We opened two bottles. It was so funny. And I felt all right the next day, which you don't if you've mixed the kinds of drink, like we did last Christmas. We all felt awful but we couldn't tell Ma why. Bags first bath."

She flung a purple paisley-printed silk dressing gown round her shoulders. "D'you like this? It's an old one of Pa's. I think it's rather fetching. I pinched it." She was out of the room before Harriet had time to speak.

Harriet started removing her own clothes slowly, thinking about Ariadne. What an extraordinary girl. So like Arabella, and yet not in the least, really. She put on her camel Jaeger dressing gown, and caught a glimpse of herself in the mirror. She looked boring and childish compared to Ariadne, she thought, so plain, with her sandy-coloured plaits and her pale face. She remembered what she had said to Arabella, and pulling the ribbons off her plaits undid them quickly, almost crossly, as if she were defying her mother. She picked up her brush and began brushing her hair hard to get out the kinks that the plaiting had left. By the time Ariadne returned she had found the navy velvet hair band that she had slipped secretly into her case that morning.

"Oh, Ari's right," said Ariadne, coming back into the room, looking exotic in the purple robe. "That suits you much better, Harry."

Harriet smiled and nodded. "Thanks." she said. She looked shyly at Ariadne." Have you got a nickname?"

"Well, I'm called Ari, short for Ariadne, by most people. And so's Arabella, which confuses everyone. That's why we do it." Ariadne laughed. "You don't mind if I call you Harry, do you?"

"That's what my best friends call me," said Harriet, feeling recklessly honest and wanting Ariadne to call her Harry, but at the same time sensing a minute, indefinable doubt.

"Well, I will too," said Ariadne. "I'll be a best friend too. Ari and Harry. It sounds nice together. You'd better hurry," she added. "You could skip the bath."

Harriet agreed, and with what her mother called a lick-and-a-promise removed the grime of the train from her face and hands in the bathroom, and pulled out her best dress, the one with tiny bright flowers on a white ground, which she loved. But its puffed sleeves and round neck looked childish next to Ariadne's calf-length navy and white spotted dress which turned her from a boyish tomboy into a sophisticated adolescent. She had taken two hairslides out of her sponge bag and fixed them expertly in her thick fair hair, lifting it on either side of her face into a graceful curve.

"Are you allowed to wear it like that at your school?" Harriet asked, awkwardly doing up the buttons up the back of her dress.

"No. They're so boring. You have to have plaits. Here ..." She had been smearing a pale pink lipstick over her lips, which made her look even older. Now she held it out to Harriet.

"D'you want to try this?"

Harriet took it tentatively. "It'll look stupid," she said. She drew it over her lips. It had a thick, sweet taste, like cheap boiled sweets. "Ugh," she said. "How can you bear it? It tastes horrible." She wiped off the pink goo with her handkerchief, already grimy from the train.

Ari smiled as she took the lipstick back. "I don't care what it tastes like if it makes me look sexy," she said, peering into the mirror. She raised an eyebrow and made her mouth into a soft moue. "Bet your father would like to kiss me," she giggled, and then said "Sorry, I forgot. We said we wouldn't talk about it."

Harriet felt the uncomfortable warm blush again pricking the skin of her neck. A picture of her mother flashed into her mind, sitting alone in her armchair in the sitting room, reading, as she so often was, the soft lamplight shining on her reddish-brown hair and her gentle, always worried, face.

"Bet he wouldn't," she said. "He's married to your sister." She hung her dressing gown over the purple silk on the back of the door. "Come on. Daddy hates it when anyone's late."

It was a sparkling evening, the champagne turning it into an occasion. Alec made Harriet drink half a glass, and she began to understand what Ariadne had meant. She felt confident and free, as if she could go anywhere and do anything. Arabella's bump stopped worrying her, and began just to seem part of Arabella. Alec directed no secret glances at Ariadne, which, Harriet realised, with the fleeting clarity which champagne had given to her thoughts, had been worrying her. Another picture came into her mind, from years ago she guessed, of Daddy with Mummy in their old house in the country. The room was full of people, and Alec, standing beside Isabel, had been looking past Harriet at someone behind her with just the look he had given Ariadne earlier. She blinked, and the picture disappeared.

"What would you call the baby, Harriet?" Arabella was saying. "It's got to have a name you like."

"Oh, I don't know," replied Harriet. "You could call it Mrs Tiggywinkle ... or Tommy Plug."

They all laughed, and Daddy caught her eye and winked, and said to Arabella, "Tommy Plug is someone only Harriet and I know about." He was referring to a story he had made up when she was small.

"You are funny, sometimes, Harry, you do make me laugh," said Arabella with a fond smile, and Harriet basked in the moment of glory.

After dinner they played cards, rummy and whist, and Daddy said she must learn to play bridge later on. Ariadne did some card tricks which she said she had learned from the gardener's boy at home, and Arabella got out some miniscule Viyella nighties and tiny white cardigans, which she called matinee coats, to show Ariadne and Harriet.

"Aren't they sweet?" she said. She smoothed the bump with her hand, looking top heavy and suddenly tired. Harriet looked at the tiny clothes and couldn't imagine a human being so small. They would fit Dinah and Dorinda, she thought. She fingered the soft wool and suddenly thought with excitement of the baby who would be her brother or sister. Tonight he or she seemed very near and she felt as if she belonged to this group, Alec, Arabella and herself – but perhaps not Ariadne who had gone to stare out of the open window. The hot summer air, smelling of trees and petrol, floated in, bringing with it a snatch of music and distant voices.

The telephone started ringing in the hall and Arabella went to answer it, saying tiredly, "Who on earth's phoning at this time of night?" They could hear her speaking, her voice lightening as she said, "Oh, hello, Mummy ..." and then Arabella came back into the room, looking excited.

"Ari," she said to her sister. "It's Ma, for you. You've been invited to Hatchcombe for the weekend, to stay with Cecilia."

Ariadne's eyes widened.

"Hatchcombe!" she said. "Oh, Ari, that's fantastic. Wizard!" She dashed from the room.

"What's Hatchcombe?" said Alec, looking enquiringly at his wife.

"It's the Griffin's place. Lord and Lady. They're friends of Ma's and Pa's, and Cecilia's their youngest. She was going to go to school with Ari, but she's got a governess instead."

"Oh," said Alec flatly. "I thought governesses had gone out with the ark."

"Oh, no. We know one or two families who still have them. Like the Royals. I don't think it's a good thing. Boarding school did me and Ari a world of good. Oh, dear." Arabella sighed. "She'll have to go in the morning. She'll have to go home first. She hasn't got the right clothes here. They're having a house party and a dance and they want her to keep Cecilia company." She glanced at Harriet, who felt the fun draining out of the evening with Ariadne's imminent departure.

"I thought she was staying a week, like me," Harriet said, a feeling of something akin to anger stirring as she realised that there would be no question of Ari staying here if she could stay with this boring Cecilia instead. Another Hon, she thought, I bet.

"I'm sorry, Harriet," smiled Arabella, putting her arm round her and pulling her close to the bump. "You don't really mind, do you? You'll have me. Not that I'm much fun at the moment, with this." She patted the bump. "But you don't turn down an invitation to Hatchcombe. Not if you can help it. She'll meet masses of people there. It's really important for her social life."

Alec raised an eyebrow at Harriet.

"Arabella will be organising your social life next," he said. "How about that?"

Harriet felt a thrill of fear run through her. How could Daddy say that? She didn't want to be organised to go to parties and dances. She would be terrified.

"No, Daddy," she said, knowing he would be angry, and wondering why she could never hold her tongue. "I don't want to go to those sort of things …"

Arabella, as usual sensitive to Harriet's moods, interrupted.

"Of course not, Harriet. You're much too young. Don't worry. By the time you're old enough for me to arrange anything, you'll want to go to dances and things. Ari's very grown-up for her age. When you're fifteen or so …" She gave Harriet a little hug, but the words seemed like a threat, and Harriet decided that she hadn't heard, and that she wouldn't go, whatever Arabella organized.

Ariadne burst back into the room.

"It's going to be the best weekend ever," she said excitedly, dancing round the room. "Come on, Alec, waltz with me."

She whirled herself towards him, and Alec put out his arms, ready to join in the infectious high spirits. He started humming the Blue Danube and together they waltzed away, round the big room and out into the corridor.

Arabella shrugged and said to Harriet. "Don't worry, we'll find some nice things to do. I'm going to bed now. I get so tired …"

She started putting the lights out, and Harriet followed her from the room. Alec and Ariadne were waltzing their way back, and Arabella put out her hand and seemed to pluck Alec away.

"Spoilsport," said Ariadne, continuing to waltz by herself.

"You'll have to catch the ten thirty-five tomorrow," said Arabella, pausing at the door to her bedroom. She smiled enviously. "You lucky thing. It's years since I've been to Hatchcombe. You'll have a wonderful time."

"I know," said Ariadne smugly. "Come on, Harry, let's go to bed. I'll tell you all about it."

Harriet slept soundly that night, lulled to sleep by Ariadne's endless chatter about dances and balls, boys and parties, who would be there, who she wanted to dance with. She was suddenly glad that Ariadne was going the next day. She couldn't keep up with this frantic social life that she seemed to lead, didn't want to know any more about her friends who all seemed to be called names like Bunny and Mouse and even Boy.

She woke to find Ariadne already dressed, and the morning passed in a rush of packing, taxis, and waving goodbye at Paddington Station. Ariadne didn't seem to mind a bit about going on a train by herself, and Harriet wondered how soon Daddy and Mummy would let her travel alone.

It was to be sooner than she thought.

Three nights later, after coming home from what Daddy had called a Show and Arabella a musical, which Harriet had found boring, though she hadn't let on, she woke to hear noises in the hall. There was not a glimmer of light through the curtains, so she knew it was very late. She crept out of bed, and opened the door a crack. Alec was pacing up and down, obviously waiting for something.

"What's happening, Daddy?" she whispered, slipping out into the hall. She heard a murmur from Arabella's room, like a sigh or a suppressed groan.

Alec looked irritated to see her. "It's the baby," he said. "I think it's, um, decided to come early. The doctor's on his way."

"Oh," said Harriet blankly. She decided she didn't want to know any more. "I'll go back to bed then."

"Well, now you're up, go and see if Arabella wants anything."

Harriet wondered why he didn't go. He'd hear the bell just as easily from the bedroom. She said nothing, and knocked tentatively on Arabella's door.

Arabella was lying flat in bed, the hump huge under the eiderdown.

"Oh, Harriet," she said weakly. "I'm sorry. Did we wake you?"

"It's all right," said Harriet. "Daddy wanted to know if you want anything." She saw that Arabella had a faint dew of sweat on her face, which was so white that it looked pale green. Harriet hoped she wasn't going to be sick. She hated seeing anyone be sick, almost as much as she hated being sick herself.

Arabella smiled faintly. "I didn't know he was such a coward," she said. "You could bring me a glass of water."

Harriet went into the bathroom that led out of the bedroom. It seemed odd to see her father's shaving things and hairbrushes next to Arabella's makeup and scent on the glass shelf above the two peach-coloured basins. The bath was peach coloured too, with gold taps, and the carpet was the same as the bedroom's, a pale oatmeal colour. She ran water into a glass, thinking as she did so that she had never seen so luxurious a bathroom. The bathroom at home had lino on the floor and a white bath and basin. She carried the glass carefully back into the bedroom. She must have missed hearing the bell while she had been running the tap, because Alec was ushering someone into the room. He gestured crossly at Harriet to get out, waving his hand backwards and forwards. Harriet put the glass down.

"Well, well, who have we here?" said a plummy voice, and she turned and found herself being looked up and down by an imposing, cheerful man, even at this hour wearing a black jacket and striped trousers.

"Yours?" he said to Alec, placing his hand on Harriet's shoulder. Harriet felt embarrassed at being in her pyjamas. Alec, nodded, irritated, but Arabella said from the bed,

"Harriet. This is Mr Swift. He's my obstetrician." Harriet wondered why he wasn't called Dr Swift.

Mr Swift patted Harriet's shoulder again.

"Well, there'll soon be a baby brother or sister for you, I think," he said cheerfully. He removed his hand and turned towards Arabella. Harriet fled back to bed.

She had not been able to go back to sleep. She left her bedroom door open a crack, and strained her ears listening. After a while, she heard the doctor come out and pick up the telephone and guessed he was phoning for an ambulance. After a long while, during which Harriet listened with dread for Arabella moaning, but could only hear a murmur of voices, she heard her father go into the drawing room. There was the chink of a bottle, and she wondered what the doctor was doing. What did a doctor do when a baby was on its way? How long would it take? She moved restlessly, tense and sleepless. The doorbell rang, and there was lot of noise as Arabella was carried out. Then there was silence, and Harriet wondered if Alec had forgotten that she was there. She crept out of bed again. The flat was empty, but the front door was open, and as she padded along the hall she heard the whine of the lift, and ran back to bed.

"Just a precaution, old boy," she heard the doctor say as he and Alec re-entered the flat. "It's probably on its way, but it won't be tonight. I'll have that drink now, if I may?" Harriet heard the door shut to the sitting room, and the comfortable deep murmur of male voices. She stretched and suddenly felt unbearably sleepy, almost sick with tiredness. She wondered faintly what was happening to Arabella, and then she woke up to find bright morning shining through the curtains, and knew by the way the sun was brilliant on the buildings opposite when she opened them that it must be late. The flat seemed silent, then far away she heard a chink of china.

Mrs Mason was busy at the sink.

"You 'ad a long sleep, Miss," she said, smiling. "Never mind, better late than never. I'll get your breakfast. 'Ad a broken night, then, didn't you?"

"Has anything happened?" asked Harriet tentatively, hardly wanting know the answer. Whatever it was, it would be embarrassing and to do with having babies.

"No, and not likely to neither," replied Mrs Mason enigmatically. She put some bacon into a pan. "Your father, Mr Alec I should say, phoned the nursing home this mornin'. She's stopped 'avin' the pains, but they're keepin' 'er in, just in case. Poor thing. It's bad enough when they come, without draggin' it out like this ..."

"Did Daddy say what I was to do today?" interrupted Harriet. She didn't want to hear Mrs Mason's comments on Arabella's labour.

Mrs Mason ladled the bacon on to a plate and dropped an egg into the hot fat. The sizzle made Harriet hungry, and she sat down at the table.

"You're to pack all your things ready, because you'll probably 'ave to go 'ome on the train, Mr Alec says." She put down the plate in front of Harriet and poured her a cup of tea from the teapot already sitting on the table. It was dark and strong.

A thrill of fear ran through Harriet. Go home? On the train? Alone?

"By myself?" she asked anxiously.

"Well, of course," said Mrs Mason, raising her eyebrows almost into the scarf tied round her head. She looked like the factory workers pictured in *Picture Post*. "A big girl like you? What are you? Ten? Nearly eleven?"

Harriet nodded her head. "It's just that I've never been on the train alone," she said. "When I go back to school there's always a teacher or someone there. And when I come here I come with one of Granny's friends."

"Well, lucky you," replied Mrs Mason, her hands resting on her hips, her whole face expressing scepticism and a sort of amazed surprise. She turned away. "Don't know how the other half lives ..." Harriet heard her mutter to herself as she started clattering the dishes again.

Alec returned at lunchtime, his big face worried and preoccupied.

"How's Arabella?" asked Harriet anxiously, putting down her book.

"She's all right. But she's got to stay in, till it arrives. Damned nuisance. You'll have to go home, Harriet. I've telephoned your mother. She's expecting you tomorrow. You're to go on the eleven o'clock train." He looked worried.

"Oh," she said flatly. Daddy obviously thought she was a nuisance, and probably she was. She shrank a little into her clothes, her fingers rubbing round the belt of her dress where she could feel Mummy's tiny, neat stitches.

Alec looked contrite.

"Sorry, old thing. Can't be helped. Don't know when the baby will be born and I've got to be free when Arabella needs me." A softened look came into his face.

"Tell you what. I'll go and visit Arabella this afternoon, and we'll go out to dinner, just you and me, this evening. Swift says he's pretty sure the baby won't come for a few days yet. The pains have stopped and it's not due till ..." He stopped.

Harriet had screwed up her face involuntarily and turned her head away as Alec seemed to be about to elaborate on this disgusting birth. Now he put his hand on her shoulder.

"Don't you bother your head about it." He pulled her close. "It's pretty boring for someone of your age. You don't want to hear about it, do you?"

Harriet shook her head.

"I just want to know about going on the train," she said. "Do I have to go by myself. Mrs Mason said I would."

"Well, yes," said Alec. "It'll be all right. You're nearly eleven. Your mother's going to see if your grandmother has a friend coming back, but it's unlikely. Even the old dragon can't arrange everything to suit herself." A strange look, half angry, half obstinate, crossed his face as he spoke of his ex-mother-in-law, and Harriet saw how much he hated her.

The thought of going on the train alone, all that way, on a Sunday, when it would take six or seven hours, filled Harriet with a sort of sick excitement. She was determined, after Mrs Mason's words, not to betray her fear.

"I'll be fine, Daddy," she said.

"Good girl," he said, dismissing the conversation. "Now let's see what Mrs Thing can produce for lunch."

Dinner had been fun that evening, with Daddy treating her as if she was quite grown-up, insisting on pouring a little wine into her glass, and showing her how to read the menu. The restaurant was small and dark, with deep red wallpaper and white-clothed tables set with gleaming silver and glasses. A silver vase holding one deep red rose sat in the middle of each table. A hum of conversation seemed to embrace them, as if they were part of a warm, vibrant, special place, and even when they weren't talking and Alec became silent and preoccupied, it didn't matter. Harriet felt she could stay there forever. Finally, though, the last piece of nutty chocolate cake defeated her. She felt suddenly sleepy and rather sick, and was glad to get home and fall into bed. She could hear Alec telephoning but was asleep before he put the receiver down.

King's Cross the next morning seemed filled with hurrying people. The dank onion smell which hung over the station filled Harriet's nostrils, and smoke and steam floated murkily above the platforms.

Alec hustled her on to the train, looking swiftly into the compartments. He found one that pleased him and slid open the door. A middle-aged woman, her hat still on, occupied one of the window seats. The other was empty and Alec put Harriet's case into the rack above it.

"Here you are, darling," he said. Harriet recognized his voice as one that he used in public, when other people were listening. It was more charming, more modulated than his usual voice. As she thought this, Alec turned to the woman.

"I wonder, Madam," he said, half bowing towards her, his charming smile directed at her. She smiled back. Alec's charm was hard to resist. "I wonder, Madam. My little girl, here, has to travel alone to Newcastle. A hitch in our arrangements ..."

The woman rose to the occasion. "Would you like me to keep an eye on her?" she said. "I'm going as far as Darlington ..."

"That's very kind of you. We'd be so grateful, wouldn't we, Harriet?" Alec said. Harriet had sat down, noting absently the harsh feel of the scratchy cloth on her bare legs. She felt very scared, and smiled faintly at the woman, nodding her head. She hoped she wouldn't feel train sick. What would she do? And what if she wanted the lav? Always before, Granny's friend had accompanied her to the lavatory, and had been waiting for her when she came out. Now, how would she know where to go? And what about lunch?

"Very well," the woman was saying. "She'll be quite safe with me. What's your name, little girl?" Two beady brown eyes fixed themselves on Harriet. A horrid brown felt hat sat on her head like a doughnut. Harriet was sure she had a nasty smell.

"Harriet," she muttered, scuffing the carriage floor with her sandal.

"There are some sandwiches in your carrier bag, darling," said Alec. He didn't usually call her darling, Harriet thought mutinously. The fear was turning to anger. Alec turned to the woman.

"I can't thank you enough," he said, crinkling up his blue eyes. The woman wriggled slightly, and smiled up at him. "A bit of trouble, plans gone a bit wrong," he continued. Don't tell her about the baby, prayed Harriet, but Alec was already launched. "My second wife – about to produce," he laughed. "Three weeks early, quite unexpected ..."

He was backing out of the carriage. Harriet leapt up, and followed him along the corridor. She passionately didn't want him to go. Fear and rising anger made her voice croaky as she whispered, "I'm scared, Daddy. Don't leave me alone ..."

"Don't be silly, Harriet," Alec said, removing the hand with which she was holding on to his jacket. "Come along now. Go back to your seat and sit down. The train's about to go. That nice lady will look after you."

"She's not nice," replied Harriet, her voice rising, rage replacing the fear. "I hate her." She lifted a foot to kick Alec in the shin, the pleasure of giving into rage blinding her to the looks and smiles coming from the nearest carriage. Alec had the door open. He stared at her, his blue eyes cold with fury, and backed swiftly away from her lifted foot on to the platform.

"Don't do this, Harriet," he hissed, as she followed him down. "My God, I'd forgotten what you could be like. Now pull yourself together, and get back on the train." He pulled a handkerchief out of his pocket and scrubbed at her face, where angry tears had sprung up. She pushed his hand away. "I hate you," she shouted. "And I hate Arabella and I hate the baby." She had been about to add that she hoped it died, when the look on her father's face deterred her.

Down at the end of the platform the guard blew his whistle. Doors started slamming and she climbed reluctantly back.

"I've got to go," Alec said flatly, ignoring what she had said. "You'll be all right." He shut the door of the carriage, leaving the window open.

Harriet had forgotten how impervious her father had always been to her tempers.

"Sorry," she muttered. The train was beginning to move. "I'm sorry, Daddy," she said quickly, "I didn't mean it ..." Alec turned back towards the window, already part of the world waiting for him from which Harriet had been excluded. She leaned out. "I didn't mean it," she repeated.

"That's a good girl," he said meaninglessly, his mind already on other things. "You'll be all right. Now go and sit down." His large, well-dressed figure was receding rapidly. Harriet waved and drew her head in, the smoke bringing more tears to her eyes. She felt abandoned, frightened and embarrassed. How many people had heard her shouting, she wondered. Luckily the carriage Daddy had put her in was three or four away from the door ... she hoped the brown-hatted lady had not heard what she had said ...

She slid the door open and made her way to her seat. All the seats had been taken now, and she felt small and squashed against a large woman who sat in the middle seat. The brown woman opposite smiled and nodded at her.

"All right?" she said.

Harriet nodded and pulled out her book from her carrier bag. She felt overwhelmed by all the things that had happened ... meeting Ariadne ... Arabella's baby ... behaving so badly just now. Daddy would probably never invite her again, she thought. Anyway, he would have his new baby. She felt the ache of tears in her throat and turned her head away, staring fixedly out of the window. The backs of houses rushed by, some with gardens planted still with wartime vegetables or overgrown with weeds, some littered with rubbish, old boxes, bicycle wheels, broken down prams. She caught glimpses of children playing, an old man stooping over some chicken wire, a boy on a bicycle riding with no hands, his arms lifted, a grin of triumph on his face. A mother and two small girls watched the train go by, the children waving. These glimpses of lives she would never know, houses she would never enter, made Harriet feel even sadder, watching them speed out of her life, just as Daddy had, just as, she faintly realised, the thought like the faintest ripple on a pool, everything always would, forever and ever, nothing ever staying, always going …

She woke with a start. The train was slowing down, coming into a station. Harriet wondered how long she had been asleep. She looked at her watch. Over an hour had passed since Daddy had left her.

"Slow train, this," someone in the compartment said. "Stops everywhere."

"Sunday travel," replied a man in the corner. "All round the 'ouses. Works on the line, they say. Works!" He sniffed contemptuously. "More like never works. Criminal, I call it. Seven bloody hours to Newcastle." He shook his newspaper and refolded it into a square. "Always gets the workin' man, what can't travel durin' the week."

Brown hat had looked shocked and shaken her head when the man said "bloody," and Harriet vowed inwardly that never, never would she be so boring as to be shocked by a swear word.

The train was moving again, now running between fields, some deep with hay, some harvested into pointed stacks. The hedgerows were thick with summer growth, the trees mighty in their dense green leaves, not yet turned towards autumn. Harriet gazed for a while, then picked up her book. This was not too bad, she thought, and Mummy would be there at the end of the journey. After a while, copying the others, she ate her sandwiches. The brown woman asked her a few questions, but Harriet's monosyllabic answers put her off. The train stopped and started; two people got off, one got on. The sun moved round and started to come in from the corridor side. The brown woman had fallen asleep. The journey felt as if it would last forever ...

Suddenly, Harriet felt the need to go to the lavatory. She willed it away. But the feeling persisted. She wished she had not drunk the orange squash Mrs Mason had packed for her. She wriggled, and crossed her legs. The feeling abated, but not for long. Soon, she knew it was inevitable. She would have to go. She looked across at the brown woman, but she still slept.

Slowly Harriet edged herself forward on her seat. Somehow, she didn't want anyone to see her have to get up and go out. They would all know why. Too bad, she told herself, you'll have to go. The urge was becoming insistent. The man in the opposite corner looked up and pushed open the sliding door for her. The rest of the compartment slept. She made her way to the end of the carriage. The train was full, and two soldiers slept across the lavatory door. Harriet pushed her way on, shocked by the sudden noise as she crossed to the next carriage, suddenly aware of the rushing rails beneath her, the terrible weight of the juddering train. Every junction seemed to be full of men, smoking, drinking beer, sleeping, many in uniform. Finally, she found an unoccupied lav not surrounded by bodies, and pushed open the door with relief. It smelt, and there was paper and damp stains on the floor, but she used it anyway.

She came out triumphant that she had managed, without disturbing anyone and without making some kind of awful mistake. Then the realisation came to her that she couldn't remember which way to go back. Had she turned left or right when she left the compartment? Had she been going with the direction of the train or against it? She had no idea. She tried to remember which way she had approached the lavatory, but it was no good. The corridor side had changed two or three times as she pushed her way along. She could feel sweat in her armpits and knew that her face would be red. She pushed halfway along a corridor, then decided she was going in the wrong direction. She turned round only to decide, a carriage and a half further on, that again she was wrong. She leant her head against the dirty window, hating Daddy for making her be here on the train, alone. She was determined not to cry, though the ache in her throat was there all too easily. She forced herself to think. What would the Famous Five do? Or the Swallows and Amazons? Or Bunkle?

After a while, she realised that the only thing to do was to go all the way to one end of the train, and work her way back, looking into all the compartments. She'd been away quite a long time. Oh God, she thought, please don't let the brown woman be flapping about me. Then she thought it might even be quite nice to see the brown woman. As she thought, she was peering into compartments, each one alien and unfamiliar. Perhaps she wouldn't recognise the brown woman, she thought. She reached the end of the train and turned round. Her heart was thumping and although she knew that her compartment must be somewhere on this endless, crowded, dirty train, her fear told her that it had gone, with her suitcase and her carrier bag, and the brown woman and the swearing man.

She walked and peered for what seemed like ages. The other end of the train was getting nearer. Her dress was sticking to her, fear making her armpits wet. One or two people looked after her as she pushed her way along, one even calling out "Not lost, love, are you?", but she took no notice.

"Little girl, little girl," a voice said insistently. Harriet peered into a compartment. A strange woman was speaking. Then she saw the doughnut hat on the woman's knee and with a sigh of relief slid the door fully open.

"Where have you been?" said the brown woman. "I've been worried sick. I was about to get the Guard. You've been away for nearly an hour. When I woke up you were gone. And I told your father ..."

"I got lost," said Harriet baldly. "I couldn't find the compartment."

"Well, why did you go?" said brown hat, her face peevish with relief, venting her worry on Harriet who looked hot, dirty and defiant.

"I had to," said Harriet, feeling the giveaway blush spreading up her face once again.

"What do you mean, you had to?" said the woman, somehow unable to comprehend what Harriet was trying to say.

"I wanted to... well, I mean ..."

"Oh, give over." The man who had opened the door for her leant forward to speak to brown hat. "Can't you see? She 'ad to go to the toilet. You thick or somethin'?" He turned to Harriet. "Come on, now, love, sit down. Here, 'ave a sweet." He held out a paper bag of Imperial mints, and Harriet took one, stories of not speaking to strange men, and not accepting sweets from strangers, mingling in her mind with gratitude that he had said it for her.

"Thanks," she said. She sat down and turned to the brown woman. "I'm sorry." She seemed to spend her life saying she was sorry, she thought.

The brown woman had tucked her chin into her chest, her head moving slightly backwards and forwards. Now she said to the man in the corner, "No need to be rude. I'm only doing my best ..."

She looked at Harriet. "You're a very rude little girl. I'm not surprised your father wanted to send you home. If you were mine I'd teach you some manners." Her hands shaking slightly, she replaced the doughnut on her head and pointedly turned her head to stare out of the window. Harriet noted that she did not have a wedding ring. So she couldn't be hers, anyway.

The man in the corner shrugged and smiled at Harriet, who grinned back complicitly. He held out the bag and she took another sweet, knowing instinctively that he had no covert designs on her. The train stopped and started, passing through stations she'd never seen before, going round the houses, as the man had said. Then after a long while Harriet realised it was stopping at a station she knew, the one where every term she got off glumly to make her way to the Bayne's bus, and from which every holiday she couldn't wait to leave. She peered out. Without the Bayne's uniforms on the platform, and the Bayne's mistresses waiting for their charges, it was transformed into ordinariness, just like any other station; but Harriet knew that the name on the board would always fill her with the mixture of fear and apprehension which had thrilled through her.

The scenery now was familiar and her earlier fears seemed foolish. How could she ever have imagined getting lost on a train? But even so, thirsty as she was, she decided against finishing the orange squash. It couldn't be too long now before they reached home. Soon the brown woman was pulling her suitcase from the rack, and the nice man in the corner was tucking his folded newspaper into his pocket.

"Bye, love," he said, and winked, as he slid back the door

The brown woman gave the doughnut a fierce last tug, so that it sat even more roundly on her head.

"Goodbye, little girl," she said sternly. "I hope if we ever meet again you'll have learned a few manners."

"Goodbye. I'm sorry," said Harriet once again, and sighed. It was no use. People didn't like her, and she annoyed them, and she kept doing stupid things. The brown woman sniffed.

"You'll be all right now. It's only another hour," she said She dragged her case along the corridor and Harriet hoped she would never see her again. She averted her eyes as the train moved along the platform; she refused to give brown hat the pleasure of nodding at her again.

The sun had moved right round, and its late afternoon beams shone through corridor and compartment window, dust moats dancing lazily in the hazy stream of light. The compartment smelled stuffy and dusty, only one other traveller remaining. More houses were passing the train, then fields, then the huge bulk of Durham Cathedral. Soon they would be swinging over the Tyne, and home. Harriet stood on the seat to heave her case from the rack. She caught a glimpse of her face in the mirror – it was streaked with grime, and wisps of hair had escaped from the sandy plaits. Too bad, she thought, relieved that the journey was almost over. She felt very tired, as if she had walked for miles.

Isabel was waiting for her. Until she saw her, Harriet had been determined to say nothing about the lavatory incident, but the familiar sight of her mother somehow brought to the surface the tears that had been hovering since she had left Alec. Instead of being the calm, competent daughter she wanted to be, she heard herself pouring all the worries, fears and hatreds out in an incoherent stream.

"I'm never going there again," she said. "I hate Daddy and I hate Arabella. And I'm not going on the train alone ever again.."

Isabel sighed and held her daughter close. The crowds coming off the train swirled round them like a river round a log. She stroked the messy hair and mopped the tears with her clean handkerchief, scrubbing some of the grime off. She felt tired and incapable. What was she to do with this bottled up anger, incoherent rage, which was Harriet? She picked up Harriet's case and together they walked to the taxi rank. Isabel had been going to take the bus, but Harriet looked so exhausted she decided that the luxury of a taxi would have to be afforded. As the door slammed she felt she never wanted to see the Central Station again, scene of so many tearful departures for school, so many overexcited meetings. She wished, more than she had ever wished, that everyone, Alec, Harriet, her mother, would just leave her alone.

***

Isabel's marriage to Alec Bolton had not pleased her mother. The Carruthers were solid northern stock, city dwellers and runners of businesses, heavily enmeshed in the politics of the town. Alfred Carruthers had been an alderman, once Mayor, and had left his wife a small fortune, a massive house, and a heavy involvement in local charities. Lilian Carruthers was chairman of two, on the board of others, and on the guest list for most.

It had begun at a twenty-first birthday dinner dance, a grand formal evening. Excitement had filled the air as the guests drank champagne cocktails before the four-course dinner. Isabel had been seated next to a man she had never met and with whom she had fallen in love over the smoked salmon: the rich and glamorous Alec Bolton.

Alec had swept her off her feet, first into every dance that evening, later at theatres, intimate dinners, and parties where she had met his friends; she had been amazed that he should have chosen her instead of the svelte, sophisticated and worldly girls who peopled his social set.

Her mother from the first did not like him. "He comes from a different world, Isabel," she had said disapprovingly. "He's got too much money, like all that set," and on that she was right. Alec Bolton's set were county, not city. His widowed mother lived in a small Georgian house near Alnwick, a pretty frail woman, diminished by the death in a hunting accident of her elder son, Simon, two years earlier. She was to die not long after they had married, of a broken heart Isabel thought, before Harriet was born. There had been a great deal of money and some property for Alec to inherit on top of the money his father had left him. Alec and his brother had not been educated locally, but at a public school in the soft south, another thing Isabel's mother had held against him.

Isabel's brothers, Frederick and Ernest, had felt the same. Frederick, the elder, was a respected solicitor, heavily into local politics, the Conservative party and the Freemasons. He'd shaken his head solemnly after Alec had been invited for Sunday morning drinks by Mrs Carruthers, to Isabel clearly, and also to Alec, though he'd said nothing, a covert vetting occasion.

"Not one of us," Fred had said. "He won't stay the course. You'd be well rid of him." Ernest, who ran the company his father had started said, "I wouldn't give him a job at the works," as if that were the final criterion of acceptability. "He wouldn't last."

But Isabel, drunk on love, didn't care. And Alec saw it as a challenge. "Your mother's a dragon," he'd said later to Isabel. "I don't think I passed the test."

Now Isabel wondered, sadly, if a challenge had been all that she'd been to him.

They'd bought a house up the Tyne valley, a house like Alec's mother's house, Isabel had realised later, and had been happy, Alec training to be a surveyor through an Uncle's up-market estate agency – *The Specialist Estate Agency for Country Houses* was its slogan – Isabel learning to run a house, become pregnant and adjust herself to her new world, and it was this which her gentle temperament found difficult. She would have liked to be left alone with Alec and later Harriet, but Alec wouldn't hear of it. It was necessary to join in, to invite and be invited. Necessary for business, necessary for social contact, necessary for his self-esteem.

But for Isabel's self-esteem it had not been good. When she had married Alec, she had been quietly confident, knew herself to be well-read, on the brink, perhaps, of widening her interests, ready to learn. But what Alec wanted her to learn was beyond her capabilities; she could have coped with anything that might have taxed her brain, but could not cope with activities that taxed her social confidence. Each new encounter was at first difficult, eventually a nightmare. As Alec became more and more the life and soul of every party, she became more and more withdrawn. Her shyness became like a sticky web, through which she could not find her way. Her remarks sounded gauche; she began to be awkward physically, dropping things, or falling over someone's feet; occasionally she had too much to drink in an effort to overcome her lack of confidence, and became ill, much to Alec's shame and silent derision. She began finding reasons not to accept, or not to go, excusing herself with a headache, a cold, a stomach ache. Alec had lost his temper. "Damn it, Isabel, you're my wife for God's sake. It makes me look a fool, turning up on my own yet again. Pull yourself together!"

Then the war came. Alec volunteered for the army, but was invalided out after a virulent bout of pneumonia had left him with weakened lungs, and he came home white-faced and weak, then after a few months of Isabel's care, and delight in having him to herself, his restlessness returned, and the social pressure began again. She told herself to pull herself together, asked people to dinner, to drinks. But soon Alec returned to Newcastle to re-open the estate agency which had closed while he was away, his uncle having died, specialising this time in finding country houses and cottages for mothers with children who were desperate to escape the threat of bombs on the city. Isabel remained in the country with Harriet, while Alec spent more and more time away, sometimes in Newcastle, more and more often in London. His business was expanding, and he was exploiting gaps left by his rivals because of the war. Towards the end of the war, he came home after a protracted stay in London and told her he thought they should separate. He wanted to move to London.

"I suppose you've found someone else," Isabel had said, her guilt at not being able to provide the sort of social life her husband needed prompting her to imagine the sort of woman who could. Alec denied this. He needed to be at the hub of things. "Property will be up for grabs as soon as this damned war is over," he'd said. "It's where the money will be. But I know you, Isabel. You won't want to move to London, you won't want to make new friends, contacts, take people out to dinner. You'd do better to move nearer the old dragon, to somewhere you know. I'll be better on my own. I'm sorry, but there it is."

Her guilt made it impossible to argue with him. She knew she could never give him the things he wanted. It was her own fault; she deserved Alec to leave her.

It was in this frame of mind that arrangements were made for them to separate. It was slow – although coming to the end, the war was not yet over, and Alec was reluctant to let Harriet be moved from the country. Eventually it was decided that Isabel would move back to Newcastle and that Harriet would be sent to Baynes earlier than they'd envisaged; this Alec approved, knowing it would push his daughter into a different level of society from his sworn enemy, his mother-in-law.

Old Mrs Carruthers had watched Alec Bolton wearing down her daughter and, for all her not inconsiderable abilities, had been unable to do anything about it. When Isabel finally confessed that the marriage was breaking up, she was half-pleased, in that she, as well as Isabel, would get rid of 'that man', as she called him, and half-worried, for she suspected that the wearing down of her daughter would be irreversible, and that this final ignominy would deal her a blow from which she would not recover.

But Isabel did seem to recover. She gathered herself together, bought a house, and started slowly to make a new life for herself. She wished sometimes, at first, that Harriet were at home, but Alec refused to hear of it.

"I don't want her under her grandmother's thumb," he'd said. "Your mother's a tyrant, you've said so yourself. She'll turn Harriet into a Carruthers, and that I can't stomach. One was enough for me." Isabel flinched at his cruelty and put the phone down.

Later, she knew that, having been granted custody of Harriet, she could have fought to have her at home, but her spirit was weary. The tussle with Alec would be never-ending. It was simpler to leave Harriet at Baynes.

She had not looked forward to these holidays much. Now that the separation from Alec was complete, and she had grown used to Harriet being away, Isabel valued her solitude, so much so that she was becoming reclusive. Her brothers, both married to solid, worthy women, had urged her to join the tennis club, do good works, play bridge. Make new friends. Isabel had refused.

"Just leave me alone," she'd said. "I'm perfectly happy on my own. Anyway, Harriet will be home soon," she would add, even if Harriet had only just gone back to school. "I have to be available for her."

She knew it was a lame excuse, and after whichever brother had been lecturing her had gone, she would feel guilty at using Harriet, and even more guilty because she simply could not bring herself to do any of the activities her family proposed. She felt, she thought, like a bruised and bent flower, which if watered and left alone might mend itself, grow tall again, but which, if touched and pulled back into shape, would die. She wondered sometimes if she felt depressed; if perhaps she should consult the doctor? But she felt perfectly well, she decided; she just did not want to venture out into the world yet. She read, she sewed dresses for her daughter, thought she might study.

The local paper advertised lectures and talks. She went once but felt that she stood out, being alone, and could not bring herself to go again. She enrolled herself into a class to study history, and paid for it, but when the evening came for the first lecture, she sat quietly in the dark at home until the hour had passed, and then put it out of her mind as something she had made a mistake about.

Lilian Carruthers worried about her, but Isabel had a stronger character than her mother had suspected, and resisted schemes her mother proposed for her re-introduction into local society.

"Do some work for my charities," Lilian had said. "It will get you out of the house at least. You could work in the office – they always need people to address envelopes," but Isabel had shaken her head, smiling slightly, and said, "I've got better things to do with my time than address envelopes."

"What *have* you got to do, Isabel?" her mother said. "Tell me just what you *do* with your time?"

It was a winter teatime, and the delicate china cups with their gold edges winked in the warm firelight. The elegant room in the massive Edwardian house smelled of expensive hothouse flowers, with a faint smell of lavender water underlying it. The polished furniture reflected the bright flames, and the soft rose pinks of the chintz sofas and chairs blended comfortably with the eau de nil walls and the thick cream net curtains that hid the bare, leafless garden. Soon Fanny, Lilian's invaluable maid, housekeeper and often companion, would come in to draw the green velvet curtains, and remove the egg and tomato sandwiches, homemade scones, fruit cake and coffee cake, and the paraphernalia of tea-making, which were set out on the low lace-covered table in front of the fire.

Mrs Carruthers turned her heavy featured face towards her daughter. She sat bolt upright in her chair, not leaning back into the soft cushions. She wore a high-necked white blouse with a cameo at her neck and several rows of pearls underneath it. Her brown wool skirt was longish, and her legs were encased in old-fashioned lisle stockings while on her feet were brown high-heeled walking shoes laced up the front. She looked like an Edwardian matriarch and in many ways behaved like one still, even though times had changed; the three maids and a cook she had once been used to had dwindled to just Fanny, and her household no longer justified the huge orders from the butcher and the grocer which had arrived each week until shortly before the war. Her big capable hands sat squarely on her knees, the many rings worn deep into the flesh of her fingers. They sparkled and glinted as she moved. Instead of answering, Isabel was thinking how her mother's talents for organizing and ordering had been wasted, and how well she would have done if she had been left to fend for herself. Unlike me, she thought, and then thought, but I won't let her bully me.

"Don't you think that's my business, Mother," she replied pleasantly, her voice soft but determined.

"Now, Isabel," replied her mother, "You know I don't want to pry."

I know nothing of the sort, thought Isabel.

"I just think you should do something useful," continued Mrs Carruthers. "You've made no life for yourself since ... well, since that man left."

"Mother, I'm perfectly happy," said Isabel. "I don't want to make a life for myself, as you call it. I just want to be left alone."

"You spend too much time alone," insisted her mother. "And what about Harriet? She's got no friends here, and she's not likely to make any unless you do something about it. It's a pity she has to be sent away to school. The Grammar School and the Church High are good enough for her cousins."

Isabel was silent. Her mother had touched her on two sensitive points, Harriet's lack of friends, and her own inability to fight Alec over Baynes. Not that she really wanted to any longer, she realised.

"Well?" Mrs Carruthers repeated. She leant over and poured herself another cup of tea, and took a piece of coffee cake. She offered the plate to Isabel who shook her head. She couldn't eat when she was being bullied. She felt her stomach contract as it had so many times when she had forced herself to do the things she didn't want to do for Alec.

"Mother," she said. "Please leave me alone. Harriet is happy at Baynes. And anyway it's a better school than the Church High," she added defensively. "But if you're worried about her, well, ask Fred and Ernest to get their children to introduce her to their friends."

Her glance strayed to the photographs of the grandchildren that were displayed on the table in the window. Harriet's waif-like face looked out of place among the square-faced boys and girls who were her brothers' children. They all looked strangely alike, as if they had come out of the same mould. Frederick's girls had straight brown hair bobbed and fringed, while his son's similar hair was neatly combed to one side; and Ernest's boy and girl were other versions of his brother's children. All five looked solid and unimaginative. They all did well at school, played tennis in summer and hockey and soccer in winter with equal enthusiasm, and passed each milestone of their growing up with no trouble, progressing evenly from school to school, the boys headed towards University, Durham of course, the girls towards domestic science or secretarial college. She doubted that Harriet had anything in common with them, but it would be better than nothing.

"Well, it would be a start," said Lilian, folding her linen napkin and placing it on the table. "But I'm not happy about you, Isabel. You still haven't told me what you do with your day."

"Oh, Mother," Isabel got to her feet. "I've got enough to do. I read. I clean the house – I haven't got a Fanny, remember. I don't want a great social life. I had enough of that with Alec." She opened the door. "I'll get Fanny."

She called for Fanny to come from the kitchen and waited until she heard her on her way before she went back to kiss her mother goodbye. Lilian would not say any more in front of Fanny. She stooped towards the heavy, worried face of her mother, and kissed her cheek and wished for a moment that she could be like her mother – strong, insensitive, firm in her belief that whatever she did was right. As she left the room she felt her mother's eyes under the worried frown following her, but Lilian said no more.

Isabel closed the heavy front door, shutting in the warmth, and set off on the walk home, walking briskly to keep warm as the evening cold coiled around her, its misty dampness making haloes round the lamps, bringing with it the smell of coal fires. She was glad she was no longer in the country, with its unlit darkness and eerie emptiness. A trolley bus went past, its bright yellow colour jolly and warm, the figures inside silhouettes against the condensation on the windows. She pulled her coat closer and shoved her gloved hands deeper into her pockets. She liked walking alone in the town, and liked even more the knowledge that she would be alone that evening. Not answerable to anyone, she thought. No Alec to harry me and hound me. No one, ever again. I'd like to be alone for ever, she thought, and felt guilty for a moment towards Harriet, who would be an intrusion when she came home, welcome of course, but an intrusion, always an intrusion.

I suppose Mother's right, she thought. I should do something about Harriet finding some friends here. The little twisting pain in her stomach started again, and she knew she would not do anything. Mother can arrange something with Ernest and Fred, she said to herself. I can't cope with it, any more than I can cope with Harriet's tempers.

As she walked, she looked, half-interestedly and half-enviously, into the lit windows of the houses she passed. Other lives always looked so much simpler, happier. She watched a mother sitting at tea with her two school-uniformed children, listening to their stories, an uncomplicated smile, or so Isabel thought, on her face. In another room, an old lady sat by her fire, a cat on her lap, her hand absently stroking. Her room looked warm and welcoming, and Isabel imagined a fond son coming home carrying flowers for his mother. Wishful thinking, she said to herself sharply, and as she looked the woman pushed the cat from her lap, and got up to pull the curtains. The face closer to was bad-tempered, and the woman shabbier than she had appeared at first. Before the curtains were fully drawn a man came in, a sullen expression on his face, carrying a tray on which sat a loaf, a jampot and a cup. He put it down with a bang and went out, switching on the centre light as he did so. Immediately, the room looked cold and inhospitable, the fire mean in the grate, and Isabel could see that the distempered walls were stained, the paintwork flaking. The woman had turned round as the door opened, and now she turned back to the window. Isabel moved away swiftly. Nothing was ever as it seemed, she thought. Nothing. I suppose others might have envied my life, married to the handsome Alec Bolton, always out at parties, dinners, functions, mistress of a pretty country house with wonderful views. She shivered as she remembered the long days that, towards the end, she used to spend gazing at the endless expanse of field and wood, the purple hills, without a human habitation to be seen. How soulless, pointless the house had seemed without Alec. How Harriet had grizzled and sulked, nagging her mother to do things with her, asking where Daddy was, why wasn't he home, when was he coming home, why, why, why? No one would have envied her that, she thought, any more than now she envied the old woman in the unwelcoming room she had just seen. Another bus was coming, and this time she ran to get on it, needing to get home to the home she had made for herself, where she felt safe, alone but not lonely, knowing that when she looked out of the window she would see other houses, other faces, not the frightening solitude of the empty, desolate fields with their dark clumps of woods.

She lit the lamps and turned on the sitting room gas fire. It wasn't as warm as her mother's house, whose fat gold radiators had poured heat into every corner, but it was home, her home, and she loved it. A photograph of Harriet was on the mantelpiece, a better one than in Lilian's gallery, and as she straightened from the fire Isabel found herself looking at it, puzzling at the expression of longing in the child's eyes. What was it she lacked, she thought? Why is she always so angry, so naughty? She thought of the last report she had had from Baynes. There was a hint in it that all was not well with Harriet. "Undisciplined ... Wilful ... Does not like to be corrected." She remembered the phrases.

"What does she want?" she said to herself, and wondered, suddenly, whether what Harriet wanted was to be with her, Isabel. She dismissed the thought. Harriet had been no better when she was at home. Anyway, it was too late. She was used to Harriet being away, didn't want her at home all the time. She picked up Harriet's letter which had come that morning, and put it into a small drawer in the desk where she kept the scrappy missives. As she dropped it in she paused. There was something, something that she was not doing for Harriet. But what was it? She didn't know. She sighed, and forgot about her daughter. She closed the drawer and went into the kitchen. She would have scrambled eggs on toast, she thought, for supper, and eat it on her knee in front of the fire, and listen to the radio play. What bliss! No one to interfere, no one to interrupt. The whole world, including Harriet, shut out from Isabel's house, and, perhaps, Isabel's heart.

She would have been horrified had she known to what extent her daughter idolised her. She knew, of course, that Harriet loved her, just as she loved Harriet, but she had no idea that everything Harriet did was done with her mother in mind, that she, Isabel, was always present in Harriet's thoughts, wherever Harriet was.

Neither did Isabel know of the objects that Harriet carried around with her, that would at a touch evoke her mother, and home, such as the lumpy gold-painted pencil which was stroked and fingered and carefully transferred from pocket to pocket, because she knew that her mother had chosen it especially for her one Christmas. In a similar way, she touched the stitches in clothes that Isabel had made, and kept untouched a handkerchief her mother had embroidered for her. Other presents, such as Alec's clock, were liked, even loved, but not in the same way as these talismanic objects.

At the end of the summer holidays she watched with relief Harriet board the train for school, her face red and weepy, unlike most of the other girls who seemed delighted to be back among their friends, and turned away, not waiting for the train to go, thereby causing Harriet's tears to well up once again.

Why could her mother not stay and wave goodbye as the train pulled out, as others' mothers did, Harriet wondered, tearful and resentful, standing at the grimy window. She fingered the pencil in her pocket again, and slumped down in her seat. Why did her mother not love her as much as she loved her?

CHAPTER Eight

Laura and Miriam drove along the dusty road, Miriam carefully avoiding potholes where she could. The drive through France had already taken three days, but Laura wanted it to go on forever. Every day, the country looked more familiar, and each day she felt more French. England seemed far away, a dream, something that had happened to someone else. They were on their way to Belay.

This was Miriam's second visit to the Bonnevilles; the first had been by train during the Easter holidays, on her own initiative but with Mrs Martin's and the Bonnevilles' full agreement.

"I'm too old to go, my dear," Mrs Martin had said. "My French is not good. And now you understand so much of Laura's story, while I feel I still only know the bare bones of it."

It was true, Miriam thought. Mrs Martin had only known up to now what she had learned from the Bonnevilles on that terrible visit to collect her granddaughter and what she, Miriam, had felt she could reveal of Laura's story.

But now, after her Easter visit, she could supplement that knowledge with some firmer facts.

She explained in detail why the deception had had to be set in motion, and told Mrs Martin of the happy family she had found, where Laura had for almost six years been the youngest sister, and how they all longed to see this youngest sister again.

"It's such an extraordinary story," Mrs Martin said. "They were so generous and so good to her. I feel a poor substitute."

"You mustn't feel that," said Miriam. "You're her only real family now, and she needs you. Don't you feel a difference in her?"

Mrs Martin smiled. "Oh, yes. You've done wonders. She's a different girl. This Easter holiday has been so much happier. But I feel I'm just beginning to know her, while you – you understand her in a different way. Of course she must go back and see them, but I feel she'd be happier with you than with me, if you could go. I know it might be considered unprofessional ..."

Miriam dismissed this with a gesture. Hang being professional, she thought, if it will help Laura for me to go with her.

And so it had been arranged, and now they were on their way. Miriam had elected to go by car because it would give her more freedom. She would leave Laura at Belay, and go on to search ... she pushed the thought of Nathan away. That would come later.

"Oh, Miriam," sighed Laura, gazing out of the window as if she could not see enough of the lush French countryside. It was very hot, and she had opened the window wide, leaning her arm out to feel the wind as they passed. "Oh, Miriam. I love France. I feel I belong here. It's so marvellous to be able to say whatever I want, and to understand everything."

"But your English is pretty good by now, isn't it?" replied Miriam, her eyes on the straight poplar-lined road ahead. They were speaking French, as usual.

"Yes, but it's not the same. It doesn't feel as easy ... it doesn't feel part of me, while French does. I wish we could drive along like this for ever."

"But you're looking forward to seeing Belay, aren't you?" said Miriam, wondering if Laura was feeling nervous. Laura's reply told her she was right.

"Well, yes and no," Laura said, pulling her arm in and turning to face Miriam. "I'm longing to see them, but it will be so strange not to call them Maman and Papa. And to know that the others aren't really my brothers and sisters any more." Her voice shook a little.

"You're bound to feel nervous," replied Miriam. "But there's no need, you'll see. They can't wait to see you." She told Laura of the telephone call she had made with great difficulty the night before from the hotel where they had stopped, to tell Marie-Claude when she might expect them. "Madame Bonneville said that the whole village knows you're coming and everyone is looking forward to seeing you."

Laura smiled. She liked the idea of the whole village wanting to see her. She wondered if they would find she'd changed.

"I bet old Madame Joly doesn't want to see me," she said. "Olivier and Sabine and I used to call her a witch. She looks like one, all black clothes and long hair."

"Well, perhaps *she* won't," replied Miriam drily. At last Laura was beginning to talk of the everyday things she used to do with the Bonneville children, not just of the shocking separation from everything she had known. It was perhaps all beginning to get back into proportion. Though of course, with what had happened to her, Laura was always going to have difficulty in knowing where she belonged.

"Tell me more of the things like that which you used to do, the silly things," she said. The sun of the last few days had browned Laura's face and arms and Miriam thought she could see the shadow of an attractive adolescent underlying the thin, sallow little girl she had first met.

It was after six when they reached St Didier, and the shadows were beginning to lengthen as Miriam negotiated her way through the hot, narrow streets of the town which lay stretched out along the deep valley, two long main streets running its length, shorter curtailed ones running cross-wise until they met the steep mountain sides. The high rounded hills loomed over the town, so that in summer the heat seemed to hover, unable to escape, while in winter the cold leached down into the valley floor and remained there. At one end of the town a heap of coal slack pointed the way to the mines.

Laura had fallen silent as she looked about her, recognizing things she had not seen for more than a year. Eventually Miriam found the signpost to Belay, and the car started up the winding road into the mountains.

Suddenly Laura tapped her on the arm. "Miriam, I'm scared," she said. "Please can we stop?"

Miriam drew in to the side of the road. When the car had stopped there was silence, and then a cricket started up with its insistent noise. A bird sang, a high repeated note. The engine ticked intermittently. In the hedgerows, pink and blue and white flowers grew, unfamiliar to Miriam after her years away.

Laura got out, and sniffed. "It smells the same," she said with delight. "I'd forgotten." Up here the air was cooler, and they could see the valley below, the town dark in the middle and straggling out towards the hills. Fields and hills looked still and peaceful in the evening quiet, the brilliant sun of midday subdued to a mellow warmth.

"Shall we go on?" said Miriam, leaning against the car and surveying the scenes of Laura's childhood. What remote perfection in these distant hills, so far removed from the Paris she had known, or the cold bleakness of the town she now practised in. How beautifully nature grew when untouched by man; how could man ever design anything so perfect as this fold of hill, these delicate trees and bushes, this gentle meander of the stream trickling down to meet the valley river?

Laura was leaning over a gate.

"Nothing has changed," she said. "This is the field we used to run down playing chase. And in winter, we were allowed to go down on the sledge. You could go so fast that you thought you would never stop, but then you'd reach that little hill" – she pointed towards a faint hump at the bottom of the field – "so of course you did."

"We must be almost there, then," said Miriam. She couldn't remember from her previous visit how far up the village lay. "Belay must be just round this corner?"

"It is," said Laura. "I'm just, well, nervous. My heart is banging. Let me just smell it for a few minutes. It's so French. Like the smell when we reached Calais. That smell of garlic, and cigarettes …"

"And drains," put in Miriam. "Drains is what France smells of."

Laura grimaced. "Mmm. Well, I suppose you're right. But you can't smell drains here!"

"No," conceded Miriam. "I can't. But I wish I could smell garlic. I'm hungry." She opened the car door. "Come on, Laura, let's go. It will be all right once you're there."

Laura climbed back into the front seat. Her heart was thumping, and it got louder as they turned the corner and saw the village ahead. There was one main street, the houses along it set close to the road. There were not many people about. Two old men sitting outside the only cafe looked up inquisitively as the car passed them. Then the church was on their left, up the worn steps whose familiarity Laura could feel under her feet, and as they passed a black-clothed priest came out and waved. Laura waved back.

"It's Père Guy," she said excitedly.

As they left the main part of the village, Laura pointed to a little cottage on the right lying slightly separated from the nearest houses. It looked empty, abandoned, its shutters closed.

"That's where my real father lived," she said. "Is it mine now?"

"I expect so," said Miriam.

"We weren't allowed to go near it. Maman used to tell us to keep away. I suppose because we might have given something away, by mistake?"

Miriam nodded, her eyes on the road. They were rounding the bend that hid the Bonnevilles' house from the village.

Suddenly Laura leant forward.

"There they are," she said. "Oh, Miriam, they're all there."

Marie-Claude and Paul stood at the garden gate. In front of them were the four children, Nathalie tall and dark-haired, almost adult, Jean-Claude now taller even than Nathalie and with a definite thickening of the neck and shoulders and, as usual, talking, Sabine more gangly than Laura remembered her, but with her blonde hair still hanging in a straight fringe over her brown eyes, and Olivier, similar in colour to Sabine, but with Paul Bonneville's more solid features.

As the car came round the corner, the group broke up, and started running towards them. Miriam stopped and Laura climbed slowly out. For some strange reason that she could not attend to at that moment, tears were beginning to run down her cheeks. The younger Bonnevilles stopped and Marie-Claude came towards her, her arms held wide. Laura took a step forward, then ran into the arms whose clasp she had missed so dreadfully. She pressed her head tightly into Marie-Claude's warm, familiar shoulder, and Marie-Claude held her tight.

Miriam got out, a smile on her face, but the shadow of a frown on her forehead. What difficulties we make for ourselves, she thought, when we love. How much simpler life would be if we had no need for attachments.

Then Fernande appeared at the gate and Laura broke away from Marie-Claude and threw herself on Fernande's ampler bosom, against which she dried the tears. Suddenly everyone was talking, and Laura was running from one to the other, clasping Paul, hugging Nathalie and Jean-Claude, momentarily embarrassed with Sabine and Olivier, but then, as Olivier said something under his breath, giggling as once again she became part of the Bonneville family.

The rest of the evening was a celebration. Paul opened champagne and they all drank a little. Dinner was a magnificent creation, Fernande excelling herself to make all Laura's favourite dishes – delicate quenelles in a subtle sauce, tiny medaillons of veal with wild mushrooms, a gratin of potatoes and cream and cheese, a salad containing dandelion leaves – *pis en lit*, giggled Laura, already working out what she would tell Harry and George – fragrant cheeses with freshly baked bread, and finally fresh peaches and apricots, golden with sun.

Laura stretched herself when the meal was over, like a cat resettling itself, and said, "That's the first good meal I've had since I left here."

Fernande had been hovering, as usual, throughout the meal, and a beaming smile spread over her comfortable face. "Nonsense," she said unconvincingly, and rubbed her hand though Laura's hair. Laura grabbed it, and pressed it to her cheek. "You've no idea, none of you, what it's like ..." her voice trembled, and swiftly Marie-Claude rose from the table and indicated to the others to move. She came round behind Laura and put her arms round her.

"We have, a little, Laure," she said, "thanks to Dr Stein." She looked over at Miriam, who had risen with the others. "I think it's too late, now, to talk about it all, but tomorrow, I promise, you and I and Dr Stein, if she will ..."

"Miriam, please," said Miriam. "I hate being called Dr Stein."

"*D'accord*. And Miriam, if she will." continued Marie-Claude. "Tomorrow, you can tell me everything that's happened to you." She hugged Laura tighter. "I've missed you so much, *ma petite Laure*," she said. "So much." She drew back. "Now, go and play with Sabine and Olivier. They've lots to tell you." Laura got up and swiftly hugged Marie-Claude before running out of the room and into the darkening garden where the four Bonneville children waited for her. Marie-Claude took Miriam's arm.

"Come, Miriam," she said. "We'll have coffee, and some of my own *eau de vie*, which we've been keeping for a special occasion. I think this is it."

Through the window, Laura watched the women leave the dining room, the thin, lively Marie-Claude with her springy hair and volatile features, and the tall, stately Miriam, her black hair drawn back into a smooth chignon, so that her features looked even sharper than usual, the long nose and high cheekbones giving her an almost oriental look. Paul was holding open the door for them, and Laura thought suddenly, I will never feel safer than I do tonight, with these three to care for me. Then the thought was gone, and the others were crowding round her, wanting to know what awful things she had had to eat in England, what the English were like, whether she could speak it – "speak some," demanded Jean-Claude, but not waiting for the reply, so that Nathalie had to put a friendly hand over his mouth to hear Laura's words – what boarding school was like – "like a prison, I should think," said Olivier mournfully, but Laura shook her head and said, "I quite like it now" – and finally, what did Laura want to do now that she was home?

"Everything," replied Laura, and they sat in the garden, planning the holiday, until it was too dark to see beyond the wall, only the lights from the house throwing a window of lamplight on to the lawn, and Marie-Claude was calling them all to bed.

As Laura climbed into bed in the room which had once been hers and Laurence's, and which had then been hers as Laurence, and which was now hers as Laura, her head was swimming. All the talk, the laughter, the tears of the evening seemed to be jumbled together, so that her head felt as though it would burst. She didn't know which piece of the day to examine first, and moved restlessly, utterly tired, but wide awake with excitement. Images of the day swam across her inner vision, Marie-Claude at the gate, Miriam's taut profile at the wheel of the car, the road running out in front of her, always more as the car ate up the miles. Then thoughts of Baynes, George and Harry, her grandmother, the cold Newcastle house, came crowding in, trying to draw her back to England. Go away, she said to them, go away. I'm French. I'll always be French. But the images repeated themselves, George standing composed under the cedar tree, Harry scrabbling in the dirt near the Pond, Matron in her silent shoes creeping up the stairs. You're English, you're English, a voice seemed to say insistently, and she sat up suddenly, sure that someone had spoken. But no one was there, and slowly she sank back into the familiar square pillow. Gradually her thoughts quietened. In the silence of the night, long-forgotten noises came to her. The tree brushing against the shutters in the night breeze. The sudden cry of Minou the cat, after a baby rabbit in the field. The mournful hoot of an owl, and, in the distance, the warning whistle of a train passing in dead of night through St Didier on its way south. Their familiarity soothed her, and slowly she sank into sleep, not to wake again until Fernande was leaning out of the windows, fixing the shutters back against the wall.

***

Georgina was bored. She had been to the library more times this holiday than ever before, passing the time reading musty books that she pulled at random from the shelves. Then she had decided to be constructive and had started to read *Great Expectations*, which Miss King had mentioned once or twice in English lessons; she sympathised with Pip, who, like her, had to tell so many lies, but after a while the dry, stuffy atmosphere made her attention wander and more than once she had fallen asleep, waking to find the librarian looking at her sternly. Once, the librarian had asked her if she hadn't got a home to go to.

Today, though, the books held no temptations, and aimlessly she walked towards Tynemouth, wondering what she could do. The weather was fine and warm, the cold east wind for once dulled to a summer breeze. She could go to see Dotty, she supposed, then remembered that Dotty was away. She climbed the hill and wandered down Front Street towards the sea. Perhaps she would walk along the pier, or buy an ice cream and eat it on the sands. Edna had thrust some money at her this morning, guilt at leaving her daughter making her generous, and Georgina pulled the tightly folded ten shilling note out of her pocket. It seemed a shame to waste it on something she could buy any day, like ice cream. She felt restless, not tempted to do any of the things she normally enjoyed. A sign at the end of the street pointed back up Front Street to the station – and suddenly she made up her mind. She would take the train to Newcastle. She knew it would be forbidden, but the fact that something was forbidden had never been any bar to Georgina.

The half hour journey passed swiftly and she soon found herself once again in the familiar Central Station. She decided she would find her way to the shop advertised on the yellow trolley buses, whose sides all read SHOP AT BINNS!

There was a map in the station on which she found Binns Department Store, and then, as she turned away, the name of the road in which Harriet lived caught her eye. Would she dare to call on her? She decided against it, not from shyness, but because she was wearing an unbecoming purply-pink hand-me-down frock which had belonged to Marlene. But she might just go and peer at the house, she thought; that would do no harm, as long as she was careful not to be seen.

The plan seemed even better than going to Binns, and looking back at the map she was able to work out which bus to take from outside the station.

The trolley bus made its silent, gliding way to the suburbs. Georgina enjoyed the journey through Newcastle's most prestigious shopping streets, and spied from the bus Binns, next to

Bainbridge's where, with her mother, they had bought the boys' house shoes. She would get off there on her way back.

The quiet suburb, dreaming in the heat, had wide tree-lined streets and big houses, each with a flower-filled small front garden. Georgina ached to live in a house like this, and for a moment imagined herself living in one, a normal middle-class child. Then she felt guilty as she realised she could never visualise Edna transported here. She pushed the thought away and instead visualised a different kind of mother, one who could come to Baynes, and talk to Miss Morrisson as an equal, as she had seen other mothers do. Then Edna's face, red, scrubbed-looking and endlessly kind, in her turn pushed the imagined mother away, and Georgina felt doubly guilty.

It was lunchtime, and there were few people about. Most houses had windows open, net curtains swaying gently in the light breeze. From the backs of the houses came shouts of children playing in the long back gardens Georgina could see between the houses. From one house came the sound of a piano being practised, a scale, then a snatch of music that she recognized from the Grade II exam book. She would take the exam herself next term. The music stopped, and an upstairs window was flung up, and a girl who might have been, but was not, at Baynes leaned out. As Georgina looked, the head was drawn in and after a moment the piano started again, desultory scales, the notes somehow mournful on the air.

Harriet's street must be two or three further on, she decided, and wondered if she was being foolhardy, inviting recognition in this select suburb where other girls besides Harriet would go to Baynes. Then Harriet's road appeared on her right, and curiosity took over.

She kept to the other side of the road, keeping her head slightly turned away until she judged Harriet's house must be opposite. She tried to look casual as she glanced across, and then saw that the house looked shut up, empty, no open windows or blowing curtains. Good, she thought, and remembered that Harriet had said something about going to London in August. She stared at the house. Its blank eyes stared back at her, silent and secret, giving nothing of its inside away. The garden was neat, and the closed front door looked unwelcoming beside the open porches of most of the other houses. Then, as she turned to go, she saw the net curtain of an upstairs room pulled to one side and a figure appeared. Shadowy behind the net, Harriet's mother, whom Georgina recognised from the station, pushed open the casement window. Georgina drew back into the shade of one of the trees. The shadowy figure had disappeared, but as she watched the front door opened, and Harriet's mother appeared again. She was wearing a dressing gown of some light, flowered material, and in one hand she held a book, which she went on reading even as she opened the door, bent and picked up a bottle of milk, and retreated. The door shut and the house looked silent and secretive again.

Georgina smiled to herself. Harriet's mother must be different from the mothers she had observed at Bayne's, none of whom would dream, she knew, of not being dressed at midday. She wondered what Mrs Bolton was reading, to keep her attention like that. She would like to meet her, she thought. She leant against the tree, still watching, but no further signs of life were given. Suddenly she felt hungry. Making her way back to the bus-stop, warily keeping an eye out to avoid anyone who looked like a Baynes girl, she decided to get off first at a café she had noted on her way up, the sort of place where you could buy a bun and a cup of tea for a shilling or less.

After her meagre lunch she explored the town's department stores, walking as though she had a purpose, which she had discovered stopped people wondering why she was on her own. Even in the unbecoming dress, she looked strikingly pretty, and one or two mothers, accompanied by plainer, duller-looking daughters, looked after her wistfully, wishing their own offspring could look like her.

Georgina was also looking, though to a different purpose. She was absorbing and storing away in her mind facts that would come in useful at some time or another. She noticed the kind of shoes that were on sale in the children's department, the sort of dresses these dull, plain daughters wore, listened to their elocution-lesson voices and their mothers' louder, more commanding tones. Other shoppers she dismissed, practised by now in picking out the ones she would emulate. She wandered into the food department and listened with interest to a woman dictating a delivery order to a black-coated male assistant, who seemed to hang on the woman's every word. Then she spent a long time at the fragrant cosmetic counters, wondering what all the different creams and lotions were for. She rode upstairs on an escalator and wandered round the fashion floors. Finally she became bored.

Outside, it was still warm, the streets now filling with people making their way home from shopping. She looked up at the clock outside the shop. It was five past four, time for her to go home if she was to be back before Edna. She had no intention of telling her mother where she had been, and wanted her asking no questions.

She sauntered down Grainger Street, enjoying the warmth, and the freedom of being anonymous in this bustling city. She decided that she would do this again, explore more of the big shops with their expensive merchandise and their extravagantly dressed customers, learn more and more, till no one would be able to tell her apart from them. Next time she would wear a less conspicuous dress, too, one of the ones she wore at school. If anyone had seen her today from school, she thought, she would just deny ever having been here. No one would be able to prove it.

The enormous, soot-darkened pillars of the station faced her. Next door to it was the Station Hotel; she went over and stared in through the revolving glass door. What looked like acres of red carpet stretched away, an imposing staircase rising from the middle of it, and a cocktail bar to one side glittered with shining brass and glass. A thin woman, dressed in a black suit, and wearing a veiled pillbox hat, sat at a high stool in front of the bar, smoking a cigarette in a long black holder while she chatted to the barman. A triangular-shaped glass with a long stem, holding a pale drink, stood at her elbow.

This was how she wanted to look one day, thought Georgina, turning away reluctantly, and implanting the picture into her head. The woman looked the epitome of sophistication, she thought; a woman of the world, travelled, experienced, rich. One day she would come here, too, she decided, and sit at that bar and drink something exotic and chat desultorily with the barman while she waited for her escort. Oh, yes, thought Georgina, I'm going to be master of this world, and others.

She just managed to slip into the house before Edna came home. Steve and Geordie were in the kitchen.

"Where've you been?" said Steve suspiciously. He had still not forgiven Georgina for her snobbishness over his threatened visit. "Visitin' yon Miss Brand?"

"Mind your own business," replied Georgina.

"You watch your tongue," her brother said, half raising his fist at her.

"Leave her alone," said Geordie.

She flung herself down on the battered sofa and looked critically at her brothers. Steve was wearing a sleeveless white vest over grey trousers, while Geordie's shirt was collarless, his sleeves rolled up. Unshaven, they looked dirty and unappealing, she thought. She was too young entirely to recognise Steve's unabashed maleness, but she recognised the sense of power that came from him, and preferred Geordie's softness. Steve was studying the greyhound racing in the evening paper, a matchstick between his teeth, rolling it backwards and forwards. Under the vest the dark hair showed, curling on his chest and in his armpits, and his black hair was sleeked back with haircream. A smell of tobacco and something male came from him.

"How's this for a name?" he said to Geordie, looking at Georgina. "Little Miss Marvellous? Could be someone we know. Thinks of herself that way, don't you?" He addressed this last remark to Georgina.

"Oh, give over, Steve," said Geordie. "Let the lass be. What you been doin', pet? Been on the sands?"

"Yes," lied Georgina. "I've been on the bloody beach again."

"You watch your tongue," said Steve again. "You let wor Mam catch you talking like that and she'll tan your bottom ..."

He stopped as they heard the front door open. Edna came in, looking tired, her hand on her back. She looked at the three of them.

"You've been quarrelling again," she stated. "Where's your Da?"

"Out. Said he was meeting Fred Parry at the pub," said Steve

"Well, we won't see him again this side of closing time then," said Edna, easing her shoes off. "Did he have his tea?"

"Said he'd get a pie in the pub, Mam," said Geordie. "What's for wor tea?"

"I'm that tired," said Edna. "Put the kettle on."

"Wor Gloria'll do it, won'tcha," Steve said. Georgina got up and went into the scullery. They heard the gas hissing as she put a light under the kettle.

"You could get the tea for us an' all, you lazy little b..." added Steve

"That's enough, Steve," interrupted Edna. She pushed her greying, frizzled hair back from her forehead.

Georgina came back into the kitchen. "There Mam, it won't be a mo'", she said, smiling at her mother and looking angelic, her cheeks pink, her blonde hair curling appealingly round her fragile face. She warmed the big brown teapot when the kettle boiled and spooned tea into it.

"Did you have a nice day?" asked Edna

"Yes, Mam," smiled Georgina. "I was just telling Geordie. I went to Tynemouth Sands, paddled a bit, looked in the rock pools, went along the pier. Had an ice cream, a strawberry sandwich."

Her mother looked pleased. "I wish you had some friends here, all the same. What about the bairns you were at school with?" she said. "It's not good for you, being all on your own all day." She stretched out her now bare, bunioned, calloused feet. "That's better. They've been that bad today."

"Mam, I like being on my own," said Georgina. She fetched the milk bottle and the sugar. "There's nothing to worry about. Here." She put a cup of strong tea next to her mother.

"She's lying," said Steve, looking up from his paper. "I saw her. Coming out of the station. Where'd you been?"

"I went in to get a comic," said Georgina, prepared for this emergency. She picked up a copy of *Film Fun*.

"You don' read that rubbish," insisted Steve. "I've seen the sort of books you read."

He turned to his mother. "Wor Gloria's up to something, I'm telling you. You shouldn't leave her alone all day. Send her to Auntie Vi. Marlene and Dee'll bring her down a peg or two." He laughed, his teeth white and wolfish against his dark skin. He hooked his shirt from the chairback. "I'll be lovin' you, always ..." he sang, rolling his shoulders and moving smoothly towards his mother the way he had seen American film stars move. He dance-stepped around a chair, and then, dropping the act, said, "I'm off, Mam. Got to see a man about a dog ..." He laughed at the truism, tucking his folded paper into his pocket.

"Here." He plucked a note from his pocket and pushed it at Georgina. "Get some fish an' chips for your teas. I'll get mine on me way ..."

"Thanks, son," said Edna, relief at not having to get up and cook evident on her tired, lined face. She wiped the sweat off her forehead. "You come into a fortune, then?"

"Why no man," said Steve, grinning. "I'm just good at choosing names. Like Little Miss Marvellous – she'll win for us tonight, just like our own little Miss Marvellous here." He put his finger under Georgina's chin and made her look at him. "Won'tcha, pet? You'll keep us all in our old age, though you'll pretend not to know us ..."

Georgina snatched her head away. He's so bloody right, she thought. I won't know him, ever again, if I can get away. Geordie looked up from the evening paper he was reading.

"Leave her alone, Steve," he said again. "Here, Gloria, give us that money. I'll go. Come on, Steve." He pushed his brother out of the kitchen, Steve still grinning his rapacious smile. I hate him, thought Georgina, hate him. She turned to her mother.

"Can't you stop him picking on me?" she said. "I hate him."

Edna sighed. "He doesn't mean it," she said weakly, knowing it was untrue.

"Yes he does, Mam. He hates me and I hate him. He's jealous, and nasty and spiteful. I won't have him coming anywhere near Baynes."

"Now don't start that again," sighed Edna, easing her aching feet. She held out her cup. "Give us another cup. Steve's got a lot of worries," she said.

"Like looking for a job," interrupted Georgina. "That's a joke, Mam. He doesn't get up early enough, and then when he does he's straight off to the pub."

"I don't want to know," said Edna. "I believe what he tells me, and that's good enough. And I don't want to hear any more from you about hating him. He's your brother."

"Maybe," muttered Georgina. "But I don't have to like him. Mam, you won't let him come to Baynes, will you?"

"I'll do me best," replied Edna. Her face softened as she thought of her daughter's triumphant progress, her brilliant reports, her changing voice and expressions. Even if these things were taking her away from home, Edna thought, it would all be worth it. The resolve that had seeped out of her with the day's tiredness returned. "No, I'll say more than that," she said, sitting up straighter, pushing her swollen feet back into their shoes. "I'll keep him away. But it'll make him worse to you, Gloria. There's no getting away from that."

"I don't care, Mam. I just don't want him spoiling things. I can't explain." Georgina sat down again.

"You don't have to, pet," said her mother. "I know why you don't want 'im to come – or any of us, for that matter?" She looked quizzically at her daughter. She would have liked to see the place which had wrought such fundamental changes in Gloria, or Georgina, as she was slowly becoming used to calling her, but nothing would induce her to embarrass her daughter in the new world in which she could climb to a freedom unattainable here.

Georgina shook her head, not wanting to upset her mother, who had never put the question directly to her before.

"It's not that I don't want *you* to, Mam, but ..." her voice trailed away. She didn't know what to say. However she put it, Mam would be hurt. But Edna knew the answer, and refused to be hurt. She knew the two worlds could not mingle without causing embarrassment, consternation even, on both sides.

"Dinna fash, hinny," she said. "Baynes is your world, not ours, and we're not going to spoil it for you." She stood up, refreshed by the tea. "Now get the plates out, and the vinegar. Geordie'll be back any minute."

She took her flowered pinny from behind the door and pulled it over her head. Then she lifted the lid on the white flour bin that stood on the dresser and took out a loaf. Holding it in her left arm, she rapidly spread the cut end with margarine, and cut the slice off, drawing the breadknife towards her with practised ease. Georgina watched her mother, always apprehensive that one day Edna would cut the bosom against which she hugged the loaf, always relieved when the exercise was over and the neat, margarined slices were on the plate.

"Come on," said Edna, "what're you dreaming of?" She set out plates and cups. Georgina, tired from the day's excitement, felt the safety of Edna's presence – the table set, the school question shelved, the bustle of food about to arrive. She got up slowly from the sofa and, going to the scullery, fetched a glass of water for herself and two empty glasses. Geordie would bring bottles of beer back for his mother and himself. As they waited, a comfortable silence filled the room. She sat down close to her mother on the sofa, nestling herself into Edna's capable red arm. The mantelpiece clock ticked, and a low beam of sun found its way through the window, lighting the faded colours of the rag rug that Edna had worked many winters ago. As the silence persisted, Georgina felt the tension of keeping up her two personalities relax. Georgina and Gloria became one, and the haven of Edna's arms became the childhood which she seemed to have left behind too early. She wondered faintly what it would have felt like never to have been taken away from this poverty, this scratched existence, unfed by books or music or culture, but instead sustained by love and the ties of blood. Even as she thought it, she knew that she could never, ever go back, could never deny now what she had learned. Just for a moment, though, she thought, in the warmth of Edna's embrace, sleep-inducing and seductive, she might forget, or not remember, become Gloria once again ...

The door banged open and Geordie came in, bringing with him the smell of fat and vinegar and melting tar from the road.

"Wake up, you two," he said loudly, dropping the newspaper parcel on to the table. "Grub's up."

Edna stretched and Georgina moved away from her. They exchanged smiles, as if, while Geordie had been away, they had achieved some kind of harmony unknown to the Charlton men. Then, the early evening peace broken, but the harmony remaining, the three of them ate their fish and chips with enjoyment, Georgina for once not comparing the food with Baynes, or thinking what her peers might be eating for supper, and, with Steve absent, Geordie made much of her, teasing her in his big, clumsy, kind way, while Edna looked on, wishing that all their evenings could be like this.

***

Laura, coming out of sleep, knew that something was going to happen today. In the restless half-sleep which preceded her full awakening, she refused to allow the knowledge to reach her consciousness; then, as she opened her eyes, the realisation of what today was came to her at the same moment as she took in the early-morning sounds and smells of Belay. This would be the last morning on which she would wake in the room which, until recently, she had assumed would be hers for ever; the last day on which the smell of Fernande's coffee would drift in through the open window; the last time she would wake to hear the soft blowing and munching of the cows in the field next to the garden, and the murmur of Fernande and Marie-Claude in the kitchen.

She turned over and buried her head in the big linen-covered pillow, which smelled faintly of the lavender bags that Marie-

Claude tucked into the shelves where the linen was kept. She pulled the sheet up over her head and tried to go back to sleep, to put off the moment of getting up, but it was no use. She was awake, and all too aware of what the day was to bring.

It had been a strange three weeks, both wonderful and upsetting. At first, after Miriam had left, driving further south on some quest which she refused to talk about, Laura felt as if she had never been away; but when the others, as she called them in her mind, not knowing what else to call them, when the others had asked her about her time away from them, a kind of shyness had come down like a transparent curtain, making her unwilling, or unable, to tell with ease the things which had happened. She forced herself to tell them the facts, the cold northern town, the grandmother whom she could now with honesty say she liked, the strangeness of an English school which seemed so odd to those used to the village school or the local Lycée, which you could put out of your mind once the gates had closed on you. The three younger ones had found it unbelievable that a school could take over your whole life, as Baynes did, though Nathalie, away from home now and studying for her entrance to medical school in a residential college in Lyon, was more understanding. But even she did not understand the loyalty that Baynes had already inspired in Laura.

"*Mais*, Laurence," she had said, "it's only a school, this Baynes. You talk as if it were your home, more than your grandmother's, more than here …"

"This isn't my home any more," Laura had interrupted, not angry but solemn and sombre in the realisation of the truth of what she was saying. Nathalie had looked surprised.

"Of course it is," she said. "You've always lived here. You're our sister – well, as if you were our sister …"

Marie-Claude, who had been half-listening to the children's chatter as they relaxed in the garden after lunch, put down her coffee cup.

"Nathalie's right, Laure," she said, getting up and coming over to sit on the grass beside them and putting an arm round Laura. "There will always be a home for you here if you want it." She looked at the other children. "But Laure is right too. We all have to understand the truth, even if we don't want to, that she is not Laurence Bonneville, as you all thought, and as Laure herself thought, but Laura Martin. And even though we all miss you, and want you back, and maybe you even want to come back ..." she smiled as Laura moved closer to her. She longed for the small, wiry, dark-haired girl to be back as her daughter, but knew that she should not encourage her. "Even though maybe you want to come back," she repeated, "we know that you have to be with your real family, for the time being, anyway, and learn to be English, which you are.

Laura made a face. "I don't want to be English, a lot of the time," she said. "They're so strange. They wear horrible clothes, and they eat awful food – the coffee is disgusting ..." She used the French word *dégueulasse*, stronger than its English equivalent, sickmaking, and Marie-Claude frowned and said automatically, "Don't use that word." Laura laughed and said, "Oh, Maman, it's the only word, if you could taste it." She stopped and corrected herself. "I mean, Tante Marie-Claude."

Marie-Claude hugged her again and Laura said, "Do I have to call you that? It doesn't sound right." But even as she said it, a cold little voice, her own voice as though from a distance, told her that she could never honestly call Marie-Claude "Maman" again.

"No, it doesn't," said Olivier, and Sabine said, "Why can't she call you Maman like she used to?"

Marie-Claude sighed. "Well ... it's difficult. Laure had a real mother of her own, and I can't help remembering her. It was different during the war of course. We had to keep up the pretence. But it's up to Laure, now." She stood up, to take her empty coffee cup into the kitchen.

After a moment, Laura followed her into the kitchen where Fernande was ironing, the smell of hot cotton and the steam from the drying clothes surrounding her like a mist.

Laura tugged at Marie-Claude's arm. "I've decided," she said unsmilingly. "I understand why I can't call you Maman any longer. So it will have to be Tante Marie-Claude – I'll just have to get used to it." Without waiting for a reply, she went back out to the garden. Marie-Claude and Fernande watched her join the other children.

"It's a miracle," said Fernande. "When you think how she left us last year – I never thought I'd see her back here accepting it."

"Nor did I," said Marie-Claude, thinking with gratitude of Miriam Stein, with whom she had found she had a good deal in common, and who she guessed was the sole reason that Laura was, or seemed to be, so well-adjusted. "But I'm not sure that she has altogether accepted it," she said. "She seems as if she has, she seems calm, perhaps too much so. It's not entirely what I expected."

She remembered the nightmare weeks last year after Laura had been taken away so summarily by her grandmother, when none of her letters were answered, and when Mrs Martin's explanations to Paul over the crackling telephone from England had sounded so remote, so lacking in understanding of her granddaughter and how she must be feeling, that Marie-Claude felt she had abandoned Laura to a wilderness from which she was now unable to rescue her.

Mrs Martin had refused to let Paul speak to Laura on the grounds that it would upset her even more, a fact which Marie-Claude had kept from Laura after Miriam's much-later description of the situation had made her more aware of the older woman's unhappy floundering, her inability to cope with the situation which she had herself manufactured. She wondered what this summer might have brought if it had not been for Miriam, and shivered for a moment in the warm sunlit kitchen as she thought of the suicide attempt about which she had known nothing until a letter had arrived from the then unknown Miriam Stein. She had wanted to rush to Laura there and then, had screamed at Paul to telephone Mrs Martin, the school, this Miriam Stein; but every move had been thwarted. Mrs Martin had refused to say anything to Paul, or to the almost-hysterical Marie-Claude, who had snatched the receiver from Paul, only repeating over and over again in her bad French that Laura was all right, that Dr Stein knew more, they should ring her, that Laura was not there. They had telephoned the school, only to have even Paul's patience tried to its limit by the headmistress's repetition that she could say nothing to someone not related, not seeming to comprehend the relationship which Laura had had with the Bonnevilles for most of her life; or not wanting to, Paul had said angrily. She would say only that Laura was well now, that he must speak to her grandmother, that there was nothing to worry about. Finally, Paul had rung Miriam Stein and had come up against her formidable medical ethics that had allowed her to say nothing more than she had said in her letter until she had had the full story from Laura. Paul had beseeched her over the phone, explained their position as quasi-parents, told her that his wife was almost out of her mind for worry about her one-time daughter, but Miriam had seemingly remained unmoved, only repeating that when she had the full story she would ask permission from Mrs Martin, who was after all Laura's grandmother and legal guardian, and who had asked Miriam to examine Laura – she would ask permission to be allowed to let the Bonnevilles know further how Laura was progressing. She had written to them, she said, on instructions from Mrs Martin, who had felt unable to explain to them herself what had happened. She had not said what Marie-Claude had later learned she had started to believe, that the Bonnevilles were the only civilised, humane participants in the extraordinary situation in which Laura had found herself, the situation which had forced her to take such dramatic action that something had had to be done. This Marie-Claude had learnt later, on Miriam's first visit that Easter. At the same time, however, Miriam had told Marie-Claude and Paul that she did not think it would be good for Laura to try to reverse what had happened.

"She has to know the truth, and to live by the truth. She cannot live in a fairy-tale, or go back to thinking that she is what she is not." Marie-Claude had felt some of the guilt lift as Miriam said this. The truth, when all was said and done, was what she had felt she needed to tell, when she had finally listened to her conscience and contacted Laura's English family. But she wondered, as she thought this, that if she had known how it would turn out would she ever have brought herself to deliver up Laura to her grandmother? Now she thanked God for producing Miriam, and sent an extra prayer to Him, to help Miriam locate whoever it was she was looking for.

In the garden, Laura also heard, in her head, Miriam's words – *"The truth, Laura, you must always listen to the truth"* – and realised that without consciously thinking of them, she had reacted to their message. Marie-Claude was not her mother, however much she might want her to be, and the only sensible thing to call her was Tante Marie-Claude. She lay on her back in the long grass under the old apple tree. A *cigale* made its furious buzzing noise close to her head, only stopping when she moved, and the hot sun dappled her with light. The sky was an endless penetrating blue above her head. She shut her eyes, half-listening to Sabine and Olivier gossiping about their friends, and wondered dreamily what Harry and George were doing. She realised they were more real to her now than the friends Sabine and Olivier were discussing, and also realised that her thoughts had reverted to English as she thought about England.

It was strange, and muddling, having these two lives, her French life here and her English life at her grandmother's and at Baynes, she thought, and realised how much she disliked the way that nothing in the two lives matched. How could she possibly explain her English life satisfactorily to the Bonnevilles? And when she was back in England, how could she possibly explain her life in France to Harry and George? The two kinds of life jarred, and she felt as if she was a connecting rod between the two, able to slide in and out of each, but belonging to neither. She remembered her desperate plan to blackmail Marie-Claude and Paul into letting her stay here, and wondered for a second why she had abandoned it, then heard Miriam's words echoing in her head again: *"The truth, Laure, the truth. You cannot escape the truth ..."* and knew that she could never slide back easily into Belay life, now that she knew who she was. Or almost knew who she was. There was something she must do, she remembered, something to be done alone.

She got to her feet, brushing the dried grass off her bare brown legs, and fastening her sandals back on. No one was looking and quietly she let herself out of the garden and ran down the dusty road towards the village.

The cottage was almost hidden behind the wisteria that had grown to cover the front, and Laura wondered who had planted it, her mother or her father, or had both of them chosen it? Or had it already been here when her father had bought the house? She pushed open the gate and went up the overgrown path. Unlike most of the houses in the village, the cottage was set back from the road, almost as if it wanted to withdraw from the life going on round the bend in the road, where women dressed in black chatted on their doorsteps and squeaky-voiced children played in the dust. Roses had been planted in the strip of land and, although overgrown and unpruned now, they still bore a few bright blooms, and the grey leaves of some straggly lavender still pushed their way between the rose bushes to line the path. The windows were grimy, the shutters for some reason fastened back against the wall, but as Laura pushed away the wisteria leaves and peered into the rooms she was able to recognise the house she had known as Oncle Robert's. She realised that she could probably have no real recollection of the times she had spent there with her father – they had been rare, she had gathered from Marie-Claude; and he had disappeared when she was only four. But still she stared at the half-remembered rooms, a new focus making her wish to imbue the pieces of furniture with meaning. She gazed for a while at the chairs covered in a pale, faded chintz, more reminiscent of an English drawing room than a French one, but they meant nothing, and nor did the table in the window gathering dust, nor the few ornaments she could see. She moved round to the next window, where she could see a dining table and chairs, a sideboard, and a small desk flanked by a bookcase. She wondered if this was where her father had worked, then realised that she really had no idea what he had done for a living. As she moved away from the window, disappointed that nothing touched a memory in her, the light glanced off a photograph hanging over the desk. It was her grandmother, she realised with a start, much younger than she was now, but recognisable, and suddenly she felt excited. This really was where her family had lived; until now she had known the facts but had been unable to appreciate the reality. She stared hard into the room again, but nothing except the photograph said anything to her, and after a while she moved round to the back of the house. She could see into a stone-flagged kitchen and through a half-open door see the stairs leading to the floor above. The kitchen was neat and empty-looking, as if no one had ever cooked there or sat at the scrubbed table, and Laura remembered that Fernande went in every now and again to clean, and rid the place of spiders and other unwanted life. She could see saucers of mouse poison on the floor, and a flypaper sticky with flies swinging over the table. She wondered vaguely how the flies got in.

Suddenly tired of peering through dusty windows at things that seemed to mean nothing to her, she turned round and surveyed the back garden. The grass was long, yellowed by the heat, and some twenty yards away from the house was the remains of an orchard and a kitchen garden, where a few unrecognisable greeny-yellow leaves had pushed their way through the invading grass. Apple trees, like the one in the Bonneville garden carried a ripening burden of fruit, and a pear tree's hard grey-green pods were beginning to swell. On the side wall was a once-espaliered peach, now springing out from the wall; wasps buzzed around the fruit lying under the tree, only a few ripe pink-and-green-streaked peaches still hanging. Laura walked to the tree and pulled one from the branches. It felt warm and soft, and wiping the skin with her hand, she took a bite. It tasted sweet and pungent, the juice running down her chin, and she thought as she ate it: I'm eating a peach from my own garden, my real mother's and father's garden. A feeling a little like sadness, but not quite, which later she would recognize as nostalgia, filled her, a feeling which she would always now associate with the taste of a white peach, and she wondered how her life would have been if her parents had remained alive. She was unable to picture it, and realised that the people she had been told were her parents were not real in her mind, were faceless, characterless robots that she was unable to give life to. She couldn't really remember the man who was her father, and however much she tried, his face, his presence, refused to come into her mind. Just for a second, she wondered if he had ever existed, and then her thoughts took the inevitable leap forward to ask, if that were so, then who was she?

A cold emptiness shivered through her and for a moment the sun seemed to have no warmth and the bright garden to be colourless. Juice from the half-eaten peach dripped unheeded on to the grass. She felt as if she could hardly breath, that she was held fast in this featureless, empty landscape forever. Then a bird sang, the sun's warmth returned and the moment was gone. She shook her head, felt the strange sense of desolation dissolve, though the cold memory of it lingered, as if it were biding its time to return. Laura pushed it to the back of her mind. She would think about it another time, perhaps tell Miriam about it, perhaps try to forget it altogether.

She threw the remains of the peach away and climbed the wall at the end of the garden. Now she could see exactly where she was, and saw that by crossing part of the field and a stream, and climbing the hilly slope beyond she could reach what she still called home quite easily, without going back into the road. She had no way of knowing that this had been Robert's way to the Bonneville's house and that the useful stepping stones in the stream had been laid there by him.

The following day, it was with some reluctance that she went back with Marie-Claude to the cottage, fearing a return of the bleak desolation she had felt in the garden, but accompanied, she felt more certain of the reality of her life and her own solid place in it, and wondered why, for that moment, she had questioned her existence?

Together they opened the creaking front door that led into a small hall, rooms on either side of it. The floor was uncarpeted and Marie-Claude explained that she and Paul had taken the rugs, which probably had some value, home to store, out of the reach of burglars and moths, and also some pieces of furniture and most of the pictures. "It will all be yours one day; in fact, it's yours now, the furniture and the cottage," said Marie-Claude.

"I'd rather the things stayed with you than came to England," said Laura, taking Marie-Claude's hand. "I think that's what ... my father... would have wanted. Can they stay here?"

"Of course," said Marie-Claude. "Let's look around, shall we?"

"I looked through the windows yesterday," Laura said. "The shutters were open."

"Fernande left them open so that the house didn't look quite so abandoned," Marie-Claude said.

Laura pushed open the doors of the rooms into which she had peered the previous day. They smelt musty and unlived in. She remembered nothing about them, only recognising the photo of her grandmother. Marie-Claude explained the part it had played in the deception they had acted out for the Germans.

"When the war was over, I put it back," she said. "It seemed wrong to keep it with our things, not with your father's."

"I never noticed," said Laura.

"Why should you have?" replied Marie-Claude. "It meant nothing to you then."

Laura lifted the photo from the wall. On the back, written in her grandmother's now familiar hand, were the words: "To My Dear Son Robert, from his loving Mother, January 1926".

"I think that was the last time Robert went back to England," said Marie-Claude. "He went back for his father's funeral, and I think there was a photograph of him too, but what happened to it I don't know."

Upstairs, the three bedrooms housed beds covered only with dustsheets to protect the mattresses. In the main bedroom, where Laura gazed at the double bed for a minute without saying anything, the rose-patterned wallpaper was beginning to droop from the wall over the window. The wisteria outside made the room greenly dark. The door of the huge wooden wardrobe had swung open to show only a few empty coathangers. Laura walked over and lifted one down; on the wood was written in still readable letters "Robert Martin, School House".

"He must have had it at school," said Laura knowledgably as Marie-Claude, puzzled, looked at the name. "My coathangers have to have my name on them, though Granny does it with a name-tape."

"Oh," said Marie-Claude, surprised at the sudden pang of jealousy that ran through her at this evidence of Laura's life away from her. She put the hanger back in the wardrobe. Laura was opening the drawers in the chest of drawers, but they were empty.

"What happened ... I mean ... their clothes ...?" she said haltingly.

Marie-Claude took her hand again. This must be quite difficult for Laure, she thought. This is the first time she has been in this house knowing it was her parents'.

"Paul and I took them to Père Guy, when we knew Robert was not coming back," she said gently. "Your mother's had already gone there, after she died. Père Guy always knows someone in need."

"I'm glad," said Laura. "It seems, well, right."

She had been pleased to be re-united with the priest who had taught her her catechism, heard her first confession and given her her first communion at the age of eight. Later she would know what a debt she owed to him for the part he had played in the long deception that had coloured the war years for so many people in Belay. But now, she was happy to see him again, to tease him at lunch after the Sunday morning mass, where at last she had been able to take communion without feeling that it set her apart from others.

She shut the drawers and went into the small room next to the main bedroom.

"This was to be your room," explained Marie-Claire.

Laura looked round as if waiting for the room to give her some message, but none was forthcoming.

"I don't remember it," she said flatly. There were no curtains at the window, for the shutters would have been closed to make it dark at night. A small bed looked forlorn and uninviting. The cupboards were empty, but on the chest of drawers stood a little shelf of books. Laura picked one up. It was a copy of *The Rose and the Ring*, a childish writing on the front page stating that it belonged to Caroline Orme, aged nine.

"That must be my mother," she said, leafing through the book. A piece of paper fell out, a scribble of colours, done by someone much younger than nine.

"I expect you drew that," Marie-Claude said, picking it up.

Laura looked at it curiously, an eerie feeling filling her as she touched the paper. She had no recollection of doing it, but on the back someone had written, "Laura. Aged 3".

"That's Robert's writing," Marie-Claude said.

Laura realised how strange it was not to know her own father's handwriting; there were so many hands she could recognize – her grandmother's old-fashioned English hand, with its carefully formed, copperplate letters; Marie-Claude's swift sloping words, and Paul's more careful *notaire*'s hand; Miriam's spiky, emphasised letters, her Greek e's and her d's that sloped backwards; the round clear boarding-school writing of Harry and George – but she had never knowingly seen her father's hand before. She put the drawing back in the book, and took down another. They were mostly English, Beatrix Potter and Alison Uttley, a book of Nursery Rhymes, and another of French rhymes, an illustrated Hans Andersen, whose pictures just touched the edge of memory – did she or did she not recognise that giant, that diaphanous fairy?

Then, hidden behind the books where it must have fallen and remained there ever since, was a tiny doll, no bigger than three inches in length, its limbs made of some pliable soft pink stuff, its primitive face no more than blue dots for eyes and a red smudge for a mouth. It was dressed in a tiny red and white checked dress and painted on its feet were white socks and black strap shoes. Laura lifted it out carefully.

"I remember this," she said softly. "I used to call it ... *Poupée*, yes, *Poupée* ..."

"You must have left it here once after being here with Robert," said Marie-Claude. "I'm surprised you didn't miss it."

"Perhaps I did, but I was too little to explain," said Laura, a faint memory of frustration connected with the doll pricking at her consciousness. She enclosed it in her hand, her fingers remembering the exact tactile sensation of the pliable limbs, like semi-hard pink rubber, but not rubber. A few wisps of pale yellow thread still clung to the head and now she could remember the feeling of stroking it as it lay in her palm.

"Isn't it strange," she said wonderingly. "All the things that have happened and it's been there all the time."

She looked at it for a few moments longer, then carefully replaced it where it had lain.

"Aren't you going to keep it?" asked Marie-Claude, surprised.

Laura was surprised herself, not knowing quite why she didn't want to move the doll.

"No. I don't want to move anything," she said, unsmilingly. A touch of the previous day's emptiness brushed her briefly, as though a curtain in her mind had been pulled swiftly open to reveal a dreadful blackness, and then as swiftly replaced. "Let's just leave it there."

Marie-Claude, feeling inadequate to deal with the emotions this exploration of the past might be exciting in Laura, wished that Miriam were here, but it would be more than two weeks before Miriam would return. She wondered if this reluctance to look at the past didn't hide something else, some denial or refusal to accept the reality of what had happened. Laura had turned away, seemingly uninterested in what other lost treasures the room might reveal.

Two single beds denoted the last bedroom's status as a guest room. Otherwise it was bare and unfurnished.

"Your mother never got around to finishing this room," said Marie-Claude. "She was going to make it really English, with curtains at the window and matching bed covers." She remembered how Caroline had discussed her plans during that long, tiring pregnancy, always saying that she would put them into operation when she felt better, after the baby had come. She began to say something about it, then realised that Laura was not listening, had disappeared into the bathroom. She wondered again if she was really uninterested, or if the lack of interest was hiding some deeper feeling. Laura had hardly mentioned her mother, though she had chattered on about her father quite easily until yesterday. Marie-Claude realised uneasily that since yesterday afternoon Laura had mentioned neither of her parents, and the reluctance she had detected but not marked in Laura to come down to the cottage suddenly struck her as strange. Something has happened, she thought, something which is making her seem uninterested, perhaps be uninterested in her parents, and her past, something which wasn't here before. Again, she wished Miriam was here, and she resolved to probe no further into Laura's past, nor push her into exploring it until she seemed ready, certainly more ready than she was today.

"Ugh! There's nothing in here but a spider," Laura called from the bathroom. "I'm going downstairs."

Marie-Claude followed her into the bleak, cold bathroom that smelled even more musty and unlived in than the rest of the house. A faint odour of mildew rose from the rust-stained bath, and a large spider squatted malevolently beside the plughole. The plug itself, its metal prong dully green with verdigris, lay on the edge of the bath, and grit and insect dirt made a faint layer of grime on the white enamel. Laura was right. There was nothing here to excite any interest. She followed her down the stairs.

"We'd better close the shutters," she said. "It's safer."

Before they left, Laura took one last look round the hall, now lit only by the sunlight that came from the open front door.

"I can't imagine them living here," she said. "I can't even remember what my father looked like."

"We'll look at the photos," promised Marie-Claude as she closed the front door, forgetting her resolution not to prod Laura's memory any further, but Laura seemed not to hear.

As they opened the gate Laura looked back. The house looked blind now, abandoned and forlorn, the shutters grey and slightly forbidding, like closed eyes behind the wisteria.

She shut the gate firmly. She had not enjoyed looking into the past, and as she thought of the little doll, still lying where it had lain for who knew how many years, a sadness welled up inside her which she knew instinctively, if she allowed it, could overwhelm her. After the events of the past year, she felt herself falter on the edge of yet one more demand on her emotions, and a feeling akin to hatred came over her for her dead parents. Why could they not have lived like everyone else's, gone on living, instead of condemning her to this never-ending muddle of who she was and where she lived? She caught up with Marie-Claude and touched her hand.

"If you don't mind," she said, "I'd rather not look at the photographs. I'm ... well ... tired of learning about the past. It doesn't seem to have anything to do with me. Can't I just enjoy being here with you, and Oncle Paul, and everyone?"

Marie-Claude this time was not surprised, the words confirming what she had guessed. She put her arm round Laura's thin, tense shoulders. "Nothing would please me more," she said. "I agree. Let's waste no more time with the past. There are so many things to do, before you go back."

Now, lying awake, resisting the call of fresh bread and homemade jam, maybe even a croissant if Fernande had been to the baker's, and a bowl of hot, sweet, milky coffee, or perhaps she'd have chocolate this morning, Laura half regretted the impulse which had made her decide not to look back into the past. She had stoically refused to discuss her dead parents any more with Marie-Claude, Paul or Fernande, all of whom had tried to broach the past, saying she was bored with things that happened long ago, a slight feeling of guilt whispering in her mind every time she said it. But now, as she approached the subject in her mind, the sense of the black empty void which had threatened to overwhelm her in the cottage garden nudged her once again, and once again she felt unable to deal with it, knew she must leave it alone for the time being. There would be other times, when she might feel stronger, she decided. The past would keep, for the time being.

Instead, she let her mind review the swift, hot days of the holiday. It had gone so quickly. Last night, Miriam had come back, browner and sleeker than ever, smiling and pleased to see her, yet with a faint sadness underlying her cheerfulness; she and Tante Marie-Claude and Oncle Paul had sat up talking long after Laura and the other children had gone sleepily to bed. Laura wondered for a moment what they had talked about, then her mind skipped back to the carefree three weeks that had just passed.

She had not gone back to the cottage and had gone on avoiding talking about her parents, turning the conversation whenever it threatened to run on the past. Instead, she had concentrated on enjoying playing with Sabine and Olivier again, revisiting their old haunts. They had followed the stream down towards the valley, paddling in its icy water, making dams and trying to catch minnows in their hands. The sun had reminded Laura of how cold and damp England was – it never shone like this, burning and relentless, so that her skin became nut brown, and she realised why Marie-Claude always insisted on them wearing sunhats. Another favourite place that they had revisited was higher up the mountain, where an old quarry had once been, and the tumbled stones made perfect hiding places or make-believe castles. They had worn rubber boots despite the heat for fear of snakes and Laura had nearly been sick with terror when she had stumbled upon one coiled, camouflaged, under a spit of rock. Olivier had wanted to kill it with a forked stick, as he had read was the correct way, but Laura and Sabine had persuaded him to tiptoe away instead.

She had been to see her old friends from the village school, most of whom were about to go on to the Lycée at St Didier in the valley, where Olivier and Sabine already were, and she had felt a pang of jealousy that she too wasn't going with them, carrying a new, bright satchel filled with the prescribed squared-paper exercise books. Talking to her old friends, she felt distanced, no longer part of the old group, as though she had moved on and away, which of course, she realised, she had. They treated her differently, too, she noticed, as though they felt some kind of deference, which Laura hated. She preferred it when she was teased about being English, and joined in with them in condemning the food, the weather, the clothes, the language and the attitude, only the faintest of guilty pangs reminding her of her disloyalty to her English friends. Harry and George would understand, she thought – they would do the same if they were in the same situation, she was sure.

One day, she went to see Father Guy, who asked her more seriously about England.

"And are you allowed to go to Mass?" he said gravely.

"Now I am," Laura said, looking round the study where she had sat so often with other village children, learning their catechism and talking about everything under the sun with the friendly priest who seemed more like a grandfather than a priest – until he appeared in his vestments at the altar on Sundays, when his everyday face became remote and withdrawn, and the sentiments expressed in his sermon were directed at a more sinful and remiss congregation than his eight-year-old catechists.

She explained that Miriam had insisted to her grandmother that arrangements must be made for Laura to see a local priest, and to join the few other Catholics at school for Mass on Sundays conducted by Father Julian.

"But he seems so different from you," she continued, trying to put her finger on quite what the difference was. It was not just the language barrier, for by now that hardly existed, her progress in speaking and understanding English having been so rapid once she had applied herself.

"It's his ... attitude. He treats me like a baby. I can't tell him what I feel, even in confession. He seems so cold. They all do. They don't laugh like you do. The one I see in the holidays is the same."

Père Guy smiled. Sometimes he felt he laughed too often, and wondered if it detracted from his credibility. He understood what Laura meant. He had met English colleagues, and had found them ... The word puritanical came into his mind, paradoxical as it seemed. Perhaps austere was a better word, or remote. Certainly a priest in a large town parish could never know his flock as he himself did, and his even closer involvement with them in dealing with the deprivations and dangers of the Occupation – those years in which trust between men and women had had to be based on instinct as well as knowledge if something as important as your life were going to be entrusted to them – had made his judgements even sharper.

He wondered what to say to Laura. It would be important for her to have a good friend who could advise her in the strange new world in which she must find herself.

"You must persevere," he said, playing for time while he puzzled over what to say.

"That's what Miriam says," Laura answered. "She says it takes a long time to penetrate beneath what can easily be left on a surface level."

"And do you understand what that means?" It seemed a difficult concept for someone so young to understand.

"I think so. For instance, with Father Julian, it's easy for him just to talk about what's in the catechism and it's easy for me just to agree with him and just do whatever penance he says. He doesn't have to go any further and so I don't either. Does that make sense?"

"Perfectly. Your Miriam must be a wise woman." He thought of the Jewish doctor who had come that Easter to see the Bonnevilles. He had liked her; in particular he remembered how she had bowed her head and stood in silence in front of the new headstone that read IN LOVING MEMORY OF LAURENCE BONNEVILLE, 1936-1940 A BELOVED DAUGHTER AND SISTER. She had been so clearly Jewish, and yet the atmosphere of his church had quite obviously affected her and she had stayed for Mass with Marie-Claude and Paul, watching with an interest that seemed more than merely inquisitive. Perhaps Miriam was already the friend Laura needed, more than this cold Father Julian. However ...

Laura had fallen silent, and had then said, rather oddly, Père Guy thought, "If you don't mind, I don't want to talk about my parents. One day I will, but ..." She had shrugged, her face, which had been open and smiling, now shut and strained-looking.

"Of course not, not if you don't want to." Père Guy was at a loss. He had been certain Laura would want to know all about her father now that she knew who he was. And he had warm memories of her mother too. Such a shy girl to start with, awkward, always blushing. Did Laura look anything like her? He looked across his desk at her. She was gazing out of the window, seemingly lost in thought. There was something, he thought, something in the set of the head on the neck, the tilt of the chin ...

he decided not to press Laura on the subject of her parents, and told her instead about various things that were happening in the parish, who was getting married, who had died. Then his housekeeper had brought in a plate of cakes, some home-made lemonade for Laura, and a tisane for Père Guy, and Laura had told him about Baynes, and he had asked sensible questions about what she was learning, and she had laughed at his expression when she explained that they learnt English history.

Suddenly a rap on her bedroom door brought Laura back to the present.

"Maman says it's time you got up," shouted Olivier, and Sabine, as usual close behind her brother, pushed open the door and pulled the sheet off Laura.

"Come on. There's croissants, and Olivier says he's going to eat the lot if you don't hurry."

In the rush of getting downstairs, kissing Marie-Claude, Paul and Miriam good morning while keeping an eye on Olivier and the croissants, beguiling Fernande into making her a bowl of chocolate, and then stuffing the warm, melting pastry spread with red currant jelly into her mouth, Laura forgot to say to herself that this was the last morning, the last time she was going to get out of her old bed.

Suddenly her case was in the hall, and Miriam's car was waiting, doors open. For a few moments, she clung to Marie-Claude, her eyes brimming with tears, huge sobs ready to swim up and overwhelm her. She opened her mouth to beg to stay when she saw Miriam watching her, a tiny shake of her head reminding Laura that it was useless to ask, not because they didn't want her, but because of the facts, the truth which she had to live by.

"Damn and blast your bloody truth," she said in English as Paul pushed the door shut and the car started to roll forwards. She wound down the window, and waved until they disappeared round the bend in the road.

Later, when she had calmed down, and was even beginning to enjoy the journey down the familiar dusty roads that quickly became unfamiliar, Miriam asked her where she had learned to swear like that.

"From Harriet," Laura said. "Her father talks like that all the time."

Miriam gave a hoot of laughter. The redoubtable Harriet once again, she thought. How Edith would disapprove.

"You'd better not say it in front of your grandmother – or Miss Morrisson," she said, her lips twitching at the vision of Edith it conjured up. She glanced at Laura, who, from the smile on her face, also seemed to be imagining Miss Morrisson. Their eyes met, and once again, as so often before, complicity bound them together.

The cheerfulness did not last, however. Both Miriam and Laura fell silent, immersed in their separate memories of the events of the last few weeks, and Miriam drove with automatic efficiency through the sunlit countryside that seemed as bright as when they came, but which autumn had already subtly touched.

"It's after the *quinze Aout*," Miriam said after a long time. "You can always tell – summer starts to end."

"It feels different," agreed Laura. "It rained on the *quinze Aout* in Belay."

"It always rains, wherever you are."

"Where were you?" said Laura off-handedly, not looking at Miriam, yet with an unmistakeable edge of curiosity in her voice.

"Somewhere," said Miriam. "I'm not sure that I want to talk about it yet, if you don't mind. I'd much rather hear about your holiday."

Marie-Claude had told her about Laura's strange unwillingness to discuss her parents, and although she felt she could guess at the reason for Laura's seeming lack of interest, she also wanted to hear what Laura herself had to say.

"Sorry, I didn't mean to be inquisitive," Laura was saying, a sad little smile on her face, and Miriam, contrite, suddenly realised how curt and cold her words must have seemed. She took a hand off the wheel and laid it on Laura's.

"You've every right to be," she said. "I don't want to make a mystery of it, and you might as well know, seeing that you already know quite a lot of my history now. Anyway, perhaps I'd feel better if I talked about it ... it's quite painful."

Laura squeezed her hand. "You don't have to."

"No, but I will. It will help to get it out of my mind, clear my head a bit," replied Miriam, putting her hand back on the wheel. Laura's touch, warm and dry and above all companionable, lingered pleasantly.

It was quite unprofessional, she knew, to talk about her personal problems with a patient, especially one so young, but everything to do with Laura seemed to have fallen over the edge of the professional into a peculiarly personal and special relationship; and Laura's own problems seemed so specifically related to Miriam's that it felt more like discussing them with a friend than with a child. In fact, when talking to her, she often forgot that Laura was so young. Professionalism told her to keep quiet about her recent journey, but sadness and the need to talk, a need that for some reason she had been unable to indulge with the Bonnevilles, had nudged her into an unusually self-indulgent mood. Who else could she talk to, she wondered briefly? Eventually, her brothers in America, she supposed. George Maxwell perhaps, but then she would have to dig deep down into her personal history to explain the circumstances, something she felt reluctant to do, while Laura already knew so much ...

"I've been trying to find my brother," she said slowly. "Nathan. The one who stayed here in France."

"And you didn't," said Laura flatly. "You've got a look, sort of ..." she hesitated. "I can't think of the word."

"Bereft? *Abandonée?*" said Miriam.

"Yes. That's the word, that's how you look." Laura glanced at her, then smiled and continued, "Oh, don't worry, no one else would have noticed. But it's a bit the way I've been feeling too."

As she said this, she surprised herself. It was only in giving a name to Miriam's expression that she had been able to name her own sense of loneliness.

"I want to talk to you about that," said Miriam. "Do you want to tell me?"

"Tell me about Nathan first. Then I'll tell you about the way I feel."

It seemed a fair exchange. Miriam nodded, her eyes far away from the bumpy grey road they were travelling on, heading north, the massive wheat fields only just beginning to come back to full production after the curtailments of the war years. Far more vivid was the face of the brother she had not seen for ten years, and which now she guessed she would never see again.

CHAPTER Nine

Nathan had been her youngest and favourite brother.

Only two years older than Miriam, he had been the one she had turned to in the emptiness after the loss of her mother. Lost and lonely, even in the over-crowded rooms of their uncle's lodgings in Paris, she and Nathan had been comfort and familiarity for each other. Of all of them, they had been the swiftest to learn French, their young minds grasping the strange sounds and syntax of the language far more quickly than they could learn to interpret its real, underlying meaning. Even now, Miriam occasionally had to translate something back into Russian or Yiddish to get at its true significance. With the language had come education, and although there had been checks and difficulties for Miriam, she had fought for her medical training, helped by the fact that Nathan had done it all two years before, so he could guide her round the pitfalls and push her towards success. David and Isaac had helped with both money and enthusiasm; but Esther, older than Miriam by seven years, who had had to shelve any ambitions of her own to take her mother's place, was bitter and envious.

Isaac, Esther and David, aged eleven, twelve and fourteen, had found it more difficult to fit in to their new country and had remained both more Jewish and more Russian than the younger ones. Miriam's father, who had once been the strength of the family, seemed by the loss of his wife and youngest son, and the long, difficult journey, to have been irretrievably weakened, unable to come to terms with their new life, incapable of joining his brother in the sweatshop where Aaron earned a minimal wage. His flesh seemed to shrink from his big frame, while his eyes searched for others similarly hopeless and, finding them, having heart only to sit over a glass of tea discussing the old days, which in his distraught memory now seemed filled with laughter and sunshine.

Miriam knew better – she remembered the fear always lingering beneath the laughter, her mother's eyes forever checking her children's presence, fearful for their safety out of her sight; she remembered the tales of the violent outrages inflicted on other villages and towns, and the feeling of helplessness in not knowing what was happening maybe only a few miles away; when smoke appeared over another town or village someone would say *'the red cock is crowing'* and everyone knew what it meant. She knew, as she watched her father's irreversible decline, that what had happened she had been expecting from as far back as she could remember. The responsibility for their wellbeing now passed silently from father to eldest son.

David from the start had been out buying, haggling, bargaining, willing to do any job offered to him, legal or otherwise; Isaac joined him reluctantly when he could, preferring to be at school, and going to Hebrew school too until his Bar Mitzvah, which when it came was an unjoyous celebration, all of them remembering too vividly David's ceremony and how their mother, holding the newly born Daniel, had been so proud of her eldest son.

By the time Miriam was ready to do her medical training, David, who had not been conscripted by virtue of the heavy spectacles without which both he and Nathan were virtually blind, joined again by Isaac, who had been invalided out of the army in 1916 with a smashed shoulder, had been running an up-and-down business for years, dealing in everything and anything, seizing any opportunity, no questions asked, which would put food into the mouths of Esther, Isaac, Miriam and Nathan, and their ever more helpless father. They had long since moved out of Uncle Aaron's lodgings; the squalor and the overcrowding there had turned Esther into an indefatigable and formidable under-age housewife who had chivvied and pushed David until he found somewhere of their own where, after school, she could scrub the floors to her own measure of cleanliness, patch and mend their clothes so that they no longer looked like nameless orphans, and stretch and improvise with food so that they never went really hungry again.

But the years of pinching and saving had left their mark on Esther, who had left school at just fifteen, and while she worked untiringly her mouth took on a sour look and her eyes gazed out unsympathetically at the world which had played a cruel trick on her, catapulting her into responsibility at an age when she should have been enjoying becoming a young woman; when she should have had girl friends to discuss marriage prospects with, she had only an ambitious younger sister for company; when she should have had a parent or brother to look for a husband for her, she was too much needed at home. When Miriam was twenty, and finally at medical school, Esther, now twenty-seven and tired of the unrelenting struggle to make ends meet, tired of cooking for the six of them, tired of seeing her father decline, left the flat one day and never returned. She had met a man, older than herself, Jewish, and fairly well off, who wanted, as Esther did, to emigrate to America. As she put in the note which she left on the kitchen table, she wanted to go as far away as possible from her family, so that they could no longer batten on her and use her as an unpaid servant. Miriam had not forgiven her.

Esther had said no goodbyes, taken no mementoes; just walked away. This second loss had finished their father. He seemed not to be able to understand what Esther had done; and his eyes searched everywhere for her now, as well as for his wife. Soon, he stopped eating, could hardly be moved out of the chair where it seemed to Miriam he remained, unmoving, from when she left in the morning until she returned at night. Tired, over-stretched by her studies, she tried to fill the space left by Esther, but she had had no practice in cooking, had no time to shop for food, no time to clean and mend. Soon, echoing their daily life, the family started to fall apart. David became angry and impotent, seeing his hard-earned money wasted by Miriam's incompetence. Isaac, always a lady's man, stayed out more and more, sometimes for the night, often for a whole weekend. Nathan dug himself more deeply into his studies, determined to succeed no matter what obstacles were put in his way, eating abstractedly whatever Miriam put in front of him, holding a text book as he forked the food into his mouth. Miriam herself, though envious of Nathan being allowed to stick to his work while she had to put hers aside to cook and clean, usually exhausted and irritable, nevertheless found herself observing with interest the effect Esther's decampment was having on each member of the family. She watched David becoming increasingly tense, the anger with Esther bottled up inside him because he knew that while concentrating on Miriam and Nathan he had let his elder sister down, had never even considered her needs. She watched Isaac become ever more frantic in his efforts to pretend that all was well, that more drink and another girl would help to make him forget his responsibilities. She watched Nathan become obsessive about his work, unable to think about anything else, morose and dispirited. She watched her father's decline; and she even watched herself as she tried to deal with the frustration of having to waste time, as she saw it, cooking and shopping instead of working. Her medical work suffered; her teachers wondered why such a promising student had suddenly become a grey ghost who no longer seemed on top of her work, but was forever catching up, who no longer stayed late to work but who rushed away the moment she could leave. She noted clinically that her appetite had disappeared, that she started at every sound and had begun to dream again of the soldiers and her mother and Daniel, a dream which had finally stopped haunting her a few years before. She saw that her hair was listless and dull and her complexion sallow and unhealthy. While she suffered, she took all this in with a cool detachment, and determined that one day, when life had returned to normal, as she assumed it would sometime, she would learn more about the human mind and how it reacted to loss, bereavement, involuntary migration, the removal of the familiar, the dictates of conscience, the guilt of omission. She also noted, and put away for future study, that perhaps none of this need have happened if Esther had told them what she was feeling, if David had not chosen to ignore his sister's isolation, and that if it had to have happened, it would have been easier to cope with if any of them had sat down and looked coolly at the situation, picking out the cold truth from the welter of hurt feelings and unexamined guilts.

What shook them out of the spiral of decline was the death, a few months after Esther's disappearance, of their father. Neither Miriam nor Nathan had realized how ill he was; their inward-looking obsessions, Nathan's with his work, Miriam's with the impossibility of running the house and studying, had blinded them to what was under their noses. Only David had realised that Benjamin Stein was in an irreversible decline; and he had said nothing, knowing in his head, if not in his heart, that once their father was dead they could perhaps reorganise their lives.

After the funeral and the long sad week when their father's friends came to condole and console – a week in which Miriam thought she would finally crack as she waited on the old, the sad and the dispossessed – David brought home one evening, shyly and tentatively, a young Polish-Jewish girl, Leah, with whom, it seemed, he had been friendly for some months. Miriam had never seen David either shy or tentative before. Normally, his hard head led him to instant decisions, often cruelly self-motivated, blinkered to any suffering he might cause others. He had become not rich, but no longer poor, and the hardship in their lives was caused not so much by lack of money but by lack of organisation. Now David proposed to change that. He would marry Leah, and Leah, whose parents had both died in the influenza outbreak, and who had been living, though hardly welcome, with an aunt, would take over running the house. Miriam could go back to studying, Nathan could occasionally smile and lift his head from his textbooks, and Isaac could stop chasing different women for long enough to take in his changed surroundings. Miriam had looked at the young Leah and wondered how she could contemplate taking all of them on, but Leah, calm, firm and efficient, had taken over Esther's mantle and brought love back into their home.

The family prospered. Isaac married 'out', marrying a petite and beautiful French dancer named Anaïs, and moved away from home, but not from the family, his personality enhanced and enlivened by contact with a more intellectual world than that offered by the business he still ran with David. Nathan finished his studies and became, to everyone's surprise, not an academic but a general practitioner, his head now firmly lifted from his books and fixed on the life around him. He wanted Miriam to work with him, but she no longer wanted to deal with bodies, preferring minds, which she found endlessly fascinating and impenetrable. Financed by David, she studied for yet more years, becoming known for her dedication to the healing of broken minds and her ability to help her patients to see how to heal themselves. She never wavered from her conviction that had first come to her in the dark months after Esther's disappearance that the key to mental calm was the acceptance of the truth, the necessity to search for what it was and look at it with detachment. By the early 1930s the Doctors Stein, Nathan and Miriam, were mild successes in the French medical world, and home-grown stars in the Jewish community.

Then, an uneasiness came into their lives. David, successful and established, father of two, possessor now of a comfortable house, came home from his office with rumours that brought back to Miriam the flavour of her earliest childhood, when that sense of an unseen menace hovering just out of sight had always accompanied her. Isaac arrived more often than usual for Leah's Friday night dinners, often without Anaïs. Some of Nathan's patients quietly disappeared to England or America, while others brought tales of more sinister disappearances of friends and relations in Germany and Austria to unnamed destinations about which it had become dangerous to enquire. Leah, whose parents had come from Poland many years before and who had not experienced at first-hand the horrors which her husband's family had fled from, began to look pinched and fearful, her expression as she held her children poignantly reminiscent to Miriam of her own mother's never-forgotten face. Miriam herself felt a hard cold anger growing within her, that once again they should be threatened by the tyranny of others, but behind the anger was fear, an unmentionable, sick, dark, primeval fear which she felt unable to explore and which she could not control. At night, in her small flat above her consulting rooms, she would wake sweating, dreams of which she could only recall the atmosphere, never the details, colouring the darkness with a sense of evil and premonition. She would force herself to switch on the light, her hand shaking, her stomach griping and her face wet with a clammy perspiration which she would see in the bathroom mirror, her face ashen and somehow reduced, as if the unnamed menace was already battening on her, attacking her, reducing her in size and status. The next morning, she would be her usual self again, only a haunting memory of the evil atmosphere of the dream remaining to remind her that the shadowy night fears might soon be matched by the only too real terrors already happening in Germany. But still she felt unable to react. She had never married, never been in love, though she had had lovers, had enjoyed a guilt-free interest in sex, knew her body's keen reactions and its ability to indulge in carefree abandonment with the right stimulation. But she felt instinctively that somehow the events of her early life had damaged her, made it impossible for her to love in the way that to her would be the only way to enter a marriage, or even a permanent liaison. She did not want to love like that, ever. She wanted no hostages to fortune, no ties that might hurt in their being broken. Her brothers had their own ties now, and had no need of her. Only Nathan remained unattached, cheerfully and untiringly looking after his patients, living in a small room near his surgery, his work his life; and Miriam wondered sometimes if he too was unable to make a relationship that, if broken, might break him. She wished he would; as it was, he remained the one sibling with whom she could not break the ties of love and family, the one person in the world to whom, if harm came, it would come equally to her. She wanted someone else to carry the burden, to watch out for Nathan, so that she could be completely free, not to love less, but to love without responsibility.

Then, while Miriam was still unresolved in her fears, still haunted by dark-coloured dreams, unsettled in what to do, as they all were, fearing the man named Adolph Hitler who shouted for death and destruction to those who did not fit into his pattern for an Aryan world – and so physically close that they carried a mental map of France and Germany in their heads, always aware of the menace of Berlin only a few hundred miles to the East – two things happened.

First, a letter came from America, from Esther.

They had almost forgotten that Esther had ever existed. She had never been in touch, and they had had no idea where she was, just hoping that she was safe with the man she had not chosen to name. At the time, David had made inquiries, but the leads had died, for it appeared that Esther had made her plans well – she had organised a passport, and opened, and closed, a bank account into which she had slowly paid the few francs she was able to save from the housekeeping, details which were reluctantly disclosed by an elderly Rabbi in whom she had partly confided, and to whom David had by trial and error found his way. Rabbi Blum had told him that it was no use his trying to find his sister's whereabouts, and he had been right, for she had given the Rabbi no address and no name, and all leads had ended with him.

Now Esther reappeared. She wrote to say that she had heard the rumours of war, and more specifically the threats being voiced against her race. She had prospered in the States; her husband had a thriving business, and she had a large house in New Jersey, two fine children and a life that she enjoyed. She sent a photograph, in which Miriam could see that the lines of envy had turned into lines of satisfaction with the big house outside which they were pictured, and with the girl and boy standing on either side of her, the girl, at eleven, the image of her grandmother, the fourteen-year-old boy more like the elderly smiling man standing beside him who had made all these things possible for Esther.

Esther went on to offer help, financial or any other, to any of them who chose to come. She did not apologize for her long silence or her abrupt departure, and the coolness that had always characterized her was apparent in the unadorned way she signed her letter, Esther Stein Brooks. Significantly, though, she had named her daughter Rachel after their mother and her son Benjamin after their father, thereby denying, Miriam decided, the break she had so firmly made.

David took the letter as a sign, and almost immediately he and Leah decided to take up Esther's offer. With his usual efficiency, he discovered her telephone number and placed an overseas call. They each spoke to her, and behind her sister's unemotional inquiries Miriam could sense a reblossoming of the girl who had come out of Russia with them. David had told her of their father's death, and Miriam heard the self-blame in her sister's voice as she spoke of him, the slight blurring of the words.

"Don't blame yourself," she said, not able to hide the unforgiving cold in her voice. "He was dying, he would have died anyway. We didn't notice, just as we didn't notice what was happening to you. We were to blame, not you."

Then it was Nathan's turn to speak, and finally, David spoke to Esther's husband, Sol Brooks, his original name, Baransky, having been Americanised. They spoke businessman to businessman, and Miriam knew immediately that David's future was assured – he would be safe and grow rich again in a new country.

Isaac and Anaïs were uncertain. Anaïs was not Jewish; she would surely be safe from persecution, and surely Isaac would be safe with her? No one knew, but Miriam felt the deep dark fear within her, and worked on Isaac to go – even without Anaïs, she thought but did not say, wondering if Anaïs, who had survived marriage into a Jewish family, would go on to survive the kind of uprootings that Jews throughout their long history had had to make.

Not that Miriam intended to go herself. The second thing that had happened was the offer of a highly-paid and prestigious job in England, at a hospital renowned throughout the world for its research into the workings of the brain, and this she had decided to accept. This would remove her far enough from the menace of Hitler, for England was seemingly not intended as a target for *lebensraum*. This would dispel the dreams, she thought, unable to visualize even in her darkest moments the Holocaust that was to come, the violence that was to erupt throughout Europe at the instigation of the living evil that was Hitler. Now her only worry was what would happen to Nathan.

Nathan refused absolutely Esther's offer. His life, he said, was with his patients in his adopted country, which had given him the opportunity to live his life doing what he wanted to do. He congratulated Miriam on the position she had been offered, but she felt his unspoken criticism that she should desert France because of the threat from Germany. She did not tell him of the dark dream that had recently begun to spread into the day, so that in the middle of some mundane activity, catching a bus or washing her hands, she would be hit by a moment of terror, an inexplicable sense of doom, strong enough to make her stop what she was doing until the dream's malevolent atmosphere dispersed. At other times, the dream's shadowy darkness seemed to persist all day, waiting for an unguarded moment when its menace would spread through her mind like fog rising from a slimy river. She made herself think about it, work out what it meant as she would have made one of her own patients work it out, but even when she understood that it was an emanation of total, unbearable fear, she was reluctant to act on it. It took one of her colleagues to open her eyes finally.

"Miriam," said the professor, now retired, under whom she had studied and to whom she had turned for advice. "I'm surprised at you – you're always so clear when looking at other people's problems. This is no aberration, this fear you have. It's the only reaction I'd expect someone of your race and intelligence to have if they have any understanding of what is happening over our Eastern border. The only way you'll get rid of it is to act on it. It's giving you a message. *You* are giving yourself a message, only you don't want to understand it. It won't go away until the reason for it has gone away." He turned his head away from her and looked from his desk out of the window, not seeing the broad Parisian boulevard, or the delicate tracery of the bare trees against the wintry sky, but rather gazing into the shadowy darkness already gathering in as the short November day began to die. Slowly he looked back at her. "And that, my dear, may take a long time, and see a lot of bloodshed. I'm apprehensive myself – and I'm not Jewish."

Miriam shifted in her chair. Professor Fournier was telling her nothing that she hadn't known. The menace would not go away, so she would have to go away from it. Neville Chamberlain's policy of appeasement in September had merely put off the inevitable, had only granted a stay of execution for which she must be grateful.

She nodded, a bleak despair filling her with a terrible lassitude. Once again she would have to be uprooted.

"Go to England. There's a job there for you. A good job, a promotion. You must take it," the Professor continued.

"I suppose I must," she said tiredly. She felt as if she could hardly get home, let alone make the move to another country. She had come, she realised, hoping that he would dismiss her fears as a manifestation of an understandable Jewish phobia. Now he was telling her that her dream was only too real, not a dream at all. This room with its warm lamplight spreading into the now dark street seemed like a haven from which she was to be excluded. Only a dark unknown in an unknown country across the Channel waited for her. She felt a tear swell in her eye and knew that the dream was breaking down her carefully built defences, eating away at her morale. She brushed it away swiftly, but not before Fournier had seen it. He moved stiffly from behind his desk, opened a cupboard and placed a glass of brandy in her hand.

"*Courage*, Miriam," he said. "Do it. Tell them today that you'll accept the job. Leave this country which I fear will not protect you from ..." he gestured towards the East, swallowed his own brandy and placed the glass emphatically on the desk. "It will come to war, Miriam, sooner or later. I've lived too long not to recognise the signs. That man, that monster – trying to maintain friendly relations with him will only make him think he can get away with whatever he likes. If he were one of my patients I would have no hesitation in diagnosing him as dangerously obsessive, psychotic in all probability, a megalomaniac, and lock him up. I needn't go on?"

"Your diagnoses are rarely wrong," Miriam said drily. "I know what you're saying makes sense – not just of the dream," – she shuddered involuntarily as with its mention its flavour flooded over her. "I've more or less made up my mind to go. But Nathan refuses to move. He shuts his eyes to anything that's not to do with his patients. I'm afraid for him. How can I leave him?"

"Have you told him about England?" said Fournier. He remembered Nathan, though he had not worked with him as he had with Miriam, and recalled how as a student he had seemed totally immersed in his studies, uninterested in and immune to life going on around him. That had been well over a decade ago ... and from what Miriam was saying he had not changed.

"No," Miriam replied. "He'll nag me to go, while at the same time make me feel guilty for considering it. First, I want him to decide to get out too."

"Don't try for too long. You may miss your own opportunity. Put yourself first, for once. It's your duty to yourself to save your skin. I'm sorry to sound so harsh, but I too have, or had, friends in Germany. Two colleagues have ..." he raised his hand expressively and dismissively, "... disappeared. Their families can find out nothing. We, they, run up against a mute, official, bureaucratic nothingness. Endless papers ... hints that any more enquiries will lead to ... other disappearances. There's a nightmare building up over there. I dread to think what might be happening ..." He leant forward. "Go, Miriam. Go. Leave Nathan here, if he's so stubborn. He's adult, he can see what is happening as well as you can. You must think of yourself."

Miriam nodded mutely. Everything Professor Fournier said underlined what she had known subconsciously. She had no alternative. She would try once more with Nathan. She was certain he could find work in England too, though maybe that would not be far enough – perhaps they should go to America too? The thoughts ran round and round as they had for weeks, and she understood now why people tortured themselves with indecision, wavered one way and then another. Never before had she been unable to come to an instant decision, and to stick by it. That was how she had run her life. Facts led to decisions, decisions to natural progression through an ordered, uncomplicated existence. Now all that was to be changed. She would not have taken the English job under other circumstances. She had not looked for it – it had come unsolicited. Now perhaps she should look on it as a blessing – or an omen.

"I'll talk to Nathan again tonight," she said, resolution in her voice, but not in her posture. Fournier thought he'd never seen her look so bruised, diminished even. Childhood horrors can bring even the strongest to their knees if they return, he thought.

"If he won't go, let me know," he said, rising as Miriam moved from her chair. "We'll stay here, whatever happens. I'm not Jewish, and I'm too old to fight. I could keep an eye on him, if he'll allow it."

"I would be grateful," Miriam said, smoothing down her slim black skirt. Thank you for the advice, and the brandy." She straightened her shoulders, forcing herself back into the brisk, decisive personality that was most of the time her true self.

Fournier escorted her to the door of the flat. "Go to England, Miriam. At least it will put the channel between you and Germany. We don't even have that." He kissed her hard on both cheeks, more an *adieu* than an *au revoir*, and Miriam wondered when or if she would ever see him again. Later she telephoned to say that Nathan would be staying in Paris.

"But I'll be leaving in the New Year," she said. "My contract is for five years so I'll have to remain there for at least that long. It'll be good for my English. I'll be back for holidays, of course," she added, trying to reassure herself that indeed she would be returning in a few months, but Fournier was silent. Eventually he said bleakly, "I hope so my dear. I do hope so. But I must tell you, I've had news from German colleagues today. It's not good. You've taken the right decision. I only wish you'd persuaded Nathan to go with you. Tell him he can come here if the disease from the East spreads."

As it turned out, Miriam never returned to France before war was declared. Her job had started at the beginning of the year and her holiday had been due to start in the first week of September 1939. Instead, Miriam sat glued to her wireless, listening, cold and shivering, as her nightmare came true and the blackness spread inexorably from Germany, first into Poland and then, inevitably she now felt, into Norway, Holland and France. The months between the onset of war and the collapse of France had been the worst she had ever spent, she thought later, worse even than leaving her mother behind in Russia, because then she had been a helpless child, and could do nothing, while now she was a capable, strong adult who could surely find a way to get Nathan out.

All her plans came to nothing. Nathan had disappeared. After September, she heard nothing from him. Fournier had not seen him, she heard eventually. No replies came to the letters she wrote. Telephone calls could not get through. The War Office could do nothing. David and Isaac in America had heard nothing. There was nothing, nothing but an immense blank. She began to understand what had happened to her father. The lack of any news, the inability to find out what had happened, the sense of irrecoverable distance between her and her second homeland, the permanent negativity began to wear her down. She felt as if a blind had been pulled down between her old life and the new. In her imagination, she saw the Channel cut in half, a dull grey impassable curtain hanging between England and France.

As the war progressed, she felt the black tide of her dream waiting to overwhelm her, held and dammed by nothing but a few miles of sea and the implacable refusal to give in against what seemed like overwhelming odds of her strange new countrymen, the English. She became resigned to Nathan's disappearance, though not accepting. But she knew that if she went on wondering what had happened, imagining what he was doing, wondering if he was safe, or dead, or imprisoned, she would crack. She did what she so often told her patients to do if they could: face up to a problem, look at it, and if there was nothing they could do about it, try to put it out of their minds, not let it destroy them. After some months, she succeeded and the active, terrifying fear became a dull, permanent ache somewhere at the back of her mind, an ache she would only look at if it became possible to do anything about it.

Her work helped: the ill minds became worse, and more complex ills became commoner, as the attrition of war continued. Her colleagues offered her silent sympathy, unspoken but nevertheless there, a continual source of help and comfort. She felt it in their help with the language, their patience at explaining their methods and their interested examination of hers. The cold northern town, so alien at first, became familiar. After a while, she took her belongings out of storage where she had at first put them, having chosen to live in a hotel room for the first few weeks and then in a bleakly furnished flat. As her cherished pictures and books reappeared she felt she had taken a bigger step than the mere renting of an unfurnished flat. She had committed herself to this strange new life, had perhaps come to terms to living with the empty space which war had created, where once there had been family, a rich and rewarding cultural and social life and a planned career. Slowly, she began to take stock of her surroundings; she began to read again, to re-study her books and texts. She went to the theatre, which was visited by the top companies for short seasons; she went to the cinema, the 'pictures' as she learned to call it, sitting sometimes through two programmes in order to see the News twice. She made herself known to the Jewish community, though she refused to join in most of its oppressively incestuous social life; she had never felt herself part of an exclusive religious sect, had in fact forgotten most of what she had learned as a child, the only religious observance she had kept having been Leah's Friday evening dinners, at which David had been made by Leah to follow the rituals of the feast, though he had baulked at anything more, treating the Sabbath as any other day and regarding Sunday as his day off. Now Miriam let herself be invited a few times to the curiously old-fashioned but richly comfortable homes, where she felt foolish as her hosts quietly expressed their disapproval of her irreligious attitudes, her regarding of food laws as outdated health rules, and circumcision as a medical and usually unnecessary intervention; and soon the invitations ceased, though the Rabbi, a highly educated man with a passion for French literature, often dropped in on her for some conversation and discussion. Through the hospital her social life became more varied – in time she met most of the town's luminaries, including Edith Morrisson, headmistress of the town's most valued jewel, Baynes. Baynes interested Miriam, as did all closed communities; she'd noted too often the damage done to the more fragile members of such communities, whether they be nunneries or monasteries, hospitals, universities, anywhere that had a structured life sufficient enough to have no need of outside activities, or where a life could be totally bound up to the exclusion of other interests. She supposed the sort of Jewish community which bound its members as close as this town's did might well produce the kind of repressed lives she often had to take to pieces for their owners so that they could put them together in a freer fashion, and wondered if it might be worth a study. But the peculiarities of the English boarding school would be even more interesting, she thought, as she listened to Edith discussing her girls and their rule-bound lives, and heard her pride in her successes and wondered what happened to the failures. She once ventured to ask Edith.

"The parents tend to realise if the child is not suited to our high standards," replied Edith.

"You mean you get rid of them?" queried Miriam, her accented English making the question sound more menacing than she had intended.

"No, no, of course not," said Edith, annoyed. "But if a parent gets a number of bad reports, or letters from me, or the child is unhappy, which she will be if she continually fails, then they realise that Baynes is not the right school for their daughter."

"And do you have many of these unhappy children, these failures?" continued Miriam, enjoying tightening the screws on this obnoxiously conceited woman – Edith's better qualities took time to learn, she realised later as she got to know her better and, although she never really liked her, began to appreciate Edith's fierce loyalties to her standards of learning and behaviour.

"Fortunately, they are very few and far between," Edith replied briskly. "Our entrance exam is rigorous, as is my interview with each and every child."

Later, Miriam was to remember this conversation, and wonder to herself how it squared up with Laura's admittance, and how the unfortunate Harriet had managed to wriggle her way through Edith's rigorous interviewing; the fact that Harriet's father was rich, and Laura's grandmother was a friend of one of the governors could surely not have had anything to do with it, she assured herself caustically.

Finally, in what she regarded only as a step in the progression of her gradual recovery after the despair and loneliness of her early years in England, Miriam took a lover. It was not her colleague George Maxwell, though he had more than once offered himself for the position, but a man Miriam had seen once or twice in the town's only large bookshop, a lean, wiry, tall, dark-haired man whom she had heard speak with pain-inflicting scorn to one of the young female assistants. "I think you'll find John Locke in the Philosophy section, not among our popular novels, Susan," she had heard him say, and had watched the girl grow red and flustered as she'd led the annoyed prospective purchaser to another part of the shop. "How was I to know?" she heard her mutter under her breath, as out loud she said, "Yes Mr Morgan, sir."

So he was the owner, thought Miriam, with interest, as she watched him make his way across the shop to the office at the back, his dark eyes darting from side to side, his swift hand pushing a book back here or rearranging a messy display. There was a second-hand section next to the office, where Miriam liked to browse, educating herself in a course of Dickens, George Eliot and Thackeray as a means to better understanding the English temperament. Now she made her way over there and waited for Morgan to reappear, but the door remained firmly shut while his assistants misdirected their customers and stood gossiping when there was no one to serve. A few weeks later she met him at one of George Maxwell's Sunday morning sherry parties.

"Invalided out," she heard him reply tersely to an inquiry, and thought again that his paleness was startling against his dark eyes and hair. "A lean and hungry look," she thought to herself, then realised with surprise that she was at last thinking, and even quoting in English, *Julius Caesar* having been one of the plays which a prestigious Shakespeare company had staged the previous winter and which she had studied to while away some of the cold, dark, empty evenings. "I'd like him for a lover, but not for a patient ..." she surprised herself again in thinking, and wondered if a similar thought had been in his mind as he made his way across to her.

"Who's this you've been keeping from me, George?" he said aggressively. George introduced them, pointing out that Sam Morgan had not long ago been in the army.

"Well, that's over and done with," said Sam unsmilingly. "Don't need me any more. Ulcers, and other things."

"In that case, Sam," said George, "you should be on milk, not this." He put out his hand to take Sam's glass of what looked like straight whisky, but Sam moved it out of his reach. "Cut it out, George," he said. "Elixir of life – my life, anyway." And turning his back on his host, he had proceeded to grill Miriam about herself, her job, her background, her beliefs, and generally to probe where she would rather he had not.

His courtship had been swift and impolite, but irresistible. His sharp mind had been on a par with Miriam's own, and she had enjoyed sparring and arguing with him, and had enjoyed too his thin, angular body with its practiced, experienced ways and its joyous acceptance of her own experience. She had been growing used to him, liking his surprise appearances and thoughtful gifts, a bottle of fine red wine one week, an old edition of *Gulliver's Travels* another.

"Read that, and you might begin to understand what makes us tick, why we don't seem to take anything seriously," he had said, and had gone on giving her pointers to what to read, poetry and prose, inspiring her with his own enthusiasms for Jonson's dark satires and Pope's elegant wit, Jane Austin's ironic insights, and T.S. Eliot's allusive and mystical works.

"Dickens is an elephant," he had said. "Too heavy, remorseless. And yet sugary. His villains are too awful and his women too sweet. He labours his themes, leaves nothing for the imagination. And Thackeray's not much better."

Miriam had disagreed, finding the strand of optimism that underlay all Dickens' dire themes heartening. She wondered if she was becoming less cynical, or if the endless horror of war produced a need to find optimism anywhere she could. But before she had time to enlarge on this thought to Sam, he had disappeared as suddenly as he had arrived in her life. One night in 1944, after a strenuous and enjoyable encounter in Miriam's bed, he had said bleakly, "This is my last night here, Miriam. I'm off to London, to higher," he gave a sardonic chuckle, "or perhaps I should say lower things." Miriam had felt, but refused to acknowledge, a black desolation. "Can't tell you what it is. Secret," he'd added.

"Will you be back? What about the bookshop?"

"That's all taken care of. Sold it to another poor sod that the army didn't want. You'll like him. But not in this way." He pulled her dark head close, so that she could see the deeply etched lines and hollows of his face, and kissed her slowly and deliberately, his lips hard against hers.

She pushed him away, even as desire for his lean smooth body rose again in her. He had undermined her defences more than she had realised, and now she must prise herself loose from him in order not to be hurt. She ignored her body's message, and merely said, getting out of bed, and putting on a thick black velvet housecoat against the northern cold, "I'll miss you."

He gazed up at her from the bed, a smile flickering about his dark face, and Miriam felt that he knew what she was thinking, knew that her indifference was a lie, as she knew too, in the hidden recesses of her mind.

"Come here," he said. "You can't deny a condemned man his favourite food." And he reached out a thin muscular arm and pulled her down on top of him. Delicately, he removed the robe, and knowing her body's requirements gave her a satisfaction she couldn't deny, deliberately holding back until she had melted under his touch.

He had gone offering no address and Miriam had not asked for one. She had missed him more than she allowed herself to know, guessing that if she admitted the empty space left in her life she might fall back into the desolation of her first year in England. Six months after he had gone, a florist delivered, on her birthday, twelve red roses accompanied by a note that read: *Don't know where, don't know when ... Sam.* Her mind supplied the missing *We'll meet again* and her heart gave an involuntary lurch as the sense of his presence invaded the flat. In an uncharacteristic gesture of sentimentality, which she would have admitted to no one, she had kept one of the roses, pressed dry and flat in one of her big medical books. She would throw it out, she told herself, if and when Sam returned, a possibility which seemed less and less likely after the war's end, although an anonymous, unsigned, bouquet of red roses still arrived each year on her birthday. George Maxwell had volunteered the information that Morgan had always been a "rum cove".

"Wouldn't surprise me if he were dead," he had said, when Miriam had asked him if he thought Sam would return now that the war was over. She kept her enquiry casual – she and Sam had been discreet, and if George knew what their relationship had been she trusted him not to remark on it. "He's done this before, disappeared. Doesn't come from around here – just turned up and opened that bookshop of his. Next thing I knew, he'd volunteered. Can't think why they took him; I wouldn't have passed him as fit, if he'd ever given me the chance. Said he didn't believe in doctors. Then he was invalided out. I was right. Well, you saw him. Treating his stomach with large doses of whisky. Those ulcers have probably killed him by now." He looked up from his drink and Miriam made her face look bland and only minimally interested, while she thought that when they were together Sam had never once mentioned his ulcers nor shown any sign of discomfort from the large number of whiskies he drank every evening.

"Well, I suppose he's got no reason to come back here," she said dismissively, and changed the subject, asking George a complicated and informed question about one of his cases which swiftly pushed all thoughts of Sam out of his mind.

After the war had ended, Miriam found to her surprise that she had no desire to uproot her life again. She had had to sign a new hospital contract a year or two back which had committed her to another five years, though she knew that they would come to an amicable agreement if she decided to return to France. But the

France she had left behind had gone forever. There was no family now, and in its absence she realised how much her family had coloured her life in Paris, making her feel wanted and needed far more than she had understood at the time. The people, whom she remembered as sharp, cynical, witty, now seemed diminished, wily rather than sharp, distrustful instead of cynical, sourness in place of wit making a remark unnecessarily cutting and in no way kind.

She wondered how she would have changed, faced with occupation by a hated enemy under whom life had to continue in some form. Would she have collaborated, found the courage to resist lacking, contributed to the atmosphere of distrust as neighbour spied on neighbour and honest men found themselves looking over their shoulders? She shrugged. The opportunity would not have arisen, she thought bitterly. She would by virtue of her Jewishness have been removed from the scene, as she supposed Nathan had. She had, of course, gone to look for him as soon as she could, but it had been a search without hope, the enquiries she had put in hand as soon as France was relieved having come back unanswered. No, there was no record of a Dr Nathan Stein after 1939. No, his name was on none of the lists that slowly came to light as the horror of the concentration camps gradually dawned on an unbelieving world.

Miriam herself could find no personal trace of her brother. The patients he had had in 1939, of whom only a few were left, told her that as the fear of Hitler built up, pressure had been put on him to leave, go into hiding, all of which he had ignored. Then, in the turmoil of the occupation, as the Germans marched into Paris, he had quietly disappeared. No one had wished to draw attention to himself by asking questions. No one knew if he had gone into hiding or been removed by the new German masters. Many people had disappeared and it soon became apparent that those who asked questions called down an unwanted investigation of themselves in place of information. Eventually, Miriam gave up and returned to England, feeling to her immense surprise that, instead of leaving her country, she was in fact returning home. Not that she would ever belong, she thought, and wondered if in fact she really wanted to belong anywhere. The facts of her life had made her into an outsider, and perhaps that was where she felt most comfortable. But she no longer wanted to be an outsider in her country of adoption, watching the society which had given her education and formed many of her opinions now floundering in the aftermath of war, unforgiving of the circumstances which had not allowed it to show the courage which England had shown, resentful of, yet grateful for, the intervention of America without which no one knew what might have happened, unsure of how it might have reacted if it had been in a position similar to England, rather than where opposition had to be carried out stealthily and under cover, never sure who was friend and who was not. She felt she no longer belonged in a country she had had to flee from; she was too tired to uproot herself again, unlikely as it might seem that she preferred a grey, English, provincial town to the glory, now tattered but soon to be mended, of Europe's most sophisticated capital.

David and Leah tried to persuade her to join them in the States. David had found his true place there, she thought, as she listened to a French now laced with Americanisms and heard the pride with which he told her of his newly acquired nationality. It came as no surprise when he called her "Sis" – she had seen enough American movies to recognise a society where David would feel more accepted than he ever had in France. America was more down to earth, less disdainful of a talent to make money, than France had ever been. But she had no desire to join them there.

"I'm staying in England, David," she repeated. "I have a good job, a nice flat, friends ... what more could I want?"

David sounded hurt. "You could want family," he said. "You've never seen our youngest two. And the eldest – they're almost grown. Rebecca wants to be a doctor – like you – and Joe ..." – his voice swelled with a pride that amused Miriam – "little Joe, as you probably remember him, Joe's become a sports whizzkid. You wouldn't believe how tall he's become on all his American milk, and strong. Loves baseball, basketball, football – the school thinks he might win a sports scholarship to university. Think of that, Miriam, anything's possible over here!"

Miriam congratulated David, though she wondered what someone on a sports scholarship would study. She promised to visit one day soon. She hesitated to say that one of the reasons she would stay in England, if not in France, was that maybe, maybe, Nathan would re-appear and need to find a family which had not disappeared totally across the Atlantic. She asked about Isaac, worried that Anaïs would want to return to France now, which David confirmed.

"They've split up," he said as if splitting up were an everyday occurrence – as perhaps it was in his new society, thought Miriam. "Anaïs wanted to go back. Isaac didn't – and, well, you know him, he's not been without comfort since she left, and if he stays I can keep an eye on him." Miriam pictured Isaac, once again in a domestic upheaval, turning for solace to a succession of women. She felt sorry for him and glad that they had had no children. She had a swift mental picture of her family: David and Esther revelling in the riches they had found in their personal promised land, Isaac using his own riches as a comfortable base from which to pursue his comforters. She dismissed the picture as unfair, prejudiced, ungrateful, but it persisted all the same, and she felt that for the time being she did not want to find out whether it was true. She knew she was right not to go, but after she had rung off she felt an almost unbearable nostalgia for the old days in France; and hatred for the war, and the man who had engineered it and who had caused her life to disintegrate and change in a way she had not willed, rose up in her like bile.

A terrible sadness invaded her, as unexpected as a storm on a summer's day, and racked her with hard, physically painful sobs in which images of her dead mother and brother mingled with memories of Nathan and her father; she felt that she had been tossed this way and that, her life out of her control, everything she loved disappearing, dying, out of reach, gone. She thought of Nathan, unfindable. She thought of Sam, who had disappeared so completely, and for whom pride had not allowed her to search. She thought of her patients and for once their problems seemed unimportant, irrelevant, beside her own emotionally empty life. She cried for the whole of humanity, for the men, women and children dead in unimaginable horror in the camps, for the pointlessness of the lives wasted in a war caused by greed and paranoia, for the children whose lives would be stunted by parents dead or damaged, or mentally crippled by the events of the last five years. She found herself sitting on the floor beside the phone in the hall, her arms wrapped round herself, her body bent in agony, the tears spilling from her eyes and wetting her skirt unnoticed, until finally she had sat so long that cold caused her to shiver uncontrollably. Slowly she pulled herself up. Perhaps it was catharsis, perhaps it would help lay the ghosts of the last few years, she thought, but she doubted it.

Not often had she felt the despair with which so many of her patients lived most of their lives; today she understood completely their disbelief in life and in man. She lit the gas fire in her study and huddled on the floor in front of it, a cardigan pulled round her for warmth, a picture of inelegant despair, her fine legs planted heavily on the rug, her upright posture collapsed in hunchbacked grief, her hair escaping in untidy locks which gave her a look of manic lunacy. Evening came, but she neither drew the curtains nor switched on the lamps. Finally she fell asleep in the fatigue of worn out tears; when she awoke, neither the sadness nor the reasons for it seemed so overwhelming. By the next day, she felt more or less normal. She was able to look back coolly on the previous day's collapse and dissect it unemotionally. Strain, tiredness, the relaxation of nerves now that the war was finally over; the frustration of conversation with David whose values seemed so different from her own, mixed with a genuine longing to see him again, and the hardly admitted guilt of wishing it were Nathan instead who was safely installed on the other side of the Atlantic; the buried hurt of Sam's silence; they had all combined to push her to the edge of misery. Doing what she forbade her patients to do, she decided to face none of these problems, but rather to throw herself into her work. It was with relief that she turned to the problems of others, which she was so good at helping to solve. None had been so fascinating as that of Laura Martin in the winter of 1947.

All this went rapidly through her mind. This last search for Nathan had been as unproductive as any of the others. She had acted on impulse, remembering one old man who had been Nathan's patient telling her that once Nathan had spoken of a friend who had gone to the Languedoc, to Uzes, someone who had been at medical school with him. The old man had not remembered his name, and Miriam had forgotten about it, concentrating her search on Paris. When she had visited the Bonnevilles at Easter, the map had fallen open at the wrong page and Uzes had leapt out at her. On that visit, she had had no time to go so far south, but this time she had determined to follow the meagre clue.

She had visited every doctor in the town. None of them had known Nathan. Some had moved during or after the war, and painstakingly she had made telephone calls to those she could trace, or visited those near enough to reach in a day. Again, she drew a blank. No one had heard of Nathan Stein. Finally, as the days passed and no trace could be found she came to realise that he was almost certainly dead. Why the realisation should have come with such certainty in the unfamiliar landscape of south-west France, its remoteness underlined by the strange tongue still occasionally used by those who lived there, she did not know. All she knew was that where once so certainly there had been hope of life, now there was an equal certainty of death. This, she supposed, was what had shown on her face. Not only was she bereft by loss of Nathan, she thought, but the feeling of being bereft was strengthened by the fact that she had no date, no grave, no papers to show his death. Just a huge blankness. A nothingness. It was as though he had never been.

Editing it as she went, she gave Laura a much curtailed and censored account of her life and what Nathan had meant to her. It would not do to tell Laura too much about the dreadful crimes which the Nazis had committed in the name of Aryan purity, especially as it was likely that Laura's own father had perished at their hands too. All she said was that Nathan had probably been killed in the war, but that there had been no record, no trace, and that now she felt certain that he was dead.

"It's too long after the war for him not to have reappeared if he was going to," she said. "I'll just have to accept it."

"You can accept anything if it's the truth," said Laura, repeating a statement which Miriam had made to her many times.

Miriam laughed. "I seem to have heard those words before," she said. "The trouble with something like this is that if you don't know what the truth is, it's hard to know what to accept. But I think he must be dead. I feel it."

"At least you knew him for thirty-eight years," said Laura unsmilingly. "I have to believe that my parents are dead when I can't remember them at all, and have always thought someone else was my mother and father." Her voice trembled, and Miriam mentally berated herself for having burdened Laura with her own problems instead of concentrating on Laura's.

"Do you want to tell me about it. What you found out?" she asked. "Or shall we stop and have some lunch?"

Laura replied in a low, flat voice that surprised Miriam with its intensity. She had not sounded like this for months.

"No. I don't want to tell you and I don't want to talk about it. I don't want to know anything about them. Why can't everyone just leave me alone and not keep trying to tell me about these people who were supposed to be my parents? I hate them."

Miriam realised that she should have known that something like this might happen. Laura was terrified by the enormity of what had happened to her. She had learned to cope with the present, but the past was too much for her battered mind to bear. To open up a new past for her now would be opening a Pandora's box of jumbled emotions.

"You don't have to learn anything about them now," she said mildly. "It can wait. You'll want to know about them sometime, and that will be the right time for you to ask questions. Why don't you tell me about the holiday – what you did, where you've been?"

"Are you sure?" asked Laura. "I really don't want to know. I'm sorry I got cross, but – Oh, it makes me shiver when I think about it. I just want to go back to being ordinary, being me – even if I'm not the person I thought I was."

"Of course it's OK," said Miriam. "I promise. You'll know when the right time comes. Now – I suggest we have some lunch." She turned the car off the main road into a lane, and there, caressed by the late summer sun, they ate the picnic Fernande had packed for them – newly baked bread, ham and *saucisson*, radishes, and a runny cheese whose smell would have disgusted Harry and George, Laura thought. Finally, there were two ripe peaches. Laura picked them out of the bag. "These come from my garden," she said, a little smile of pride lightening her dark features. "My father planted the tree."

So she has learned something, thought Miriam to herself, carefully saying only that peaches like this could never be found in England, but noticing the faint shiver that seemed to touch Laura for a second as she bit into the peach. One day, she'll tell me, she thought, not guessing it would be three full years before Laura finally had to face up to and come to terms with what had happened to her.

CHAPTER Ten

Autumn, 1947

When Harriet, Georgina and Laura returned to Baynes in the autumn, all three were subtly changed by the events of the summer.

Harriet now had a half-brother, who had been born three days after she had returned from London, and whom she had not yet seen but was determined to dislike. She had been told of Simon's birth by her father, over the telephone. She took the receiver from Isabel's hand reluctantly, waiting until her mother's whispered entreaty to speak was too fierce to disobey.

Alec's voice was tinny and loud in her ear. "You've got a new brother, Harriet. We're going to call him Simon. Simon Alexander Canmore Bolton. What do you say to that?"

Harriet did not answer. She could hear her father's breathing over the faint noises of the telephone line. The announcement, expected though it had been, shocked her as if she had known nothing of Arabella's pregnancy, and a cold, black dread seemed to grow into her stomach as she heard his words.

"Harriet, are you there? Did you hear what I said?"

Alec's voice was becoming irritated.

"Yes."

"Well?"

"It's very nice. His name, I mean. Simon."

Alec started telling her about the baby's size, and hair colour and how he looked like him, and how Arabella had wanted to call him Crispin, but had been overruled by Alec. "No soppy names like that for my son. Anyway, Simon was my brother's name," he said firmly, and as she listened Harriet knew from the way he had said "my son" that she would no longer come first in her father's affections, no matter what he said. He was telling her that Arabella sent her love, that they would see her soon, that she must come and stay and meet Simon in the Christmas holidays. Harriet held the receiver away from her ear as if she wanted, or perhaps was being forced, to distance herself from her father. She interrupted his flow of confident words.

"I have to go, Daddy," she said loudly, shouting into the receiver. "I'll get Mummy."

She passed the receiver to Isabel without waiting for Alec to say goodbye, and feeling tears that were somehow both unexpected and at the same time not surprising, she pulled open the door and ran up to her room.

As she went, she could hear Isabel saying, "Well, I don't know what you expected, Alec – I'm not particularly thrilled about it myself ..." The bitter tone of her mother's voice registered with Harriet as it faded behind the door which Isabel now kicked shut, and some of her painful, unstoppable tears were for her mother as well as for herself. When she went downstairs, however, her face red and still wet, her eyes swollen under smarting lids, Isabel looked composed and distant.

"You must try to accept it, Harriet," she said. "Your father has a new wife, and you have a new brother."

"I won't," Harriet stormed. "He's not ours. I hate Daddy, and Arabella, and babies ..." The hot tears streamed over her cheeks again and she scrubbed at them with her sopping hanky. She wished she didn't cry so easily, she thought, not quite able to articulate the idea that such easy tears might seem to others to detract from the strength of the emotion felt, but suspecting something of the sort. She tried to stop the gulping sobs.

"It's just that ... well, it's the end ..." She didn't finish the sentence, noting the expression that flickered on Isabel's face, and ashamed that she had not thought that Isabel must feel that it was the end too, though of what Harriet was not sure.

"I know, darling," said Isabel, making an effort to control the bitter thoughts which had surprised her as much as Harriet's reaction had surprised Harriet, and trying to ignore the empty feeling that Alec's selfish excitement with his new life had given her. There could never be any question of him coming back now; and Isabel realised that always, underneath, a buried hope had lain hidden, that Alec would return and life could go on. Hopes like this ignore the facts, and wait in desperate patience until, finally, a fact is too great to be ignored. A fact like a new baby cementing a marriage which might, until that point, have been discardable.

Isabel felt shaken and utterly weary, but knew that she must comfort Harriet; and she spent the rest of that bleak evening coaxing her daughter back to cheerfulness, making her favourite supper and playing Snap and Beggar-My-Neighbour until Harriet's swollen eyelids began to droop and Isabel could safely tuck her up in bed. Harriet's dependence on her was becoming too much, Isabel found herself thinking, and she felt a new hatred for Alec in his easy leaving of Harriet to her alone. She longed to leave the house, walk in solitude in the cool, autumn-smelling streets where the faint tang of bonfires mingled with the musty scent of wet leaves and the sooty smell of coal fires.

***

Laura returned to Baynes with the knowledge that she had chosen to return, was no longer being forced to. Her relationship with her grandmother had improved greatly with her knowledge of where she herself fitted into the complex intertwining of two families. She still, however, refused to explore her English family background, though once or twice Mrs Martin had caught her examining the photographs of Robert and others that stood upon the grand piano in the drawing room. When she tried to explain who the figures were, though, Laura always turned away, professing lack of interest and changing the subject. Mrs Martin had described this reaction to Miriam, who had told her to follow Laura's lead in this.

"She'll ask when she's ready," Miriam said. "She's accepted the idea now, but we must give her time to get used to it. I think her mind is telling her not to try to take in too many new facts at once. It's like a too-rich meal – too much of it will make her ill."

So Laura had been allowed to spend the few days left of the holidays exploring the huge, detached house set in its dark, rhododendron-filled grounds, and its rabbit-warren of rooms, most of them unused. Harriet had come to tea once, with her mother, and Harriet's grandmother had also come, separately; Laura, reading outside the open drawing room window, had heard her tell Mrs Martin of Harriet's upsetting behaviour over her father's new baby.

"Though of course it's the father who's to blame for all of this. I never liked him, though I can see why Isabel might have found him attractive. Much too much of a social climber – I believe this new wife of his has some kind of title." Here Harriet's grandmother had lowered her voice and Laura, who felt slightly guilty at hearing what she was obviously not meant to hear, moved quietly away from the window.

***

Georgina came back to Baynes with relief, thankful to get away from the house in North Shields where the atmosphere had become very uncomfortable for her. She had spent most of the last two weeks – except for one important encounter with Steve – at Dotty's flat, now that Dotty was back from her walking tour in Scotland, in the first place to get out of the house, but also to take in with great gulps the civilised air of a place that echoed the atmosphere of Baynes. She could browse among Dotty's books and recharge her intellectual batteries with an infusion of the generous, unaffected knowledge that Dotty constantly exuded, every sentence, or so it seemed to Georgina, filled with treasure to add to her store. They talked of music, listening to records and even sometimes reading a simple score, a talent Georgina found she possessed and enjoyed. They explored books, Dotty lending her some of E. Nesbitt's magical tales and Louisa May Alcott's *Little Women* and *Good Wives;* she had begun to discover from these how 'proper' families, as opposed to her own dysfunctional, radically split household, behaved, and that magic and mystery could be a part of life.

They discussed pictures, leafing through Dotty's big, shiny books full of reproductions, and when Georgina described the jewelled picture, with its dots of shimmering colour, that illuminated Miriam's sitting room, Dotty brought out a book on the French Impressionists and they identified the style – pointillist, perhaps Pissarro or Seurat. Or at least of that school, mused Dotty, wondering who this woman could be to possess something so valuable. "And she's beautiful," added Georgina reluctantly, still suspicious of her putative unveiling, as she saw it, by Miriam. "Well, perhaps not beautiful but striking. Strange. Like someone from the east."

***

All three were now, in the autumn of 1947, in the top form of the Junior School, all now eleven, Harriet making it by the skin of her teeth. Edith had pondered the idea of keeping Harriet down a form, her late September birthday putting her into that ambiguous position where she could be youngest or oldest of her year. It would solve the problem of having to give her the privilege of sharing a dormitory with Laura and Georgina, both rapidly becoming possible Baynes stars in Edith's view, a future not envisaged for Harriet, for whom Edith was developing an irrational dislike, an emotion she kept almost, but not quite, hidden from her conscious mind. But could she justify not having notified her parents sooner, she wondered; she could deal with Mrs Bolton, she knew, but Harriet's father was more of an unknown, and perhaps more formidable, quality, she thought …

"Harriet really isn't of the calibre of the other two," she'd grumbled to Miriam, who had telephoned to make sure that her protégé would remain bolstered and protected by her chosen friends. "I'm thinking of keeping her down; she has a year in hand – she'll only just be eleven when term starts."

"Edith!" Miriam expostulated, pronouncing it in the French way, Aydeet, which Edith felt made her name, which she did not particularly like, seem exotic and foreign, which in consequence made her more open to suggestions from Miriam.

"Edith! How can you say that when you have only just awarded the child the Junior English Cup? What possible justification could you have for, what did you call it, keeping her down? Or perhaps that is exactly what you want to do? Keep her down, break her spirit – it's an interesting expression, keep her down, *n'est-ce pas*? With more than one meaning … I get strongly the impression that in fact you don't like Harriet?"

"Miriam, please do not insult me by demeaning my motives," replied Edith, stung by the truth of what Miriam said, and, to her credit, somewhat shocked at her own mental duplicity. She had not truly admitted to herself the strength of her dislike of Harriet, and now, having had it pointed out by Miriam, would not let it make her come to an unfair decision.

"Harriet is young for her age, and naughty with it. She seems to resent any kind of discipline and order. On the other hand, her English work is very good, and her other marks …" She glanced at the report she had pulled out as Miriam was talking. It was full of comments about unruly behaviour, but it was undeniably, from the point of view of marks, a more than acceptable report. "Her other marks are not at all bad. In fact, they're well above average. Perhaps you're right, Miriam, though I know you're biased because of Laura ... Very well, somewhat against my better judgement – and you must allow me to be the judge, I do know my job – I'll allow Harriet to move up to Form III with her friends. And yes, she can remain with Laura and Georgina and Alison in that privileged little dormitory at June's." She laughed, somewhat maliciously Miriam felt. "I can't do anything, however, about Matron's attitude. I gather she finds Harriet rather a trial."

"How you can allow a monster like Matron to have jurisdiction over all those helpless little girls, I don't know," said Miriam crossly. She had not forgotten Matron's unhelpfulness towards and lack of understanding of Laura.

"Don't be silly, Miriam. She's not a monster, only a woman who likes to rule her charges with the will of iron that they need. She keeps June's in tip-top order."

"A little compassion never hurt anyone," Miriam replied. Pictures of the uncompassionate women who had helped so many Jewish children to a dreadful death with the excuse that they were only obeying orders, doing their duty, flashed unbidden into her mind. It was a ridiculously exaggerated comparison, she told herself, but all the same ...

"That sort of woman can be very hard on timid children like Harriet, you know," she said. "Now Georgina is a different matter – she would never be intimidated like Harriet. What's her background, Edith? Is she one of your scholarship children?"

"I never reveal which of the children at Baynes are here on scholarships," Edith replied firmly. "And neither do I divulge information about their families, Miriam. It would be unfair and unprofessional. You of all people should know that. I don't suppose you would tell me about any of your patients' backgrounds, would you?"

For a moment Miriam felt the scorching shame that had so often been felt by Baynes pupils as Edith kick-started them into self-knowledge, forced them to examine their moral stance; then she laughed, though not aloud. She had been trying to force Edith into admitting something about Georgina that she shouldn't, and perhaps inadvertently she had admitted it in the force of her refusal. "You're absolutely right, Edith," she said. "I shouldn't have asked."

Edith felt victorious; and having regained the high ground felt she could perhaps bend a little. She was proud of what Baynes had done for Georgina, or Gloria as the child had originally been called. She had had no difficulty with Georgina's insistence on the change, understanding completely that a name like Gloria would start her off at a disadvantage. She remembered with pleasure the little note from the scholarship girl, thanking her for her scholarship and stating that her second name was Georgina and that she would prefer to be known by it alone ...

"You're very astute, Miriam," she now said. "You're right – there is something about Georgina's background which might differentiate her from the other girls, but I doubt that anyone could tell now, after two years here. She's going to be a star ... perhaps Oxford, certainly university somewhere."

Miriam was silent. She would rather she had not been right about Georgina, convinced though she was that some kind of secret lay behind that perfect little face. Edith and the whole Baynes ethos was beginning to sound to her like the quest for perfection, for a stereotypical Aryan norm, which was what had lit the fires of Europe ... She shook her head; she was exaggerating again. Matron as Camp Commandant, Edith as gene selector? Nevertheless, Miriam herself had been forced out of her country just as Harriet, if she did not learn to conform, would be forced out of Baynes; as Georgina no doubt would have been if those two years of Baynes influence had not produced the desired chameleon-like change by which Georgina blended unnoticeably into the social world around her while at the same time standing out scholastically. Brains without the required accent were not something which Edith could deal with successfully, Miriam thought, and as she rang off she filed away, for future examination, the notion that perhaps Georgina came from a very different background from the Baynes norm.

The three girls were pleased, and Harriet secretly relieved, for she suspected both Matron and Miss Morrisson of being against her, to find themselves still in the attic dormitory with Alison. The relief made the tearfulness, which always overwhelmed Harriet for at least a week after the beginning of term, prick more strongly at her eyes. She fixed her eyes unseeingly on the view out of the window, willing herself not to give in to the huge empty sadness that bleakly threatened to overcome her. Why, why, why did she have to leave home and Mummy and come here? Even seeing Laura and George did not compensate ... and there was an added horror: the thought of the new baby, the hideous embarrassment of it, as well as the fact that it had probably displaced her in her father's affections. She fingered the new fountain pen, smooth and shiny and smelling of Bakelite, which sat in her blazer's top pocket, its gold clip bright against the dark green, its presence somehow reassuring, reminiscent of home in these alien surroundings. She wanted to scream and shout, stamp her foot, anything to get out of this place ... but then she remembered Morry's threat last term, and the displeasure which Alec had voiced over the telephone at the tone of the remarks on her report, all the references to being unruly, disobedient. She swallowed with difficulty the sob that was rising painfully up her throat. She was condemned, as she saw it, to stay here if she was not to bring down Daddy's anger on her head, knowing that her special place as eldest child was being usurped, that Mummy's place had already gone, and that it perhaps would not take much to lose hers entirely, and the exciting world of Arabella and Ariadne, of shows and ballets, expensive restaurants and staying up for dinner and champagne, be gone, unattainable, for ever. A pang of disloyalty to Mummy shot through her, and with it a weariness, a tiredness of wrestling with the problems of split loyalties, jealousies of new babies, denials of certain sides of herself depending where she was. Perhaps it would be easier, she thought, just to concentrate on being here, get through the term without incurring the Bun's rage or Morry's disapproval?

Georgina too, after the first pleasure of being back at Baynes had swept through her, was consolidating her position. No one must ever know, she thought once again, of the home she had left behind. How could she ever live down a visit by Steve, who had been vociferous in his threats to visit his sister's school, or explain Da's uncouthness, or excuse Mam's huge hips, scrubbed red arms and faint odour of fish? The gap between home and here seemed wider than ever, and the assumption of her Georgina character not exactly more difficult, but more important, and thus more wearing, than it had ever been.

But she had found something to threaten Steve with, something that would make him lose his will to visit her.

"If you come to Baynes or anywhere near it, I can and will do something to you that you won't like," she had said one day last week, waiting on the doorstep for Steve to come home and knew he had felt the chill of cold determination behind the words. He'd tried to laugh it off.

"Get away, man. I'll do as I want and you canna stop me, you stuck up little bitch," he'd said, half expecting her to run at him, goading her into rage.

But Georgina looked at him coldly, a steely glint in her blue eyes.

"I have those pictures and photographs you hide in your room," she said.

The pictures were in a magazine, but not one from even the highest shelf of a newsagent's. They showed children, little girls, even some looking like five year olds, posing provocatively, lewdly, some with old men, some with muscled studs. Some were in positions Georgina could never have imagined, and they made her feel cold and sick, as Laura's story of Nordhoff had, and as the man in the park had.

Steve went red, then white. A muscle tensed in his cheek, and his face looked thin and vicious.

"You little cunt," he said, moving towards her. She stood her ground.

"If you come anywhere near me *you* won't find them, but Mam will," she said. "And calling me names won't help you."

Steve moved nearer to her. "I'll get you for this," he said, raising his fist. "You tell me where they are."

"You touch me, and Mam will get the pictures," replied Georgina indomitably. "And you'll never find them."

Determinedly, she turned away from him. He moved as if to come after her, and then stopped, frustration lending the vicious cast of his face a looming menace. "I'll get you for this one day," he repeated, so quietly that she hardly heard him, and a shiver went through her, a premonition that one day he would.

It had been sheer chance, finding the magazines. She'd been in the bedroom Steve shared with Geordie when, as usual, she was alone in the house, poking around more for something to do than actively looking for some way to give her a hold over Steve. The boys' room, small and cramped with the two beds was neat and clean. Steve's doing, thought Georgina, opening the rickety chest of drawers that the brothers shared, and ruffling through the socks, underpants and singlets neatly laid in piles. Steve's, clearly. Geordie's drawer was more untidy, his underwear and socks thrown in anyhow. The room otherwise contained only the two beds, at right-angles to each other along two walls, two chairs serving as bedside tables, with a mirror over the chest of drawers. There was no wardrobe, but some shirts and jackets hung from hooks behind the door.

She poked through the pockets, but there was nothing to interest her. A dirty handkerchief, a greasy comb, a betting slip. She turned towards Steve's bed, which faced the door. Nothing under the pillow. On the chair beside his bed was an unshaded lamp, an empty ashtray, a box of matches, and two shilling's worth of loose change. He'd know if she pinched that, she thought, putting it back. The piece of old carpet that covered the middle of the room was rucked-up where it stopped at the edge of Steve's bed. Absently, she put her foot on it to push it flat and felt something move. Intrigued, she pulled back the carpet. It was only a loose floorboard, she thought at first, but then saw that something was preventing it from lying flat. She pulled on the board and it came up easily, revealing a small cache filled with magazines, one of which had been put back carelessly, so that the board could not fit back properly.

She pulled out the magazines, and opened one. Its innocuous cover gave her no warning, and she gasped out loud at the lewd and graphic photograph which confronted her, a double-page spread of a young girl, legs wide open and pulled up, showing all, a rampant, naked man leering above her. She snapped the magazine shut, blood rushing into her face, her heart banging. It was foul, disgusting and, she knew instinctively, forbidden. She felt as if she was holding dirt, but dirt with an obscene fascination. Slowly, she opened the magazine again, her eyes gazing unbelievingly at the photographs. Some of the girls were her own age, and it was as if she and Harriet and Laura were spread out there for her filthy-minded brother to drool over. She felt sick, and yet excited in a horrible, inquisitive way. After a while, she pushed the magazines back, knowing that she would remember every detail of what she had seen, and knowing, too, she could never tell anyone. Yet another thing she had to hide, she thought, and thought how much she hated Steve for his threat to come and see her, and that she would now hate him even more for what he had hidden in his room. Rage began to take over from disgust, and as an idea took hold of her, she pulled out all the magazines. Underneath them was an envelope, addressed to Steve. Inside were photographs, black and white, detailed and disgusting, two of them of Steve himself with a girl who looked no older than six. She put it to one side, willing her mind not to take in the images she had seen, and from the middle of the pile of magazines – called *Nature's Way*, she now saw, and disguised to look like a nature-study magazine – she put aside three, replacing the rest in their hiding place, and carefully putting back the board and smoothing the carpet down over it. She looked round the room; there was no sign that she had been in it. She pushed the magazines into the envelope, went into her own bedroom, and slid it under her mattress. If Mam saw them, she thought, that would be the end of Steve as far as his mother was concerned, but he'd know who'd shown them to her. Might it not be better, she mused, to have some hold over him herself? To threaten him with showing the material to Mam, rather than doing so? In that case, she must find somewhere really safe to hide it, she thought. She couldn't conceal it from Steve in her room, or in fact anywhere in the house. He would go through everything savagely.

It took her some time to work it out, but finally she hit on a solution. Leaving the envelope under her mattress, she sauntered down to the library and made her way to the music section. It was as usual empty; Georgina had only found it after looking at scores with Dotty when, fascinated with her new skill, she had thought she might try it on her own, only to find that it lost its magic without the music itself to listen to. Nevertheless, she had noted the huge old books of Mozart and Beethoven sonatas and piano concertos, so big that they were piled sideways on the shelves. Now she looked more carefully. One pile looked as though it were made up of identical volumes, and proved in fact to be so. Who, she wondered fleetingly, had thought the library needed five copies of Bach's *Preludes and Fugues*? She pulled out the bottom one. Its ticket at the front had never been stamped. Slowly she replaced it under its identical companions. That would do very well.

When she returned, she was carrying the incriminating envelope in a brown paper carrier bag, along with her library books, which she handed in. Slowly, careful to look as if she was searching for a book, she made her way back to the music section, its few shelves hidden at the back of the big, airy room. She slipped the envelope into the copy of *Preludes and Fugues* and replaced the book at the bottom of the pile. No one would take it out; if one did go, it would be from the top, though judging by the dust, no one except herself had looked at these books for years. Anyway, if someone did find it, it would be Steve whose name was on the envelope, and he who would be exposed, not her. She laughed to herself. That would be a sight worth seeing, she thought, the strait-laced, prissy librarian and her dirty-minded, revolting brother confronting each other. Almost worth engineering, except that the longer she kept the magazine hidden, the longer she would have her hold on Steve.

When she got home, Steve was in, affable and friendly for once. "Well, wor Gloria, what have you been up to today?" he said, ruffling her hair. She pulled away from him, his touch, his whole being, making her feel sick.

"Nothing. Reading," she said, knowing it would annoy him with its overtones of school and learning. He gazed at her. She wondered if she was imagining the leering, knowing look in his eye. She could never look at him again, she thought, without thinking of those images that had burned themselves onto her brain.

"Been book-readin', have you?" he said. "Could fancy a bit of that meself. I'm goin' up for a kip – don't you disturb me." All his words had double meanings now for Georgina. She remembered that he often went upstairs for a kip, as he called it, when he came back from the pub in the afternoon. Now she wondered if he slept, or just read his sickening magazines.

"Suit yourself," she said. "I'm off to see Auntie Vi in a minute."

She waited until he had gone upstairs, and then slammed the door without going out, a burning and unstoppable curiosity about what he did in his room giving her courage as she crept up the stairs. She put her eye to the keyhole. He was lying on his bed, which faced the door, holding a copy of *Nature's Way* in one hand, blocking her view of what he was doing with the other. An image from the magazines sprang into her head, and without actually knowing, she knew what he was doing, and that it was forbidden, disgusting, and because of the magazine, worse than anything a normal man could do. Her stomach heaved and it was only by superhuman effort that she stopped herself from retching there and then. She must keep absolutely silent, she knew. If he knew she was there, she would not be able to escape his violence. Inch by inch, she moved away from the door, trying not to hear the faint creak of the bed or the hiss of his breath as it was finally released. After a while, she heard a snore, and was able to move more quickly. Downstairs, she let herself out silently, closing the door slowly and carefully.

"Hello, Gloria," said a voice as she pulled it to. She jumped, amazed that she was back in the outside world, where life was continuing as if it was a normal day, not one that had to be conducted with stealth and secrecy and shame and fear, and forbidden, sickening knowledge.

She forced herself to smile at their next door neighbour. "Hello, Mrs Minto," she said breathlessly.

"You look pale, hinny. Are you all right?" Mrs Minto looked concerned. "Is your Mam at work?"

"I'm all right, Mrs Minto," Georgina said hurriedly. "Just a bit tired with reading indoors. I'm going to the beach."

"That's right, hinny. You get some fresh air. You're turnin' into a proper bookworm, spendin' your time with your nose in a book instead of out wi' your friends." The friendly Mrs Minto let herself into her house.

Georgina set off at a run, aching for some truly fresh air, some Baynes air, not this foetid, fishy-smelling atmosphere that surrounded her home. She made for the pier and sat at its end, letting the cold wind that always blew off the North Sea clear her head of the hot forbidden images. After a long time, she rose and slowly walked back, wishing she could be anyone but herself, envying the wheeling gulls overhead for their freedom, and the cosy families eating their picnics on the beach for their unity and safety. When she got home, her mind was made up. She would confront Steve tomorrow; then at least one of her worlds could remain uncontaminated by his threat and filth.

Now, back at school, she tried to get rid of the fear she felt, which was spoiling her return to Baynes. Why, oh why, did Steve have to be her brother? She knew that it was unlikely now, with the hold she had over him, that he would come here. He would be too frightened of Edna's rage and disgust, and too sure that Georgina would do as she had threatened. But some day he'd get his revenge. She shook her head as if to get rid of these dark thoughts and turned resolutely away from the window through which she had been unseeingly staring, back to the realities of Baynes.

Laura was the most equable of the three, having been, last year, the most emotionally damaged. It was as if she had come out onto a high plateau of acceptance of what had happened to her. She felt able to cope, after the summer, with leaving Belay, which she now thought she clearly understood was not a banishment. She wanted now to please her grandmother, to please the Bonnevilles, to please Miriam, and to please Miss Morrisson. She had become tired of the sense of exclusion that had earlier overwhelmed her, and tired of the searing emotions that had racked her since being made to leave France. Now she wanted peace and acceptance, to enjoy becoming part of a world that she was beginning to admire. She felt years older than she had at this time last year, at peace with herself and, mostly, with her memories. It no longer pained her to think of Belay, or Sabine and Olivier, or Tante Marie-Claude and Oncle Paul, whom she no longer, she told herself, thought of as her parents. She ignored by an act of determined self-will the fluttering sense of darkness and void which sometimes, fearfully, threatened this sense of wellbeing, reminding her of the cold moment in the garden, eating the peach, when she had doubted her own existence. When she felt tendrils of this feeling floating into her mind, she clamped it down, refusing to look at it. She had not told Miriam about it. It was the second secret she had kept from her, but intuitively she felt that if she took it out, examined it, the happiness and sense of safety that had been returned so unexpectedly to her through Miriam, would once again be shattered.

Mundanely, it was Matron who now shattered her reverie, padding silently up the stairs to open the door with a bang. She must have worked out which step creaked, and stepped over it.

"Harriet, get your case unpacked," she snapped. "Time waits for no man, let alone you. Where's Alison?"

"In the bathroom, Matron," said Georgina.

Harriet opened her overnight bag and took out her pyjamas, Dinah and Dorinda, and the precious photograph of Mummy. To this she added a new photograph of Daddy with Arabella and Simon, a mixture of feelings sweeping through her.

"Who's that, Harriet?" said the Bun, picking up the photo frame.

"That's my business," said Harriet rudely, a red flush rushing into her cheeks.

"No cheek from you, Miss," Matron replied tartly. "I asked you a civilised question. That's your father, isn't it? Married again has he? A nice looking woman. And that's your new baby brother, I'll be bound?" She looked questioningly at Harriet, who looked back stubbornly. Georgina came to the rescue.

"Can I have a look, Matron?" she said, reaching a hand up for the frame.

She turned to Harriet. "What's his name, Harriet, the baby?"

"Simon," muttered Harriet, taking the photo from Georgina and placing it on her chest of drawers. Georgina had defused the situation and her flush was subsiding. She felt the hot rage she had felt as Matron touched the picture begin to disappear. What did it matter? They'd all have to know sooner or later, so they might as well know now.

"My parents are divorced, Matron," she said as coldly as she dared. "My father's now married to the Honourable Arabella Canmore, if you must know, and that's their new baby, Simon."

"An Honourable, you say, Harriet," said Matron, an unctuous tone coming into her voice. "Well, well ...". She was clearly trying to think of something nasty to say. She smiled, and looked Harriet up and down as if, Georgina said afterwards, Harriet were something the cat had brought in.

"Well, let's hope some of it rubs off on you, Harriet. You could do with it. Now come along all of you. It's nearly time for supper." She padded away on her silent soles.

Harriet, Georgina and Laura fell into each other's arms, giggling helplessly. "Did you hear her voice when she said 'Honourable'?" said Laura. "What does it mean?"

"Oh, it just means that Arabella's father is a Lord," said Harriet, making it sound as though she spoke of lords every day. "Arabella's actually quite nice."

"And the way she couldn't think of anything horrid to say," giggled Laura. "It took her ages to come up with something."

"Something stupid, too," said Georgina. "'Let's hope some of it rubs off on you.'" She mimicked Matron's voice.

"Have I missed something?" said Alison, returning. "What are you all giggling about?"

As Georgina explained about Matron, the photograph and the Honourable, Harriet thought with relief that the information about her new brother and her father's new wife had somehow been released without her having to say much, and without her feeling as embarrassed as she had thought she would. Thanks to George, she thought, and felt the faintest tremor of happiness run through her at the prospect of another year with George and Laura. She walked over to the window and gazed at the familiar grounds.

Perhaps it would all get better now, she thought. Perhaps the future might be better than the past.

Georgina and Laura joined her; and looking at the soft twilight of late September, seeing the faint evening mist rising from the water meadows running down to the river, they all had a sense that something hidden and exciting was waiting to be revealed in the years to come. If they had been able to see into that future, perhaps they would not have been so sanguine.

Made in the USA
Lexington, KY
29 May 2018